Stonewall Inn Mysteries
Keith Kahla, General Editor

Also by Grant Michaels

A Body to Dye For
Love You to Death
Dead on Your Feet

Grant Michaels

Mask for a Diva

St. Martin's Press
New York

MASK FOR A DIVA. Copyright © 1994 by Grant Michaels. All rights reserved. Printed in the United States of America. No part of this book may be used or reproduced in any manner whatsoever without written permission except in the case of brief quotations embodied in critical articles or reviews. For information, address St. Martin's Press, 175 Fifth Avenue, New York, N.Y. 10010.

Library of Congress Cataloging-in-Publication Data

Michaels, Grant.
    Mask for a diva / by Grant Michaels.
       p.   cm.
    ISBN 0-312-14120-3
    1. Kraychik, Stan (Fictitious character)—Fiction.   2. Beauty operators—Massachusetts—Boston—Fiction.   3. Opera companies—Massachusetts—Boston—Fiction.   4. Gay men—Massachusetts—Boston—Fiction.   5. Boston (Mass.)—Fiction.
I. Title.
PS3563.I2715M37   1996
813'.54—dc20   95-39343
                                                  CIP

First published by St. Martin's Press

First Stonewall Inn Edition: February 1996
10 9 8 7 6 5 4 3 2 1

for all divas,
operatic and otherwise

Thanks to the many friends who once again kept my body and spirit nourished.

Special thanks to Paul Nagano, in whose Boston studio this book was born, and to Mike Dively, in whose Key West cottage it grew.

Thanks also to David Stockton and Roland Guidry of Boston, and their associates, for sharing their expertise in opera production. Likewise, thanks to Adam Harris of San Francisco.

And finally, with all respect, thanks to il signor Verdi *for his great legacy to all divas and their disciples.*

1

I should have known better.
   All the signs were there.
   I should have gone straight to Italy as planned.
   But I figured working the wigs for the first season of the New England Summer Opera Festival would be easy, glamorous work. I'd be breathing fresh ocean air instead of the recycled fumes of a Newbury Street salon; I'd be among real celebrities instead of so many Back Bay pretenders; and my esthetic talents would be challenged far more than any Beacon Hill dowager had required of them lately. To top it off, I'd net myself a tidy little bundle to spend in Italy later on.
   The train should have been my first warning. No silvery sleek Metroliners depart from Boston's North Station. The commuter rail is more like the Livestock Local—cramped and decrepit, better suited for the outer bounds of Siberia than a regal excursion to the opera.
   The coach was especially stifling that day, jammed with noisy people eager to escape from the city to the north shore on the first Sunday in June. Beach chairs and beverage coolers blocked the aisles; tote bags and straw hats spilled from the overhead racks; and adults and children hovered everywhere, yacking and whining and sparring nonstop. I was lucky to be getting off at the next town, Abigail-by-the-Sea, the oceanside hamlet where the new opera festival was based. The riffraff would stay on to the end of the line, or so I thought.
   The train rounded a shallow curve and blew its whistle as if to recall the lost romance of the rails. The conductor announced Abi-

gail, and we headed into the once sleepy town that would soon be a shrine to international opera and all its worshippers. Relief, comfort, and luxury were just moments away.

But as the train approached the station it jolted and screeched to a halt, throwing many of the standing passengers off their feet. A large man in a soiled sweaty shirt fell onto me, and I cringed at his rank wetness. The conductor ordered everyone to remain seated, which seemed pointless since so many people either had no seat or were now sprawled on the floor. The coach became eeire and still, as things do in the first moments after a catastrophe. There was a communal sense of something gone badly wrong. Twenty suffocating minutes later we learned that we would have to vacate the train and walk along the rail bed for the remaining distance to the station. And then we all saw what had stopped the train.

A young woman had apparently thrown herself onto the rails, and like that tragic Russian heroine, had been decapitated. The local police had already set up barriers around the first two coaches, but it was easy, too easy, to peer beyond them and catch glimpses of the body sans head.

First the train ride, and now this.

Inside the small station house, which had been freshly painted and restored in honor of the opera festival, the townsfolk were quickly gathering. Oh, the horror! The tragedy! The delicious scandal! I gathered enough snippets of various conversations to learn that the young woman had been a singer, a local soprano who had failed to get a part in the festival.

"Poor thing," they said. "Such a voice. Such promise."

Announcements informed us that shuttle buses would arrive to take the holiday travelers to towns further north along the coast. But I had already reached my destination—the Sidney Blaustein Center for the Performing Arts, brand new, never been used before, located just outside Abigail's town center. I left the station and scanned the main street for a taxi, but with no luck. Then I heard the sound of a car horn, a four-note chord in perfect tune. I turned toward the sound and saw a petite silver-haired woman waving from the driver's seat of an immense cardinal red convertible. The top was down, exposing to the New England elements four plump seats upholstered in soft leather, near-white, and trimmed with red piping to match the car's bold lacquer paint.

"Jonathan!" cried the small woman.

Me? My name is Stan. I looked behind me. No one was there.

"Jonathan!" she called out again in a high raspy voice. She motioned me toward the car, so I went.

She smiled brightly at me, although her eyes were concealed by wraparound sunglasses as dark as a bandit's mask. "I forgot to send word," she said. "Parker stopped driving last month. Can you imagine? I expected some kind of natural calamity would follow, but the only thing that happened is that I'm driving myself now."

I stared blankly at her. She was easily over seventy years old, spare as a sparrow, and pale, wearing a white cotton sun dress with big black polka dots. She could have been idling on a boulevard in Monte Carlo, awaiting some prince to dash from a casino, laden with bounty, and settle in next to her.

"Well, get in," she said. "Let's go!"

"But—"

"We'll send the jitney to pick up the rest of your bags."

"But—"

"Quick now. Lunch will be ready."

Why argue? I placed my two pieces of luggage on the back seat, then opened the door—the automotive equivalent of a Swiss bank vault—and settled myself into the seat. Aromatic leather enveloped me like those ponderous armchairs in gentlemen's clubs in London and Boston. The woman eased the heavy car away from the curb and slid it into the traffic lane, oblivious to the oncoming cars. We just avoided a collision, and I bristled. She seemed to be looking everywhere but in front of her, and she seemed to be having trouble seeing. Maybe her chic opaque sunglasses were part of the problem.

"What is all this hubbub around the station?" she said.

I told her there'd been an accident on the tracks.

"Oh, dear," she said. "Was it serious?"

"A young woman apparently killed herself."

"Oh, *dear!*" The woman shook her head. "Well there isn't much we can do for her now."

She drove the big convertible at a deplorable crawl along the main street, allowing it to weave languidly in response to her tendency to turn the steering wheel in whatever direction her gaze fell at the moment—toward a colorful shop window on the left, toward a pedestrian couple strolling along on the right, toward me sitting beside her. And ever obedient, the car meandered gracefully to the whim of her visual attention. An oncoming vehicle honked loudly at us, and the woman swerved us back into our lane of traffic.

She said, "What an unfortunate welcome for you, Jonathan."

"Ma'am, my name isn't Jonathan."

She smiled. "Oh, don't worry. I know most theater people have stage names."

"I'm Stan Kraychik," I said.

"You're Czech, then!" she said, as elated as if she had discovered America.

"Yes, but—"

"Well, it's no wonder you took a British identity. It makes international work so much easier. Although I love Czech theater. It's so daring and dynamic. Would you prefer me to use your real name?"

She faced me again. The car followed the direction of her eyes and veered slightly to the right. I was just about to put my hand on the steering wheel when she swerved us back on course.

"No," I said. "As long as you're comfortable with it."

"Whatever you like," she replied.

What I would have liked was to know who Jonathan was. And who she was too, for that matter.

The woman said, "I know it's an outrage to own a car like this, especially with the economy so uncertain, but when Sid died two years back—my dear, I had no idea how wealthy my second husband was—frozen foods, of all things!—and then Parker failed his eye examination last month—and, well, here I am, driving again."

"I'm afraid that—"

"Oh, don't be," she replied. "I'm quite capable." She pressed her hand warmly over my forearm. "And I've always wanted something sporty."

I gave up on the identity crisis for the moment and tried to share her delight with her new car. "What is it exactly?"

"Don't you know? It's a Bentley, dear. A Bentley Continental. It's made in your country, by the Rolls-Royce people, but it's much faster—turbocharged, they say—but you'd never know by the way I drive, always below the limit. It's the one place where I just can't seem to break the rules. How nice that you're here, Jonathan!"

"Ma'am, you've really mistaken me for someone else."

The woman turned her gaze toward me and once again the car followed her line of vision. She lowered the sunglasses away from her eyes. They were a clear pale blue. She studied me with the alertness of a fox. This time I did casually place my hand on the leather-wrapped steering wheel to keep us in our lane.

"Now that I look at you," she said, "you don't look quite like Jonathan Byers at all. You have the red hair, but . . ."

"I tried to tell you."

"And you're so much better mannered than I remember."

"There are some who would disagree."

"Well!" she said, then laughed heartily. "It seems I've made a big mistake. How do you do? I'm Daphne Davenport."

Daphne Davenport? Was that a real name? Or was I caught in a John Waters hallucination of *Some Like It Hot?*

"I'm Stan Kraychik," I said.

"Yes, you told me, you naughty boy. Did you just want to ride in my new car? I wouldn't blame you one bit."

"Actually I was looking for a taxi."

Daphne lifted her sunglasses back over her eyes. "Well, now that we've met, would you like to have lunch with me?"

"Sure," I said. People have sex knowing less about each other. "But I'm supposed to report for work at the opera house."

Daphne said, "I think they'll make an exception if they know you're with me. I *am* the opera festival, after all."

I looked at her askance. I was still steering us.

"My second husband was Sid Blaustein," she said.

"As in the Sidney Blaustein Center for the Performing Arts?"

"That's right, dear. You could say I own the plantation." She laughed again. She seemed to be amused with her own life.

"But you just said your name is Davenport."

"Yes. That was my first husband's name, and I liked the sound of it so much that I kept it through my second marriage."

"Well, then," I said. "If it's not any trouble, let's have lunch."

"No false courtesy with me, young man. We'll have a nice time and pity poor Jonathan who's missing all this fun."

Daphne pulled a small telephone handset from the console between us. I wondered what might have happened if I hadn't been steering the car for the last few minutes. She punched in some numbers on the phone and waited a few moments. Then she spoke in a loud voice, fairly yelling into the small handset.

"Parker? Tell Maurizio to pick up Sir Jonathan at the train station." She paused, then said, "Yes, I've missed him! But I've got someone else with me, so there'll be one more for lunch. What? I can't hear you. Oh, never mind!" Then she slid the telephone back into the console. "Imagine that?" she said. "Me, using a car phone. Times really have changed."

Once again Daphne laughed, and then she finally brushed my hand from the steering wheel. "Thank you, dear," she said. "I'll take over now." She aimed the big Bentley onto a winding road that climbed upwards high above the water. The Bentley was perfectly at home tracing the craggy coastline, just as it might have been along the *Grande Corniche* that skims the hilly coast of Monaco. But that late spring day it was the Atlantic Ocean that hypnotized me, and with the noonday sun on my head, I was lulled into a dreamy torpor.

I thought of my lover Rafik, who was en route to Europe. He was the one who had insisted that I take the gig with the opera festival. It would supposedly look good on my curriculum vitae. I protested that hairdressers don't have such things, but as usual, Rafik charmed me into his way of thinking. We would rendezvous in Paris, where I was to meet his parents. They know he's gay and they're cool enough about it, but then, he's never been enspoused before. (Etymologists, compare enslaved, ensnared, and ensnarled.) And

6

since Rafik is the elder male scion of a dynasty of epicurean food exporters, they may not be ready for a working-class American son-in-law who does hair. Whatever the outcome of our Paris summit, we would continue to Firenze together, guests of a duchessa no less. But that's another story.

I also thought of my best friend Nicole, who owns Snips Salon where I usually work. She had grumbled enough about giving me time off for the vacation in Italy, but when I was invited to do wigs for the opera festival she agreed to give me that time as well, probably because she figured I'd be working at least. Nicole tends to view the work ethic as just one more supervisory role for her. But she did agree to board Sugar Baby, my taupe-colored Burmese cat the same hue as the candy, even though Nikki is adamant that animals have no place in a household.

Daphne's voice intruded on my mental meanderings.

"Are you a singer?"

"No," I replied lazily. "I'm assisting with the wigs."

"You're a hairdresser then?"

"Yes."

"How nice," she replied, and somehow conveyed in those two words a sincerity and kindness that neutralized all the nasty things anyone has ever said or thought about male hairstylists.

Daphne chattered on. "And I'm thrilled that the festival is finally coming to fruition. It was Sid's wish too, you know, even though the poor dear hated opera. But he did insist that I do something for the arts when he died. I think he would have liked this festival. It's ecumenical—is that the right word? I've insisted on singers and musicians of all ages from all countries. I want to create the spirit of a new Verona or a new Spoleto, not another Lake George. We have a wonderful lineup of operas. Verdi's *Un ballo in maschera*, Puccini's *La bohème*, Mozart's *Die Zauberflöte*, and my concession to a modern work, P.D.Q. Bach's *The Stoned Guest*. Oh, but I'm boring you."

"Not at all," I said halfheartedly, for I am hardly an opera buff.

Daphne continued, "It's quite a program. And the performance center came out beautifully. I insisted on hiring an Italian architect whose specialty is designing opera houses. It's a rare person who can balance beauty and function on both sides of the proscenium. And it's got the latest technology too. Have you seen the opera house yet, dear? No, of course you haven't. Well, you'll see plenty of it soon enough."

"By the way," I said, abruptly changing the conversational tack. "Who is Jonathan Byers?"

"Don't you know?" said Daphne with a chortle. "Sir Jonathan Byers is the stage director for our main production, Verdi's *Un ballo in maschera*. A masked ball. Do you know it?"

"A bit," I said. My lover had forced it on me.

"Wonderful opera," said Daphne. "And we've got a wonderful cast. We're doing it in the original Italian, of course. And Sir Jonathan—" Daphne let out a small whoop. "Well, some say he goes straight for the jugular, and he certainly does do and say some very controversial things. But he's not like those brats who insinuate their own silliness onto someone else's work. Sir Jonathan seems to be on a quest to purify the music, to hack away at the layers of interpretation that have congealed over the years since the composer wrote it. He's quite an idealist, and an absolute beast. I've met him only once, and he does behave rather badly, not at all well-mannered like you. But I hardly consider him dangerous, except perhaps to one's own calcified thinking."

Daphne completed her peroration just in time to turn the Bentley onto the long curving driveway that led up to the front of a sprawling old summer mansion.

"Here we are," she said, sounding oddly triumphant.

2

It was a massive three-story ocean house, a hodgepodge of architectural disunity on the outside. All the ground floor windows were actually French doors with fanlights over the lintels; the ceilings inside looked about twenty feet high. The second floor windows were similar, but without the fanlights; and the third floor windows were paned and shuttered, just like an ordinary seaside cottage. Above all that was the attic, riddled with dormers. And finally, like a ridiculous tiara, a spindly widow's walk sat atop the crest of the roof.

Blocking the front entrance to the mansion was a small white Japanese roadster that resembled an oversized hygiene device.

Daphne said, "Someone is here already."

"Silly little car," I said, and noticed the New York plate.

"Don't you like sports cars?" said Daphne.

"Something loud and Italian, sure. But not those."

Daphne turned off the Bentley's motor and studied the little car in front of us. "New York," she mused. "It must be Bruce David."

"Who's that?"

"Who else?" she said wearily. "Our tenor."

We were greeted at the door by a man Daphne introduced as Parker, her former chauffeur. Parker attempted the lofty manner of a British butler, but he couldn't conceal his truer self—the docile and malleable old gent.

Daphne asked him, "Has Maurizio gone to pick up Sir Jonathan?"

"No, Miss Davenport. I tried to explain earlier to you on the telephone, but our connection was bad. Sir Jonathan had called to say that he would not take the train after all, but would drive here directly."

"How odd," said Daphne with a hint of vexation. "He told me he didn't drive."

Meanwhile I gazed around the foyer. It felt cool and light and airy, with walls of palest green and woodwork painted glossy white. Unlike the outside, the interior of the summer mansion showed the marks of a good designer.

Parker continued, "I've been receiving calls all morning, Miss Davenport, ever since you left the house. Each of your guests has telephoned at least twice to ask if any of the others had arrived yet."

I recognized that game: Arrive late and with great fanfare to proclaim your supreme importance.

Parker said, "Bruce David drove in half an hour ago, and to his chagrin,"—Parker chuckled politely—"he found himself the first one here. I took the liberty of inviting him to lunch."

"Of course," said Daphne.

"But he apologized that he was too tired to eat."

Brucie was obviously lying low until someone else arrived. Such fragile egos, tenors. All *mi, mi, mi.*

"What about the maestro?" asked Daphne.

Parker answered, "Apparently he is traveling with Madama Ostinata, and they will arrive together."

"All very odd," said Daphne again. "And not a propitious start." Then she turned to me. "Shall *we* eat then? I hope you like fresh lobster salad."

She led me from the foyer through a large reception area. A broad curved staircase descended from the second floor. And I was right about the ceilings. They were stratospheric. The French doors opened onto a broad piazza set in a checkered pattern of black and white marble slabs. From there we descended a few steps and crossed a vast manicured lawn to a screened-in gazebo that looked out over the ocean. The breeze carried the scent of salt, while picture-perfect sea gulls embellished the clear blue sky. Not a bad setting for lunch.

We sat and Daphne asked me, "Iced tea? Or champagne?"

"Your choice," I replied.

10

She turned to Parker. "A bottle of the Roederer then."

I noticed that the back of the house had a broad balcony that ran most of its length and extended out partway over the marble piazza on the ground floor. The edge of the balcony was supported by pillars running up from the piazza. Like the ground floor, all the rooms along the balcony had French doors that opened out onto it.

Lunch arrived, a splendid lobster salad arranged on a bed of mixed California greens. While we ate, I learned that Daphne and I shared a background in human psychology, although I had survived less than two years in clinical work, while Daphne had made a brilliant career in psychiatry under her maiden name of Wattis. It was only then that I realized who my hostess really was: Daphne Wattis had written numerous authoritative texts, some of which I had even read in college. I told her so, and she smiled.

"It pleases me that my old work is still relevant," she said. "Even with those 'inner child' folks running their mouths off."

Daphne Wattis had been a colleague of such luminaries as Karen Horney and Helena Deutsch. Decades back she had even done some original and pioneering work on the psychology of arrested childhood development. But at the time her theories had been callously dismissed by the psychiatric community as too lightweight. Daphne had maintained that the men in power simply couldn't bear hearing a young blonde woman from southern California tell them things they hadn't imagined on their own. It would take a German to spout the same ideas before they were taken seriously. Perhaps the Teutonic weight of language had lent credence to identical if not plagiarized theories. But by that time Daphne had moved on to her research with the chemical basis of mental illness. She was just as content *not* to be lauded as the founder of "inner child" psychology, since it had been so defiled by popular culture. The occasional lecture at Harvard or consultation at McLean Hospital kept her professionally active.

She asked, "Have you lost all interest in clinical work?"

"I shrink 'em at the sink now," I said. "But if I ever go back to school, I'll do my thesis on the bond between hairstylists and their clients. God knows I have the case studies."

The main course finished, Parker cleared the table and prepared

11

to set out fresh fruit and small cakes. It was then we heard someone's voice exclaiming loudly, resonating from within the big house and out through some of the open windows. Before Parker could attend to the disturbance, a man in his late forties burst from the mansion and strode angrily across the lawn toward us. His hair was dyed that awful red some men believe conveys a youthful look. But in the bright sunlight it looked as though someone had rinsed his hair with Brasso. How could Daphne have mistaken the natural coppery sheen of my hair for that? The man shouted with a heavy British accent as he approached us in the gazebo.

"What a piss-awful mess your country is!"

"Oh dear," murmured Daphne. "It's the real Jonathan Byers."

He stormed into the gazebo and threw himself into the empty chair next to her. "Your bleeding trains have no first-class compartments. I had to hire a car in Boston—if you think *that* wasn't a bloody bit of work! I'm adding it to my expenses."

"Of course," said Daphne. She was about to introduce me, but Byers interrupted her.

"Is this it?" he said with a reckless flutter of his hand across the table. "You call this lunch? Bloody fruit and cake?"

Was he referring to me?

"If you're hungry," replied Daphne, "Parker will serve you."

But speaking of blood, mine was already simmering from the man's boorish behavior. Yet Daphne somehow remained unruffled and objective. She'd obviously handled plenty of aggressive patients and succeeded, something I could never do easily. I could never maintain a safe distance when facing open anger. I tended to absorb it and then get launched on the same savage ride as the instigator.

Meanwhile, Parker calmly set up a table service in front of Jonathan Byers. He made up a plate of lobster salad and set it before the man. Then he filled a glass with champagne, which Byers guzzled in seconds. Before Parker could return the bottle to the cooler, Byers grabbed it from his hand and refilled his glass.

"Bloody cheap bastard," he muttered at Parker.

"Bloody asshole," I muttered back.

Jonathan Byers whirled at me. "I'll ream you bloody."

Daphne didn't flinch. Parker didn't flinch. And I was saved by deus ex machina, a blond man in his mid-twenties who emerged from the house at that moment. He was clad in skimpy denim shorts, a striped cotton jersey, and white leather sneakers. He was tall, tanned, smooth, and muscled. In short, he was the perfect facsimile of a hustler.

Jonathan Byers motioned for the young man to join us, and yelled to him, "Over here, you bugger!" Then he said to Daphne, "That's young Ricky Jansen," adding with a leer, "my personal assistant. Lucky thing I pulled him out of computer school. Raw talent like that belongs in the theater, where more people can get a good look at it."

When stalwart young Ricky joined us at the table he said to Byers, "I pahked the cah in th' shade like ya tole me," I recognized a Boston accent. He'd not been Sir Jonathan's personal anything for very long. And with his lips insistently puckered as though ready for a kiss, Rick Jansen seemed less a fascimile and more like the real stuff of a hustler.

Byers gazed at him and moaned faintly, as though he'd just tasted something delicious. Then he said to Daphne, "Where's the rest of the lot then?"

She told him calmly that Maestro Toscanelli and Madama Ostinata were on their way, and that Bruce David had arrived but wasn't feeling well.

"Not feeling well?" said Byers. "What is he, a withering mayfly? We've got a show opening in less than two weeks. I've been trapped, bloody *trapped* in Boston rehearsing every screaming piece of shit in this opera *except* the principals, and now you tell me that our tenor's gone pansy on us! Where the bloody hell is he?"

"He's resting in his quarters," said Daphne.

Byers retorted, "I'll be *on* his quarters if he's not ready to sing tomorrow."

Ricky-thing flinched at that remark.

I happened to glance up at one of the second floor windows and saw that a man had been watching our dramatic vignette through a parted curtain. Our eyes connected. Immediately he vanished, and the curtain fell closed. No one saw but me.

Daphne said to Jonathan Byers, "I've reserved the guest cottage for you."

"The what?" he said, newly provoked.

Daphne continued with the well-practiced tranquility of a veteran shrink. "Jonathan, when we spoke, you emphasized your need for complete privacy. Naturally I assumed you'd prefer the cottage, where you can be utterly alone if you want."

"Where are the others staying?"

"Here, in the big house."

"All of them?"

"Yes. Madama Ostinata, Maestro Toscanelli, and Bruce David. They each have two rooms and a private bath. And you have the cottage all to yourself."

"Why am I being separated?"

"Jonathan, you are not being separated. I've given you special consideration."

Byers wasn't convinced. "I don't like being separated unless I decide on it."

Daphne maintained her equanimity. "If you want, there's plenty of room in the house—"

"I'll solve this my own way," he said. "I'll find some real privacy." He pushed his plate away, then stood up abruptly and grabbed the young Ricky-thing by his shoulder. "C'mon, you bugger. Let's go get a place in town. I'll take a whole bleeding floor of that fancy hotel." He squinted his eyes at Daphne. "You hear that?"

"Whatever is best for your work," said Daphne.

He pointed a finger at her. "And you're paying for it."

"Naturally," she said. "But I can't imagine why you'd choose to isolate yourself like that."

I could. Jonathan Byers wanted quality time with his bugger.

He marched Rick back across the lawn toward the mansion. Though the older man led the younger, the phrase "a boy and his dog" still came to mind.

"Don't forget," Daphne called out after them. "Reception tonight at six."

Jonathan Byers turned back toward us and yelled, "It's not in my contract!" He cuffed his young consort smartly on the shoulder, then pulled him close into a snug buddy-hug.

Parker gave a disdainful little snort. Daphne studied the two men and made a quick analysis. "Despite their outward familiarity, I suspect those two are nearly strangers."

"Not in the biblical sense," I said.

"Oh dear," said Daphne. "I suppose I'm paying for that as well."

I asked her why she tolerated Byers's behavior.

She shrugged and shook her head. "What can I do? He creates brilliant theater."

"But at what cost?"

"Ironically, the people he most abuses are the very ones who beg to work with him again."

Did that include former psychiatrists?

Daphne went on. "But Sir Jonathan never uses the same cast twice."

I added, "Like the best predators, he needs fresh kill."

Daphne smiled. "A good observation. And I hope you'll forgive me. I don't know how I mistook you for him. You have nothing in common, except for your hair color."

Again I was about to object, but Daphne continued.

"That man troubles me so much that I find myself denying the extent of his antisocial behavior. I'm ready to defend him, and almost to admit that he has a certain charm." She chuckled and said, "Imagine that? Still gullible at my age."

And I'd always thought great psychiatrists were immune to such foibles.

Then the great psychiatrist said, "But look how well it's turned out. *We* got to meet each other."

"I'm pleased too," I said.

I thanked her for the excellent lunch and excused myself. I really did have to get to the performance center and meet the production crew. I was there to work, after all. Daphne told me that her handyman Maurizio would drive me back to town.

Out in front of the mansion, when I went to get my bags from the back seat of the Bentley, Daphne stopped me.

"Oh, no. Leave your bags here."

"But—"

Daphne's eyes beamed as she explained. "Since Sir Jonathan wants to choose his own accommodations, I'd like you to stay here on the estate with me, in the cottage." Then she added with a hearty laugh, "That is, if you don't mind camping out with an old fogy and the would-be luminaries of opera."

I replied quickly, "Not at all."

"And I could use some fresh young company," she said.

And if there's one thing I can usually supply, it's fresh.

Daphne said, "Maurizio will set you up in the cottage, then drive you down to the performance center in the jitney."

She summoned Parker to get Maurizio. No sooner had Parker come and gone than a huge black limousine entered the circular driveway and pulled up to where we were standing. The uniformed driver got out and opened the back door. I felt a rush of cool, conditioned air escape from the passenger compartment.

The first person to appear was a shriveled and dour woman in a plain black dress. She had that innate quality of looking older than she actually was. Her gray hair had been yanked into a masochistic chignon, and her dark desperate eyes seemed to cry, *"Salva me!"* She quickly and silently moved out of the way to make room for the others.

After her followed a much older man, but he was spry and slender and impeccably dressed in a creamy white linen suit. His complexion was ruddy, with taut pink skin and a big white moustache and bushy eyebrows. His eyes were bright blue, and his hair a wavy mane of white. He quickly took in the mansion and the grounds, then gave a quick approving nod and smiled broadly toward Daphne.

"Buon giorno, bella signora," he said.

Daphne replied with a smile, *"Buon giorno, Maestro."*

Then from within the limousine came a shrill cry.

"Angelo! Aiutimi!"

The old man rolled his eyes upwards, then turned back toward the limousine and stooped into the open door. He held out his arm and a plump, bejeweled hand took hold of it. The maestro helped the hidden person get to her feet and finally emerge from the plush compartment. Her hair was expertly frosted, a pale ash blonde that glistened in the sunlight. It complemented her golden eyes perfectly. The makeup was professionally applied but heavy-handed, and unfortunately emphasized her big mouth and snouty nose, giving her face a porcine quality. She set herself firmly on her feet and sniffed at the air as if to make sure it was safe to breathe. Then she threw back her shoulders and puffed up her bosom like a pouter pigeon. She tossed her head once and delivered the line she'd probably been practicing all the way from the airport.

"How do you do, Miss Davenboat."

Daphne gave a dubious smile and replied, "How nice to meet you, Madama Ostinata. I hope your trip was pleasant."

Madama consulted with the maestro for a quick translation, then answered with a forced stagy smile.

"It was horribly."

Horribly what, I wondered.

Daphne murmured for my ears alone, "Oh dear." Then she spoke to them all in what sounded like fluent Italian, and which I made out to be an invitation to come in and get settled and then have some lunch. Madama and the maestro nodded and smiled and made approving sounds to Daphne. But to me Madama shot a disdainful glance, followed by an accusing flick of her fat little fingers.

"Who is?" she said to Daphne.

I answered her directly. "I'm doing wigs." Then I gestured with my hand to my head, as if to remove my hair.

Madama Ostinata tittered, an obvious stage mannerism, then dismissed me with a wave of her hand. "I do not need. I bring for me."

"But they'll still need dressing," I said.

Madama quickly consulted again with the maestro, then replied to me, "Mathilde will do."

I looked to find Mathilde, the severe woman in black who had withdrawn behind the rest of us. Long-suffering and apparently devoid of free will, she nodded toward Madama Ostinata. She would do her bidding.

Then Daphne said blissfully, "Here comes Maurizio now."

3

When Daphne had referred to Maurizio earlier, she had said simply "my handyman." But now a strapping youth was standing before us. A big grin showed off his large white teeth. His amber-colored eyes danced as he took us all in. His dark curly hair was tousled and his brow was beaded with moisture. Chest and shoulders were dense with muscle, and his jersey clung to his skin, tracing the deep contours of his flesh and his slightly erect nipples. In one of his large hands he balanced a two-wheeled hand truck. He looked like the young version of a Boston cop I've had dealings with—strictly business, of course.

As if recognizing a compatriot, the maestro greeted Maurizio in Italian, and the young man responded with hand gestures that indicated he could neither hear nor speak. Daphne regarded him with obvious affection while she explained that he was *sordomuto*—deaf and mute—but that he could read and write English and Italian, and could read lips in both languages as well. Maurizio seemed to receive Daphne's remarks as personal compliments, which is exactly how she had delivered them. But Madama Ostinata was clearly distressed by Daphne's familiarity with her help. Her gold-colored eyes met with Maurizio's amber ones, and a fiery jolt surged between them and held them rapt with each other. Then their response transformed itself to surprise, which then evaporated strangely to cool acquiescence. It was as though Madama Ostinata and Maurizio had recognized each other, then realized that they hadn't.

Daphne invited me to join the others for a second round of lunch, and though I sensed that she wanted and needed my company, I explained that I had to get back to town for work. I was already too late.

She said, "Then Maurizio will take you, and I'll see you at the reception later."

"You want me at the reception?"

"Yes. Six o'clock. When everyone meets everyone else."

Then she took her other guests inside.

Meanwhile the hired chauffeur had opened the limousine's trunk and was snapping his fingers at Maurizio to unload the luggage. When that didn't work, he poked the young man on the shoulder and then pointed to the numerous bags waiting to be removed. The chauffeur evidently handled live cargo only. He went and sat in the driver's seat while Maurizio wheeled the hand truck into place. I watched the interplay of his back and shoulder muscles, the tensing of thighs and loins as he lifted the heavy bags out from the limousine's trunk and piled them onto the hand truck. When he was done, he slammed the trunk lid closed. Within seconds the chauffeur started the limo and drove off. Maurizio made a lewd gesture toward the departing car and driver. Then he motioned for me to follow him as he wheeled the hand truck to a service entrance off to one side of the mansion. I waited there for him while he took the bags inside and up to the rooms.

I was enjoying the ocean air and the sounds of distant surf when I realized how quickly and wonderfully everything had changed because of a simple mistaken identity. I hadn't even started the work I'd been hired for, and already I'd met a near-operatic cast: a retired psychiatrist; a lunatic stage director and his catamite; a secretive tenor susceptible to the vapors; a benign operatic conductor; a virago of a prima donna and her hostage maid; and finally, a hunky-chunky Italian handyman. On top of it all I'd had a champagne and lobster lunch.

Then I had a sobering thought: I'd also seen the remains of a young woman whose life had apparently been so frustrating that even death was preferable to her. And she had taken that last irreversible step.

Maurizio reappeared and put my single bag on the hand truck. Then we walked together toward the far edge of the front lawn where

19

we turned onto a flagstone-paved path. The low verdant growth along the path had been meticulously cultivated to resemble an English country garden, replete with bronze statuary, a verdigris-covered fountain depicting Neptune and his consorts, and a filigree iron bench flanked by marble urns and set into a secluded alcove. Frozen foods had obviously endowed Daphne's second husband with extraordinary means to exercise ordinary bad taste. But one thing all the froufrou couldn't lessen was the soft tumbling sound of ocean waves from far below, a constant soothing whisper carried by the clean sea breeze. As Maurizio and I strolled along the path, the low shrubbery gave way to borders of higher, denser greenery, pruned and shaped to create a secluded arcade that neither wind nor ocean sounds could penetrate. Only our soft footsteps were audible now.

Just ahead of us the path split. The fork was marked by a statue, a generously muscled and endowed young Orpheus with his lyre. I paused in front of it. It could have been my lover, whose firm ex-dancer's body was still as sculpted as the polished bronze of that statue. Maurizio's eyes met mine and he winked. I saw the dilemma already: My godlike lover was three thousand miles away in Paris, while the salt of the earth was standing and grinning not two feet from me. I'd need a new mantra, and fast. I wanted to be faithful. I really did.

In the clearing ahead was the cottage that would be my home for the next two weeks. It had been freshly painted a pale green, the color of spring buds. It was a salt box style, but all on one level and with numerous multipaned windows all around. To the right of the front door was a cozy screened-in porch. Maurizio opened the door, and in we went. The scent of fresh-cut flowers pervaded the main room. A round table near one wall was graced with an extravagant bowl of fruit. Lucky for me Jonathan Byers had passed up the cottage.

I wandered into the bedroom and Maurizio followed me. He laid my heavy bag down at the foot of the bed without a sound. He's considerate too, I thought as I watched his haunches flex and harden under taut denim. The young man surveyed the room as though he'd never been there before, but I sensed it was a tactic to prolong my admiration of him. What long eyelashes! Then he smiled a mischievous smile and winked again. But I made a sign that we should drive to town. He shrugged and nodded, and away we went.

4

The jitney, as Daphne had called it, turned out to be a sleek air-conditioned minivan. Maurizio drove fast, which didn't surprise me, but also with intense focus, which did. His driving was the polar opposite of Daphne's, whose attention wandered constantly from the road in front of her. In fact, Maurizio barely glanced my way at all, which gave me plenty of time to enjoy his profile: sensual lips, straight nose, meaty chin, strong brow, and those long lashes, soft as sable.

Before leaving me off at the stage door to the opera house, Maurizio gave me a riding tour around the performing arts center. It was an old mill complex that had been completely gutted and now comprised four huge brick buildings that interconnected around an open quadrangle, formerly the mill's truck yard. The entrance to the complex was an archway built into one of the buildings. The main structures facing the quadrangle were the opera house, a concert hall, a theater, and a building of studios and residences for visiting artists. The quadrangle had been landscaped and terraced to provide pleasant views for the clientele of the ground-floor businesses, among which were an epicurean restaurant, a smart café, and various posh ateliers. All that was left to test this wild experiment in *haute luxe* was a successful opening season.

At the opera house I opened the stage door and immediately encountered the tinny sounds of a chorus and piano coming over the house PA system. Rehearsal was obviously in progress. I asked the security guard in his glass booth for directions to the wig room. He told me the way, the first leg of which was a long stairway going down. Once in the subterranean world I passed through a hallway lined with many small rooms. Through the closed doors I heard the sounds of singers vocalizing. Some were singing actual music, but most were singing scales or other warm-up exercises, a lot of which resembled barnyard noises more than operatic grandeur. I guess it's true that the best vocal technique is purely natural.

Unlike the seaside quietude of Daphne's mansion, the bowels of the opera house were alive and seething with music. It seemed the entire cast was there preparing to work, everyone except the two principal singers, Madama Ostinata and Bruce David, who at that moment were probably lunching in Daphne's gazebo.

The wig room was at the far end of a corridor. I went through the open door, and before I could get my bearings a voice barked at me, "Yes?"

I looked around, but my view was blocked by row upon row of industrial shelving filled with dummies and wigs. I couldn't see the man who'd already seen me.

"I'm looking for Dan Carafolio," I said into the air.

"I'm Daniel," said the haughty voice, still concealed among the rows and racks of wigs.

"Where are you?" I said.

"Who are you?" he said back.

"Stan Kraychik."

I heard him struggle to his feet. Then he came out from behind one of the high shelving units. Now I'll admit to having a small weight problem, fifteen or so pounds that linger around my rump and midriff. But this guy had let himself go to slop. Even his clothes were repulsive. An oversized Hawaiian-print shirt hung outside some ratty plaid Bermuda shorts, and filthy canvas sneakers showed his fat dirty toes poking through holes on top.

"First rule," he said. "When you work for me, you show up on time."

Bad start.

"I meant to call," I began, then caught myself. Was I about to grovel? I continued more assertively, "I was lunching with Miss Davenport."

"Sure you were. And I'm Anne of Romania."

"It's Marie, doll, not Anne. If you're going to quote Dorothy Parker, do it right."

"This isn't a literary contest," he snapped. "This is opera, and you're working for me." His feral eyes glowed within the doughy flesh of his face. "I requested two assistants for this production, but the costume designer determined that I needed only one. And now it looks as though all they could find was some beauty school dropout to help me."

"I have clients from the social register," I said.

"I don't care. I don't care what you claim you've done before this, and I don't care what you thought you'd be doing here, but this is your job description while you're in this opera house and working for me. Are you ready?"

Would I ever be?

Daniel said, "You will carry the hairpieces for me." He paused as if to impart weight to the words, then went on. "I have spent the last eight months creating these works in my New York studio. I then had to arrange their transport here at great expense. And now I will style them, and I will dress them. And you—" He said the word like it was a disease. "You will carry them. *That* is your sole function here, your only job. You never touch a hairpiece. If that's not clear I'll say it another way. Keep your hands off the wigs."

"I think I understand, Daniel. But how am I supposed to carry them if I can't touch them?"

He shot me a venomous glance. "They are stored on dummies. You should know that. Who hired you anyway?"

"I was referred by a client," I said, struggling to be cool.

Daniel said, "If this was New York, you'd be out of work."

If this was New York, I thought, you'd be in a cage.

He said, "They're just finishing the first scene of act one upstairs. I'm going to have a few words with the chorus, then we start the first fittings down here. Do you think you can handle that?"

"I'm at your service," I said, but I couldn't help wondering once again, Did that young woman throw herself in front of a train because she was missing this?

I followed him upstairs, but instead of going backstage with him—I wasn't sure I wanted to consecrate our association—I found a door that led out into the house auditorium, where the audience would eventually be. The stage was full of singers, including some of the soloists. A piano accompanied them all from a front corner of the stage. Finally, with the live music and the singers onstage, everything seemed fine again, as though the sun had come out and all the bad manners I'd encountered so far—the insanity of Jonathan Byers, the noblesse oblige of Madama Ostinata, and the bitchiness of Daniel Carafolio—all of it vanished in the presence of Verdi's music. Despite the petty power struggles that were endemic to an opera company, there was a point to it all: the glorious music.

Those very sounds roused me to the point where I didn't even care if I lost my charge as slavey to the keeper of the wigs. Daphne had already invited me to stay with her on the estate. Why not just attend rehearsals every day and enjoy myself? I'd always wanted to learn about opera, and what better way than to watch a production in progress?

The chorus had just finished singing, and already my life was back on course. A husky young woman dressed in jeans and a plaid flannel shirt came onto the stage. She sported a boyish brush cut.

"Break!" she barked. "Twenty minutes."

The singers were about to disperse when Daniel Carafolio waddled out from the opposite side of the stage in his grotesque clothes. He clapped his hands loudly and shouted, "People! People, don't leave yet. I want your attention here."

The chorus stopped while Dumpy Daniel addressed them all.

"I'm the wig master."

That's the word he used. Master.

Daniel continued, "You are all scheduled for a fitting later on, after this rehearsal session. I have just two simple rules for you, which should be easy enough even for chorus singers." That was apparently another term for disease in his vocabulary. "Number one," he said, "you don't open your mouth to me. And number two, you never touch your hairpiece. Is that clear? One, two. Very simple. Shut up and don't touch. Don't make me nail a sign to your skulls to remind you."

Dead quiet followed.

"Good. See you all after rehearsal."

He stalked off the stage and immediately the chorus members were murmuring among themselves. Then I heard a familiar voice shout from the back of the hall.

"Bloody fool!"

It was Jonathan Byers. He came forward into the light and addressed the chorus from the rail of the orchestra pit. "You listen to me now, all of you. Pay no attention to that pathetic little grub. You just tend to your blocking, if you can remember any of it. Once you've got that all straight, you can sing that idiot's wigs off your bleeding heads for all I care."

It was going to be some two weeks.

During the break I wandered into the main lobby of the opera house. There was an exhibit out there about the history of the performance center, how it had originally been a woolen mill owned by Chester Wattis in the late 1800s. Wattis had created the famous "Abigail" brand sweaters, named after his wife. So dear old Daphne, in spite of her youth in Santa Barbara and her stellar career and her two marriages, had come from Yankee stock after all.

I went back downstairs to help Daniel set things up for the fitting session that afternoon, and I was promptly berated.

"Where have you been? Are you here to work or to fuck around?"

"Look," I said, "I'm sorry we got off on the wrong foot."

"I thought maybe you'd gone for tea with Miss Davenport."

"You and the wigs have pre-empted all my prior engagements."

"It's too bad you showed up at all," he said. "I need professional help."

About ten years, doll.

Thus began an afternoon of enforced labor, carrying wigs for her bitter highness. Later on I did try to lighten up the chore and banter with some of the singers, but was quickly reminded by Daniel to shut the fuck up. Finally I *gave* the fuck up and claimed I had a headache. I called the estate and asked Parker to send Maurizio to come and get me. When he arrived in the minivan, I was pleased to find that the sight and the scent of him, like the sounds of Verdi's music, had restorative powers. But that didn't mean I had to fool around, did it? Hell, before meeting my lover I'd spent eons alone, languishing without so much as a trick. Surely I could wait two short weeks to be with him again. And just in time, my new summer mantra came to me: *monogamy, monogamy, monogamy.*

5

Back at the cottage I unpacked my bags, then did a few token exercises and showered. It was around six-thirty when I set out for the reception at the big house. The sun was nearing the horizon and streaking the evening sky with bold strokes of mauve and magenta. I found an alternate path to the mansion, one that led out to the ocean cliffs. A lookout platform surveyed the world from high above the sea, while far below the surf crashed on huge rugged rocks, some of them big as boxcars. Billows of cool salty mist ascended the cliffs and swirled around me, cleansing me of my recent ordeals with the raging queen of wigs.

As I approached the big house, I saw small groups of people gathered along the circular driveway chatting and drinking and smoking, creating an air of refined civility. From the open windows of the house came the lights and the voices and the clinking glasses and clattering plates of a festive event in progress. And yes, there was music too. I realized that anyone even vaguely associated with the opera festival was probably in there now, and I had the sudden urge to bolt. I wanted to be home again, in the quiet familiar comfort of my lover and my cat. But my lover was in Paris, and my cat was with my friend Nicole. So the hard facts were that home was here for now, and there wasn't a soul back in Boston pining for me.

I continued my way toward the entrance of the mansion, preparing and coaching myself to face the crowd of people inside, wondering, Who shall I be tonight? Though on the surface I may appear to be confident and sociable, that's all a mask, part of my work as a hairstylist. Underneath it, inside, I have terrible stage fright. I'm always unsure of myself among strangers. Fortunately though, I'm a Gemini, and we are blessed with malleable, adaptable, and capricious personalities. Some would say it's our bane as well.

As I passed by the loitering smokers I greeted them politely. I thought I even recognized a few of them from the orchestra that plays for the ballet company where my lover works. One young man smiled and waved to me. He was rosy-cheeked and sturdily built, wearing a tuxedo and holding a long tapered cigarette holder. "Hello again," he said, but I had no idea who he was. I waved and smiled politely, then moved on.

I stepped up to the front door and pressed firmly on the doorbell button, holding it down a second or two longer than necessary. Nerves, I told myself. I tend to forget quantum mechanics and misjudge time when I'm nervous. Witness the rare crimped perm walking out of Snips Salon.

Parker answered the door. From behind him came the raucous energy of a large party approaching its peak. He greeted me and said that Miss Davenport had been expecting me.

"I'm afraid I was delayed," I said, and then thought, What does he care about my timeliness?

Parker replied, "I shall alert Miss Davenport of your arrival."

While he went off to fetch Daphne, I surveyed the large reception hall and took in the crowd. It looked as though all the celebrities of the Boston musical world were in attendance, and all their hangers-on as well.

Daphne appeared in the foyer wearing a cotton jersey dress, cut full and pleated, pure white splashed with bold graphics of red, yellow, and blue. She opened her arms to me and exclaimed, "My dear, I missed you. I was afraid you'd forgotten."

"I lost track of time," was all I could offer. I didn't want to tell her what hell I'd seen at the opera house that afternoon.

"We've already lost one guest," she said. "Bruce David is still upstairs sick. But here *you* are, and my friends are all looking forward to meeting you."

She took my arm and led me into the main reception room. We snaked our way through the well-heeled crowd and passed by many tables laden with colorful and exotic foods.

Daphne said, "The punch is especially good tonight." Then she gave a sly wink. "I added the London gin myself."

I ladled us each a glassful. Then I made a toast.

"To new friends," I said.

"To new friends," said Daphne.

We drank, and then moved on. That's when I noticed standing off in a corner of the room apart from the crowd and looking alone and abandoned, Rick Jansen, or Ricky, as Jonathan Byers had referred to his young bugger-assistant. Rick had doffed his sun suit for black leather jeans and a white silk shirt, the latter worn open to show off his tan and his torso. I noticed Jonathan Byers in another part of the hall, holding court in his contemptuous way with a small retinue around him. For his part Byers was all in black: a black cotton jacket over a black T-shirt, with black slacks and shoes. It really set off his brassy hair. Standing close beside him was a tall, handsome man with matte brown skin the hue of a *doppio cappuccino*. At one point Byers leaned toward the dark man and whispered to him. Then he pointed toward Ricky-thing in the far corner. The other man glanced that way too, then smiled and nodded approvingly. Perhaps they were negotiating a time-share deal for the generically desirable Rick.

Daphne's voice entered my perverse meanderings.

"The handsome man with Jonathan Byers is Adam Pierce."

"What does he do?" I said, intrigued by a name that conjured a twelve-step guru for the impotent man.

Daphne replied, "Adam is the set designer for *Ballo*."

Then a glamorous middle-aged couple approached us, and Daphne introduced them as old friends. The woman said to Daphne, "Did you hear about young Sonia Hatfield?"

Daphne said no, but her face showed grave concern.

The woman went on, "It was certainly tragic for her, but it's unfortunate for you as well." Her husband tried to intervene, but the woman persisted. "I thought surely you'd heard by now."

"What happened?" said Daphne, with an impatience I hadn't expected from her.

Her friend explained with barely suppressed triumph. "After all those years and bungled tries, Sonia finally did it. She killed herself this morning—just put her head down on the tracks as the train from Boston came round the bend. There was no time to stop her or the train."

"Oh dear," said Daphne. "The poor girl. So tortured."

"I was on that train," I offered.

The woman ignored me. "Sonia had a suicide note on her."

Daphne said, "And?"

The woman reported smugly, "It said that Jonathan Byers was a bisexual rapist."

Daphne frowned. "Handwritten?"

Both the man and the woman nodded.

Daphne said, "Sonia's writing?"

Again a nod.

The woman said, "So you see, you're indirectly involved."

"Who knows about this?" said Daphne.

"Apparently everyone in town but you," said her so-called friend.

As if to counter his wife's impertinence, the husband said, "Sonia was a very sick young woman."

"I know that!" snapped Daphne. "I'd been consulted on her case." She pressed her lips tightly together for a moment, then said, "Sonia had wanted so badly to be a singer. I'd never met anyone with such burning desire. I always sensed that if her dream wasn't realized, it would destroy her. The poor creature finally lost the will to keep dreaming. Now her pain and struggle are over."

I scanned the reception hall and once again saw Jonathan Byers flirting brazenly with Adam Pierce. One final time it struck me that denied access to such absurdity as this, a young woman had killed herself.

Then through the storm of party noise, through all the attendant rush of laughter and conversation and music in the air I heard a distinctive high-pitched coloratura giggle that drove itself directly into the temporal lobe of my brain. Mercifully it passed quickly. But then it was there again, slicing its way through the crowd and into my skull.

Daphne must have sensed the slight jolt in my body because she remarked, "Ah, Madama Ostinata has arrived." She excused herself and went to greet the woman, who had just entered the reception hall with Maestro Toscanelli.

A marked change had taken place in the two people. They were no longer the tired travelers who had arrived earlier with their baggage and a maid. Now they were performers who represented a world beyond ordinary human existence. They were the stars of a formal summer reception among opera aficionados. The maestro was dazzling enough with his mane of white hair and equally impressive white moustache against a healthy glowing complexion, but Madama Ostinata even surpassed him. She seemed to emanate light—from her hair to her makeup, to the white sequined dress that emphasized her voluptuous figure, to the gauzy white boa of sheerest silk she had draped over and around her shoulders. Her throat and ears and wrists glittered heavily with diamonds and platinum. Everything about the woman was light and reflective. There was no opportunity for shadow, no visible line or wrinkle on her face and neck. Now she held a glass of champagne in her free hand, and she took great pleasure in letting it slosh and spill as she emitted that metallic penetrating laugh at anything or even nothing that was said to her.

In another part of the reception hall the salon orchestra had launched itself into a passionate tango. The throbbing music caused a sudden shift on the dance floor, and those who had been enjoying the more sedate dance forms now went off to socialize or to find food and drink. The dance floor became the domain of those who were eager and willing to partake of the sensual tango.

I was drawn toward the music and the dance floor, where five couples were sliding and strutting their way through a musical maze of domination and submission. I was surprised to see Daphne in the arms of Maestro Toscanelli. The sight of two older people daring to be so physical in public triggered mild amusement and mild outrage. I'm jealous, I thought, then smiled. Also on the dance floor were Madama Ostinata in the arms of that paragon of virility, Adam Pierce. Madama followed her partner's elegant lead—he'd obviously learned his moves in the school of tasteful seduction—then she whispered into his ear, and he responded by lowering her into a dip. She threw her head back and exposed her throat, stretched her neck out long and vulnerable, unconcerned for the moment about the fragile vocal mechanism within. The diva then arched her back sharply, so that her breasts swelled and pressed against the bodice of her sequined gown. From that precarious position she giggled with hedonistic pleasure as the observing crowd applauded her. With the tango it was never clear who was really in control.

I found myself looking beyond the dancing couples to the people who stood and watched from the opposite side of the dance floor. Among them was Jonathan Byers, whose attention was fixed on the dancers and on one couple in particular—Madama Ostinata and Adam Pierce. Sir Jonathan looked troubled by what he saw. Was he jealous? Then his eyes flashed toward me and our gazes met. My heart raced unexpectedly, and I felt oddly fearful. With great effort I managed to keep my expression stony. Byers did the same, but then he narrowed his eyes as if to focus the heat of his rage through them and sear a pathway into my mind. My forehead got sweaty and I was disoriented for a moment. I felt my brain swell under the assault of his stare. Then Byers turned away suddenly and vanished into the crowd, and my own vision returned. The tango ended just as abruptly with that characteristic unresolved cadence, a musical implication that love prevails despite the pain and damage it might inflict.

General applause followed the end of the music, and four of the dancing couples took modest bows. Madama Ostinata indulged in deep, extravagant stage bows.

The maestro excused himself from Daphne, and she watched him longingly as he departed into the crowd. I went to her side.

"What a delightful man," she said.

"And a good dancer," I added.

"And," said Daphne, almost glowing, "still a bachelor."

"Where did he go?"

Daphne beamed. "He's a man who likes his cigarettes."

Madama Ostinata was still taking curtain calls when the crowd insisted that she sing for them.

"Oh, I cannot," she demurred. "You will hear me soon."

Her English seemed to have improved remarkably since that afternoon. Perhaps the tango had helped. It often cured as many troubles as it created. More applause, more bows followed, yet the woman had done little more than refuse everyone's request to sing.

The small orchestra took its break, and most of the crowd began to disperse toward the food and drink as well. It was then that a young woman approached Daphne and myself. She was about my height and almost the same build, which for a woman meant she resembled a Valkyrie. Daphne introduced her to me as April Kilkus, Madama's understudy. I recognized the name of a fellow Slav, this one a Lithuanian. April had the robust figure of someone raised on buckwheat groats and cultured cream. Her complexion was smooth and glowing. So was her ambition, I found, as she spoke unassumingly to Daphne.

"I know it's unusual for singers to perform at parties like this, but since the crowd was asking for something, I wouldn't mind doing an aria if you'd like me to."

Daphne was taken slightly aback, but she replied with aplomb, "I'm certain they'd all love to hear you, and I would too. Let me announce it."

"Thank you!" said April. "I'll go get my accompanist."

And off she ran. Daphne and I exchanged glances.

I said, "She must really want to sing if she's willing to do it at a party."

Daphne said, "She's an understudy, my dear. She has nothing to lose."

Within moments April Kilkus returned with her accompanist, a plain woman named Carolyn Boetz, whose melancholy eyes appeared shrunken behind the thick lenses of her eyeglasses. April consulted with Daphne for a moment. Then Daphne stepped up onto the dais and got the attention of her guests. She announced that April Kilkus would sing the aria *"Morro, ma prima in grazia"* from the festival's opening production of Verdi's *Un ballo in maschera*. It was one of the few operatic arias I was familiar with, thanks to my supercultured lover. The clattering sound of applause brought other people back into the salon near the dais.

April Kilkus faced her audience almost defiantly. She stood alone, without support from the piano. From the keyboard Carolyn Boetz played the opening bars. Her mouth fell slightly open, and a sadness appeared on her face as she played. In the score those first doleful lines of music are played by a solo cello. But somehow, through her love and affinity for Verdi and the piano, Carolyn Boetz persuaded the huge instrument to resonate and sing with the same mournful quality of a cello tenderly caressed. She may have appeared plain on the outside, but Carolyn's inner life certainly had depth and richness.

And then April Kilkus sang her first notes. From the initial sound it was clear that she was a talent to be reckoned with. The crowd was enthralled with every phrase, every breath, every nuance the dramatic soprano made. I noticed standing in the doorway to the salon the same chunky tuxedoed man who'd been smoking outside earlier. His attention was now fixed on the singer with wide adoring eyes. Standing next to him was a tall Asian man with the same smitten look on his face. How strange love is! Already two sides of a triangle were forming.

Among the audience I also saw Jonathan Byers, who was openly entranced by April's voice. It was strange to see him so tranquil. His catamite-bugger-thing was nowhere near him. But Adam Pierce was, and he was listening to April's voice with cool detachment, as though the music she was creating was something he realized he was supposed to appreciate.

Daphne was beside the maestro again, and their responses to the aria paralleled each other. Only Madama Ostinata on the maestro's other arm was shooting daggers toward the dais, looks that seemed to say, How dare she sing? Madama toyed with her necklace, rattling the heavy jewels and precious metal, and creating a mild nuisance. The maestro patted her arm gently as if to calm her.

The aria closed with a shimmering sotto voce cadenza. While April sang it, time stopped and world peace was achieved.

In the quiet moments after the last note, nothing was heard throughout the entire salon save the careless rattle of Madama Ostinata's necklace and a noticeable clucking of her tongue. Maestro Toscanelli then applauded heartily toward both performers and encouraged the audience's enthusiasm as well. Everyone clamored for another selection, but April refused them. She'd made her point.

"Pity she's only the understudy," said a voice behind me. I turned to see who it was. The tall Asian man had moved beside me and was now cheering April with calls of *"Brava!"*

The party had reached its climax. There was nothing to do but leave at the crest of excitement or else stay too long and pick up the debris. I made my way toward Daphne, who was still applauding with Maestro Toscanelli while Madama Ostinata was still fuming.

"I'm going," I said.

"So soon?" asked Daphne.

I nodded and made excuses about tiredness.

"See you in the morning then," she said. "Breakfast here at the big house, eight o'clock sharp."

Minutes later I was almost out the front door when I heard from the music salon a terrific tremolo of chords from the big piano. Some ham-fisted player had replaced Carolyn Boetz. Then followed a wave of applause and loud cheers from the crowd. I looked back inside and saw Madama Ostinata standing on the dais and preparing to sing. She had cleverly seized upon April Kilkus's enraptured audience for her own purposes. But her accompanist was the real surprise. It was none other than Rick Jansen, Jonathan Byers's personal assistant driver-thing, or perhaps ex-thing was more correct, considering Byers's recent behavior with Adam Pierce. Who would have thought Rick Jansen could play the piano as well as drive? But once he began, I realized he was all fist and no wrist. He pounded out a bombastic introduction to Madama's chosen selection, a circus version of Johann Strauss's "Voices of Spring." Between the two of them, it was sure to be a travesty of real music, with trills and frills and interpolations. But what truly puzzled me was how they even knew each other.

And then I saw Daniel Carafolio cheering from the front lines, *"Brava,* Marcella! *Bravissima!"* So I quickly learned which side of the musical bread he liked to butter.

At the door I caught Parker's attention and spoke like a conspirator.

"You'd better cushion the crystal for this one."

"Very good, Mr. Kraychik," he said. "Ho ho."

Outside the door I saw the young man in the tuxedo, and once again he waved to me. It was only then and to my embarrassment that I realized he was really a woman, and vaguely familiar at that.

She said, "I saw you at the opera house this afternoon."

I apologized that I didn't recall seeing her.

"Sure you did. I'm the stage manager."

Then everything clarified in an instant, and in my mind I saw her again at rehearsal, in her stage manager's duds—plaid flannel shirt and jeans.

"I remember now," I said.

"My name's Ronda Lucca," she said. "But people call me Ron."

"I'm Stan Kraychik."

"I know," she said. "You're a hairdresser."

"How did you know?" I asked.

"It's a small world," she said. "I know your partner, from the ballet and all."

"Oh," I said, nodding.

"It's going to be some festival with that Italian cow singing," said Ronda. "She's a sonic health hazard."

"But her understudy is good," I said.

"She's the best," replied Ronda.

"Well, see ya 'round," I said.

"Damn right," said Ronda.

I moved away from the light and onto the estate lawns. Then I continued into the darkness, onto the broad expanse of soft grass. As I moved over the lawn, I felt the urgent need to be away from the house and those people, to be back safely inside the cottage. In my haste I moved a bit too fast and found myself stumbling, breathing quickly, gasping almost, running away from something I couldn't identify, but something heavy and oppressive. Far across the dark lawn I saw the dimly lit path that led to my cottage. I made a dash for it, running faster than I should have on unfamiliar ground. But I couldn't slow myself down somehow, had to go faster, had to get back to safety before something caught up with me. Then I lost my footing and crumpled onto the cool moist grass.

I rolled onto my back and looked up at the sky. It was blazing with stars. I lay there a few minutes and caught my breath. Why had I panicked? What had come over me? It was as though I had wanted to be afraid, had wanted to run away from something, and so I had purposely created a feeling of fright within myself, and then had run witless to escape from . . . nothing.

I watched the stars until I lost track of time. Eventually I felt a chill, and I got to my feet. I pulled myself up straight and tall, then strode toward the dimly lit path that would lead me home. I passed through the dark convoluted tunnel of foliage and trees and finally saw the soft glow of light ahead, the light from the cottage. I would be snug and safe. I could lick my imaginary wounds in solitude. I unlocked the door and entered.

6

It was only when I was inside the cottage that I realized the significance of the lamp being on, for I hadn't turned it on when I'd left earlier. An automatic timer, I thought simply. But there was no device attached to the lamp's power cord. Someone had purposely done it, perhaps Maurizio the young handyman. Like a thoughtful hotelier, he had switched on a lamp to make the empty cottage seem more homey on my return. Perhaps he'd even turned the bed down for me. I smiled at that thought.

Then my nostrils flared, for through the flower-drenched air of the small cottage I perceived another scent, another person close by. I went toward the bedroom, but stopped short in the doorway. In the faint glimmer of lamplight from behind me I made out the form of someone on my bed. It was Maurizio, lounging comfortably in skimpy white briefs. His appealing scent filled the small bedroom. The air went still, save for a fierce pounding in my chest and against my eardrums. I saw his smile in the dimness. He swung his big-muscled legs over the edge of the bed, then he stood up and faced me.

I would never clearly recall the step-by-step moments of what happened after that. It was a dream that switched abruptly from sanity to madness, from restraint to recklessness, without any of the intervening moments. My memory allowed only the dark image of his face in ecstasy, and the sensation of his rough hairy thighs against my smooth skin, and his sounds—*uhnff, uhnff, uhnff*—as he thrust himself against me.

Then it was over and he was gone.

7

I slept like the dead until my alarm clock went off at seven-fifteen. I got up and showered, then headed to the mansion for breakfast. I found Daphne already out in the gazebo enjoying the cool morning air and the glassy green ocean. Parker had just set out a huge basket of fresh-baked scones—classic currant, tangy ginger, and decadent pecan praline—along with a platter of sliced fruit and a big French-press coffee maker.

"Good morning," Daphne chirped happily to me. "Our musician guests are taking breakfast in their rooms, so you're stuck with me."

"That's my good luck," I said. I sat down and dove into the basket of scones. I chose a pecan praline and slathered it with butter and orange marmalade.

Daphne pressed the plunger on the coffee maker with a dramatic gesture. "Voilà!" she said. "I just love doing that." She filled my cup first. Then as she filled hers, she cleared her throat and attempted a casual tone as she said, "Are you romantically involved with anyone?"

"Yes," I answered.

"That's too bad."

"Not at all," I said, thinking of my man in Paris.

Daphne explained, "I think Maurizio likes you."

I sighed. Before the great conjugal drama of my life had begun, it seemed I was always playing Anna Magnani, causing dread and loathing in anyone I dared to pursue, no matter how simple my approach. I mean, I'd ask someone out to a movie, and they'd run for the airport. But then, after settling in with my lover, the tables somehow turned, and occasionally I found myself involved however unwillingly in the bizarre sport of Fuck Me, I'm Married.

"I get more attention since I met my lover," I said.

Daphne replied, "That often happens. Just be kind to Maurizio. He may seem strong, but he's timid and vulnerable."

Not last night he wasn't.

Daphne went on. "He'll be driving you all down to the performance center in a little while." Then she inhaled deeply and exclaimed, "To think that today marks the beginning of the home stretch. Everyone is finally here, and the rehearsals can start taking place in the opera house. Less than two weeks to opening night. Imagine!"

All I could imagine was my grueling work in the bowels of the new opera house, toting wigs for Daniel, the demon diva.

We finished our breakfast, then Daphne walked with me to the front of the mansion. There under the portico stood Madama Ostinata and Maestro Toscanelli chatting in Italian. Maurizio was trying to coax the two musicians to board the minivan. They didn't seem to understand that the limousine was long gone and the minivan was now their mode of transport. Mathilde stood by silently.

When Maurizio saw me he left the others and came to me. He was as frisky as a puppy. I was friendly, but reserved. As rousing as his impromptu visit had been the previous night, I didn't want to encourage a repeat performance. I wanted to be faithful to my lover in Paris, though I suppose it was a bit late for moralizing. Still, it had been innocent and playful with Maurizio, sort of. And I hadn't really hunted him down. It all just happened. So in my heart, if not my mind and body, I was still faithful.

Maurizio must have sensed my thoughts, because he stopped himself short of touching me. I knew all he needed was a sign, some molecular clue that I wanted more of what had transpired just hours before. And I did feel a strange affection for him and especially his direct approach to sex. Or was it pity I was feeling because of his impairments? I was about to extend my hand to him and touch his arm, a simple friendly gesture that honestly would have meant much more to both of us, but then I heard my new mantra—*monogamy,*

monogamy, monogamy—and I pulled back too. Immediately Maurizio's eyes filled with tears, and he turned and ran off. It all took but a few seconds.

Daphne said to me with a fleeting grimace, "I warned you he was emotional."

I was about to go after Maurizio but Daphne stopped me.

"It's best if you let him be. He'll reason it out in his own way. But for now, would you mind driving the others into town?"

"Not at all," I said. It was the least I could do since I'd scared off the designated driver.

So I herded the others—Madama, the maestro, and Mathilde—toward the minivan. The maestro asked me for a light for his cigarette. *"Hai da accendere?"* I pointed to the minivan.

"I'm sure there's one in there," I said.

He nodded amiably and went to light his cigarette.

But Madama Ostinata looked at me uneasily. "You are coming too?" she said.

"I'm driving you, doll."

"I hope you will not make us late."

Her English was getting better and better.

Then Daphne said, "Where is Bruce David?" She called Parker and asked him to get the tenor.

But Parker replied, "Mr. David apologizes that he is not quite ready, and he will join you all at the performance center."

"Oh dear," said Daphne. "I'm worried about him. It's one thing to miss the reception last night, but he simply cannot miss today's rehearsal. It's the first time the principals will be singing together."

I saw Maestro Toscanelli's eyebrows rise dubiously, as if he recognized a behavior pattern that was familiar among the precarious male voices known as tenors.

Daphne said that she would drive Bruce David down to the opera house herself when he was ready. I felt a slight twinge of jealousy. My place as her favored guest was already being usurped by a temperamental if invisible tenor.

The maestro helped Madama Ostinata onto the minivan's plumply cushioned middle bench, then Mathilde scrabbled her way into the cramped back row, and finally we were off.

During the drive to town I tried to catch bits of the subdued conversation between Madama Ostinata and the maestro. My Italian is limited, but I've learned that the true message is often carried by the inflection as much as the words and grammar. It seemed that Madama was concerned about her career, especially with this new production of *Ballo*. It was too controversial, she complained, *"Troppo controverso e moderno."* Madama seemed to require extraordinary encouragement from the maestro, which he seemed only too willing to give. She sounded almost like a child, while the old man cooed comforting words to her and called her Marcella and *mia cara*. But despite his concern I gleaned that the maestro believed his *cara* had grown dependent on him. "Too much," he said. "You must rely on yourself again, like the old days. After all, who will be there when you are Tosca next fall?"

Madama answered with operatic intensity. *"Tu, Angelo,"* she declared. *"Tu me salvarmi."*

I sensed the maestro would easily succumb to her feminine wiles. Then the minivan jolted to a halt.

Madama shrieked, then began jabbering in English, of all things. "I will be late for the press!"

The press? What about rehearsal? What about food and water?

The maestro made some remark about how all machines break down, including himself, he added with a hearty laugh.

I tried to restart the van a few times, but nothing happened. No starter motor. No click. No nothing. Zip. Which I quickly diagnosed as no electricity. Now, there are some laws of electromagnetics that even a hairstylist can savvy, such as when there's suddenly no juice, you check the fuses. Fortunately, since it was a new model van, the fuse block was inside the passenger compartment, which meant no dirty fingers for me. I checked the fuses, and sure enough, the one that protected the electronic ignition was open. I tried to remove the fuse, but it had been forced in place too tightly, and I wasn't about to split a nail prying it out.

"Does anyone have a nail file?" I asked.

My three passengers looked at me blankly. I mimed the motions of a manicure—we Geminis are born actors—which caused Mathilde to speak from the distant regions of the back seat.

"I have," she said, and she rummaged through her beaded reticule until she produced a fine French nail file. I'd have to be careful not to bend it. An artist has respect for his tools.

When I did get the old fuse out I found that it was the wrong type for the slot it was in—too low a rating and too big a circumference. No wonder it had failed, and no wonder it had been stuck tight. I checked the glove box for spare fuses. None. If we were going to get moving again, I'd have to make a decision. I assumed there was nothing wrong with the ignition system, but only with the wrong fuse. It was show time.

I asked Mathilde, "How about a hairpin?"

"Eh?" she said.

Once again my Marcel Marceau imitation worked, and I was soon filing the vinyl coating from a simple hairpin and fashioning it into a temporary fuse. There was a big risk in my ingenuity however: My hand-fashioned fuse would probably withstand more current than ten minivans could produce. It was like putting a penny in the fuse box at home. I hoped I wasn't about to melt the van's entire electrical system.

I installed the makeshift fuse. Then I said a silent prayer to the god of voltage regulators as I turned the ignition key. I heard the faint whir of the electric fuel pump as it filled the small reservoir in the fuel injection system. I turned the key further and the engine leaped to life.

"Bravo," yelped the maestro. "Very clever."

Madama Ostinata sighed with relief. She wouldn't miss her date with the papparazzi after all. *"Grazie a Dio,"* she exclaimed.

"You're welcome," I muttered back. But I wondered if Maurizio had purposely installed the faulty fuse to set the stage for him to display his mechanical prowess and save us all. Especially me.

When we got to the performance center, there really was a small pack of reporters waiting to rush Madama Ostinata and the maestro.

Madama seemed to encourage them. Strangest of all was that by that time her English had become almost fluent.

I traipsed downstairs to my dungeon, but found the door to the wig room locked. A note taped outside read: SICK TODAY. DON'T TOUCH THE WIGS!

Things were looking up.

8

With my newfound freedom I went upstairs to watch rehearsal. As Daphne had said earlier, it was the first time all the principal singers would be together, and I certainly wanted to witness that. Rather than go backstage though, I decided to watch from out front, in the opera house itself.

I found one of the doors that led into the house near the pit, along the left aisle wall. When I opened the door I met a pleasant rush of cool air from the auditorium. Along with it came the sounds of a piano, though not so pleasant. Someone was attempting a difficult passage from the opera, but fumbling it every time. The piano player would stop and try again and again, pounding at the keys mercilessly and stupidly, trying to vanquish the technical snag with the subtlety of a bulldozer. Well, I used to play the piano, and I was pretty good too. In fact, I won the prize for serious music at my high school talent show all four years. I hardly play now, but one thing I still know is that music and piano keys will always resist brute force. You can't just knock down a musical hurdle. You have to coax it and entice it, ply it with analysis and respect and even affection, both for the instrument and for what the composer wrote. And for your own physical equipment too. All that loving attention usually entices the problem to yield its secret willingly.

The house lights were off, but the work lights onstage were bright. The air all around bore the smell of new lumber and fresh paint and recently laid carpeting. A shiny brass railing separated the orchestra pit from the first row of audience seats, and velvet draperies the color of fresh-drawn blood hung from the railing. Those yards of dense, luxuriant fabric would stifle most of the light and movement within the pit, but the sounds of music would still fly up gloriously free into the audience.

The stage was devoid of scenery except for a few chairs and a background of artificial rock. The stage crew was bustling about with clipboards, referring to them with clinical precision and then marking the floor with strips of masking tape.

Through it all the pianist persisted with that same passage, obtusely making the same mistake over and over, treating the piano like a keypunch machine instead of an instrument of music.

Finally someone called out, "Can it, will ya!"

Amen, doll.

The musical torture stopped for a moment, then resumed with new vigor. The piano itself was downstage right on the very precipice of the orchestra pit, which put the pianist just out of my sight line. I shuffled quietly along my row toward the aisle at the other end. I wanted to see who'd had the lobotomy at the keyboard. It turned out to be Rick Jansen. Why didn't he stick to things he was better at? Things like driving and buggery? At least one hoped he was better at those. Instead, there he was, lost in a labyrinth created by his own fingers. The piano lamp cast odd shadows on his angular young face, giving it a stark and sinister look. His eyes appeared to vanish into deep sockets under his brow, and his usual too-eager smile resembled a demonic leer.

A door at the back of the house flew open letting in a stream of light. Rick and I both looked back toward the open door. Madama Ostinata called out from the back of the house, "Rick, darling! You are here!"

So it was "darling" now. Madama rushed down the left aisle. As she passed me, she glanced my way from the corner of her eye. She approached the orchestra pit, then leaned on the rail and stretched herself up toward the stage. "You saved me last night," she exclaimed to Rick-darling, then blew him a kiss. "I owe you my life."

Through my nausea I wondered again how they knew each other, and how was Madama's English improving so fast? Moments later Sir Jonathan Byers entered through the same doorway and rushed down the same aisle. He was accompanied by Adam Pierce. Rick watched Jonathan Byers hopefully, as if he expected the same bountiful and impassioned greeting from his bugger-daddy as he'd just got from Madama Ostinata. But Byers was so preoccupied with Adam Pierce that he didn't even acknowledge his discarded, previously driven model. I almost felt bad for Rick.

"Let's get to work," bellowed Jonathan Byers. "Act two, scene three, Renato's entrance heading into 'Odi tu'. Places now! We have work to do."

The soloists converged quickly onstage. I recognized the same handsome Asian man I'd seen at Daphne's reception the night before. I assumed he was the baritone who would be singing the role of Renato. Madama Ostinata would sing Amelia, of course, who is Renato's wife in the opera. Standing in the wings was Mathilde, always close by in case her mistress needed her. The maestro was sitting at a chair close to the piano. Also present onstage and seated at the front edge were the festival's prompter and the resident language coach. Sir Jonathan took a seat in the audience, just in front of the production table that had been set up midway in the house. At the table were seated Ronda Lucca alongside the production's technical director, then the lighting designer and his assistant, and finally, a gerbil-like man who was supposed to be Jonathan Byer's assistant director, but who seemed to have no clear official function, at least not with Rick Jansen and Adam Pierce vying for Sir Jon's unofficial attentions. There was a place at the production table for Adam Pierce as well, but instead he sat next to Byers in the audience.

When he began giving stage directions, Sir Jonathan spoke with an austere directness that showed little emotion or vulgarity, quite a change from his usual style of address. At least that's how he started.

"The first-level motivations for this scene are easy," he said. "*You* are the club owner . . ." Byers's voice trailed off as he scanned the stage for a particular face. Then he said with great exasperation, "Where's the bleeding tenor?"

Ronda Lucca answered from the production table, "He's on his way."

Byers said, "Understudy, please!"

Please? Jonathan Byers had said "please"?

From the wings a plump but sturdy young man quickly took his place onstage with the other singers.

Byers went on. "This is where Riccardo and Amelia are caught together by her husband Renato, who with his cohorts has been planning a fag bashing."

Madama Ostinata said, "What is that?"

"Wake up, love," said Byers. "Your boyfriend Riccardo owns a nightclub that caters to a mixed clientele. Some of the townsfolk don't approve and they want the place closed down. Renato, your husband, is their leader, so he wouldn't be too happy to see you consorting with the enemy. We've changed the plot a bit, love. You did know that, didn't you?"

"But where is the king?" said Madama.

"There is no king," said Byers, his patience already spent. "Riccardo owns a nightclub now."

Madama began babbling incoherently about *un cane in chiesa*—a dog in a church—and then about poor Verdi, until Maestro Toscanelli finally got up from his chair near the piano and went to console her with verbal bromides: It was the modern world. The old traditions were dying. Youth would be served.

Then followed a slight disturbance back at the piano, where Carolyn Boetz was trying to take her place.

"Excuse me," she said too loudly to Rick Jansen, who was still sitting at the keyboard. "*I* am the rehearsal pianist," said Carolyn. But Ricky-thing wouldn't budge. Carolyn turned to Jonathan Byers. "Why is he here?" she demanded. But then her face and neck reddened under the work lights, and she looked suddenly lost, as though she hadn't really meant to speak so sharply to the big daddy director.

Jonathan Byers whirled at Carolyn, but it was Madama Ostinata who explained in a heavy accent, "Rick-darling plays for all my solos."

Carolyn Boetz replied shortly, "There is no solo now."

Madama went on. "*Non te ne fare una testa.* Don't be upset, my child. You will receive full pay."

"I don't care about that," said Carolyn. She turned her imploring gaze to the maestro. "Who decided this? When?"

Maestro Toscanelli seemed confused by the suddenness of her questions and was unable to answer.

Meanwhile Marcella Ostinata's eyes glittered wildly. She was enjoying herself. Carolyn Boetz stared back without flinching. Then she turned once again to Maestro Toscanelli, who now simply shrugged and shook his head like Pontius Pilate.

Jonathan Byers settled the debate quickly. "You!" he said, snapping his fingers and pointing to Rick at the keyboard. "The car needs petrol. I'll want a long drive after rehearsal."

"I can fill it then," replied Rick, cool as a lime rickey.

"But *you're* not driving me, love. Now just do as you're told, and let the young woman play the piano. There's a good boy."

I had a little dog and his name was Fuck.

Rick Jansen got up and left the stage in an angry huff.

Work on the scene resumed.

As I watched the rehearsal I discovered that Jonathan Byers's directorial method was basically to volley stage directions at the singers, challenging them or else outright demanding that they do his bidding. "Of course you can ask me questions," he'd say encouragingly, but then his standard reply would be, "Just try it my way, love." His goal seemed to be to frustrate and confuse the singers to the point where they could not or would not think anymore. The odd thing was, during those brief lapses when I myself stopped thinking and could almost overlook his abrasive style—though walking on water might have been easier—I did get inklings of the dramatic intent that Jonathan Byers had in mind. At this early stage though, the moments of truth were like optical illusions, fleeting and ephemeral. You thought you saw something, felt something, but then you didn't. Or did you? And then there'd be a flash of intense clarity that caused a very real shiver of delight and even fear. If the noxious Sir Jonathan could get these folks to enact those aberrant visions of his, which seemed to lurk just under the surface of the story—much the way an alternate world exists on the reflective undersurface of water, separated from the top side by a transparent film just a molecule thin—then the audience at the New England Summer Opera Festival was in for the kind of wild ride the world hadn't seen since the Messieurs Stravinsky and Diaghilev presented their scandalous collaboration in 1913, *The Rite of Spring*.

But who should arrive at that moment and shatter a dream in the making but Bruce David, the tenor. He wore sunglasses and a fedora, and his throat was wrapped with a white silk scarf.

"Here I am," he said in a barely audible mezza voce, which was further obscured by his noisy sucking of a pastille. "I am ready to sing now. Where are we?"

"You just sit and watch," ordered Byers.

"But I'm perfectly warmed up."

"We're working without you at the moment," snapped Byers.

"But this is my opera!" said Bruce David, expelling the pastille and revealing his version of a full voice.

"Yours!" said Byers.

"I demand to sing, or I will consult the union."

Ronda Lucca's voice came from the production table. "You're not *in* the union."

"Oh bleeding Christ," muttered Jonathan Byers.

Meanwhile Daphne, who had arrived with Bruce, slipped into the seat beside me in the darkened audience. "Did you sneak away from work, you naughty boy?"

"No, ma'am. The boss called in sick today and had the wigs locked up. So I figured I'd come up here and watch."

"Isn't it exciting?" she said. "Has Hwang Yung Cho sung yet? He's our Renato."

"No one has sung a note," I replied. "They've been working out the blocking. The piano has been playing, but so far everyone has just been humming their part."

"They're saving their voices," said Daphne. "Just wait until you hear Hwang! A voice like burnished teak. We were so lucky to get him. He's in demand all over Europe."

Meanwhile Jonathan Byers had stopped the rehearsal and was painstakingly reiterating for Bruce David every gesture that he'd just shown to his understudy in the previous hour. Madama Ostinata stood by impatiently, although she could certainly have used the extra rehearsal time. Only Hwang Yung Cho seemed to relish the chance to rehearse his acting movements once again. At one point I saw him make a furtive little wave to someone offstage. I looked in that direction and saw April Kilkus standing in the wings, smiling at him with the unmistakable look of love.

Finally it was time to try a run-through of the whole scene with voices and music.

Jonathan Byers moved to a chair at the production table. Adam Pierce joined him there. The maestro sat near the onstage piano and conducted Carolyn Boetz, who followed his direction perfectly. But Madama Ostinata, who was to open the scene with the exclamation *"Ahimé!"* missed her cue three times—once for pitch and twice for timing. Bruce David sang every note sotto voce and acted out none of the blocking as he'd been shown. It seemed that only Hwang Yung Cho had prepared his music thoroughly before rehearsal and had also absorbed Jonathan Byers's stage directions during the preceding hour. One professional singer out of three wasn't bad.

Then the crucial moment arrived. Madama Ostinata had to begin the trio *"Odi tu."* Both the maestro and Carolyn Boetz tried repeatedly to help her with the attack on the quick, light upbeat that starts the trio. The two notes are sung without accompaniment. It's a difficult cue, because those two little notes set the tempo for the entire trio that follows. But Madama Ostinata botched it again and again. Finally in frustration she turned to the maestro and said, "That girl is confusing me." She glared at Carolyn, then pleaded desperately with the maestro. *"Angelo, caro Angelo, te imploro.* I need Rick."

Once again Maestro Toscanelli cooed and coddled Madama Ostinata for many minutes, and once again managed to placate her without yielding to her request. The trio finally got off to a stumbling start, but by that time Jonathan Byers had just about lost interest in the rehearsal and was finding more reward in the attentions of Adam Pierce. Through sheer willpower Maestro Toscanelli and Carolyn Boetz kept the trio going, which was a major feat, since Madama would bring the music to a grinding halt by sustaining every one of her high notes. To keep the tempo up the maestro began pounding on the top of the piano, which only caused a look of wide-eyed panic on Madama's face. Bruce David was completely inaudible. And though Hwang Yung Cho sang beautifully—Daphne's image of smooth, oiled, deeply grained wood had been accurate—the whole scene came off unbalanced, a shambles.

When it was over, Madama Ostinata spoke in a loud voice to Carolyn Boetz.

"Young girl, you should perhaps give up music and find a husband who will buy you a nice dress."

Carolyn Boetz was speechless, as was the maestro.

Daphne murmured beside me, "Oh dear."

Jonathan Byers was so busy whispering and flirting with Adam Pierce that he completely missed Madama's insult. But up from the production table sprang Ronda Lucca to the rescue.

"Hey you!" she said to Madama as she made her way down toward the stage. "That's my stage. You don't talk like that to anyone while you're up there. I don't care who you are."

Ronda quickly ascended to the stage, then escorted Carolyn Boetz away from the piano and offstage. The maestro and all the other musicians, all except for Madama Ostinata, dispersed backstage as well. There was an aura of revulsion over what had just transpired onstage, both musically and socially. Oblivious to all though, Jonathan Byers and Adam Pierce were still whispering to each other with great animation at the production table. It was embarrassing to watch them.

Then Adam said aloud, "I'll show you what I mean, Jon."

He got up, walked down front and made his way to center stage, then beckoned Madama Ostinata to join him there. He said to her, "We're considering a new light cue for your aria 'Ma dall'arido'. Can you stand here?" He pointed to the spot and Madama complied.

"Special lights for me?" she said coyly.

Adam ignored her and spoke excitedly out toward Jonathan Byers. "It really will work, Jon. She'll be singing about guilt and fear and the forces of evil, but we'll bathe her in pink light to show what's really on her mind."

Jonathan Byers left the production table and headed toward the stage too, as if being closer to Adam Pierce would help him understand the proposed lighting change. Then again, Byers might have wanted to consider the whole idea away from the lighting designer, who was still at the production table and who was clearly irked to see his own theatrical visions being challenged by the stage director's latest darling.

Once onstage, Byers said discreetly, "I think it may be a bit much, Adam."

"No," replied the other man. "You'll see. If you get her down on the ground, the message will be clear."

Madama looked horrified. "I do not sing on the floor."

But Jonathan Byers was seriously pondering Adam Pierce's proposal.

"Perhaps the message will be a bit too clear," he said to Adam.

Then I felt Daphne's hand grip onto my forearm. I looked up and saw a scrim the width of the entire stage dropping down from the flies. Stupefied and entranced, we watched it plummet toward the stage floor like a surprise special effect. Not a single voice called out to the people onstage, not even mine. Then I saw the heavy pipe that carried the scrim strike Adam Pierce on the head. He fell to the stage floor, and some of the crew came running out from the wings to help him. Jonathan Byers stood motionless with disbelief. Madama Ostinata was trapped on the other side of the scrim, looking ridiculous and wailing, *"Soccorso! Maleficio!"*

Within moments I was up on the stage myself. Adam Pierce was still down, but he seemed to be talking jovially to the people who had gathered around him. A few of them had hunkered down and were asking how he was. He said he wasn't hurt at all, just stunned. And there appeared to be no blood on his head. But when Adam tried to lift his arm, nothing happened. His face grimaced in panic. Then, to everyone's horror, his body began twitching violently, like a rabbit whose neck has just been broken. His eyes rolled upward and his limbs shook erratically. Ronda Lucca knelt down quickly and rolled him onto his side to lessen the seizure. Someone ran to call an ambulance. Everyone else in the cast and crew had formed a wide circle around Adam and Ronda, who now resembled a grotesque pietà.

The stage became suddenly silent. Adam's long limbs jerked and shuddered, then his body contracted into an acute spasm. He gasped. His breath rattled. Then he died in Ronda Lucca's arms.

9

The ambulance arrived along with two officers from the Abigail police. The opinion of the medics was that a portion of Adam Pierce's spine had been crushed by the impact of the pipe. As if to absolve any feelings of guilt that we in the opera house might have felt for failing to save Adam, the medics assured us that injuries like that were always fatal, and nothing could have saved him. But they were also careful to remind us that the official cause of death would be determined by the county medical examiner.

While Adam's body awaited further examination, the police sergeant ordered us all to remain in the opera house for routine questioning. "No big deal," he said impassively. "I'll just need to interrogate you all for a little while." He lingered on the I-word and savored each syllable. In-ter-ro-gate. He acted like the head of security for a country club, moving too deliberately, relishing every micron of power in his tiny domain. He was nothing like the Boston cop I knew, who often seemed plagued by his own authority.

We were all to wait out in the auditorium where we would each be called in turn to be questioned by the sergeant. The house lights were brought up, and we all dispersed from the stage. Madama had since been rescued from behind the fallen scrim and was babbling to Mathilde and the maestro. I caught words here and there, things like *malocchio* and *la vendetta*. And the maestro seemed to be having trouble finding a light for his cigarette.

As I headed into the wings Ronda Lucca caught up with me. In a whisper for my ears alone she murmured, "Too bad that pipe didn't hit the cow instead."

I glanced sharply at her. She'd uttered my exact thought.

Out in the audience Daphne was sitting in the same seat where I'd left her.

"Were you too upset to come up on the stage?" I said.

She answered, "I'm sorry I couldn't help. The sight of blood unnerves me. Even a paper cut makes me woozy. Show me a mind that's laid open with gaping, fatal wounds, and I can dive right into it, to the deepest darkest places, and try to fix it. But the sight of blood or broken bones ..." Daphne shuddered. "That part of medical school was a nightmare for me."

"But there was no blood up there," I said before I could edit myself.

"Still," said Daphne.

"It's all under control now," I offered quickly, as if to retract my insolent gaffe.

She chortled. "Oh, I hardly believe *that*."

"Neither do I," I said.

Daphne sighed heavily. "I wonder what will happen now."

"The police will question us."

"I meant with the festival," said Daphne.

"Is that why you didn't go up onstage? The police?"

Daphne explained, "Since the beginning I've tried to maintain the spirit that the festival would be smooth sailing, as if everything should fall magically into place because it was all for the sake of art. But that's hardly the truth. Just getting the town fathers' approval was a major hurdle. Then there was satisfying the building inspector's infernal safety regulations about the performance center. And then followed the countless requests from local charities I never knew existed."

I said, "And since you knew the police would be here now, you chose not to face them so soon after that suicide yesterday."

Daphne gave me a cold stare, then said, "Young man, you may yet be a psychologist."

"Or else a very suspicious detective."

"The best mind healers are," she said, then continued. "You're quite right though. The chief of police was adamantly opposed to an opera festival in our cozy enclave of Abigail-by-the-Sea. The increased revenues to the town were hardly needed to maintain our privileged existence. But beyond that he felt that the increased tourism, especially the fussy opera lovers, would require too much attention from him and his men. After Sonia Hatfield's suicide and my connection to her, this accident is exactly what the chief has been waiting for—something that might make the opera folks pack up and go away for good."

Daphne's words raised all kinds of new questions for me, whose imagination is always raring to run wild. I wondered, Could Adam Pierce's death possibly have been intentional? Then who had released the scrim to drop onto him that way? Jonathan Byers's catamite, Rick-darling-thing? He was supposed to be out filling the car with gasoline, but he could have sneaked back into the opera house and done the deed. But did he have the capacity to be jealous enough to commit such an act? Or was the "accident" meant for one of the others who was onstage? Jonathan Byers himself? Or Madama Ostinata? Or was it an act of random terrorism to subvert the opera festival? But perpetrated by whom? The police? And then another troubling question arose: Had Sonia Hatfield, the tragic suicide, perhaps been pushed under that train?

When my turn with the police came, I was giving them a clear account of what I'd seen when I had an insight that surprised even me. I discovered that my subconscious mind had made its own observations in the first microseconds after that pipe hit Adam Pierce, even before my reflexes had propelled me from my seat to go and help him. A part of me had surveyed the opera house and registered exactly who had been visible at that moment and who was not. I don't know why I did it. Maybe some dormant genome for inductive reasoning had been activated by my previous involvement with bizarre murders, and my mind had already made the leap that Adam Pierce's death might not have been an accident. Whatever the reason, I'd made a quick mental catalogue of everyone who was out of sight and perhaps somewhere backstage at the moment of the accident. That list included Ronda Lucca, Hwang Yung Cho, April Kilkus, Rick Jansen, Bruce David, Mathilde, Maestro Toscanelli, Carolyn Boetz, and the countless nameless members of the crew. I told the Abigail police all this, but they didn't seem too impressed. Too much speculation, I guess. But I had also observed that the only people with irrefutable alibis concerning the accident were Madama Ostinata and Jonathan Byers, who were both onstage with Adam Pierce, and Daphne, who was in the audience with me. Anyone else could have released that deadly scrim, including the ailing Daniel Carafolio, who was presumably recuperating in his room, or the heartsick Maurizio, who was presumably back on Daphne's estate awaiting my troth.

When I returned to the auditorium I found Daphne and the maestro still trying to placate Madama Ostinata. The maestro was lighting his cigarette with what looked to be a solid gold lighter. Perhaps Daphne had supplied it to him. But then, once the cigarette was lit, rather than smoke it, ever the maestro, he seemed to conduct the conversation with it. Surprisingly, no one told him to put it out.

Mathilde stood by, voiceless as usual, awaiting an order to fetch whatever exotic elixir might be needed to calm Madama's nerves. For her part, Madama Ostinata was ranting that she had been the intended victim of the accident. I could tell the woman was truly terrified because her hair was almost standing on end. Then, as if to give credence to my observation, she said, *"Far rizzare i capelli,"* as she tried to smooth down her frazzled fleece. She was certain that someone had purposefully let that scrim drop, but it had missed its true mark. It was disquieting to realize that she and I shared the same lunatic interpretation of the facts. And her version even had religious overtones: It was not Lady Luck who had saved her, but *il buon Dio* himself. And now, since Madama obviously wanted to live quite a bit longer, she was saying over and over that she would have to leave the festival. There was no choice. Yes, she understood that she would be breaking her contract, but what was a scrap of paper when her life was at stake? I swear I saw obvious relief on some of the other faces among the cast and crew. That wasn't too surprising though. From what I'd seen and heard so far, the festival's production of *Un ballo in maschera* could only be improved by Marcella Ostinata's hasty retreat to Italy.

I waited for the police to finish questioning Daphne. I hoped to ride back to the estate with her. Perhaps she might even offer the real dirt about how she had convinced the town fathers to approve the opera festival. When she saw me, she seemed relieved that I had waited for her, but then just as we were leaving the opera house, she stopped and said, "I must find Maurizio first."

"Is he here?" I said.

Daphne replied, "He came along with me when I brought Bruce David. He's going to drive the other guests back to the house."

"Then maybe he's waiting in the minivan," I offered.

"It's more likely that he's been wandering around inside. He spent a lot of time here when the theater was being built, especially the stage house." Then Daphne laughed and added, "I think he might have grease paint in his blood."

Which caused me to wonder, Had Maurizio been backstage when the accident occurred? As it turned out, no one inside had seen him, but the police did make a point of getting his name from Daphne for questioning later on.

"You'll need a sign language interpreter," she told the sergeant, barely concealing a haughty tone in her voice. "He's deaf and mute."

The cop made a disapproving grimace and said, "Then maybe you can help us when we question him."

Daphne gave a condescending smile. "You know I'm only too glad to cooperate, Sergeant."

Once more Daphne and I left the theater, and once again she stopped us before we got out the main door. "I hope you'll forgive me for asking you," she said. "But since Maurizio has disappeared again, do you think you might drive the others back to the house? It would mean your waiting around here for them to finish with the police, but I don't know what else to do. It would help me tremendously."

"I'd be glad to," I said, even though I wanted to get away from the opera house myself. Enough of these folks was enough.

"Thank you," said Daphne. "And if by chance Maurizio does reappear," she added, "remember to be gentle with him."

"I'll do my best," said cream puff Kraychik.

Daphne drove off in the Bentley and I went back into the opera house. It was strangely quiet inside the vast auditorium, and it had become cooler as well. I made my way silently down an outside aisle, hoping the cops wouldn't notice me, but it didn't work. One of them saw me and called me up to the front of the house. I told him that I'd already withstood the Inquisition and was just waiting to drive some of the musicians back to Daphne's estate. He told me to wait outside. I told him it was too hot out there. He told me he didn't care. I told him I'd keep out of the way. I promised. Okay, so I groveled. I tried to explain to him that some of these people were world-class performers. They weren't common criminals. (Then again, one of them might have been exactly that.) But I was their escort, and part of my job was to ensure that they received the deferential treatment they deserved.

The cop made a sour face—I don't think he appreciated my vocabulary. He told me to sit down and shut up. I quickly surveyed the audience for the most fertile site to conduct my own kind of interrogation.

The maestro and Mathilde were sitting far apart in the front row, silent as stone, yet I could see they were both anxious. The maestro was lighting another cigarette with the gold lighter, still heedless of any no-smoking rule. Madama Ostinata was apparently being questioned at the moment, and no doubt the maestro and Mathilde were preparing for her return in their respective ways. Bruce David was sitting a few rows behind them, alone and looking lost and worried, sucking on another pastille and stewing in his own precious juice.

Already I could tell that the ride back to the estate with those four people together in the minivan was going to be an adventure in hypocrisy. I felt myself salivate.

Meanwhile Jonathan Byers was leaning against the rail of the orchestra pit and trying his "congenial Brit" act on one of the cops, but to no avail. Ricky Jansen was nowhere in sight. Presumably he was still out buying gasoline.

And then I spotted April Kilkus and Hwang Yung Cho sitting together about twelve rows back, off to one side. They appeared relaxed, as though they were taking a break from rehearsal, as though nothing bad had happened that morning—no scrim, no death, no cops. They could have been discussing the rise and fall of nineteenth-century opera. But one thing was obvious: Hwang Yung Cho was in love with April Kilkus. I don't know what he was saying to her, but when someone shows that kind of passion and animation, they don't want to prove a point. They want sex. Besides, even from where I was standing, I could see that Hwang's eyes were on fire.

The quarry of choice in that auditorium was easy.

10

When Hwang and April saw me walking up the aisle toward them, they stopped talking. I waved casually. April stared back dubiously, then glanced toward Hwang, who was trying to determine whether I was friend or foe.

"I'm with wigs and makeup," I said, and told them my name.

"Oh," said April with a deadpan face. I sensed she was relieved to pigeonhole me along with the rest of the festival staff, the nonsinging pedestrians. To her I had been reduced to no threat, no bother, and with any luck, no further contact.

Meanwhile Hwang was forcing an overfriendly smile that carried a different version of the same message: Nice to meet you, go away.

I said, "Pretty awful what happened, eh?"

They both nodded glumly and replied simultaneously.

"Tragic." "Horrible."

"Did you know him?" I said.

They both shook their head no, but Hwang said, "He was the assistant director."

I corrected him. "Set designer."

They nodded quickly in agreement. I could tell I was making them nervous. Perhaps they were hiding something, or perhaps they were just feeling guilty, as if I'd caught them in flagrante—in thought if not in action.

I went on. "Kind of ironic that he was hit by a piece of his own stage work."

Then April scowled and said, "Are you an undercover cop or something?"

"Hardly. I'm just curious. I was wondering if either of you recall seeing anyone suspicious backstage just before the accident."

"Sure," said Hwang. "I saw you."

"Me!"

He nodded. "Yeah, I saw you hanging around back there just before it happened."

I protested, "But I was sitting out here with Miss Davenport. I heard you sing. She can verify it."

Hwang shrugged. "Then it's my word against hers, but I'm sure I saw you back there, or someone who looks just like you." Then that big fake grin reappeared on his face, and he almost snarled when he added, "So why don't you just mind your own business and tend to the wigs and makeup."

Hwang Yung Cho was taking his role of Renato too seriously.

April Kilkus said, "If you're not with the police, you have no business asking us questions."

"Doll," I said, "I'm just making conversation. We've all been through a major trauma together. Sharing the stress helps dissipate the negative impact of the event and starts the healing process."

April stifled a laugh. "You sound ridiculous."

Hwang said, "If you don't stop harassing us, I'll get one of those officers to evict you."

Fine, I thought. Wait until it's time for your wig fitting.

I walked toward the rear exit of the auditorium, wondering why they had behaved so guiltily when I approached them, and then turned on me so suddenly. All I did was invade their privacy. Perhaps they were already clandestine lovers. That might explain their irritation. And if they really didn't know Adam Pierce, there was no reason that his death, no matter how sudden or bizarre, should bother them at all. Unless . . . unless their intended victim was one of the others who'd been onstage at the time, and they had bungled their chance. God, what was wrong with me? I was too ready and eager to accuse someone, anyone, two secret lovers even, of Adam Pierce's accidental death. Maybe it was the result of too much opera all at once.

At the upper end of the aisle, just before the foyer and the doors to the lobby, I saw two people sitting in the last row of the orchestra, where it was dark in spite of the house lights. They were Ronda Lucca, the stage manager, and Carolyn Boetz, the rehearsal pianist. Carolyn had removed her eyeglasses, and even in the darkness I could see that her big round eyes were teary.

Ronda saw me and said, "You still here?"

I replied, "I have to wait around. I'm driving some of the stars back to the estate. Have the cops questioned you yet?"

Ronda said, "Me, yeah. But they don't bother me. I'm used to them. But Carolyn is still waiting her turn, so I'm giving her some pointers on how to deal with them."

"Just don't put words in her mouth," I said. "Cops always know when you're lying, and they'll shake you down."

Ronda snapped, "Who said anything about lying?"

"Sorry," I said. "Must be nerves."

"Not mine," said Ronda. "Maybe yours."

Carolyn Boetz said nothing, but gazed at me wide-eyed.

I left them and was just about to open the lobby door when I turned back for one more question—just like Columbo. "By the way," I said to Ronda. "Do you know anything about minivans?"

Ronda answered, "Are you kidding? I can drive an eighteen wheeler."

"Then maybe you can tell me if I did the right thing today," I said. I explained to her about the blown fuse earlier that day in the van, how it had seemed rigged to fail, and how I had fixed it.

"I'd get a real fuse in there soon," she said. "Before you blow out the whole ignition system." Through the dimness I sensed her eyeing me curiously. Then she added, "I wouldn't expect you to be so mechanical."

"My father always wanted a son," I replied.

"So did mine," said Ronda.

"But yours got one."

She gave a small laugh in spite of herself.

I went out into the lobby, where the glass-panelled walls were letting in the bright afternoon sunlight. Within minutes a huge white sedan pulled up in front of the opera house. The young driver leaped out. It was Rick Jansen. He came into the lobby, gawked at me, then scowled. As he opened one of the doors to the auditorium, I said, "The police are in there. You might want to wait out here for Mr. Byers."

He jeered, "You can't scare me, faggot." Then he marched proudly into the jaws to hell and left me wondering: If I was a faggot and he was being buggered by Jonathan Byers, what exactly distinguished us?

I wandered around the lobby awhile, passing time until the police finished interrogating the operatic big shots. I kind of hoped that Maurizio might show up, but he never did. Finally I got tired of waiting around, so I went back into the auditorium. I got there just in time to see Madama Ostinata coming out from her lengthy session with the police. She must have told them her life story. Mathilde rushed to her side and offered her a pill and a glass of water. Madama refused the pill but took some water with a dramatic toss of her head. She grimaced at the aftertaste, and then muttered loud enough for everyone in the house to hear, *"Non è San Pellegrino!"*

I went down front and told the four of them—Madama, the maestro, Bruce David, and Mathilde—that I would be driving them all back to the estate. Once again the maestro asked me for a light, but I couldn't help him. But then he snapped his fingers and reached into his jacket pocket to produce the same gold lighter he'd used earlier, as if it were a new toy he'd momentarily forgot about, then remembered. Still, I made a mental note to arm myself with a Bic Flic just to keep the old man lit and happy in the future. With Madama Ostinata's questioning finished, they were all ready to go.

During the ride back Bruce David sat up front with me and rattled on about the violation of his rights. "As soon as we're back on the estate I'm going to call my agent and my attorney. I expect compensation for this kind of abuse. We're artists, not dogs."

Meanwhile the two Italians murmured quietly from the seat behind us. I caught occasional phrases that I could understand, but the gist of their talk seemed to be focused on Madama's flight back to Italy, and her contract be damned. Again what impressed me about the language was that the message seemed to be carried in the pitch and the dynamics—the music—as much as in the actual words. They kept their voices low, just beneath the hum of the minivan's motor and Bruce David's prattling, so that all I could hear from behind me were the sounds of muffled Italian vowels, as though they were speaking in another room. Then suddenly Mathilde blurted something from the back of the minivan, which caused Madama to exclaim, *"Taci!"* It must have been the superlative equivalent of *silenzio*, because we rode the rest of the way in utter silence, while I wondered when and if my makeshift fuse would melt the minivan's electrical system.

That night I telephoned Nicole from the cottage to let her know what had happened, and that I was all right. An association with corpses seemed to be becoming part of my life. Nicole wanted assurance that Adam Pierce's death was an accident.

"As far as the facts go, doll, it was an accident."

"But what do you think, darling."

I paused. "Nikki, I hope my instinct is wrong."

I switched the talk to something more agreeable. It turned out that

Sugar Baby—my truest one and only—was adapting just fine without me.

"She *loves* fresh crab," said Nicole. "You told me she didn't eat it."

"No, doll. I told you not to give it to her. Now I'll have to wean her off it again."

"Have you called Paris yet?" she said. Like me, Nicole often changed subjects willy-nilly. It was usually a way to prevent boredom, hardly ever to avoid conflict.

"Should I?" I said.

"Don't you want to?"

"I might look insecure."

"Don't fight your destiny, darling."

We said good-bye. Then I fought my destiny and won the current round: I didn't call Paris. For the time being I would appear strong and independent to whoever it was I was trying to impress. I turned in for the night and was just entering the realm of the nether senses when Maurizio arrived soundlessly. He shucked his clothes and then slid between the sheets, where he snuggled and cried and finally slept with his arms around me. There was no sex this time, so I guess you could say I was faithful again.

11

The next morning I awoke alone. Maurizio had vanished as stealthily as he had appeared. I got up and showered, then headed to the big house for breakfast. The sky was overcast, and a dark storm was gathering out over the ocean. The gazebo was empty. I looked around and saw Parker standing at one of the back doors to the mansion. He waved and called out to me.

"Breakfast inside today!"

In the big house I found Daphne at a table in the garden room. Parker had just set out the last of the breakfast trays.

"Good morning," chirped Daphne as she pressed the knob on the coffee maker and plunged the filter down through the murky fluid, miraculously creating perfect coffee once again. "There's a bad storm rising," she said. "So I thought we should have breakfast indoors. And besides—" Here she nearly smacked her lips. "Parker is making waffles this morning."

"But it's not Sunday," I said.

"That's a silly tradition," said Daphne. "If Parker wants to make waffles on Tuesday, it's fine with me. I just wouldn't want to electrocute him out in the gazebo with all the rain."

Parker acknowledged her lame joke with a raised eyebrow, then he asked me whether I wanted buttermilk or buckwheat.

"Can I have one of each?"

Daphne exclaimed, "You must be a Gemini."

I nodded.

Daphne said, "I'm a Leo, and Parker is a Libra. A trine and two sextiles. No wonder we all get along so well!" Then she leaned toward me and murmured secretively, "Astrology is my secret hobby, but don't breathe a word of it. Can you imagine what the boys at Harvard would say?"

Meanwhile, Parker, with perfect aplomb—balance being one of Libra's hallmarks, indecision one of its banes—dispatched his task of pouring two separate batters onto the hot waffle grids. And not a drop of either ran over the common border.

Daphne said, "The other guests are all taking coffee in their rooms again."

"They don't seem very sociable," I said.

Parker concurred with an audible snuff.

Daphne said, "They aren't, and it displeases me. But wait until Madama learns about the latest development." Daphne chortled as though she had gained an easy point in a round of cat and mouse. Then she told me that the festival administration was going to advise Marcella Ostinata against breaking her contract. If she insisted on defaulting, the board of directors would file suit. "And the woman can ill-afford it at this point in her career," said Daphne with that odd triumphant sound in her voice again. "In her *younger* days, the notoriety might have helped her. But now it can only lessen her chances for future engagements." She smiled the smile of victory.

"Your esteem for her seems to have fallen," I said.

"Yes," replied Daphne with a sly wink. "Well, I've just discovered something about Madama Ostinata that puts her firmly on my 'not very nice' list."

I waited a suitable time for Daphne to dish the dirt, but it was not forthcoming. All she offered was, "When this business is cleared up and the festival is launched, I'll tell you all about it. The important thing now, at least from the festival's standpoint, is that the police determined Adam Pierce's death was officially, absolutely, and without doubt an accident. They closed the files last night after running batteries of tests on the stage equipment. All to my great relief."

And all to my great suspicion, for I wondered how it had happened so fast. Weird deaths like Adam Pierce's usually got more than a few hours' investigation. Had Daphne lubricated the bureaucratic process with a generous contribution to the police retirement fund? Rather than pursue the subject, I decided to be a good little Gemini and make light conversation while I enjoyed the two crusty brown waffles Parker had just placed before me. There'd be plenty of time for impolite candor later on.

After breakfast Maurizio arrived to drive me and the maestro to rehearsal. As it turned out, Bruce David the tenor was indisposed again, and Madama Ostinata and Mathilde were resting while Madama awaited an overseas return call from her *avvocato*.

The ride to town was very quiet in spite of Maurizio's tendency to drive fast. The maestro sat calmly and watched the scenery whizzing by. Perhaps in Italy a blur of countryside greenery is the norm. He seemed pleased by everything he saw, including the ever-darkening storm clouds, which more and more resembled a foreboding opera set. At one point the maestro leaned forward and propped himself between the two front seats. I sensed he was about to ask me for a light for his cigarette, and so I activated the van's lighter. He smiled, and then offered me a cigarette, which I graciously refused. The maestro looked at Maurizio and then at me, then waved a gnarled old finger back and forth at us while he said in halting English, "You both boys are . . . er . . . *omosessuale?*"

Maurizio nodded quickly and enthusiastically. I guess he'd read the maestro's lips, or else his version of sign language and eye contact. Then Maurizio signed something with his right hand, which I didn't understand. But when I looked into his eyes, the meaning was clear: He was telling the maestro that he loved me.

The maestro smiled agreeably and repeated the sentiment in his own language. *"Ah, sì. Lei amarlo. Bene."*

Here I'd thought I was just taking a two-week job doing wigs—at the insistence of my lover, no less—and look what had happened already. Like I said, I should have known better.

We arrived at the opera house at exactly nine o'clock, which was the hour of rehearsal and the beginning of my day in the wig room. Maurizio gave me a viselike desperate hug, as if he would never see me again. I caught my breath, then got out of the van and slid the back door open for the maestro. But instead of reaching for my arm, the maestro was grasping and shaking Maurizio's hand and saying something to him, something I couldn't hear. Maurizio nodded, then made two sharp nasal sounds, as if to agree with the maestro. Finally I helped the maestro out of the van, closed the door, and waved good-bye to Maurizio. He zoomed off. I escorted the maestro as far as the opera house auditorium. Then I went downstairs to face my day of drudgery with that other prima donna, Daniella of the dungeons.

Luck was still with me, though. Daniel Carafolio wasn't there yet and the door was still locked. In fact, the note from the day before was still taped to the door. I waited about ten minutes, until I heard the muffled sounds of music from the stage. Then I went up to watch the day's festivities.

The show was going on in spite of Adam Pierce's death. I suppose as set designer his work had been pretty much completed already. Anything more he might have done to the sets would be ultrafine-tuning anyway. Everyone onstage that day seemed unfazed by his death, as though it was truly the unfortunate accident the police had determined it was. These people were there to create tomorrow's opera; Adam Pierce was yesterday's news. Well, call me biased or call me bored, but I was still ready to believe that someone had intentionally killed the guy, or had meant to kill someone else on that stage. Even in a brand-new theater, scrims don't plummet from the flies like that, not without a proper cue. There was no clear motivation yet, but I was on the alert for the culprit—if there was one—to get sloppy and leave a hair on the soap, or something else that might point an accusing finger between now and opening night.

That day was to be a musical rehearsal, which meant the opera house would be the maestro's domain rather than Jonathan Byers's. A musical rehearsal provides an opportunity to focus solely on that aspect of the production. If a bit of staging was bungled at the expense of the music, so be it. The conductor was God that day. The stage director would get equal time to tell the singers to forget about the music and concentrate on the blocking. Eventually, there was supposed to be a perfect balance between music and acting. Eventually.

On stage was the day's cast: Maestro Toscanelli perched on a high chair at a makeshift podium; Carolyn Boetz seated at the grand piano; Hwang Yung Cho singing Renato; the stand-in tenor for the indisposed Bruce David, singing Riccardo; April Kilkus singing Amelia and covering for Madama Ostinata, also indisposed; a small wrenlike woman singing the chirpy "trouser" role of Oscar, Riccardo's page; a men's chorus; and off to the side, the prompter and the language coach.

I decided to go and watch from backstage for a change, which turned out to be a good idea. That's where I found Ronda Lucca, sitting in front of a computer at her stage manager's desk in her own little booth. She was wearing her usual blue jeans and plaid shirt. She must have had a whole closetful of that same ensemble. Next to her computer screen was a bank of five small video monitors that showed various aspects of the stage and backstage area. A big sheet of paper was clipped to a holder near the main screen. It read: ACT 1 SCENE 5.

Ronda was busily typing at the computer keyboard. I watched her for a few moments while I listened to the music out front. Even from backstage the stand-in tenor was sounding good, maneuvering his way through some really fast singing, all very light and rousing. Combining the energy of the men's chorus and the brilliant coloratura of Oscar, the scene's overall impression was that a good time was imminent. God knows we needed that.

I spoke quietly to Ronda. "If Bruce David doesn't shape up soon, his cover will be singing on opening night."

Ronda looked up from the computer screen. She winked at me and said, "Then let's pray that Brucie can't find his balls."

"You're not out at the production table today."

"It's a musical rehearsal so I get to work at home, back here in my cozy nest."

"Do you have a minute?" I said.

"For you I got time," she replied. "What's up?"

"I heard that the police were here last night checking out the stage equipment for possible foul play."

Ronda said quickly, "That's not exactly right. They were checking for faulty operation. We had the company who installed the equipment and the computer out here. Four hours of testing, and all they could say was everything was fine. No damaged cables, no faulty servos, and a flawless control program. Everything was tip-top, just like the day it came through the door."

"Did the police check for fingerprints?"

"Huh?" said Ronda.

"Usually they search a crime scene for clues and other evidence."

Ronda eyed me uncertainly. "Who said anything about a crime? It was an accident."

"Or an act of God," I added.

Hmph, went Ronda. Then she said, "The cops put in their report that the scrim came down because of a bug in the control program—which is technically incorrect, but I guess they had to blame it on something. So last night I reinstalled the software from brand-new disks, which is also why I have to sit here today and re-key all the cues for the tech director. Pisser."

"That's it?" I said. "New software and the case is closed?"

"I already told you," said Ronda. "There ain't no case! The only thing this festival's gotta worry about is whether that guy's heirs will sue for damages."

"Heirs are unlikely for Adam Pierce. Creditors, maybe, like the folks at Emporio Armani."

Ronda smirked and said, "Well, just for your information, the cops did order me to mark the stage floor with reflective tape wherever there's scenery or lights flying overhead, just in case something else wants to fall down. We're supposed to change a lot of blocking too. What a pain."

"Not to mention a stage floor covered with bits of reflective tape."

Ronda laughed. "Leave it to you boys to worry about décor."

I wondered why the local police hadn't checked the computer keyboard for fingerprints. Any latent prints would have narrowed down the suspects considerably. But then I remembered, I was the only one pursuing Adam's death as a murder and not an accident.

I said, "Could someone have just thrown a lever to make that piece of scenery fall down?"

"That would be nice and simple," said Ronda. "But you can't do it that way, not on this stage. The old stages work like that, with manual ropes at the lock rail. But now it's all steel cables, and they run by computer." She patted the machine in front of her. "This little baby takes care of everything."

I wondered, Including murder?

I said, "So that scrim was released through this computer."

Ronda replied, "No one knows how it got released."

"But this is the only place it could have happened."

"No," said Ronda. "That cable could've been released from the computer, or else from the lock rail."

"Didn't you just say it had to be done from the computer?"

"There's a manual override."

"What does that mean?"

Ronda made an impatient frown. "It means you can tell the computer you want to override the automatic controls and release the cables manually."

"So it might have been released by hand?"

Ronda persisted with her original stand. "Not likely."

"Where would you do that, release the ropes by hand?"

"They're not ropes," said Ronda. "They're cables."

"All right, cables then."

She groaned impatiently. "If you were gonna do it, you'd go to the lock rail," she said. "Over there."

She pointed behind her to the inside wall of the stage house itself. Extending the full length of that wall was a huge metal framework that organized the innumerable steel cables that controlled the flying scenery. It looked like a monstrous loom in a weaving mill.

Ronda said, "But like I told you, with this computerized system, if you want to release a fly from the rail, the system has to be switched to manual override. And I never do that. If something's going to fly, I want it to happen right from here." Once again she touched the computer as though it were part of herself, a private part. "And I always keep the manual override turned off."

"Maybe yesterday afternoon you forgot."

"I don't forget things like that!" she snapped.

She was getting huffy. And who could blame her? I wasn't exactly charming her.

"Look," she said. "You need a password to use manual override. The whole purpose of it is to prevent exactly the kind of accident that happened yesterday."

"Oh," I said, feigning ignorance. "Well, that makes sense. Safety first and all that. Too bad it didn't work though. Who knows the password?"

Ronda said, "Hey, I'm real busy right now, and obviously you're not. But just for your information, I'm the only one who knows the password so far. No one else. Not even the guys who installed the system. Okay?"

"Wow," I said. "So you're kind of a god back here."

Ronda corrected me. "Goddess."

"Excuse me. Goddess. Just one more question. Where is the other end of the cable attached?"

"The cable goes up through the grid and connects to whichever fly it's supposed to operate." She pointed overhead and I looked up. High above us, up in the stratosphere of the stage house, just below the roof of the very opera house itself, was a gigantic maze of metal beams and grilled flooring as big as the whole stage and backstage area. It looked like celestial filigree.

"I wouldn't want to climb up there," I said.

"Not too many people do," replied Ronda.

"But maybe someone did yesterday," I said. "Crawled up there and cut one of the ropes."

"Nah," said Ronda. "They would've just done it at the lock rail. And like I already told you, none of the cables were damaged." Then she said, "I know one thing for sure. That scrim didn't get released from here." She patted the computer again.

"How do you know that?"

"Because I was sitting right here when it happened, and I didn't give the command that put that scrim into free-fall."

"Are you sure?" I said. "I thought you were out at the production table."

"I was. Then I came back here."

Her face glowered in the reflected light from the computer screen.

"Sorry," I said. "I get carried away sometimes. It just seems odd that the computer and all the controls checked out perfectly last night, but yesterday afternoon a scrim fell down and killed someone."

Ronda said, "I think you need to chill out, babe—maybe get yourself a date."

What I needed was a lot more explicit than a date.

The scene onstage finished with loud voices and crashing chords. Ronda Lucca said, "I'm back to work." She put up a piece of paper that read: ACT 2 SCENE 1. Then she started typing again.

I stood in the wings and watched everyone scurrying to prepare for the next phase of rehearsal. It was then that Madama Ostinata arrived in the auditorium, escorted by Bruce David and Mathilde. She ascended the temporary stairs to the stage floor, and as she passed the maestro, she gave him a chilly greeting. The maestro nodded back politely, as though nothing unusual was happening. Perhaps he'd seen so much in his long life that he'd learned the easiest response to any situation was to be docile.

Madama strode downstage center, then with a grandiose flourish turned her body to face upstage. She waited for absolute quiet on-stage, then she addressed us all with a control and authority that were unusual for her.

"Good morning," she said. "How nice to see you all today."

Meanwhile Ronda Lucca had left her computer and was standing beside me in the wings. "What's she mooing about now?"

I whispered back, "I think we're going to find out."

Madama Ostinata continued her declamation. "You all see yesterday an attempt is made to my life on this stage."

She was forgetting her English again.

"I have taken much time and thinking about this, and today I decide to stay here at the festival. I *will* sing Amelia." She paused for dramatic effect, of which there were several among the people on-stage: The maestro nodded submissively; April Kilkus looked as though she had just lost a talent show prize; Hwang Yung Cho muttered disgustedly, just the way his character Renato would have over his wife's infidelity; Bruce David gazed at Madama with a veneration known commonly among my crowd as diva worship; Ronda Lucca simply said "shit"; Carolyn Boetz lowered the keyboard cover on her piano; and Mathilde stood in the wings, biding time patiently. After the hiatus in Madama's monologue, Mathilde referred to a piece of paper in her hands and vocally prompted Madama Ostinata to continue. Apparently Madama's *avvocato* had dictated a script to her that morning, all contingencies covered. Madama nodded gratefully toward Mathilde and continued her speech.

"Yes, I will stay and sing," she said. "But it is with the condition that the festival will pay for me a bodyguard. Do you all hear that? I must have witnesses to hear me. I am demanding a bodyguard for all hours, and then I will sing."

From out in the orchestra seats came a familiar stentorian voice exercising its familiar vernacular. "Oh bleeding fuck!" said Sir Jonathan Byers.

I peeked out from the wings just in time to to see Sir Jonathan storming up the aisle on his way out of the theater. Scampering close behind like a faithful hound was none other than Ricky Jansen. I guess with Adam Pierce dead, Sir Jonathan and his bugger had taken up where they'd left off, wherever that was. Then I wondered if Rick might have hastened his reunion with Sir Jonathan. All it would have taken was finding a way to circumvent the computer controls to release that scrim onto the skull of Adam Pierce. *Poof!* Jonathan Byers's romantic diversion would be history. Even a muscle-brained hustler might manage it.

I was brought back by the sound of Madama Ostinata's voice. "I *will* stay!" She was unfazed by Jonathan Byers's outburst, and I wondered what had become of the creature who would have been shrieking at such an insult by now. Instead she seemed utterly in control of herself and the situation. I wondered if some outside agent might be the genesis of Madama's strong new personality. A drug perhaps? Something readily prescribed, like the miracle personality in a bottle, Darzac.

Madama then turned to the maestro and said, *"Caro Angelo,* please. Now I will sing my aria, *'Ma dall'arido stelo divulsa'."*

The stage was cleared—April Kilkus made an unlikely ruckus by knocking over a chair on her way offstage—and then Madama took her place near the piano. When Ronda Lucca corrected her stage position according to Byers's previous directions, Madama said, "No. I will sing here."

It was hardly surprising that her performance was more melo-drama than music. Though to be fair, I knew that Darzac could nullify any vestige of vocal technique Madama might yet retain. In fact I remembered seeing it among the list of possible side effects and complications. Right there in the *Physician's Desk Reference* it had said that Darzac could cause "loss of vocal control in aging dramatic sopranos." So perhaps that morning Madama Ostinata couldn't be held completely to blame for the sounds she was making. Still, the maestro didn't bother conducting her, and Carolyn Boetz at the piano didn't bother following her. In a way, I felt sorry for Madama. No one was on her side. She was alone. True, she'd brought most of it on herself, but then too, she was just another poor mortal struggling against destiny to make something of her life, hoping for some kind of genuine acceptance from a small corner of the world, and probably realizing from the shallow depths of her soul that aside from her wardrobe, a furnished villa, a caseload of jewels, a town car, and some tattered old reviews, there really wasn't much else for her to get. And in the meantime she'd forgotten to be faithful to her art.

When she finished singing Bruce David joined her for the ensuing love duet. His cover, who had sung so well earlier during rehearsal, was listening keenly, as if hoping for a disaster. He wasn't disappointed. For all of Bruce David's introspective solitude, by now the man should have considered a new career. The duet was so unbearable that I left the theater and returned to the wig room. It was that bad.

When I went down to the wig room for the second time that day, Daniel Carafolio had finally arrived.

"Nice of you to show up," he sniveled.

"Look, doll," I said. "When I got here, the big hand was on twelve and the little hand was on nine. So the question is, Where were you?"

"Don't take it all so seriously," he said with a flick of his hand. "I'm surprised you even came back here at all, after what happened yesterday. A death onstage! I always miss the excitement."

"It wasn't very pleasant," I said.

"But didn't it spook you, seeing him get killed like that? I love to be spooked."

I said, "The things that spook me usually come from living people, or the ones who pretend to be alive."

"You don't have to be so catty," he said.

"I think I'm getting a headache. I should go home."

Daniel snarled, "You just got here!"

"Then do us both a favor and fire me."

"But I need you today. I'm way behind schedule."

I suppose with everyone else at the festival behaving so selfishly, I felt obliged to be magnanimous, or philosophical, or plain stupid. So I stayed the afternoon and helped Daniel. It's what I'd been hired to do, after all. He must have really been desperate too, because he actually let me work on a few of his sacred wigs. True, they were the wigs for the supernumeraries—the living scenery—but it was a lot better than being his lackey. And getting my hands back into hair, even if it was on a dummy, had a meditative effect. I found myself relaxing and expressing my creative side again, my better self.

At one point Daniel was watching me work, and he remarked, "That's for a waitress, not Marie Antoinette." It might have been backhanded, but it was still a compliment, and coming from him it was a small miracle. Maybe he was on Darzac too.

At five o'clock I went upstairs to catch a ride back to the estate with Maurizio in the minivan. Being down in the bowels of the opera house, I hadn't realized that the storm had arrived in full force. The wind was gusting and driving sheets of rain against the huge glass panels that lined the front of the lobby, rattling and shaking them. It was the kind of storm that comes in the dead heat of a New England August, not in the fresh warmth of early June. I peered through the blur of water running down the glass in front me, but couldn't see the minivan anywhere. What I did see was Daphne's red Bentley with its bright white top. She flashed the headlights and sounded the horn. When I discerned her white-gloved hand waving at me through the windshield, I made a run for it.

12

The cockpit of the Bentley was cool and dry, almost tranquil despite the raging storm outside. Even the windshield wipers performed their duty with quiet, regal grace. We could have been in a serene mahogany-paneled library taking tea.

Daphne said, "Maurizio is driving the others back to the house. I told him I'd come for you myself. How was work today?"

"Just fine," I answered quickly. I couldn't tell her that I'd asked to be fired. It might appear ungrateful.

She pulled the car out into traffic without looking. Another car honked loudly at us. Daphne was unfazed.

"I think from now on I'll drive you," she said.

"I don't mind the van."

"But it will give them more room if you come with me."

That sounded lame. There was plenty of room in the minivan for everyone, even for the extra fifteen pounds I carry.

"Am I bothering Maurizio?" I said.

"Not at all," said Daphne, then she laughed lightly. "In fact, I think he'd like nothing better than to drive off into the sunset with you." Then she turned her head and looked at me intently with her pale blue eyes. Reflexively my left hand reached for the steering wheel. Daphne said, "Please try to understand, dear. Madama Ostinata told me this morning that she feels uncomfortable riding with you."

"Is it my driving?"

"I think, dear, that it's your personality."

"You mean my sexuality."

Daphne winced. "I'm afraid that Madama has an extremely limited view of life, despite all her years in the theater."

And to think I'd had a moment's pity for the old cow during her aria.

Daphne continued, "But look on the positive side. If I drive you now, we'll have more time together." She tapped my hand away from the steering wheel. "Thank you, dear," she said. Then she explained that she had just come from the police station, where she had finally placated the chief regarding Sonia Hatfield's suicide note, the one accusing Jonathan Byers of being a rapist. "I convinced them that poor Sonia had written 'rapist' when she'd probably meant to say 'sybarite'."

"How did you know that?"

"I didn't. I have no idea what she meant. But I *had* treated Sonia as a patient, and I did know that she was a voracious reader, and that she loved words, especially big fancy ones. But she was also slightly dyslexic, and if she couldn't remember the word she wanted, she often substituted one with similar sounds, even though the meaning was very different."

"Like saying pedophile for pedagogue?"

Daphne looked skeptical. "Something like that. Anyway, I got the police to drop the rape charge, but then I had to keep them from arraigning Sir Jonathan for sodomy. It was a mess."

"How did you finally resolve it?"

"I reminded them that Jonathan Byers was not only a British subject, but was knighted as well. As his host, the town of Abigail was in the position of goodwill ambassador, and arresting Sir Jonathan could well be construed as an act of international aggression. And who were we to judge the man when the queen of England herself had chosen to overlook his basic nature?"

"I wish I could have heard you," I said.

"I was wonderful," said Daphne. "Just like Perry Mason."

I sighed. "My hero."

"And best of all, it worked!" she said.

But I wondered, What had it really taken from Daphne to win the police over this time? A contribution to their uniform fund?

We rode most of the way in silence, with just the sound of the rain and wind against the windshield, and the reassuring hum of the Bentley's powerful engine. Then I asked her, "Do you know anything about Darzac?"

"My goodness! Where did that come from?" said Daphne.

"I was just wondering."

"I know that it's commonly prescribed, perhaps too much."

"Did you by chance give any to Madama Ostinata?"

"Why ever would I do that?"

"To calm her down after yesterday's accident."

"Hmmm, yes," said Daphne. "It might have helped her."

"But you didn't give her any."

"My dear boy. What do you take me for? A drugstore?"

"No. I just noticed that Madama's behavior was markedly different today, and I wondered if she had taken something to calm her nerves."

"I suppose she did," said Daphne. "But she didn't get it from me. She's perfectly able to take care of herself. She only pretends to be a helpless, brainless soprano."

"Why do you say that?"

Daphne replied, "I told you this morning, I've found evidence of something that displeases me a great deal."

Again I waited to hear about it, but all Daphne said was, "I'm sure she has no idea that I know. How would she? And I suppose it all happened so long ago that it really doesn't matter now. But I see through her, and she's a sly one."

Let the games begin.

As we pulled into the driveway to the mansion, Daphne said, "It looks as though the power has gone out. We have a generator, but we'll still be dining in subdued light."

"Sounds romantic," I said.

Daphne replied, "Well, as far as that goes, I'm afraid your cottage will be dark except for kerosene lamps. If the power doesn't come back on, you can stay in the big house tonight."

"Let's see what happens," I said. A dark and stormy night in a secluded ocean cottage had a certain appeal, especially when comfort and security were only a short distance away. Then I had a pang of longing for my lover. I wanted to entwine our limbs under the sheets in that cozy cottage while Mother Nature was howling outside. But for all I knew, he was off carousing with some French sailor in Montmartre.

We got inside and Parker greeted us. Cocktails were being served in the library since that's where most of the low voltage lighting was. Also, there was a fireplace. Parker took my order—a parched martini up with a twist—then opened the library door for us. Daphne and I entered and found the rest of the house guests already there: Maestro Toscanelli smoking by the fireplace; Madama Ostinata and Bruce David assuming their respective airs; and Mathilde as usual portraying the life of the party. We all exchanged polite greetings, but Madama was clearly displeased to see me arrive. She turned her attention back to the maestro and to Mathilde, rudely ignoring Daphne and especially me.

Parker entered with the cocktails—a second round for the others and doubles for Daphne and myself. We'd waste no time in catching up. But no sooner had Madama Ostinata gulped her second cordial than she complained of not feeling well. She announced that she would take her meal upstairs. And instead of bidding us good night, her last words were, "Mathilde, attend me."

Daphne murmured, "Cunning bitch," which was so out of character that I wondered what *had* she found out about Madama?

Dinner began with a chilled puree of fruit garnished with crème fraîche, then proceeded to grilled swordfish en brochette served with individual polenta soufflés and a grillade of artichoke and red pepper, and finished dramatically with a bombe of bitter chocolate sorbet with tiny hazelnut meringues. With a menu like that the kitchen obviously had a gas stove and oven. Every course was accompanied by a different wine from Daphne's excellent cellar.

"Did Parker do all this?" I said.

"His daughter comes in to prepare dinner," replied Daphne. Then she added, I felt for my benefit, "Maurizio assists her."

The conversations throughout dinner were light and polite, with hardly a mention of politics or the opera festival, as if to deny the awful intrigues at the opera house. At one point we even sank to that low conversational denominator, the New England weather, which was still showing off outside. The maestro had been smoking and offering me cigarettes throughout the evening. Oddly, he was using matches and not the gold lighter he'd had earlier. He interspersed our meteorological discussions with tales from his many years of apprenticeship under the great Arturo Toscanini.

"They think I take his name," said the old man. His eyes sparkled capriciously in the candlelight. He had enjoyed his share of the wine and then some. "But I am Toscanelli," he said. *"Not* Toscanini." Apparently it was some kind of joke, because he laughed very hard and then he began coughing, and then lost his breath for a moment. When he regained his composure, he said it once more, as if to taunt another coughing fit. "I am *not* Toscanini!" And this time he chuckled cautiously.

Bruce David remarked off-handedly, "I feel like I'm the only one here who takes opera seriously."

Well, that got our attention. The next question was, What was he going to do with it?

"I mean," said Bruce, "there's a depth to all this music that no one at the festival seems to appreciate. It's almost sacrilegious what everyone is doing."

"Bah!" said the maestro. "We have in Italy a word for you. We call you *il finocchio dell'opera*. You know what it is?"

Bruce David didn't answer because his jaw had fallen into his sorbet. I was pretty shocked myself. Up till then the maestro had appeared to be a docile, agreeable old man. That kind of insult was unlike him. Then again, both Daphne and Madama Ostinata had said and done things that were out of character as well. More Darzac? Or was the Abigail water supply contaminated with truth serum?

The maestro addressed the room at large, waving his cigarette like a baton. "*Il finocchio dell'opera* does not sing, but he worships the opera. He knows every note, every line, every prima donna, every performance, all history of all opera, but he cannot sing on the stage himself. He is too delicate. So perhaps he can write a book and he can teach at the university." The maestro turned his gaze to Bruce David and said, "You think about it." Then he drained the last of the wine from his glass and banged it emphatically on the table. "*E sía!*" he said. He rose from his chair and said to Daphne, "*Perdona me, Madamigèlla. Buona notte.*" He bowed to her then he tottered away from the table and departed errantly through the kitchen door. Within seconds he returned and, smiling amiably to the three of us, found his way back out of the dining room and upstairs to his chambers.

Bruce squirmed uncomfortably in his seat and looked imploringly at Daphne. "Should I resign now?"

Daphne said, "You were hired to sing, not run the decathlon. Maybe if you'd stop keeping so much to yourself, including your voice, the maestro would have more confidence in you."

Bruce David turned to me and said, "What do you think?" His eyes had a look that said, Save me, sweet Jesus.

"Who cares what I think?" I said.

"I do," said Bruce, his eyes boggy with need.

"I do too," said Daphne.

With the maestro's departure the storm had finally broken. All was becoming calm outside, except for an occasional gust of wind that brushed the residual rain from the trees.

I said to Bruce, "I think your closet door is ready to fall off its rusty hinges, and it's time to let in the light."

My brilliant insight disclosed, I excused myself and retired to the cottage. I thought of calling Nicole. Then I thought of calling Rafik. Then I decided to write to him. I knew how much he liked receiving aerograms from Europe, so I had brought a small stack of them with me, assuming that I would write passionate tropes to him every day. But once I set myself to the actual writing, I found my truest feelings oddly blocked. Without the dramatic advantage of a flesh and blood encounter with my man, all I could muster was talk about the weather. I decided to continue the letter the next night.

Then I settled on waiting for Maurizio.

13

As it turned out, Maurizio never showed up that night. I confess I was a little disappointed, but at least it put me firmly back on the road to monogamy. Over breakfast Daphne told me that he had gone home with Parker's daughter the previous night.

"She lives alone," said Daphne. "And Maurizio is very handy with electric generators."

Among other sources of energy, I thought.

He arrived just in time to drive the others to rehearsal. He was cordial enough to me, but that puppylike eagerness was gone. The first fine careless rapture had passed.

I reported for duty in the wig dungeon, but no sooner had I arrived than Daniel Carafolio insisted that we go upstairs and watch rehearsal for a while.

"Marcella is doing her act three aria this morning," he said. He exuded an enthusiasm usually attributed to mood-lifting pharmaceuticals.

I replied, "I didn't know you were on a first-name basis with her."

"Not to her *face*," said Daniel. "But everyone calls her Marcella."

"I don't."

Daniel glowered at me. What did it matter if a pedestrian operaphile didn't refer to a has-been diva by her first name?

He went on, "You probably don't know the aria either, but it's—"

"I do," I interrupted. "April Kilkus sang it at the welcoming reception last Sunday."

Daniel said, "If you can call that singing."

But thanks to my lover's patient tutelage, I knew that Amelia had one of the opera's big moments with her third act aria, *"Morro, ma prima in grazia."* All the elements of Italian opera exist in that aria: patrimony, religion, deception, delusion, adultery, murder, sacrifice, and forgiveness—all the family values. It also shows how clever Amelia is in saving her own neck. In the setup for the aria, her husband Renato believes she has been unfaithful to him with his best friend Riccardo, and now he intends to kill her. She pleads for mercy, since her sin, if it existed at all, was in thought and not in deed. But Renato doesn't yield. So Amelia launches into this aria, where she submits to her inevitable death, but first begs Renato, by God's grace no less, to let her see their son one last time—if not as his wayward wife, then as the boy's mother—so that she can embrace him and kiss him with a mother's pure love. And then, after Renato kills her, he must let their son close her eyes for the last time. She plays it to the hilt, as if knowing that her husband, though violent, is also vain, and will spare his son the brutal shame of knowing his mother's death was by his father's hand. Verdi understood family dynamics long before the misnomer "dysfunctional" was applied.

Daniel and I went upstairs, where rehearsal was just starting. He stood in the wings to watch, but I slipped out into the house and sat a few rows behind the production table, where I had a clear view of everything. Since it was a stage rehearsal that day, God was being played by Jonathan Byers. And like Gabriel, Ricky-thing was at his side at the production table, taking notes and keeping the wireless handset ready for his lord and master. Carolyn Boetz waited patiently at the keyboard and peered about myopically for cues from the maestro, who was sitting nearby and was looking a bit bleary-eyed from last night's indulgences with the grape and the tobacco leaf. Onstage were Madama Ostinata and Hwang Yung Cho, playing Amelia and Renato respectively. Daphne had been right: Ecumenical opera it was.

The maestro gave the downbeat and Carolyn Boetz played the introduction to the aria. But somehow she didn't produce the lingering sonorities she had when she and April Kilkus had performed the aria at Daphne's reception. And when Madama Ostinata sang her first phrase, it rang empty. Instead of resonating with the desperate need to save her life, the aria sounded like the insipid bleating of a wife begging to keep a ridiculous party frock. It finally became clear to me that Madama Ostinata and her so-called artistry were the same: She was a singer who performed from the outside in, as though the words and the notes could be applied onto a role like costume and makeup. And when a character is created that way, what lies beneath the decorations is hollow and empty, like a mannequin.

I looked around to gauge the other reactions to Madama's singing, but by this time no one was paying much attention to her except for three people. One was Daniel Carafolio, who stood beside me enraptured with Madama's musical guile. The second was Hwang Yung Cho who, despite the libretto and stage directions, seemed eager to dispatch Madama on the spot. And finally, April Kilkus stood in the wings watching and listening anxiously, hands clenched tightly, as if she expected or hoped that Madama's voice might break at any moment and open the door for her to sing the role properly. When I recalled how April had sung this very aria at Daphne's reception, I sensed she would create a brilliant Amelia onstage as well.

During the final unaccompanied cadenza Madama Ostinata missed the initial high C. From there she lost all sense of the musical key, and tumbled headlong into an abyss of atonality. She crashed at the bottom in the yawning chasm of chest tones, from which she sang the last notes of the aria. Alas, not only were they a few steps lower than what Verdi had written, but Madama had migrated into a major key as well. There were random cringes among the cast and crew. Through it all I noticed Carolyn Boetz shaking her head and becoming flustered. She must have had perfect pitch too, because her hands fluttered over the keyboard, searching frantically for the best way to conclude the aria. I could almost see Carolyn struggling with the conflict: Should she play the final notes that Verdi had originally indicated, even though it would create a jarring cadence to the aria? Or should she modulate to the bizarre tonality into which Madama had stumbled during her cadenza? With only seconds to decide, Carolyn Boetz resolved the musical calamity at Verdi's expense. She looked disconsolate.

Meanwhile, standing beside me, Daniel Carafolio had uttered an odd, almost lascivious little moan of pleasure, as if Madama's lapse had been intentional, had been a spontaneous rush of genius that carried a symbolic meaning far beyond the fact that she was tone-deaf. Daniel was the only one to applaud until some of the others joined in feebly. The scattered noise stopped quickly though, and he turned to me and said, "I'm going downstairs. I want to keep those last luscious sounds in my head. You can stay and watch more if you want."

Apparently Madama's lowing had softened Daniel's heart and won me some extra time away from the cellar. Then we all heard the blasé voice of Jonathan Byers, who even this early in the rehearsal could not hide the fact that he was overcome by tedium.

"Thank you Marcella very nice please review your blocking. Now I'd like to do the act three finale. Places please quickly."

Marcella looked confused. She had expected a longer ovation perhaps, but instead she was being herded into the finale along with the others who were making their way onto the stage.

I sensed someone standing just behind me in the wings, and I turned to see Bruce David. He spoke quietly. "Thank you for being so honest last night. I needed someone to tell me the truth. And now for the first time since I got here, I feel as though I can sing with all my strength."

The only reply I could muster was, "Break a leg, tiger." But my heart wasn't in it, and I'm sure it showed.

Bruce was the last to go onstage, and finally they were all there, ready to sing the finale to the opera, the masked ball for which it is named. Verdi had composed the scene with brilliant musical irony. An onstage string quintet plays a delicate minuet, which is not only the dance music for Riccardo's elegantly costumed guests, but is also the background music for Amelia's desperate warnings about an assassination plot. Against the steady charm of music in three-quarter time, Amelia sings her fevered pleas in syncopation, while Riccardo replies fearlessly—and rather stupidly—that as long as she is there with him and loves him, then nothing can harm them. And the music plays on.

Bruce David was actually singing with a new strength that morning, though it could hardly be called vigor. He'd need a lot more therapy before that would happen. And to no one's surprise, Madama Ostinata stumbled through her part. Tone-deaf and couldn't count— how had the woman got as far as she had in the opera world? If she had ever been a good singer, there was no sign of it now. Older performers usually show some vestige of what had made them great. But Madama Ostinata was barely the shadow of a musician.

The scene progressed, however crippled emotionally. Hwang Yung Cho (Renato) stabbed Bruce David (Riccardo) on cue, and the chorus expressed their horror appropriately. Madama Ostinata (Amelia) reacted as though she had been the one to receive the death blow. But then, she had maintained from the start that this was *her* opera and not Riccardo's.

The problem came when Bruce David was singing Riccardo's last lines, when his character is in the throes of death but somehow finds the wherewithal to tell Renato not to worry, that his wife has been faithful. Since these are his last words before facing Judgment, they must be perceived as utter truth. But without warning, as Bruce took a final breath before his last *"Addio"* to the world, Madama Ostinata leaned close to him and planted a big full-mouth kiss on him.

Bruce David cringed and shook his head violently. After that he couldn't sing his last notes. He didn't even bother to die. Still, the chorus finished the opera, railing, "Night of horror! Night of horror!" They'd come expecting a nice party and found murder and mayhem instead. I could relate to that.

Carolyn Boetz played the last crashing chords of the opera. Then followed the voice of Jonathan Byers.

"Marcella, what the bloody hell was that all about? I never told you to kiss him."

Madama Ostinata glared angrily out toward the production table. "I was inspired," she said. "I want to kiss my Riccardo farewell. But now I see how this Bruce David really is. And if I am to sing, I must have another tenor. A *real* man."

I was near Jonathan Byers's end of the table, and I heard him mutter, "I'd love to cut her throat and shut her up, once and for all." Then he spoke out in his full voice, "Thank you, Marcella. Thank you, Bruce. You can leave now. I won't need you anymore today. I'd like to do the same scene with the covers now. Places, please!"

A big hubbub ran among the cast members. Apparently that kind of thing was not done while the principals were still present at rehearsal. But April Kilkus and the stand-in tenor quickly took their places onstage. And despite the earlier evidence of Bruce's newfound confidence, the finale went remarkably better with April and the other tenor singing it. Even Hwang Yung Cho and the chorus had more verve. Even Carolyn Boetz did. In fact, when she played the last chords that time, there was a disquieting sense of destiny fulfilled.

And when all was done, Jonathan Byers yelled, "Yes! That's more like it."

He glanced toward Madama Ostinata and Bruce David, who had stayed to watch their seconds perform—from opposite sides of the stage. Both singers were livid with each other and with Byers.

Meanwhile the maestro was beaming happily, along with Carolyn Boetz at the keyboard. For once that day, Verdi had been properly served. Even Ronda Lucca was applauding from her place at the production table. When everyone had quieted down, she yelled, "Twenty minutes!" And the union rules were obeyed.

Ronda turned toward me in the audience and said, "Got a minute?"

I replied, "For you I got time."

She must have recognized her exact words to me the day before, because she smiled.

"Let's go outside," she said.

We went out the stage door and leaned against the loading dock. Out there the sun was bright, and the sky was blue and clear. Last night's storm was already forgotten. Ronda pulled out a pack of slender plastic-tipped cigarillos and offered me one. I was about to refuse—I'm a dud of a smoker—but then I realized it might create a kind of bond, a buddy-trust, if I took one and smoked with her. So I did. The small cigar turned out to be, if you can imagine such a thing, vanilla-flavored. What had the smoking world come to?

Ronda created a billow of smoke in front of her, something like what a truck driver might do. Then she said, "I think maybe that set designer's accident was intentional."

I gave her a "do tell" look, and said nothing. Anyway, if I'd spoken at that moment, I would have coughed.

Ronda cocked her head and jutted her jaw forward slightly. It was a confrontative stance, though why she was displaying it with me wasn't clear.

"See," she said. "This morning my computer didn't boot up with my preset defaults. Again."

"What does that mean?"

"That means that someone got into the system and changed something. But I haven't been able to figure out exactly what."

"Are you sure?"

"Oh yeah," she said, and made another big cloud of vanilla-scented smoke in front of her. "So I reinstalled the software again before rehearsal. Pisser is I'm gonna have to retype all those damn cues again too. That makes three times." She watched me fumble with my cigarillo. "You're not a smoker, are you?"

"I inhale enough to feel it," I said. But in truth, the vanilla-flavored tobacco was disgusting.

Ronda shook her head disdainfully.

I said, "Was the manual override on or off this time?"

Now it was her turn to give me the "do tell" look.

"I don't recall," she said.

"Maybe it's time to put in a new password."

"Good thinking," she said, and eyed me suspiciously. "I already did that. But for someone who says he knows nothing about computers, you seem to know an awful lot."

"I guess I'm a quick study. See, I have this client who's a programmer at John Hancock, and that's all he talks about when he's in the styling chair. I must have picked up some of the jargon by osmosis."

"Sure," said Ronda with a nod, but her smirk meant that she didn't believe me. Then she changed the subject. "What do you think of the production so far?"

I told her honestly that I thought the stand-ins for Madama Ostinata and Bruce David were better than the first singers.

"You ain't shittin' about that," she replied. "It would be great if we could just dump those other two. Then we'd have a chance at getting some good press. The way it stands now, any critic who comes to the full dress next week will shred us."

"You think so?" I said.

Ronda said, "Between that Italian cow and—you'll pardon the expression—that twink of a tenor, this show's gonna bomb."

"I got the impression that Madama Ostinata was a favorite with operagoers."

"Maybe," said Ronda. "But this is a new festival, first season. We're trying to attract a young upscale crowd, the next generation of opera lovers. Most of them won't even know who Marcella Ostinata is or where she came from."

"But they'll know April Kilkus?" I offered.

Ronda nodded. "They may not know her yet, but they're going to love her when they hear her. April is on the verge of being a hot piece of property, and this festival could be her big break."

"So it would work both ways," I said. "April would get her big chance, and the festival would benefit from introducing her."

"You got it now," said Ronda. "Except that Marcella isn't about to give April a chance to sing. She's desperate for a comeback, and she's nobody's fool. She knows if April sings onstage even once here, word will spread like fire. You don't know those opera people. They are a world unto themselves."

I played devil's advocate. "But surely there are enough of Marcella's fans—I mean Madama's"—I was slipping into the casual reference myself—"to fill the house for her."

Ronda shook her head no. "You're wrong there. Everybody's waiting for a chance to pull her down."

"Typical hero worship."

"I don't know about that," said Ronda. "It's just that Marcella isn't very generous to her audience."

"Nor to anyone else, from what I've seen."

"Right," said Ronda. "And that kind of attitude toward your public might work for a while—that superior diva act she does so well. People eat that up because it's so nervy, and they like to see someone saying and doing things they don't have the guts to try. But the truth is, they eventually get tired of it. And if Marcella's fans ever got a load of April's singing, with that voluptuous, ravishing voice of hers . . ." Ronda's eyes were starry. "They'd make the switch in one performance. I've seen it happen plenty. April is a woman with a heart and a soul and a great talent. Marcella is just a bitch who sings, and she'll eventually get what she deserves."

A goddess pedestal was under construction for April Kilkus.

Ronda went back inside. I stayed out a little longer and did some deep breathing to try and clear my lungs of the dreadful vanilla-flavored smoke. Minutes later, my bronchioles refreshed, I headed back into the opera house. On my way I noticed April Kilkus and Hwang Yung Cho strolling toward the stage door as well. I waited for them, though they weren't too thrilled to see me there.

I said, "You both sounded really good this morning."

April and Hwang nodded warily. Perhaps they sensed that my compliment, though utterly honest, was also a lead-in to a few questions. To put them at ease, I said, "I'm really sorry about yesterday. I didn't mean to intrude on your privacy."

April replied coolly, "I suppose it's forgivable. We've all been under stress these last few days." Even through her defensive barrier, she couldn't hide the rich warm quality in her voice.

I said, "I hope you'll get to sing some of the performances. You certainly deserve to, even though it would be at Madama's expense."

"I hope so too," said April.

Then Hwang added, "Marcella never cancels a performance, so there's little chance of that happening."

"You never know," I said.

"Sure," said Hwang. "You never know. Someone might cut her throat."

April grabbed his forearm. "Don't say that! It's bad luck."

"But that's what it would take," replied Hwang. "Marcella's not about to retire on her own, even though she's years overdue."

April tried to be generous. "She still has a certain quality to her performance."

"I couldn't agree more," said Hwang. "The certain quality of a has-been hag soprano."

"Hwang!" said April. "I hope you won't say that about me some-day."

He replied, "If you never sang another note, April, you would still be an angel. But Marcella shouldn't be singing at all. Anyone with ears would agree with me."

April shifted her eyes toward me, as if to tell Hwang that he'd already said too much.

"Amen," I said agreeably. And then, since we all seemed to concur about Marcella Ostinata's voice, I took the liberty of putting another question to them. "Do either of you know how to use a computer?"

"What kind of question is that?" said Hwang.

"A straightforward one," I replied.

"Not for a singer," said April.

"I guess I'm just inquisitive."

"You mean nosey," said Hwang.

"Sorry," I said.

"No you're not," he said.

April was already nudging him to go inside with her and get away from me.

In their wake I said to her, "I really meant what I said about your singing." But my weak attempt at re-establishing trust only chased them away faster.

"Yes. Sure. Thanks," they both said as they vanished into the opera house.

It was no wonder I'd failed as a therapist.

I gave April and Hwang a suitable head start, then entered the stage door myself. In the backstage area I saw them both talking with Carolyn Boetz. But when the two singers noticed me approaching, they moved off quickly again, leaving Carolyn alone and vulnerable. I smacked my lips as I stalked my quarry.

"You play beautifully when the singers are right," I said.

She studied me through the thick lenses of her eyeglasses, which shrank her large eyes into keen little beads, making her look like a bird of prey.

"I try to play beautifully all the time," she said curtly.

"I meant that when April sang this morning—"

"What do you want?" she said suddenly.

"I just want to ask you some questions."

"Why? By whose authority?"

Her eyes disarmed me and I faltered. "I . . . by . . . it's a hobby," I finally said weakly. "Like that woman on Sunday night television."

"I don't watch television," said Carolyn. "And I have no interest in your inane hobbies. Aren't you supposed to be working on wigs?"

Where was the gentle soul who'd played so sweetly at Daphne's reception?

I said, "I was just trying to compliment you on the beautiful music you create. You and April seem to have a soul connection."

To what depths would I plummet to find a clue?

"We ought to," said Carolyn. "We're planning a concert tour next fall."

I encouraged her. "That should be wonderful."

"It could be," replied Carolyn. "It could be the turning point for both of us, for our careers. And so much of it depends on what happens here at the festival."

"Meaning?"

Carolyn shook her head. "They warned me not to talk to you."

"What harm can it do?" I said. "As you said, I'm just working on the wigs."

Carolyn removed her glasses, revealing her sensitive and vulnerable eyes. "I didn't mean that the way it sounded," she said with a sigh. "I guess I'm still upset by that accident the other day, and I'm frightened by what could happen next."

"Frightened?"

"Yes," said Carolyn. "If April doesn't get to sing in performance this summer, she'll miss the best opportunity of her life for good publicity. That could affect our tour either way, and it will definitely affect our careers."

"All based on singing here?" I said.

"*Yes*," said Carolyn, giving the single syllable the weight of an operatic pronouncement. "If April can sing Amelia just once onstage, it will pave the way for both of us. You heard her. You know the truth."

I nodded more solemnly than I had intended.

"So," I said. "You believe that your future can be determined by this festival."

"I know it," she said. "In the arts, all it takes is one missed chance, one wrong turn, and you can lose everything. Before you realize it, you're off the career path, and the rest of your life is wasted. You end up teaching and giving occasional recitals for women's clubs. But your dream of greatness is gone forever. It belongs to somebody else then."

It sounded so bleak. The only hope I could offer was veiled in humor.

"Maybe one of these days Madama Ostinata will overindulge at lunch, and something will disagree with her, and April will get her big chance."

"Yes," said Carolyn. "I suppose we could wait around and hope for something ridiculous like that to save us."

Then we heard Ronda Lucca's voice over the PA system announcing places for act one, scene six, traditionally the fortune-teller's cave, but in Jonathan Byers's version a New Age healing workshop.

"I've got to go," said Carolyn. "I apologize for being so curt with you earlier."

"And I apologize for being rude," I said, though the more correct word would have been "deceptive."

I went back downstairs to work on the wigs.

Daniel Carafolio was still waxing euphoric over Madama Ostinata's singing earlier that day, which even for an opera queen seemed too long for the afterglow.

"I don't care what anyone says," he gushed. "I think Marcella is the greatest dramatic soprano alive today, perhaps ever. She may have her off days. What genius doesn't? But today she was magnificent."

Hmph, I went.

Daniel said, "You're a tight-ass, aren't you?"

"As if you'll ever find out."

He went on. "You're one of those people who limit themselves to what they hear. But with Marcella . . ." His eyes were suddenly luminous with wonderment. "With Marcella . . ." His elocution rose toward the exalted heights of Divine Liturgy. "With Marcella . . ." He looked about ready to genuflect. "With Marcella, you must listen beyond the notes."

I replied, "You mean the half she gets?"

Daniel retorted from his lofty place just below the diva's throne. "You'll never understand greatness."

"Maybe not," I said. "But I know bad singing when I hear it."

Daniel gave a look of dire distress, then one of profound pity, as though my soul was doomed beyond all redemption.

"You can go now," he said pontifically. "I'll take care of things here myself."

Then the self-appointed high priest of diva worship turned and lumbered back into the rows and racks of steel shelving, the cloisters wherein he would seek solace and refuge from my plebeian sensibilities.

14

I quickly took my leave of the wig room and the opera house. It was just around noontime, so I had about five hours to wait before Daphne came to drive me back to the estate. I felt as though I needed an afternoon devoid of operatic intrigue. It was losing its charm for me both on and off the stage. And what better way to reconnect to mundane reality than by going shopping? Whatever clever architect had designed the Sidney Blaustein Center for the Performing Arts had the good sense to reserve a major portion of the ground-floor perimeter for luxury retail space, a demi-mall that had been dubbed The Plaza. Even opera lovers needed relief from the emotional rigors of the stage, and opera lovers—*especially* opera lovers—love to shop.

I was in luck too. From my vantage point in front of the opera house I could survey all of Retail Row, which was my name for it. Some of the spaces were ready for business, with their window displays complete, doors open, and wares laid out for sale. Other stores were still working against the clock before the festival's opening day—arranging windows, installing awnings, unloading delivery trucks. On the one hand it was all an appetizing sight, a string of new stores for me to explore. On the other hand, I sensed they were mostly those absurd boutiques that sell things you'd never think of buying except when on a glamorous vacation—things like a cotton turtleneck jersey from Switzerland, or a solid copper *zabaione* pan with a Delftware handle, or a tiny flashlight wrapped in lizard skin, perfect for reading opera programs. It was the kind of merchandise that relied on the ultimate marketing ploy: You don't need this stuff. No one in the world ever did or ever will. But since you're here pretending to be royalty, why not squander those shekels and buy something anyway?

Before hunting for the afternoon's unlikely bargain, I went for coffee at the chic café I had spied across the plaza. When I got there I was surprised to find Maurizio, Daphne's resident *ragazzo* and my own occasional catamite. I guess Sir Jonathan's libido was contagious. Maurizio was entertaining a hot little friend of his own, a blond, smooth-skinned young man with big worshipping eyes. They were signing to each other. Their fingers, hands, and arms filled the air with a high-energy field that might have implied an argument. But I'd learned from Daphne that the most animated signing was the most expressive as well.

Maurizio saw me and beckoned me to where they were sitting. He wanted me to meet his friend, who, as it turned out, was a hearing, speaking person. We exchanged polite greetings, and I got the unsettling sense that Maurizio was hoping his cute friend would arouse some jealousy in me. But since I was supposed to be the model of monogamy, I improvised my own sign language to tell Maurizio that I thought the two of them were a handsome young couple. He didn't quite understand me, so his friend showed me—a bit overzealously I thought—how to sign my message properly. Once I'd done it, Maurizio shook his head emphatically no. I asked, "Aren't you a couple?" while I crossed and recrossed the first two fingers of my left hand over and under each other.

Maurizio glared at me. I asked his friend what was wrong.

He said, "You asked him if we switch roles when we fuck."

"Do you?" I said.

Maurizio abruptly got up and stormed off. His blond friend ran after him, leaving my question unanswered.

Coldhearted Stanley then found an empty table and sat down. I ordered a double cappuccino, nothing on top, just to appease the voice in my mind that alleged, "Every calorie counts." I wanted to arrive in Paris with as little extra baggage as possible. When the coffee arrived though, I couldn't resist sinking two big lumps of raw sugar into the firm foamy head of steamed milk. As I sipped the bittersweet brew I recapitulated the impressions of the people I'd met and the events that had transpired since my arrival in Abigail-by-the-Sea three long days ago. Hell, I could create my own grand opera, a thumbnail version, with a bit of soap stuck under it just to keep the ordinary folk interested.

My hostess, Daphne Davenport, had invested a lot of money and emotional energy in this festival. She may not have said it explicitly, but I knew she wanted its success to be big—front-page big—maybe even garner a feature story in *Opera News*.

Marcella Ostinata was an aging dramatic soprano whose past glories were dubious given her performance so far. Though she excelled at playing the temperamental diva, her capricious behavior and unreliable voice could subvert the festival's success.

Angelo Toscanelli was venerated as an opera conductor, yet so far he'd rehearsed the singers like a lamb. Maybe he'd suffered a breakdown at some point, or maybe he was just old and tired and didn't care anymore.

Jonathan Byers, the stage director, seemed more intent on buggering Americans than on directing opera. Perhaps that was his Stanislavskian motivation. He also seemed to detest all singers. Then again, Sir Jonathan seemed to detest everybody. But at least he didn't apologize for his behavior or blame it on a dysfunctional family or unresolved childhood issues. That alone made him almost bearable to me.

Rick Jansen had a bit part in my opera of Abigail-by-the-Sea. He was a public utility, taken and used and paid for by anyone who needed what he had to offer. Was there more to him?

Mathilde was Madama Ostinata's dark-eyed, brooding maid who seemed to take everything in and let nothing out. If she wasn't careful, she was going to explode with all those nasty secrets building up pressure inside her.

Adam Pierce never got to see his sets in actual performance. Yet the other players in my opera regarded his untimely death as something insignificant, as though he'd simply left town before opening night. But something wasn't right there. No operatic death is insignificant.

Bruce David was a homegrown lyric tenor, but somewhere along the way he'd lost the fortitude—that all-American strength that had made our country great (all stand and salute as the orchestra sneaks in a phrase from our National Anthem)—the fortitude needed for a major career on the opera stage. Bruce was living proof that musical sensitivity and good vocal equipment were not enough. An opera star also needed the genes, however latent or blatant, for industrial strength bulldozing.

Ronda Lucca, an exemplar of the tyrannical stage manager, seemed genuinely and personally concerned about the outcome of this production of *Ballo*. Was she really so dedicated to opera? Or had she perhaps invested money in the festival? Was she a closet venture capitalist? Could Ronda be one of those heiresses who tries to conceal her vast wealth by portraying a wage slave in the workaday world along with us plebeians, when the real challenge of her life was figuring out what to do with those million-dollar dividend checks? That portrayal proved that a clinical dose of caffeine and sugar were surging through my already hyperactive imagination.

Carolyn Boetz was the sensitive soul who seemed attuned to an-other time and place, with gas lamps and horse-drawn carriages. She was a musician's musician who survived the harshness of the modern world by viewing it through the extremely thick and distorting lenses of her eyeglasses.

April Kilkus was probably America's great hope for the next world-class dramatic soprano. Among musicians it would someday be agreed that not since the young Leontyne Price did a singer possess the fine balance of voice, music, technique, instinct, presence, and sheer will. But what good would it all do if audiences and critics never got a chance to hear her?

Hwang Yung Cho was already known through operatic Europe for his rich baritone voice, but that didn't ensure his popularity among American operagoers, who were fickle in their idolatry.

Daniel Carafolio, my beloved boss, had already had his moment of brilliance as flunky to the jet-set hair designer Cornelius Haupt-Bettlesmann, affectionately called "Betty" by his devoted flock of countesses, duchesses, and marchionesses.

And finally, like the deaf-mute in *Out of the Past*, Maurizio seemed to hear and to know all, but as far as I could tell, his only suspect behavior was an unlikely infatuation with me. I may have Slavic genes, but I'm hardly Robert Mitchum.

I finished my coffee just in time for the final curtain of my imaginary opus. It wasn't yet one o'clock. I still had over four hours before Daphne would come for me. I considered telephoning her, but instead decided to do my shopping first. After that maybe I'd splurge and take a cab back to the estate.

During my perusal of the boutiques on The Plaza I found a music store, a real old-fashioned specialty store that sold only vocal and operatic scores and recordings. It was the kind of place you might find in London, a place that would probably know the answer to a question that had come to me while I was having coffee and opera earlier. First I checked all the catalogs of opera recordings they had, including the historical ones. Then I asked the clerk for assistance. But the answer was the same both times: There was not now and there never had been available in the U.S. a single operatic recording conducted by Maestro Angelo Toscanelli, which seemed kind of odd for a hotshot conductor, no matter how old he was now. The clerk agreed and claimed that he could have sold a carload of the maestro's recordings during the festival. But there were none to be had.

As I continued my shopping tour of The Plaza I did succumb to Madison Avenue tactics: I bought a chamois leather shirt for my lover Rafik. It was a velvety pale aqua, with a band collar and an open buttonless front cut just low enough to reveal the meat of his furry chest. Yes, it was extravagant and foolish, but isn't everything when you're in love? Besides, when I saw Rafik in Paris it would be out of my hands and onto his body, which is exactly where such a piece of costuming belonged.

An hour later as I left the last of the boutiques, I felt the need for a pick-me-up before heading back to the estate. I returned to the chic café, and this time I ordered a sumptuous dessert with my coffee, something called a mocha-nocciola tart, which consisted of espresso-flavored Bavarian cream piled high in a crumbly, buttery hazelnut shell, topped with—what else?—freshly whipped cream and then drizzled with melted chocolate. Damn the extra calories! I needed sustenance after shopping.

While I indulged my innermost needs, I wrote postcards to Rafik, to Nicole, and to my mom in New Jersey. Nicole got an honest message. The other two got a weather report. I considered sending a postcard to Lieutenant Vito Branco of the Boston Police Department, but I stopped myself. He probably wouldn't remember me anyway. Then again, how could he forget? Instead though, I sent one to Sugar Baby, care of Nicole, even though I was certain that in Sugar's eyes, Nicole had already displaced me as the resident can opener.

When I mailed the postcards it was just three o'clock. I still had two hours to kill. I bought a cigarette lighter for the maestro's habit. That took one minute. I still had too much time to wait, so I phoned Daphne, but she wasn't home. I told Parker I'd be returning to the estate on my own, and that Daphne should not come for me. I was about to call for a cab, but then realized it was a perfect afternoon, and why not walk back to the estate? I knew the way, and I could certainly use the exercise, especially after the mocha-nocciola tart. But it was a big mistake. The estate was much farther and the climb up to the bluffs much higher than I had recalled. It was over an hour later when I finally arrived at the big house. Daphne was just getting into the Bentley.

"I was coming to rescue you," she said. "Did you walk all that way?"

"Yes," I gasped.

Daphne clucked her tongue. "Silly boy," she said. "When I got home Parker gave me your message. We both assumed you'd be taking a taxi, but then you should have been here long ago."

"I was going to," I said, still panting and sweating. "But I decided to give my legs a workout."

"It's a difficult walk if you're not used to it," Daphne replied. "You'd best go have a lie-down before cocktails."

"Sounds good," I said.

I headed toward the cottage, where I took a long hot shower. Clean and refreshed, I lay down on the bed and let the ocean breeze from the windows cool and caress my body. Just as I was dozing off I wondered, Who's been messing around with Ronda Lucca's computer?

15

By six-thirty I was back at the big house for cocktails. Daphne and the maestro were in the library, where a welcoming fire was burning in the fireplace. Even in early June, a fire helped break the chill of the ocean air at night. Daphne was pacing on the Persian carpet while the maestro lounged in a tufted leather armchair, smoking. From Daphne's tone of voice, I sensed a storm of artistic temperament was looming with one of the guests, namely the diva. Madama Ostinata had returned to the estate earlier that day, incensed that Jonathan Byers had rehearsed the second cast singers in exactly the same scene that she and Bruce David had just done. Without so much as a hello to Daphne, Madama had stormed upstairs to her quarters and had spent the remainder of the afternoon on the telephone, transatlantic to her lawyer in Milano.

"And at my expense!" roared Daphne.

Apparently Madama was seeking adequate grounds for suing Jonathan Byers for mental cruelty, and the festival itself for unprofessionalism.

"She told you that?" I said from the liquor cart. I had just poured myself a martini from a crystal decanter that was set in a matching bowl of shaved ice.

Daphne replied sharply, "I heard her on the extension. And don't look at me like that! I didn't listen in purposely. I do have the right to use the telephone in my own house, you know." Then she spewed, "Unprofessionalism! Why, the woman could hardly pronounce the word."

I'd never seen Daphne in such a highly charged state. And the cheap shot at Madama's accent was so unlike her that I knew there was more at stake than just a telephone bill. To show Daphne whose side I was on, I remarked that Madama's fluency in English did seem to change according to whoever's patronage she was soliciting at the moment.

Ignoring my comment, Daphne went on. "Here I am, an opera lover, wanting simply to be a good hostess and a patroness of the arts—to *do* something, finally, for the performing arts that I have loved throughout my life. And now one of my distinguished guests wants to sue me. Oh, if only I'd known!"

I could relate to that sentiment.

The maestro meanwhile turned his gaze from the fireplace and looked toward Daphne with warm caring eyes. *"Cara Madamigèlla,"* he said serenely. "Do not worry. There will be no lawyers. Marcella sees herself growing old. She hears it in her voice. And she is angry. She wants to be a young girl again, and she cannot make that happen. So now she thinks the lawyers can fix it. But she has no power. It is her destiny. You are safe."

Daphne stopped pacing and threw herself into the armchair opposite the maestro's. She looked miserable. I knew I was on shaky ground, but I wanted to help her, to comfort her. I pushed forward tentatively.

"Daphne, is any of this related to what you discovered about Madama Ostinata the other day?"

Daphne whirled at me as if I had betrayed her. Her eyes blazed with reflections from the hearth. Then she let out a long sigh of resignation that almost ended with a small laugh.

"You *are* a devil," she said. "And I could despise you for seeing what I've denied myself. Of course that's it. And here I thought I'd put that squalid business away for later, after opening night. But you're quite right. That's very likely what's driven me to this condition."

"Do you want to talk about it?" I said almost reflexively. There I was, a hairdresser, shrinking a world-famous shrink.

"I doubt the maestro wants to hear about it," she said.

Maestro Toscanelli said, "I know Marcella for many years. I can have no surprise with her. It is better if you talk."

Daphne said, "Well then, here goes. Madama Ostinata made her daily grand descent from her rooms after coffee the other morning. She was glamorized and accessorized in her usual way, but that particular time I couldn't help noticing her brooch. It was solid gold inlaid with onyx. It was a beautiful piece of jewelry, and I commented on it. Madama fondled it for a moment and then giggled coyly and said, 'From an admirer.' But you see, I had recognized that brooch as one of my very own pieces, a gift from my first husband."

I blurted, "Are you saying—?"

Daphne stopped me with her hand. "That brooch had disappeared from my jewelry case long ago, and it was never recovered. When I saw it again the other morning, my first guess was that the stolen piece had been transported to Italy, where Marcella might have purchased it, or even received it as a gift. It was shocking, but then quite stimulating to think she had among her admirers international jewelry thieves. Italians are so hot-blooded. But then I had the next guess, and it was very unsettling: What if my second husband Sid had taken the brooch from my jewelry case and sold it? He was always jealous of my first marriage, when I had a young vibrant body to give to my husband. Sid and I barely nuzzled. And once my imagination had been set on that path, I went all the way and wondered: Had Sid *given* the brooch to Marcella himself?"

"It's so unlikely," I said, though my own imagination had often taken similar flights of absurdity, unrelated to facts and logic.

"Not at all," Daphne said quickly. "Sid was often in Milano on business. Perhaps he met Marcella there."

"But you said he hated opera."

"Yes," said Daphne. "But now I see that his intense dislike of opera might have been a defense for his guilt over Marcella."

Daphne got up and went to the fireplace. She held one hand toward the flames as if to warm it. Then she spoke her next words like a confession into the fire.

"I asked her how long she'd had the brooch. She hedged and said she didn't recall. I told her it reminded me of one my first husband gave to me, his last gift to me. And she said, 'How quaint. You must show it to me sometime.' And I told her I didn't have it anymore. And she said with great theatrical pity in her voice, '*Akh!* I once had to sell some of my jewels as well. It is horrible what a woman must do to survive.' And I agreed with her. Horrible."

The maestro said, "Perhaps Marcella does not know the brooch belongs to you."

"Oh, she knows," said Daphne, turning back toward us. "She's too sly not to. But then, as if that whole business wasn't distressing enough, she had the gall to announce that something very personal and valuable was missing from *her* room, something that no one else would have any use for."

"What was it?" I said.

"Well, that's the final slap," said Daphne. "She wouldn't even tell me."

I offered, "Maybe she knows the brooch is really yours, and that's her way of saying, 'Don't try to get it back.' "

"Or maybe there was nothing missing to begin with," said Daphne.

"Which is probably more likely," I said.

"Well, thank you for that, anyway!" said Daphne. "I was beginning to wonder who's side you're on."

"There's no question about that," I said.

Daphne lowered her eyes. "I know," she said quietly. "I apologize."

I gulped the remainder of my martini and then asked Daphne and the maestro if they wanted another cocktail.

"Dinner will be ready soon," said Daphne. "I'm fine now."

But the maestro held up his empty glass. "Please," he said.

I took it along with mine to the liquor cart. There was just enough left in the decanter for half a drink each. As I refilled the glasses I said offhandedly, "Where's Bruce David?"

"Oh, him!" said Daphne with a dismissive wave of her hand. "He's taken to bed again, exhausted from rehearsal today."

"But he sang only one scene," I said.

"I'm afraid the maestro was right," said Daphne. Her voice was calmer now, as though she'd finally recognized and surrendered to the facts of life for an opera festival benefactress, if not a betrayed wife. She said, "Bruce David simply isn't strong enough for opera."

"Surely this isn't his first role," I said.

"No," said Daphne. "But his previous experience has been in concert performance, and he's been fine there, occasionally thrilling, in fact. But he's never sung a major role in a full stage production. And now it's clear that the stage action and the costumes and cues and everything else have been too much for him. With all he has to think about, he barely has the wits left to sing."

The maestro nodded dolefully. "I know this thing," he said. "I have seen before."

So had I, I thought, in my abbreviated and imaginary melodrama at the café that afternoon.

Parker appeared and announced that dinner was ready. The maestro and I toasted Daphne with our glasses, then downed the silver bullets. Then the three of us went to the dining room.

On the long Hepplewhite sideboard Parker had laid a silver tray bearing a whole fish baked with its head intact. The huge sea creature was set upright on its ventral edge, its long body curved gracefully as though taking a leisurely swim among the braised vegetables and the wine sauce on its serving tray.

"Oh, wonderful!" said Daphne. "Fresh sea bass."

"It was caught this morning," said Parker. "And dressed this afternoon."

And eaten tonight, I thought.

With surgical skill Parker cleanly separated one whole side of the fish from its central bone. Then he cut the tender white flesh into suitable portions for the three of us at the table. The rest of the fish remained on the serving tray, its cooked eyes unfocused on our plates, its mouth agape, and its entire spine exposed against the other half of its body. It looked like something from a biology class, and my appetite was fading fast.

We were just about to tuck away when Madama Ostinata's maid Mathilde appeared at the dining room doorway. The dim candlelight emphasized the hollows of her eyes and the points of her cheekbones. Her hair was pulled back into a chignon so tight that I wondered how she managed to talk. Her teeth were clenched and her lips barely moved.

"Madama wishes no further disturbance tonight."

"We hardly intend to," said Daphne. "Is she ill?"

"She is resting," said Mathilde. "She has taken her sleeping potion." Then she glared accusingly at Daphne and added, "Madama required an extra dosage tonight because she was so upset today."

Daphne said, "Well, I hope Madama is feeling better tomorrow, and I hope she is able to sing after taking all that medication."

The maestro shot a cryptic glance to Mathilde, who raised one eyebrow and then nodded solemnly back to him. It all looked absurdly comical, like a travesty of Mrs. Danvers in *Rebecca*.

The maestro said to Daphne, "I think Marcella will not sing here again."

Daphne said, "You mean at the festival next season? I should say not! Not after today's performance."

"I mean," said the maestro portentously, "no more."

I thought I heard sounds of distant thunder, but then realized it was my stomach, newly impatient for dead fish. The last food I'd had, if you could call it that, was at the café that afternoon. And though mocha-nocciola tart may tarry at the hips, it doesn't stick to the ribs.

Daphne shook her head at the maestro's remark and said, "If Madama chooses not to sing, then who is being unprofessional?" No sooner had she said it than she clucked her tongue. "Silly me," she said. "I should realize I'm dealing with a child now." Then in a last attempt at hospitality, Daphne asked Mathilde, "Would Madama like her dinner brought to her room?"

But instead of answering Daphne, Mathilde's eyes wandered to the sideboard where the sea bass had been laid open for human consumption. As if responding to the dead animal's extinct gaze, her own dark eyes bugged out and her body became rigid. Then she said to Daphne, "We are not hungry," and she departed quickly.

After that, dinner went nearly without a hitch. Daphne fretted a bit about what would happen to the festival's opening production if Madama Ostinata broke her contract and refused to sing. But the maestro placated her by contending that April Kilkus would sing Amelia beautifully, and that the production of *Ballo* would be a great success.

"Even without a world-known diva in the role?" said Daphne.

"More important to worry," said the maestro, "is who will sing Riccardo."

The maestro's allegiance to his singers had changed camps.

"But Bruce David hasn't cancelled," said Daphne.

The maestro shook his head. "You must take him out."

Did he realize what he'd said in slang?

After the fish and vegetables came a salad, followed by strawberry shortcake with homemade biscuits. I had two helpings. Then we went our ways to bed. I read for a while, but couldn't get sleepy. I kept thinking about the dead fish, and the way it seemed to be watching us eat its body. Then I thought about Rafik and what he might be doing in Paris. I took out the aerogram to add some more to it, something beyond the weather, something about life and love. But instead I found myself worried that I might be falling out of love with Rafik because I was having so much difficulty being honest and open with my pen. Maybe it was the spectre of his parents' imminent disapproval of me. Or maybe it was Rafik's very absence that caused the confusion, the withdrawal symptoms. His love and his body were like an addictive drug whose presence dictated use and indulgence, and whose absence often caused a temporary anguish that usually gave way to independence and strength. It was shocking to think that maybe I secretly wanted to leave him. But truthfully, I enjoyed the exhiliration of being on my own, to work and to investigate and to meet people without having to answer the call of love. The responsibility of it. O ugly word! Maybe I was just projecting my old fear that

Rafik would ultimately leave me. But maybe that too was just a projection of my desire to flee from him. Caught in a vortex of worry, that night I could manage only a continuation of the weather report to my lover. But, alas, no love.

16

The next morning Daphne and I were having breakfast outdoors in the gazebo. After the turmoil of the previous night, peace had been restored with the help of Mother Nature—a mild morning sun, a quiet blue ocean, a soft cool breeze—and by Parker's breakfast spread—warm brioche, crushed raspberries, and freshly whipped butter. Daphne had just given the coffee maker its ritual plunge, but with a tranquil, almost reflective gesture that was in keeping with the morning calm.

And then came from the open French doors of one of the second-story bedrooms a wild animal-like shrieking—cries and screams and wailings in a woman's voice. The howls of distress excited a flock of seagulls on the beach far below, and they took flight, squawking and cawing and further heightening the sense of alarm.

I ran from the gazebo and rushed into the house and up the stairs. The vision from the doorway to Madama Ostinata's bedroom seemed to be frozen from some ancient period of time, like an old daguerreotype, except in modern-day color and accompanied by the bestial cries of Mathilde the maid. Madama was lying on her bed in a rumpled cloud of blood-soaked sheets. On one side of the bed stood Maestro Toscanelli, his face ashen and his body rigid. His two hands were held as if in holy supplication. In one hand was a large chopping knife, its blade red and sticky with blood. Bruce David was kneeling at the side of the bed, his torso thrown facedown over the bloody sheets. His awkward position implied that he had either fainted or died there. All else in the room was still except for Mathilde, who stood at the foot of the blood-soaked bed screaming savagely, barely pausing for breath.

My skin went cold and damp. My eyelids fluttered and I realized I had stopped breathing. I leaned against the door frame to gather my wits and keep myself from fainting. I forced my breathing to resume by taking deep controlled breaths. In a few moments I recovered, but then the awful scene caused another more visceral response: tummy squitters. Once again the deliberate slow breathing revived me and kept that one mingled bite of brioche, raspberries, and butter where it belonged. I heard Daphne coming up the stairs behind me. I turned and was about to warn her to keep away—step back, don't look!—but it was too late. She'd already entered the room and seen Madama Ostinata on the bed, her throat slashed open so deeply that the pale bones of her neck were visible even from the doorway, like ivory nubs amidst the soft wet folds of bloody flesh.

Daphne fainted in my arms. Her body was extremely light, like a small bird's, almost fragile. Parker was standing directly behind her. When he saw what was in the bedroom he said, "I'd best call the police."

I carried Daphne out to a divan in the hallway and laid her down. I elevated her legs slightly, then went to get a cold wet towel to revive her. And through it all, Mathilde continued her wild screaming. Minutes later Daphne regained consciousness and immediately instructed Parker and me to bring Mathilde from the bedroom into the hallway. There she managed to administer a hypodermic sedative to the hysterical woman, and within moments the savage noises stopped.

Back in the bedroom, the maestro remained rigidly fixed at Madama's bedside, although he had dropped the big knife onto the bed. Bruce David remained draped over the dead woman's body. I went in and tried to pull him off, but his hands gripped tightly to the sheets. It was either catatonia or rigor mortis. I spoke quietly into his ear and told him he had to get off the bed. He whimpered, "No." I suppose it was good news that he was still alive.

The local police arrived and spent less than two minutes in Madama Ostinata's bedroom. The sergeant came up to Daphne and said, "Looks like we'll have to call in the big boys on this."

"The Boston Police?" said Daphne almost hopefully.

"Yeah," said the sergeant. "Homicide. They'll know how to handle it."

"What happened?" said Daphne.

"That's what I'd like to know," said the cop. "Two of the witnesses in there are in shock, and the third one you got sedated already, so they're all useless at the moment."

"I had to sedate her," said Daphne.

"Oh, I'm sure," said the cop, holding up his hand. "But the way it stands now, I don't know what's going on here."

He made a sour face toward the bedroom, as though the dead soprano had shown exceedingly bad manners by getting herself murdered within his jurisdiction, and with an old man standing by and a younger man clinging to the sheets.

But Daphne looked relieved, as if she knew the Boston police would conduct a bold objective investigation without the long-standing bias of the local police. Still, it was odd how willingly the Abigail police had surrendered their control of the case. Perhaps they recalled their mishandling of another murder a while back, one connected to a chocolate company in Boston. Why bungle another one? Then again, folks in a country club town always called in someone else for the menial work—painting the mansion, tending the landscape, sponging up the blood. The local sergeant had no way of guessing that he and his elite peacekeepers would soon be playing grunts to the Homicide Division of the Boston police Department. But I did, because I had an intuition who was driving out from Boston that very moment at ninety miles an hour on Route 128 to head up the investigation of Marcella Ostinata's murder. And when I heard the throaty growl of a vintage Alfa Romeo pulling into Daphne's front driveway, along with two Boston police cruisers and the county medical examiner's van, my heart raced a bit, and I knew I was right.

17

When Detective Lieutenant Vito Branco of the Boston police entered the mansion, I was still upstairs in the second-floor hallway with Daphne. The small gang of local police up there provided a kind of cover for us as we watched Branco coming up the stairs. When he arrived at the second-floor landing he stood for a moment and surveyed the scene.

Daphne gasped in my ear, "Goodness!"

I had to agree with her. Branco's six-foot frame always seemed larger than life, partly because of his classic proportions, and partly because of his absolute masculinity. His clothes barely concealed a musculature that would have kept Michelangelo busy at the chisel. And depending on the light and Branco's emotional state, his eyes could be an austere and impenetrable gray, or else a cool but more inviting slate blue. His big white teeth luminesced occasionally through one of his rare wry smiles. Hair? Dark and curly, in spite of being trimmed short and neat. And his skin glowed with a lustrous Mediterranean olive tone that complemented the bluish cast of his beard and the sleek black hair on his forearms.

I could write a book.

But that morning I watched him from the safety of Daphne's company. Yes, safety. For with Branco I always felt on the brink of emotional danger, like Tatiana trembling at Onegin's arrival. It wasn't as though Branco and I didn't know each other. In fact he and Nicole had dated for a while. So in a sense Branco was like family, or so I tried to convince myself. But my nether instincts—the ones unrelated to familial bonds—always seemed inclined otherwise.

The Abigail cops filled Branco in on what they'd done so far, which was very little. Still not noticing me or Daphne, Branco went into the bedroom, and I heard him say loudly, "Who are these people?" Bruce David and the maestro were still in there. Apparently the Abigail police had been too zealous about not touching or moving a thing for the Boston cops, including the two people still in the bedroom and very possibly in shock. Their laissez-faire decision bordered on irresponsible.

Daphne whispered to me, "We'd better go help the maestro."

"Are you sure?" I said.

"I'll be fine," she replied. "Just keep my face turned away from the blood. Don't let me look at it, or I may go out again."

She set herself in a self-protective stance by turning her head and looking over her right shoulder. "I'm ready," she said, as though prepared to undergo a session of semiconscious neurosurgery. I led her by her left hand to the doorway of the bedroom. But there I had to pause for an unexpected tableau before me. Bruce David was still kneeling at Marcella Ostinata's bedside with his torso thrown over the bloody sheets. Lieutenant Branco was crouched over him, straddling him from behind, tugging at his arms and trying to untangle his hands from the sheets. I could hear Branco talking softly to Bruce, murmuring persuasively with a father's care, urging the prostrate tenor to come on and be good and let go and everything would be all right if he'd just listen and cooperate. Only a fool would comply too soon.

"What's wrong?" Daphne murmured, her head still turned away from the scene.

"Nothing," I answered with a strange green-eyed hoarseness in my voice. The other cops were moving the maestro away from the bed. That was our cue. "Here we go," I said.

As I led Daphne into the bedroom, Branco changed his stance and was now grasping Bruce David's body in a full bear hug from behind. Then in one mighty haul he lifted him off the blood-soaked sheets. Damn lucky bastard, that tenor. Meanwhile I kept Daphne's head averted from the bed, so she missed Branco's pas de deux with Bruce. She and I had just intercepted the other cops and were trying to balance the enfeebled maestro between us when I heard Bruce David let out a loud wail. I looked his way and saw that he had turned himself around to face Branco and had thrown himself into the lieutenant's arms. To an uninformed viewer it could have appeared a passionate embrace, at least from one party's side. That's precisely when Branco looked over Bruce's shoulder and finally saw me.

"Stan?" he said, amazed.

"Hi, Lieutenant." I tried to wave, but both my arms were occupied, one supporting the maestro and the other averting Daphne's head from the sight line of center stage. "Looks like you've got your hands full," I said.

Branco smirked and replied, "What the hell are you doing here?"

"Wigs for the opera."

Daphne managed to glance toward Branco, and I quickly steered her and the maestro away, like waltzing two people at once around the floor. But Daphne, like any mortal who tries too hard to avoid something, found herself facing directly toward the forbidden *letto di morte*. She got herself a good eyeful of the bloody remains lying there, and once it all registered, she lost her footing and began to slump and sink toward the floor. In an instant Branco saw what was happening. He dropped Bruce David and ran to Daphne's rescue. Before her body touched the floor Branco caught her in his powerful arms and scooped her up. Daphne gazed into Branco's eyes and gave a beatific smile.

"Thank you, officer," she said.

Branco led the way out, carrying Daphne in his arms. He had miraculously escaped Bruce David's clutch with nary a smudge of blood on him. Easy work for a god. I followed close behind Branco and Daphne, with the maestro still leaning on me. Meanwhile, abandoned by his savior, Bruce David lay blubbering on the bedroom floor. I glanced back at him. Easy come, easy go, pal. The local cops then hauled him to his feet and dragged him wailing from the bedroom behind the rest of us.

Branco settled Daphne onto the hallway divan, while I put the maestro in a nearby armchair. I asked him if he wanted a cigarette, since I was finally prepared to light it with the Bic Flic, but he waved me off, as though irritated with himself for requiring so much attention. Didn't he see that attending him and Daphne was a welcome respite from the only alternative at the moment—the messy corpse on the bed?

With the bit players all safely out of the way, the long slow arm of the law—in this case the county medical examiner—could perform her duties with the star attraction, Marcella Ostinata, deceased. And I got to rekindle the connection between me and the lieutenant.

"We've missed you at the shop," I said.

Branco nodded ruefully. "I lost my parents a few months ago, about two weeks apart."

"Wow," I said quietly. "I'm sorry."

Branco said, "There was no sickness, and nobody suffered. That's how they lived their whole lives—clean and orderly."

"I wish I'd known."

Branco waved me off. "It's over now."

"Nicole will feel bad."

"I wanted to be alone," he said. "I took some time off, went away, didn't tell anyone where I was." He forced a smile. "It didn't help much. Anyway, they left a little money for me and my brother. My sister got the house. So I bought a small place in the South End." He laughed and shook his head. "A real fixer-upper. It needs a lot of work, but it has a nice back yard, so someday I'll have a garden and a clothesline."

This was a beefy Italian cop talking.

"And one good thing," he went on. "I spend so much time making it homey, I can't get too bogged down thinking about other things. It's better that way."

"Maybe Nicole could help you decorate."

"When the time comes," said Branco. "Maybe. But for now ..." He faltered a moment, looking for the right words, usually a sign that someone is trying to temper the emotional content of his message. Branco finally said, "Nicole is a wonderful woman, but I'm sure you'd agree that she isn't very domestic."

"True," I said. The only household appliance Nicole could operate was the telephone.

Branco said, "All I've been doing for the past month is hammering and sawing and painting. As far as I can recall, that's not her idea of a good time."

"But when day is done, Lieutenant, she's still a woman."

A mischievous gleam appeared in Branco's eye. "And I'm sure we'll still be friends."

The Abigail county medical examiner interrupted us to say that as far as she could determine, Marcella Ostinata had bled to death from a fatal wound in her neck. (She sure had learned a lot in medical school.) The wound had been inflicted with an extremely well-honed, high-quality knife, like the ones found in any gourmet's kitchen. And whoever had done the deed had wielded the knife like an expert. One sure swipe was all it had taken.

"No jagged edges," she said. "No amateur sawing. Just one nice clean cut—like gutting a fish."

Branco looked at her coldly, without a word.

The examiner continued her barbaric saga with obvious relish. "The spillage was contained by using the sheets as sponges. Otherwise those jets of blood from the carotids could have hit the ceiling. The whole area around the bed would have been splattered."

"Enough!" said Branco. "Just tell me how you're so sure of the murder weapon."

"Didn't you see it?" said the examiner.

Branco gave her a seething look.

The examiner responded with a smug grin. "How could you miss it? It's right there by the pillow."

"Thank you," said Branco. "I'll take over now."

I was about to tell him about the knife, that the maestro had been holding it earlier, but the police sergeant from Abigail interrupted. He'd apparently overheard the exchange, and either he was embarrassed by the county examiner's behavior or else he wanted to gain brownie points with the big shot Boston cop. He said to Branco, "I'll help you any way I can, Lieutenant."

"Good," said Branco.

Then he went into the bedroom and I followed. A police photographer had set up lights and was preparing to take pictures of the death scene. Elsewhere officers were looking for evidence, dusting for fingerprints, taking notes. Branco studied the dead woman with what seemed like more than clinical interest, the same way people often look at corpses at a wake, as though they are trying somehow to associate with the body. Then he looked up suddenly toward the French doors that opened onto the second-floor *terrazzo*. He aimed his question to everyone working in the bedroom.

"Were these doors open?"

The cops replied variously like obedient schoolchildren, saying things like "Yes, sir," and "We haven't moved a thing."

Branco went out through the French doors and I followed. The broad *terrazzo* ran along the entire back of the house. While Branco surveyed the open space out there, he stroked his chin. He seemed to enjoy palpating the strong angular bone under the flesh.

He said, "Anyone whose room opens onto this balcony could have got into that bedroom."

"But why would she leave the doors open?" I said. "I thought any diva worth her diamonds avoided the night air."

"Maybe she was expecting someone," said Branco.

"Who?"

"That's what I intend to find out." He faced me and added, "Could've been anyone in this house, for that matter."

"Don't look at me, Lieutenant."

"Where were you when this happened?"

"Having breakfast outside with Daphne. Her man Parker can vouch for both of us."

"At least for the time the body was found," said Branco.

"Lieutenant, I get my revenge with scissors, not a knife."

"Easy, Stan. I don't suspect you."

"Three strikes and I'm out, eh?"

Branco sniggered. "This isn't a game."

I told him what I'd seen earlier, that the maestro had been holding the bloody knife at Madama's bedside.

"I figured that," said Branco. "I saw some blood on his hands when I walked into the room."

"But you told the examiner—"

He cut me off. "I know what I said."

He looked over the edge of the *terrazzo*, to the soft grass of the lawns far below.

"You think someone climbed up here from down there?" I said.

Branco countered, "There's no evidence of an anchor for a rope, no scratches or chips in the marble."

I reminded him of a wacko rock climber I'd once met in Yosemite National Park. He could have scaled the columns to the second-story *terrazzo* with one arm and leg tied together. Branco responded to my theory with one of his manly grunts.

"Lieutenant, there's a whole cast of characters connected with this opera festival, and they're not even staying here at the house. Maybe one of them drove up here and killed that woman, then went back to town."

He dismissed it. "Someone would have heard the car."

"Maybe they drove part way and then walked."

"Possibly," he said. "Maybe going into town now and meeting those other characters isn't a bad idea—give these folks a little time to settle down before I question them. They're in no condition to talk now anyway." He turned to go back into the house, then he said to me, "You want to come along?"

"With you?"

Branco's eyes glittered in the morning light. "No one else," he said flatly. "Maybe you can tell me your version of things on the way to town."

"Sure," I said, eager to play *His Girl Friday*.

Branco instructed his assisting sergeant to begin questioning the people at Daphne's place as soon as they could tolerate it and still give coherent information. Then he and I left the house together and headed toward his car. When Daphne saw me walking out with Branco, a wary frown wrinkled her brow. I waved back cheerily to assure her I was still her ally and that this escapade with the police, or more specifically with Lieutenant Branco, was on friendly terms. For his part, Branco seemed to have loosened up since the last time I saw him. Maybe the recent brush with mortality and the death of his parents had caused it. Or maybe being out of Boston, out of range of headquarters, he felt he could relax his cop behavior a little. One thing was sure. He'd become more humane.

As we approached Branco's car, Maurizio spied us, gave a look of fright, and then vanished into the nearby greenery.

"Who's that?" said Branco.

"The handyman," I replied.

The corners of Branco's mouth curled slightly. "Another conquest?"

"Hardly," I said in full denial of the facts.

"What is it with you and these ethnic rascals?" said Branco. "You got some kind of magnet for them?"

"Yeah," I said. "A big bar magnet."

Branco grimaced, and I regretted my remark. It was a leftover reflex from those times when every word was intended to provoke him.

Branco said, "I thought you offered something a little closer to the heart."

"I've got that too, Lieutenant."

He nodded toward where Maurizio had vanished into the shrubbery. "I'll question that guy later."

Meanwhile my higher self screamed, Change the subject!

Getting into the Alfa and closing the doors didn't help at all though, for I suddenly found myself shoulder-to-shoulder with the cop. Now, I don't own a car. But no sooner was I seated in the passenger seat of Branco's Alfa Romeo than I understood all those movies and songs that ever used a car as a prop, a kind of aphrodisiac setting for romance and adventure. Maybe that's why it had taken me so long to find love, because I didn't own a car. Yet there I was—right in Branco's love capsule. I could feel the warmth of his body near me, and smell the clean starched cotton of his shirt and the scent of balsam that always seemed to emanate from the man. Like Sophia Loren trapped with Gregory Peck in *Arabesque,* I pressed myself against the door, trying in vain to put a little more space between us.

He said, "Got enough room?"

"Sure," I lied.

He put the Alfa into reverse and grazed my knee roughly with his hand. I flinched, but not out of fear. My face flushed and I turned my head toward the open window. With the cool air blowing on my face, it was only a few moments before my left-brain functions were restored. Then I saw and smelled that the Alfa's seats had been reupholstered in soft tan leather, and new carpeting and sisal mats had been laid on the floorboard. Not all of Branco's money was going into his vine-covered cottage.

While we zoomed toward town and the performance center, I gave him my version of what I'd seen and heard at the opera house in the preceding days, an Anna Russell-like sketch of the production and the cast of characters. The ridiculous soap opera I'd imagined at the café the previous day had prepared me for that stellar moment in Branco's sports car. And when I finally recounted the dramatic and accidental death of Adam Pierce, Branco almost choked.

"There was another one?"

"It was an accident," I repeated. "At least that's what the local police say."

The Alfa's engine roared as Branco downshifted into a tight curve. At the next stretch of straight road he turned toward me.

"What do *you* think?" he said, and he kept his face on mine, as though he wanted me to register all his strong dark Mediterranean features at close range.

I had to clear my throat before I answered him.

"After this morning, Lieutenant, I think Adam Pierce's death was a mistake, but it was no accident."

18

When we arrived at the performance center the Abigail police were already there as well. I fairly burst from the intimate confinement of Branco's car. For me, physical proximity to that man would need a lot more rehearsal. Baby steps. Time. But what did any of it matter, since I was already partnered? And Branco, from all earthly indications, was straight, even though his presence always caused that enjoyable if troubling tingle.

On the way into the opera house Branco stopped to confer with the local cops. They'd already told the cast and crew what had happened to Marcella Ostinata and that the Boston police had been summoned. Branco nodded approvingly, and then without another word he and I entered the auditorium together.

A stage rehearsal was in progress with Jonathan Byers in charge. Carolyn Boetz was at the piano. April Kilkus, Hwang Yung Cho, and the cover tenor were all singing onstage. No one seemed to notice or care that neither Maestro Toscanelli nor Bruce David were present, nor that Madama Ostinata had been permanently detained. Within seconds of hearing the music Branco murmured, *"Un ballo in maschera,"* in perfect Italian. I glanced at him and saw half a smile curl up on one side of his mouth. "I'm Italian," he said with a small shrug. "We all like opera," he added, as if to excuse any mote of culture in himself.

We stood and watched rehearsal for a few minutes from the back of the house. I identified the various personalities for him, both on and offstage, and explained the controversial setting of this production in a New York nightclub. At that, Branco leaned close to me and whispered, "I've seen this opera set in a lot of places, but never in modern-day New York."

I replied, "The director wants to make his mark."

Branco grunted quietly.

April Kilkus seemed remarkably well prepared for her role. She proceeded through the rehearsal confidently, as though she had known all along that she, and not Madama Ostinata, would be portraying Amelia. Still, Jonathan Byers stopped her abruptly mid-phrase.

"Darling," he exclaimed. "You are a jewel, and your voice is pure velvet, and I love everything you're doing. But do you think you might put a bit more worry in your voice? You *have* been caught red-handed with your husband's best friend, you know."

The break in action was Branco's cue to move down the center aisle toward the front of the house. He stopped at the orchestra pit rail and introduced himself boldly. Then he made his big announcement.

"We have a serious problem here, folks. As you probably know, one of your colleagues was found dead this morning. For everyone's protection, I'm putting the performance center under police guard until further notice. Beyond that, you can come and go as usual, except that no one will be allowed to leave town without my permission."

There were mutterings of outrage among the cast and crew, but it was Jonathan Byers's voice that cut through the muddle.

"Maybe under a police state we'll get some work done."

I thought I saw him smack his lips at the sight of Branco.

Branco addressed Byers directly. "There's going to be a lot of questioning and interruptions today. You might want to cancel rehearsal." Then he added, "Maybe out of respect for the dead woman, if nothing else."

Byers answered him defiantly. "We don't have time for respect here, Inspector Branco. Marcella Ostinata was a bothersome bitch, and it's a relief to know I won't have to hear that voice again."

"Since you're so eager to talk," said Branco, "I'll question you first."

"Fine," said Byers, showing an unlikely air of cooperation. He instructed his assistant director to run the scene according to his notes, then he left the auditorium with Branco. I half expected Byers to join arms with the cop.

Rehearsal continued with the assistant director fumbling hopelessly with his first assignment. Carolyn Boetz rescued him and ran the show from the piano. She seemed optimistic and fully in control of the situation. Once again she accompanied April Kilkus with that special sensitivity I'd heard the night of Daphne's reception. And I heard an extra vigor in her playing whenever the tenor or the baritone sang. Perhaps it was the maestro's absence, or perhaps it was the news of Madama Ostinata's demise, but Carolyn Boetz had acquired a new freedom in her music-making.

There wasn't much I could do but listen and observe while rehearsal was in progress, so I went downstairs to see if Daniel Carafolio was in the wig room. It was a work day, after all, even if the prima donna's throat had been cut. I found Daniel down there, all right. He was sitting upon a huge square of cardboard and contemplating a wreath of artificial leaves, probably something he'd found in the prop department. He was shaking a can of black spray paint when he saw me.

"This is a dark hour in the history of opera," he said. "Marcella's death concludes an era of greatness."

He began spraying the wreath with glossy black paint.

I asked, "Is there anything you want me to do here?"

Daniel continued spraying the wreath until it was evenly coated. Then he turned his tear-streaked face to me and said, "Just go home. We should all go home. But you especially. You've been a mistake from the beginning."

"Your diva's death is not my fault," I said.

"But the migraine headaches certainly are." He turned the wreath over and began spraying the back side of it. "None of that matters now," he said. "It's all over. The production will be cancelled. You might as well go and apply for unemployment. I'll sign anything they want."

"I don't run away from problems," I said, which was one version of the truth. "I'll work here until I'm let go."

"Suit yourself," he said. "But there'll be nothing for you to do." He finished spray painting the wreath, then he aimed a hair dryer on it. When it was done he stood up and went and hung it on the door to the wig room. "I'm closing up shop," he said, then added with finality, "Until further notice."

"I guess I'll have to take over then."

Daniel glared at me. "Over my dead body," he said.

It seemed a particularly ill-chosen cliché. But hell, consider the source. And I know when I'm not welcome. So I left Daniel in his dark and dismal dungeon and went back upstairs to the auditorium. I entered quietly by one of the side doors, and was just in time to hear the finale to act one. During that music, the singing was so exciting and the ensemble work so tight that I realized that Marcella Ostinata's death, and perhaps even the subsequent absence of the maestro and Bruce David that morning, might be a blessing to the festival after all.

The music had just about stopped reverberating in the hall when Jonathan Byers entered from the wings, downstage right. He was applauding the singers, and he appeared slightly flushed under the work lights. Whether it was from the thrilling finale or from his first round of questioning with Branco, I could only guess.

At the same time, from the opposite side of the stage Daniel Carafolio made an entrance. His eyes were red, and the tears were running freely down his cheeks. He addressed the entire cast and crew with a loud and tremulous voice.

"I am announcing my intention to boycott this production, based on Sir Jonathan Byers's arrogant refusal to recognize the loss of one of opera's greatest voices ever. If any of you have any brains or feelings, you will join me in solidarity and leave the premises now."

I expected to hear Lieutenant Branco tell Daniel Carafolio who was really in charge now—who could say "leave" and who could say "stay"—but I didn't see him anywhere. Instead, it was Jonathan Byers who addressed Daniel from his position, downstage right.

"And if you're still here on opening night," he bellowed, "you can lick my arse. But today I've got work to do." Byers then faced the audience and addressed the production table. "Stage manager, would you please remove Humpty Dumpty from the set?"

Ronda Lucca scurried up onto the stage and crossed to where Daniel Carafolio was still standing, apparently transfixed by Sir Jonathan's opening night proposal. It's not often that an invitation to a rimming is made public. Ronda grabbed Daniel's arm to escort him off, but he jerked it away from her and turned to walk off himself, stage left. But who should emerge from those wings at that moment but Lieutenant Branco. He confronted Daniel, there was a moment of freeze action, then Branco took him offstage left for questioning.

Improvisational theater was still alive.

Then Jonathan Byers announced for all the cast and crew to hear, "Act three, scene one. Places please in twenty minutes."

As the singers dispersed for a break, I wandered backstage myself. By this time, I was becoming a familiar enough face in the opera house so that people accepted my presence in the auditorium and backstage, even if they weren't quite sure what I was doing there. As I passed by one of the prop tables, I noticed a big knife lying there. Before I had a chance to study it, one of the stagehands grabbed it and took it to Hwang Yung Cho, who was onstage practicing his role of Renato, the character who murders the tenor in the last moments of the opera.

I found Ronda Lucca in her booth, backstage right. She was consulting her cue sheets for the next scene in rehearsal, and she was instructing various people over her wireless headset as to which lights and sets would ultimately be in place during performance. She seemed to enjoy being in charge, as though giving orders to other people was her natural place in the world. Marcella Ostinata's death hadn't affected her much.

I went to her and, during a moment between orders when she paused for a breath, I said, "How's your computer running today?"

Ronda glanced up from her cue sheets.

"Oh, hi there," she said. "The computer is fine. It's me who's feeling fried today."

"Because the sacred cow is dead?"

Ronda gave me a quizzical look.

I said, "Isn't that what you called Madama Ostinata?"

"Not sacred," replied Ronda. "Just cow." She spoke into her transmitter regarding the placement of a glass-topped desk onstage. Then she looked back at me and remarked, "One good thing about a dead diva—she can't sing."

"That seems to be the general consensus," I said.

"All it takes is two ears," she replied.

I noticed that Ronda sported a heavy ring of keys hanging from a metal clip on her wide leather belt. Also attached to that clip was a Swiss army knife. It was larger than the standard issue model, with what looked to be a five-inch blade folded into the black housing. It hung from her belt like a slender phallus. I'd never seen a knife like it and I said so.

"Picked it up in Europe," she said simply. Then she unclipped it from her belt and handed it to me. It was heavy, and it did have an extra-long blade concealed within. Ronda said, "Open it up. Or are you afraid of knives?"

"No," I said.

She grabbed it from my hand and flipped open the blade. It was long and sharp, with a mirrorlike finish that glinted harshly even in the dim backstage lights. The blade looked dangerous enough—you could do some nasty carving with it—but it was hardly the implement to slice open someone's throat as deeply as Madama Ostinata's had been. Still, Ronda Lucca was pretty handy with the knife, especially the way she snapped the blade closed with one hand. I'd never try a trick like that. I'd never even want to learn how. Maybe that's the kind of thing that separated gay boys from gay girls.

Ronda had just finished her show-and-tell with the knife and was heading back out front to the production table when Lieutenant Branco approached us. He'd been as quick with his questioning of Daniel Carafolio as he had with Jonathan Byers. Perhaps Branco was doing his first sessions fast, to get the lay of the land. Or perhaps he was using efficient new police methods.

"Are you Ronda Lucca?" he said to her.

"Call me Ron," she replied.

Branco introduced himself and told her he wanted to ask a few questions.

"Fire away," she said.

Branco said, "Not here—"

But Ronda's receiver beeped before he could say anything more. Ronda told her caller that, no, the glass-topped desk hadn't arrived at the opera house yet, but to make a note where it belonged onstage once it did. Then she turned to Branco and said, "Sorry."

"Not at all," said the cop. "By the way, you aren't related to Tony Lucca, are you?"

"Who?" she said.

"Runs a fish market in the North End."

"In case you hadn't noticed, Lieutenant, Lucca is a very common name."

"You could almost be a relative," he said.

"It's the blood. You oughta know. You seen one wop, you seen 'em all." Ronda laughed, and I realized that she had lapsed comfortably into tough-guy talk with Branco, something I could never quite pull off.

For his part, Branco dismissed her remark, as if he knew he was in a class by himself, apart from every other Italian who ever walked the earth. He asked Ronda to go with him for questioning. She agreed easily, and called her assistant to take over for her. When Ronda walked away with Branco, I noticed a pair of old suede work gloves jammed under her belt in back. Ronda Lucca had executed her butch costume to perfection.

With no one else available for me to torment at the moment, I went out into the opera house lobby. The afternoon sun had warmed the broad glass-enclosed space, and cast long slender shadows across the carpeted floor. Standing far away in a dark corner designated for smokers—an endangered architectural detail in smoke-free America—was Rick Jansen, alias Ricky-thing, Jonathan Byers's very own wonder-slut. He was having a smoke. I felt my investigative claws emerge from their protective sheaths and I headed over to him. As I approached the smoker's nook, I heard and felt a superefficient ventilation system at work, almost like a wind tunnel, but on the suck end instead of the blow. The vacuum tugged at my hair, even though it's cropped fairly close to my scalp. Any secondhand smoke in that corner would be taken and sent far, far away from the rest of the opera house lobby.

Ricky blew a lungful of smoke toward me, a certified aggressive gesture. But instead of hitting me in the face, the smoke flew directly from his lips and up past his own face toward the overhead ducts.

He said, "Don't you belong downstairs?"

"They let me up for air today," I answered.

"Too bad," he said.

"I see you've regained your footing with Jonathan Byers."

"What's that supposed to mean?"

He tried blowing another puff of smoke at me, but with the same ridiculous effect.

I said, "It looked like you were playing second fiddle to Adam Pierce. Until he was killed."

"That was an accident."

"So say the police. But I wonder—"

"Look," said Ricky. "Why don't you mind your own business and tend to the hairnets?"

"It gets kind of lonely. Besides I like to watch people, what they say and do, especially when they're provoked. It's my nature, the same way it's your nature to hustle."

He took a step toward me.

"You don't know my real nature," he said. The cigarette dangled from his lips. It might have looked tough if he wasn't so blond and if the smoke wasn't being sucked upward in a thin whispy stream.

"I can guess," I said. "Or is the tough guy just a façade for the puss underneath?"

"I'll beat the shit out of you," he said.

"Would that give you a hard-on?"

He braced himself and swung at me, but his preparation gave me plenty of time to duck. His whole move was too calculated, and I sensed it had been a feint. I also sensed that if Rick had wanted to connect, he would have.

I said, "There are other ways to make a point besides violence."

He sneered. "Violence works fine for me."

I backed away cautiously but he followed me.

"Are you afraid yet?" he said.

"Why do you hate me?"

"Because you're a faggot."

"And you're not?" I said.

"I'm a man," he replied.

"Explain the difference," I said, still backing away.

He was trying to seethe, as if to imitate his mentor, Jonathan Byers. "The difference is," he said, "you want to suck my thing. But I'd just as soon beat your face with it."

"You sure know how to sweet-talk a guy."

He lunged toward me with a jab and I leaped back, but his fist caught the fabric of my shirtfront. The force knocked me off balance, and I stumbled. He jumped onto me, and we fell to the floor. We grappled each other, two sissies of opposing viewpoints engaged in unmanly combat. I aimed to roll us over, to get myself on top, where my extra weight would give me an advantage. All that playful wrestling with my lover had taught me how to use leverage to overcome his sheer muscle strength. And that's how I got Ricky pinned down, by yielding to the manic pressure of his arms and torso for a split second, so that in that momentary empty space of his pressing against nothing, I could change the angle of my shoulders slightly and get a new footing with one leg, and then give one good push with that leg and roll Ricky over in exactly the same direction that he was still applying pressure onto me. It's really simple. Cats do it all the time, where the squirmy ones can always overtake the bruisers. It's all timing and leverage.

So I got Ricky pinned to the floor and applied my weight just heavily enough to keep him restrained. I didn't press all of it onto him because I wanted something to maneuver with. That's when I told him he should be nicer to the less fortunate faggots who didn't have his pretty looks and nice muscles. We have feelings too. That's exactly when two of the investigating cops finally showed up and broke up the fight—if you could call it that—just when I was scoring a victory for all the unsung sissy heroes among us.

Like two schoolboys after a tussle, we told the cops that neither of us was hurt, which was true, and that the fight was all about nothing, which was false. Ricky headed quickly into the auditorium, retreating in shame I wanted to think. But I stayed in the lobby, for someone else had come out there as well. It was Carolyn Boetz.

She told me she had just entered the lobby for a break when she noticed the trouble between me and Rick, so she alerted the police. I thanked her and then complimented her on what I'd heard of the rehearsal. She peered at me through her thick eyeglasses. Her myopic eyes seemed keener and more daring than before.

She said, "The maestro isn't coming in today, so I'm in charge, at least musically."

"It's obvious that you're qualified."

"It's all I've ever wanted to do," she said blissfully.

I said, "It's too bad about Madama Ostinata."

"Yes," said Carolyn, suddenly without emotion. "Too bad. But we'll manage. The show will go on as scheduled."

"And from what I heard today, it may sound even better."

Carolyn's eyes flickered nervously. "I have no doubt about that. Did you hear the new tenor?"

"Yes."

"Then you know that he's much better than Bruce David."

"It's obvious," I said.

"And it doesn't take a psychoanalyst to see that Bruce David doesn't have what it takes for an operatic career."

I thought that was a cheap shot at Daphne.

Carolyn continued. "He can barely get through one aria without problems, never mind a role like Riccardo."

"And the other tenor can?"

"I'm sure of it," she said. "He and I rehearsed all night."

"Where?"

She looked at me suspiciously. "In one of the rehearsal studios here in the performance center."

"Was anyone else there with you?"

"No. But neither of us went out again. You can check the security report. It will show that we never left the performance center last night. We all have electronic keys, and they automatically record who goes in and out of where, and when."

"I didn't ask you for an alibi," I said.

Carolyn blushed. "I'm sorry. I guess I'm a little nervous with the police around."

"And a little defensive," I added.

But I was intrigued that she knew or even cared about the high-tech security system around the performance center. I asked her why she'd spent so much time with the second tenor the previous night. Had she known that Bruce would not sing?

She answered, "I was preparing for the inevitable."

"Was Marcella Ostinata's death inevitable?"

"That," said Carolyn, "was a blessing." Then she quickly added, "I know that sounds cold. I'm truly sorry about what happened to her, but Marcella caused much more trouble than she was worth. We were all running around trying to sustain a glamorous legend instead of collaborating with a great artist. The fact is, I wonder if she ever could sing." Carolyn made a small grimace. "Perhaps her vocal gifts came to light during performance."

"We'll never know that now," I said.

She looked at her watch. "It's time for me to go back in."

"You haven't had a very restful break."

"I'm fine," she said blithely. "You probably wouldn't guess, but I like excitement. It refreshes me." And she returned to the auditorium to make beautiful music again.

At that point I'd done all the investigating I could at the opera house. Except for Jonathan Byers, Hwang Yung Cho, and April Kilkus, who were all rehearsing again, I'd either offended or vanquished anyone else who could possibly be considered a suspect in Marcella Ostinata's murder. And I wasn't quite ready to return to Daphne's house. So with time on my hands, I telephoned Nicole, who I knew would be at Snips Salon in Boston.

When the receptionist answered the phone I could hear the comforting homey sounds of a busy salon in the background. I almost felt the familiar sting of perm solution in my nostrils. I asked the receptionist to send Nicole to the phone in my office at the back of the shop. I wanted her to have privacy for this little chat. She eventually came on the line in her usual brusque manner.

"Stanley?" she said. "Is everything all right?"

"Yeah, doll." My throat choked up at the sound of her voice. I didn't realize how much I was missing my best friend.

"We're extremely busy here today, darling, so there really isn't time—"

"Nikki, the diva was murdered this morning."

"No!"

"It was awful. The local police couldn't handle it so they called in the boys from Boston. Lieutenant Branco is out here now."

"Ah," said Nicole. "How is Vito?"

"I just found out that his parents died recently."

The line went quiet while I heard her light up a cigarette. That's unusual for her, to smoke on the telephone. Nicole is one of those rare creatures who smokes in ritualistic pleasure, not mindless habit. She is always seated, and she smokes actively. For Nicole, a cigarette is a focus, not a secondary prop. That she was lighting up now meant her emotions were charged.

"When did it happen?" she said.

"A few months ago."

"That explains the long hiatus."

"Branco says he purposely kept to himself, didn't tell anybody. But apparently the retreat didn't help much. The odd thing is, Nikki, he seems friendlier now."

Nicole puffed quietly.

"Doll?" I said.

After a brief pause she spoke. "I think Vito probably is better off when he's by himself."

"How can you say that when you dated him, Nikki?"

"That's exactly why I know, darling." She puffed some more, and somehow I knew not to talk. And when she spoke again, she finally answered an old question that had plagued me during all the time she'd spent with Branco. "I assume by now," she said, "that you realize Vito and I never had sex."

"I could only guess, doll. You kept the fog pretty thick."

130

"It was always platonic between us."

"Not for lack of your trying though."

"You're wrong there, Stanley. I took all my cues from him."

"Everyone does."

"There's no other way with a man like that. But I sensed from the beginning that Vito Branco is the kind of man who has difficulty getting close to people, especially to women." Another pause. More puffing. "He confessed to me once that whenever the loneliness became unbearable, he would pay for sex. He thought it was healthier than being alone."

Wow, went my silent voice.

Nicole went on. "He stopped it when he realized he was beginning to enjoy getting rough with the women."

"Nikki, enough."

As though wakened from a trance, Nicole changed her tone of voice and said, "Stanley, you realize what I'm telling you is in utmost confidence. You must never let Vito know what I've just said."

"Don't worry, doll."

"I do worry. I've just broken a promise to him. I've said too much, and you're not very good at keeping secrets."

"Mea culpa."

"But Stanley, this time you must."

"I will, doll. I will. I do have some control over my mouth."

Nicole tried to stifle a laugh. Meanwhile, I was already setting up differential equations that might explain the true nature of Lieutenant Branco's sexuality.

"He never hit *you,* did he, Nikki? I recall that time when your arm was bruised—"

"Vito never approached me physically," said Nicole. "Except for a chaste kiss on the cheek, he was always the perfect gentleman." She sighed heavily into the receiver. "Please give him my condolences."

"I will, Nikki."

There was a long pause, and we both seemed to realize that unless we had about six hours and a litre of cognac, there was nothing more to say about Lieutenant Vito Branco at the moment.

"How's Ramon doing?" I said.

Ramon was a former shampoo boy at Snips who was handling some of my clients in my absence.

"He's coming along quite nicely," replied Nicole. "Not as good as you, darling. But who could be?"

"Thanks, Nikki."

"You know I mean it."

"Kind of."

"When are you coming home?"

"I'm not sure, doll. The investigation just started."

"But isn't the opera closing down?"

"No."

"So you're staying out there?"

"For a while. Maybe I can help. Like I said, Branco seems friendlier now."

"Stanley, please don't call him Branco."

"But that's who he is, Nikki. He's Vito to you, but he's Branco to me."

Nicole said, "Maybe someday he'll be Vito to you too."

"When cows fly and horses sing, doll."

"There was that talking horse on television," she said.

"I'll call you with updates," I said.

"You call me every day, Stanley."

"Yes, ma'am," I said, though I knew I wouldn't.

"And remember to give my regards to Vito."

"Just regards?"

"That will do," she said. "For now."

"Ciao, doll."

There was a moment's silence when I expected the line to go dead, since Nicole never says good-bye. But instead I heard her say quietly, "Take care, Stanley."

"I'll try, Nikki."

Then came the familiar click.

19

I had just hung up the receiver when Branco came out from the auditorium. He saw me standing at the public telephones and waved me over. I had to keep myself from running to him.

"Nicole sends her regards," I said. "I told her about your parents."

Branco acknowledged my message with a nod and a slight smile. "I'm just about done here," he said. "Are you hanging around to work?"

"The wig room is officially closed," I replied. "I was heading back to the estate myself. Any chance I might bum a ride?"

Branco considered a moment. "Probably."

"I mean with you," I said. "In your car."

"I know," he said. "I'm sure there's room."

God forbid the guy should just say "yes." I guess I should have been satisfied that all the words he danced around with came out meaning the same thing. I wanted to ride back with Branco so I'd have a chance to compare notes with him. Honest, that was the real reason.

On the ride up the winding road to Daphne's house, I again studied the cop's powerful hands. They embraced the wooden steering wheel with an almost haughty confidence. The long heavy fingers formed sharp angles as they grasped the arc of burnished walnut; the huge thumbs, loosely connected to the palms like those of the best concert pianists, were strong sculptures of curves and planes; the nails were large and pink, with perfectly trimmed white tips shining against the olive tone of his skin. But now Branco's big beautiful paws disturbed me too, for I wondered how many women he had struck with them. His voice broke the spell.

"How is your partner doing?"

"Rafik is in Paris, preparing his parents to meet me."

Branco chuckled quietly. "Sounds like every other couple in the world."

"Except that—"

Branco interrupted, "You've got nothing to worry about, Stan. His folks are going to like you just fine." He turned his face toward me. "Look at me," he said with unlikely surrender. "You even won me over. I mean, in a manner of speaking."

Aberration of logic! screamed my left brain. A cop is flirting with a hairdresser. I focused on his big manly hands, the ones that had beaten women. That way I could despise him just enough to maintain a safe psychic distance between us.

I told Branco that Carolyn Boetz had mentioned a security report that recorded all the comings and goings around the performance center based on electronic keys. Branco said he knew about the report, and had already consulted it while questioning the people in the opera house.

"But it doesn't record the stage door," he said. "There's a security guard there twenty-four hours."

"Supposedly," I said.

Branco had a copy of the report with him in the car. I asked him if I could see it. He said sure, it was in the back seat. I fished it out from a pile of papers that was fast overtaking the Alfa's tiny back seat. The report would require some decoding, so I refolded it and placed it on my lap for later on.

Branco said, "You can't keep that."

"I know," I said. "I'll give it back."

"Today," he said.

"Sure, boss."

Branco smiled.

Then I said, "Did you talk to April Kilkus or Hwang Yung Cho?"

"You mean the soprano and the baritone?"

"Yeah," I said, still somewhat bewildered that Branco knew anything about opera and singers.

"What about them?" he said.

"They're the only two people I didn't get a chance to bother today."

Branco smirked. "It sounds to me like you've already been mucking around pretty deep in this thing."

I hesitated. "I guess you could say that."

"Stan," he said. "What if I told you this time that I'm considering using your help? That I actually want it?"

"I'd wonder what you have up your sleeve, Lieutenant."

"What if I make you a deputy?"

"That would really complicate it."

"It's just common sense," said Branco. "In the past you've meddled and I've resisted, but you've always ended up helping the case. So why not just skip the first two steps and register you as a civilian deputy?"

"Can you do that?"

"I'm the boss, like you said."

"Do I get a shiny badge?"

Another smirk from the cop. "A badge is something else."

We had just climbed the final ascent to Daphne's place where the road leveled off. Though the afternoon sun was bright and the sky clear, the ocean far below us was choppy and dusted with whitecaps. We'd be at the estate in a few minutes.

I told Branco I was surprised that he knew about opera.

"Nothing wrong with that, is there?" said the cop. Then to my surprise, Branco divulged another bit of his personal life to me: His mother had been a singer. She had often taken him as a boy to New York to the opera, and he had heard Marcella Ostinata sing many times.

I told him I thought he seemed to recognize her that morning.

Branco replied, "You've got a good eye."

And, I reasoned, that's why Marcella's death had affected Branco so strongly—because of the association to his recently dead mother.

I asked him, "Do you remember how she sounded?"

He nodded. "Marcella was young then, and extremely dramatic.

For her, opera was more visual than musical. Her voice was never secure, and never really what you'd call beautiful. But her personality was strong enough so that it worked."

Then he recalled that there was some scandal about Marcella, that she had stopped singing smack in the middle of the season. But the next year she was back again in her usual form. Branco said, "My mother always spoke obscurely about the brief pause in Marcella's career, but I think she really knew what happened. I have a hunch she was too ashamed to tell me."

"It must have been sex-related," I said. Hell, from my skewed view of the world, everything was sex-related. "Maybe Marcella had a baby out of wedlock," I said.

Branco shrugged. "I never found out. But I still go to New York for opera. There's almost nothing in Boston now." Then he made an ironic little laugh and said, "I sure hope there's not a potential conflict of interest here. I bought a subscription for the festival."

"This one? In Abigail?"

"Yup," said the cop. "I want to encourage opera in Boston. I don't talk about it at the station though. Why give them any ammunition?"

As he turned the Alfa onto Daphne's curved driveway, I wondered, Ammunition against what?

The Abigail police had gone home, but the Boston police cruisers were still parked in front of the house. According to Parker, the local force had left the premises hours ago. Madama's body had been taken back to Boston, since that's where the investigation was based. And things had generally quieted down.

Daphne came into the foyer looking bright and refreshed, a marked reversal to the horrors of the morning. She came to me with open arms. "I'm so glad you're back. I didn't realize how much I would miss the comfort of someone young and friendly around here with me." She embraced me tenderly. Then she said to Branco, "The same goes for you, Lieutenant. It's a relief to have you here again." However, rather than greet Branco with a big hug, Daphne grasped his upper arm and gave it a reassuring squeeze. It was something I'd always wanted to do, but the older woman could get away with it, while a grope like that would probably have landed me a slap.

"I'll bet you're both famished," she said. "Parker is standing by to serve lunch in the garden room."

"Thanks," said Branco. "But I'll want to question everyone first. Where have my crew set up?"

Daphne said, "They're all in the library." She looked a bit crestfallen. "Don't you want any lunch?"

Branco's eyes betrayed his cool manner. He wavered for a moment, then said to Daphne, "Would it be any trouble to get some sandwiches and coffee in the library?"

Daphne beamed at him. "Consider it done. And Lieutenant, you and your crew are welcome to stay at the performance center in town for as long as you need." She was already in thrall with the cop.

Branco considered her offer, and then said, "That would help us out a lot."

Daphne continued, "There's even room for one more here at the big house, if you'd like to stay with us. It's very comfortable."

"I'm sure it is," said Branco. He looked at me. "Where are you sleeping?"

Daphne and I exchanged glances.

"In the cottage," I said.

Branco turned back to Daphne. "It's probably better if I stay in town with my crew."

I guess my residency in the cottage was still too close to the big house for Branco's comfort. But he did invite me into the library with him. His crew from Boston was waiting in there—a male sergeant and a female officer. They were arranging the statements they'd taken while Branco was at the opera house. Branco introduced me to them, and I was pleasantly surprised when they greeted me hospitably. I was only a civilian, after all, even though I knew Branco from previous cases. Perhaps my dubious reputation with the Boston Police Department was beginning to serve me well.

Parker wheeled in a cart bearing a platter of sandwiches, a thermal decanter of coffee, and a big porcelain cookie jar in the shape of a clown. Branco laughed out loud when he saw it. That was a rare moment when the dark brooding cop laughed like that, in genuine amusement, in spite of himself. It made me almost want to rescue him and take care of him until he could do it more often—loosen up and laugh at more things, even the most serious ones. But his laugh had also opened a tiny loop in the stranglehold of his self-control, and Branco was suddenly identifying the cookie jar as a caricature of Enrico Caruso, costumed for his famous role as Canio, the clown in *I pagliacci*. Branco's two crew members looked at him curiously, and he caught himself. "My uncle had one just like it," he said quickly. And after that he was all business.

Before the cops had lunch, Branco took Parker's statement. It was a simple session with few surprises. Daphne's butler had heard and seen nothing unusual between the time he locked up the house the night before until the shocking moment that morning, when Madama Ostinata's maid had discovered her lady's mutilated body on the bed.

Branco said, "You're certain that every window and door was locked then?"

"Yes, sir," replied Parker. "My standard routine is to secure every window and door. It takes me a good half-hour."

"What about the windows and doors in the guest quarters?"

Parker's face showed a minuscule flinch. "I'm afraid you've caught me there, Lieutenant. I did not check any of the guest rooms, nor do I ever check Miss Davenport's quarters."

"That's all right," said Branco. "I wasn't trying to trip you up. I just wanted to make sure."

But I saw a small, self-satisfied gleam in the cop's bright gray-blue eyes.

That brief interrogation finished, Branco told Parker to gather everyone else in the household in some convenient place close to the library so that he could call them in one by one for questioning. Before dismissing Parker, Branco snapped his fingers at me.

"Stan, what's your young friend's name?"

"Who?"

"The one hanging around my car this morning. Your latest conquest," he added smugly.

Parker intervened. "That would be Maurizio, sir."

Jeez! Even the butler knew about me.

"Good," said Branco. "Be sure to get him in with the others."

Parker nodded and set off on his mission. Meanwhile the three cops and I had lunch, and I got to watch Branco's big square jaw work its way through two slabs of thick-cut dark bread, laid heavy with nearly raw meat.

I took a dainty bacon-lettuce-and-tomato sandwich on crustless white bread, then settled down to study the security report, the one that showed everyone's comings and goings from the performance center residences the previous night.

20

Before Branco began his serious questioning, he had one of his assistants draw the draperies across the library windows to darken and enclose the huge room. Meanwhile Branco himself went about the room and turned on some of the reading lamps, choosing them strategically to give a gothic, sinister feeling to the place. He seated himself directly center along the length of the library's study table, which was a long, broad slab of solid mahogany. On either side of him sat the assisting officers, looking very much like they were preparing for an afternoon fête at the Grand Inquisition. The inquiree's chair was placed opposite Branco's seat, on the other side of the wide expanse of tabletop. I was out of the way, slouching in one of the leather wing-back chairs off to one side, where I could quietly and almost invisibly observe the goings-on while I also perused the security report. A Gemini prefers to do two things at once.

The first person Branco called into the library for questioning was Mathilde, the late Madama Ostinata's personal maid. Mathilde entered the wood-panelled room with her head held confidently high. Even in the subdued light, her eyes appeared clear and open, with no sign of redness. The shadows under them had somewhat faded as well, but that could have been an effect of Branco's dramatic lighting. Most noticeable was Mathilde's keen awareness of everyone and everything in the library. She had obviously recovered from her screaming jag that morning.

Branco began with some standard questions, and Mathilde's answers provided some standard facts. Her last name was Morçeau. She was forty years old, although she looked and acted like a woman whose life had been a much longer succession of disappointments. She was an orphan, and Marcella Ostinata had rescued her long ago and had become like an aunt to her. Mathilde claimed the one great fortune of her life was to have been Madama Ostinata's personal companion for twenty-five years. She even pulled herself up higher from her already ramrod-straight posture to make this pronouncement, and she purposefully looked Branco straight in the eye as she spoke. And I detected a lie. Mathilde may have enjoyed the luxury of traveling the world with a great diva, and packing her trunks, and setting out her costumes, but I didn't sense any genuine gratitude there. Mathilde was, after all, no matter what fancy label you gave it, a piece of hired help.

Branco asked her about the previous night. Was there anything unusual from the usual pattern of things?

"No," said Mathilde. "I gave Madama her nightly potion. Then I opened the doors to the balcony, and I left her."

"You say you opened the doors?"

"Yes," said Mathilde. "Just a tiny crack."

"Were they open all night?"

"Yes. Whenever she was in the country Madama liked to sleep in the fresh night air."

Branco fiddled with his pencil for a moment. The library became dead silent. There were five of us in there, and you couldn't hear a single breath. Branco finally spoke.

"Ms. Morçeau, isn't it unusual for a great singer, especially an Italian—you see, I'm Italian myself, so I'm somewhat familiar with these things—wouldn't a singer be afraid of the night air getting into her lungs? The night air is dark and often damp. Some people say it carries the forces of evil with it. Perhaps Madama was superstitious?"

Mathilde considered Branco's question carefully. She sensed a trap, although what he'd said was true: Morning, noon, and night, singers are extremely wary of the air.

Then she answered him simply. "Madama was not afraid of the night. She was not afraid of anything."

"Then perhaps she was expecting someone," said Branco. "Maybe that's the real reason Madama wanted the balcony doors ajar. Eh, Ms. Morçeau? Was she expecting a guest?"

Mathilde glared at him. "You are a pig!"

"Where did you sleep?" said the cop, quickly changing tack.

"My room is next to hers. Always, wherever we go, I am next to her."

"Do your rooms connect directly?"

Branco already knew the answer to that question. Even I did, since we'd both inspected Madama's room and the outside *terrazzo* earlier that day. So why was he asking it?

Mathilde said, "No. There is no door between our rooms."

"Except for the balcony," said Branco. "Your rooms both face out on the balcony."

"Yes," said Mathilde, a bit uneasily.

Branco got up from his chair and walked around the table, then sat on one edge of it to continue his questions, which placed him above and over her. Mathilde shifted in her chair so that she wouldn't have to twist her neck to face him, although she'd still have to look up to see him. She seemed to be familiar with Branco's kind of sport.

Branco said, "Tell me about Madama's potion."

Mathilde answered flatly. "The potion was to give her sleep. She had much distress from the rehearsal yesterday. Some people did not treat her with the respect deserved by the great."

"So it was a sleeping pill?" said Branco.

"No," said Mathilde sharply. "No pills. Madama did not like pills because they might hurt her throat. Her medicine was always a potion."

"A liquid then?"

"Yes," said Mathilde. "I mix it for her every night."

Branco nodded silently, then asked, "Are you a pharmacist, Ms. Morçeau?"

Mathilde looked at him blankly.

Branco went on. "You say you mixed the potion for her. How did you know how much to mix?"

Mathilde said, "It was the same every night. The doctor explained it to me."

"And last night's dosage was the same as usual?"

"Yes," said Mathilde, but her voice extended the syllable uncertainly.

"Was that a 'yes'?" said Branco.

"Yes," replied Mathilde more resolutely.

"Ms. Morçeau, by tomorrow morning I'll have a full report of the contents of the dead woman's stomach, as well as a complete rundown of her blood chemicals. Do you understand that?"

"You are like an animal," she said.

Once again Branco ignored her insult. "Do you want to reconsider your answer one last time?" he said. Was the dosage of Madama Ostinata's sleeping potion the same as usual last night?"

Mathilde squirmed uncomfortably in her chair. "I will tell you again," she said defiantly. "The potion I mixed for Madama last night was correct." She stared at Branco and he stared back. Mathilde had called Branco an animal, yet there *she* was, facing him like a stray cat trying in vain to claim its territory. She didn't realize that she was challenging another cat, the king of all cats, an astrological Leo, just like Daphne. As if finally recognizing her error in judgment, Mathilde shrank back slightly and mewed, "Except for one thing."

"And what was that?" said Branco with a big grin.

Mathilde's answer was strained. "Madama insisted. What could I do?"

"The question to answer is, What *did* you do?"

Mathilde's eyes had suddenly reacquired that pained look, the look they'd always shown before Madama Ostinata's death, the look that said, "I cannot help what I am. It is my destiny." She turned those eyes up toward Branco and spoke in a hoarse whisper worthy of a Macbeth witch.

"I mixed Madama's potion, and she took it and drank it as usual. But then she demanded that I mix it again. She wanted to take the potion a second time last night. I told you, she had great distress from the rehearsal."

"Yes," said Branco. "You did tell me."

Mathilde's voice became more animated as she spoke. "And now I think if I did not do that, Madama would be alive." Her words came louder and faster. "Madama would have awakened and called out for help, and I could have saved her." The crescendo and accelerando continued. "But instead, someone came into her room, and she never woke up, and they killed her!" Climax.

Mathilde broke down into tears and sobbing.

Branco let the woman cry for a few moments, as though his book of police rules had instructed him to display some compassion toward witnesses in distress. Then he asked her, "How can you be so sure, Ms. Morçeau?"

Mathilde looked up at him. "I told you that I gave the potion to Madama two times. I mixed it myself."

"Yes, I know. But how can you be sure that Madama Ostinata didn't cry out for help? You were in the room next to hers, and the room on the other side of hers was empty. Perhaps she did cry out, but you paid it no heed. We know that Marcella Ostinata was an extremely difficult and demanding woman. Perhaps after twenty-five years of waiting on her night and day, perhaps this time you just didn't feel like running to her side."

Mathilde glared at Branco. "You are a monster to say such things. I was ready to die for her."

Branco changed tack again.

"Tell me how you found Madama Ostinata this morning."

Mathilde squirmed uncomfortably. "It was not the usual way," she said.

I should say not, doll.

"Madama always was awake with the sun, and every day she checked the voice. But this morning I did not hear her singing. So I went to her room. I thought it was the extra potion that made her sleep. But then I see . . ." Her chin began to quiver.

"Was anyone else in the room?"

Mathilde replied with a quavery "No."

"All alone then? You're absolutely sure?"

"Yes!" she snapped.

"And then you started screaming and that's when the others came in?"

"Yes!" she cried. "Yes, yes, yes!"

Branco flipped his notebook shut. "Thank you, Ms. Morçeau. That's all for now. You can go."

"No," said Mathilde with a sneer. "There is one more thing you should write in your disgusting report."

"We'll be taking your written statement shortly," said Branco. "You can mention it there. Thank you."

"But I want to say it now," said Mathilde. "I want *you* to write it in your report that one of Madama's brooches is missing from her jewelry box."

Branco said with a sigh, "Describe it please."

Mathilde described the missing piece as solid gold inlaid with onyx. Unique. One of a kind. From an admirer. And I recalled my recent conversation with Daphne. I didn't want to think what I was thinking—that Daphne had slipped into Marcella's room during a lull in the police investigation, and had recovered the stolen property back to its rightful owner, herself. Daphne couldn't have done a thing like that, could she? It was more likely that Mathilde was lying and had appropriated the brooch for herself. Perhaps she even knew the sordid story of its intercontinental travels, and was now taking advantage of a convenient opportunity to incriminate Daphne. Marcella Ostinata's death seemed to have released Mathilde from more than mere servitude. Her newfound confidence bordered on criminally brazen. Then again, I suppose Daphne could just as well have made up her version of the story too. She did tend to create drama where little existed. Like me.

When Mathilde finally left the library, I mentioned to Branco the apparent contradiction that Marcella Ostinata would fuss about liquid potions scratching her throat, but then sleep in the night air.

Branco agreed but added with a shrug, "She was a soprano. They're made of inconsistencies."

"I guess you'd know. Your mother was one."

Branco said curtly, "My mother was a mezzo. That's a whole other ball game."

I forgave his flawed though manly metaphor.

The assisting sergeant on Branco's right asked him what he thought of Mathilde's story. Branco replied that whatever truth she'd told them still didn't amount to much. What he was after was the stuff Mathilde was obviously holding back, the little truths lurking between the big lies. "The kinds of things a woman might tell her hairdresser," he said. The female cop on Branco's left guffawed, but Branco looked my way with a steady gaze, and I knew I'd been assigned my first mission as his deputy—to conduct a private session with Mathilde using a hairstylist's special techniques for getting the Real Dirt.

Branco called Maestro Toscanelli as his next witness.

The maestro must have recognized Branco as a *paesano,* because his first words were, *"Posso mi interrogare in Italiano?"*

"No," replied Branco. *"In inglese."*

"Bene," said the maestro, and then fished through his jacket pockets until he produced a small package of cigarettes. "I can smoke here?" he said.

Branco nodded, while the other two cops grimaced. As usual though, the maestro was without a light. None of the cops could help him, so I leaped from my chair, Bic Flic in hand. As I held the flame for the maestro, Branco looked on with surprise.

"Closet smoker," I said sheepishly. Then I fetched an ashtray and placed it on the table near the maestro. And just as he had done those other times, he offered me a cigarette. And just as I'd done those other times, I declined.

Branco addressed me impatiently. "Finished?"

"Yes," I replied, and skulked back to my chair.

He asked the maestro how long he'd known Madama Ostinata.

"Ah," said the maestro. *"Molto piu tragico.* Is a big loss, no? Marcella has a long career. She was more famous in Europe than in America. I know her since her debut at La Scala—was nineteen-sixty, er, something."

Branco said, "Then you knew her well?"

"I have no children," replied the maestro. "But Marcella was my daughter."

"You mean she was like a daughter to you?"

The maestro considered the question while taking a big drag from the cigarette. "I think that is right—like a daughter. Yes."

"Tell me why you were in Madama Ostinata's room this morning."

"I hear screaming, so I go to see what is wrong."

"So it was Mathilde's voice that woke you up?"

"Er, yes," said the maestro.

"And then?"

The maestro shrugged. "I see her there. What else? I have no thoughts, only shock."

"Did you touch anything while you were in the room?"

"No, no."

"I thought I saw blood on your hands this morning."

"Me? Blood here?" said the maestro showing his palms.

"Yes," said the cop. "Maybe you touched something with blood on it, and you don't remember. The knife maybe? Did you pick up the knife?"

The maestro chuckled. *"Tenente,"* he said, acknowledging Branco's rank in Italian. "You make a bad joke. Why would I take the knife? I see Marcella on the bed like that, and I am in shock. It is like a scene on the stage, but worse."

Branco grunted. "Much worse. But we have a witness who says you were holding the knife."

"Oh, it is not so," replied the maestro.

"Tell me," said Branco. "Did Marcella have any enemies?"

I sensed Branco used the diva's first name to imply a common bond with the maestro, a trust based on operatic familiarity.

Maestro Toscanelli's eyes danced with amusement. *"Tenente,* every person in opera has enemies. The singers, the musicians." He chuckled, then tapped at his chest with both hands and sent a tiny volley of ashes fluttering to his lap. *"I* have enemies, *tenente.* Even the stage workers—we all have enemies. It is natural in opera."

Branco said, "Tell me about Marcella's enemies here."

"Ah, Marcella. *Povera Marcella."* The maestro shook his head sadly. "Her enemy in this country was herself. Marcella does not understand how to be—how you say?—*diplomatico."*

"But someone killed her," said Branco.

The maestro shrugged helplessly. "Maybe it was a terrorist? Or else, they say in your country you have many, er . . ." He paused uncertainly, searching for a phrase that wasn't going to come easily. Branco was fast losing patience with the old man, though I sensed his conscience was directing him to respect his elders.

"Ehhhhh," went the maestro until finally he could say proudly, "acts of random violence." He overenunciated every syllable, as though he enjoyed the sensation of the strange English sounds in and around his mouth.

Branco said curtly, "Her death was not random violence."

Then he stood up just as he had done during his questioning of Mathilde, and came round to the maestro's side of the big study table. The maestro followed the cop with his eyes, but then turned his attention back to his cigarette. Branco sat on the edge of the table and said, "Maestro, how will Marcella's death affect you? What will be different now?"

"It is obvious, no?" said Maestro Toscanelli. "I have a new soprano. April Kilkus. She is young. She has not learned how to be a prima donna yet. She will sing Verdi the way he writes, not the way she feels. Who cares what the soprano feels? Verdi knows, and he tells you what to do. You see the score, and you do it."

"And that wasn't the way with Marcella," said Branco.

The maestro chuckled. "Marcella was inventive." He seemed to like that word too. "Inventive. Too much invention. First she uses the Ricci cadenzas, then she makes her own—much, much worse. And poor Verdi is like circus music."

"Why didn't you stop her?"

"Hah! Who can stop Marcella? *Cantarla ai sordi.* You sing to the deaf. They call Callas *La divina,* but they call Marcella *La tempesta."*

"So in a way," said Branco, "you're a lot better off with her out of the picture."

"Eh?" said the maestro.

"The performance will probably be better without Marcella."

The maestro made a little grunt, the same as Branco might have, and then extinguished his cigarette.

"I think," he said, "this *Ballo* is the last time I conduct. I am old now, and I am tired. But I have enough force inside me for one more time." He shook a clenched fist strongly in the air. "This will be the best Verdi I have done for my entire life. I have a dream it should be *Falstaff,* but . . ." He shrugged like an old philosopher. *"Ballo* is good too. It is Verdi's big love story. The setting we are using here is somewhat, er . . ." The maestro bobbed his head from side to side. "Is peculiar," he said, relishing the word. "But I know Verdi is watching over me. He takes Marcella away and gives me instead April Kilkus. She will be *la migliore Amelia."*

Branco snorted loudly and said, "I hardly think it was Verdi who cut Marcella Ostinata's throat!"

The maestro shrank visibly under Branco's words.

"Thank you," said Branco. "That's all for now."

When the maestro left the library, Branco told his sergeant to arrange a personal guard for Jonathan Byers. From my place in the armchair I asked him why. Branco was just about to tell me, but then he considered his two assistants. And so, instead of answering my simple question, he snarled, "I can't explain everything to you!"

His next witness was Bruce David. But instead of a self-absorbed and hypochondriacal tenor entering the library, in walked Daphne Davenport. And truthfully, it felt as though the wind had changed and was now carrying fresh air into that room.

Daphne walked directly to the broad wooden table and stood opposite the place where Lieutenant Branco sat.

"Excuse me, Lieutenant," she said. "I hope you'll forgive my show-ing up out of turn, but I must tell you that Bruce David has suffered a serious nervous collapse. He's in no condition to speak to anyone. I've sedated him and I'm looking after him now. I didn't realize what had happened until after I'd recovered myself this morning, but now

I see that his condition is tenuous at best. A police interrogation at this point is not only impossible, but the strain of it would put him over the top. As it is, depending on what I observe in the next twelve hours, I may be admitting him to McLean Hospital."

"That bad?" said Branco flatly.

"In vulgar parlance," said Daphne, "Bruce is a mess."

Daphne had somehow rocketed to a new level of action. Who would have guessed at this point in her career that she would respond so readily to someone in psychological need? And here was Bruce David, conveniently fallen flat on his emotional face. His collapse had launched her back into full force as an attending psychiatrist. Watching Daphne, I recognized yet again why I had failed as a therapist. She could relate to the patient with absolute objectivity and focus on the sickness. She even seemed able to engage her compassion, as if she knew it could withstand the voracious needs of a patient in emotional distress. I'd always worried that my patients would suck me dry and then turn me crazy like them. That was basically why I left the psych clinic and took up hairstyling. Now, whenever that old feeling creeps in, that someone is trying to snack on my emotions, I just turn the blow dryer up high and pull hard on the styling brush.

"Well, then," said Lieutenant Branco. "Since you were next on my list, why don't I question you now, Ms. Davenport?"

"Of course," said Daphne.

And as I had hoped and expected, Daphne began with a clear and simple statement of the facts. Like Parker, she had neither seen nor heard anything unusual around the big house until that morning, when Mathilde's extended and horrified screams came from Madama Ostinata's bedroom. It probably helped the tone of Daphne's statement that Branco seemed partial to her, and that was probably because Daphne was just a little older than his own recently dead mother. Of course, that same logic wouldn't apply to his earlier, more brutish treatment of the maestro. But that was a man, and psychobabblists could argue that the cop had unresolved father issues there. For my part, I'd challenge them that Branco was simply impatient with the histrionics of a sly old man who was trying to distract an investigating cop.

When Branco asked Daphne if there was anything personal she felt the police ought to know regarding Madama Ostinata, Daphne said, "She was a wonderful singer, Lieutenant. She would have been an asset to the festival. And she was a guest in my house. I think that sums it up."

"No emotional upsets or difficulties of any kind?"

"None at all," Daphne answered firmly.

"According to some, the woman was quite temperamental."

Daphne brushed his comment off. "She was an artist, Lieutenant. It's part of their nature."

"Just the way it's part of a psychiatrist's nature to be cool and collected in times of crisis."

"Yes," replied Daphne without a second's hesitation.

"Did you and the dead woman ever argue?"

Daphne's eyes flashed away from Branco and toward me for an instant as she replied, "Never, Lieutenant."

Of course, I hadn't really expected Daphne to tell Branco about her long-lost brooch, the one she'd seen Madama Ostinata wearing, or about the heated scene that had followed. I wondered if Mathilde had already confronted Daphne about its sudden disappearance from Marcella's jewelry case. And then I began to feel uncomfortable. Branco had deputized me, and at the time it had seemed a major coup. I mean, how many hairdressers do you know who fetch for a super-macho cop? But now I saw trouble ahead. Daphne had befriended me, and that too was a major coup, simply because she was such a wonderful, energizing person. But already there were big holes in her answers to Branco's questions. So what was I to do? Snitch to Branco now? Confront Daphne later? Both choices were loathsome. The only clear action at the moment was no action.

Some detective I was going to make.

Branco thanked Daphne for her time. I realized that during his session with her he hadn't stood up and gone round to her side of the table. Maybe there was no pattern to his terror tactics after all. On Daphne's way out, as she passed my armchair, she winked at me. I almost winked back, but my face was directly in Branco's sight line, so I just smiled.

For his last witness in the household, Branco called Maurizio, the young handyman. Moments later Maurizio entered the library. He was wide-eyed and frightened, like a small nocturnal creature. And he wasn't alone. Daphne accompanied him.

"Lieutenant," she said. "Since Maurizio is deaf and mute, I thought it would help if I stayed here as his interpreter."

"Can he read and write?" said Branco.

Daphne said yes at the exact moment Maurizio nodded.

"Looks like he reads lips too," said Branco.

Again, a simultaneous nod from Maurizio and a yes from Daphne. But as it turned out, one of Branco's assistants, the female officer, was fluent in American Sign Language, and would be able to interrogate Maurizio that way. Daphne insisted on staying in the library, if only to comfort him. Branco resisted.

"We're hardly going to hurt him," he said.

Daphne retorted, "And I'm hardly going to put words in his mouth, Lieutenant."

Branco finally yielded, probably out of mother-guilt, or else plain weariness from the long day of interrogations.

Before Maurizio sat down in the chair opposite the lieutenant, he gazed around the library and caught sight of me. I gave him a small friendly smile, but in return I got a squint-eyed scowl. Maurizio nudged himself closer to Daphne as if to get further away from me, now perceived as a consort to the cops. Then he sat down, and Daphne stood near him.

Branco asked his first question. "Where were you last night?" His assistant re-created the query with hand gestures while she mouthed the words silently to Maurizio.

Maurizio answered the assistant cop with a flurry of hand motions, and then the cop said to Branco, "He says he was with him." She gestured toward me with her thumb. Branco raised an eyebrow.

"No!" I protested.

Branco held up his hand. "Quiet, you!"

Branco asked Maurizio, "Where was that?"

Arms, hands, mouths moved between Maurizio and the female cop. Then she interpreted to Branco, "In his cottage."

"What time did you leave Mr. Kraychik's cottage?"

Maurizio's interpreted reply: "I stayed with him until we had breakfast."

I stood up and faced Branco. "Wait just a minute," I said.

Branco snapped, "I said be quiet!"

Daphne said to Branco, "There *is* a discrepancy, Lieutenant."

"I don't care!" said Branco. "Quiet now, or else."

Next question: Did Stan leave the cottage at any time during the night?

Answer: An emphatic no.

Question: How can you be sure?

Answer: My arms were wrapped around him.

Branco looked my way with a smug grin. "I think this young man is trying to protect you. I wonder if you'd do the same for him."

"I thought you wanted the truth," I muttered.

Branco replied, "I think I may be getting it now."

"Lieutenant, I did not kill that singer."

"Oh, I know that," said Branco. "I was referring to the truth about your escapades."

"He's embroidering," I said. "I was alone last night."

Branco was about to ask Maurizio his next question, but first turned to me for one more jab. "How long did you say your partner has been away?"

"I didn't say, Lieutenant. But it's been about a week."

Branco shook his head ruefully. "Doesn't seem long at all," he said.

Then he asked Maurizio his next question: Did you know the woman who was killed?

Maurizio looked confused by the question. He gazed up at Daphne for reassurance. She placed her hand on his shoulder and nodded kindly. "It's all right," she said. "You can tell the lieutenant."

But Maurizio had no answer. His eyes flashed around the library, first at me, then at Branco, then up at Daphne again.

Branco repeated his question.

Maurizio's eyes became panic-stricken.

"It's very easy," said Branco. "Yes or no. You knew her or you didn't."

The interpreting cop sent volleys of hand signs to Maurizio, who responded by holding his hands up in front of him, as if protecting himself. By that point, he'd begun to cry.

Daphne interceded. "Lieutenant, I assume you're going to take a written statement from all of us."

"That's right."

"Then why not let Maurizio just write his statement now?"

"Because I want that question answered," said the cop.

"But you've upset him."

"Ms. Davenport, I agreed to let you stay here while I questioned this young man, because you insisted that he needed the comfort of a familiar person. But I can't let you rise to his defense every time he gets a little flustered."

"Why not?" said Daphne. "Someone has to. He certainly doesn't understand his rights, not in a criminal case like this."

"There are specific questions I want to ask him."

But I sensed that Branco was purposely trying to disarm Maurizio, who was an easy target for his bullying. Branco had a cruel streak that showed itself at odd moments. I'd experienced it myself back when he first discovered I was involved with Rafik. But for Branco to terrorize someone like Maurizio who was already challenged by daily life seemed despicable.

Branco pressed his question once more to Maurizio.

"Did you know the woman who was killed?"

But Maurizio was no longer paying any attention to the interpreting cop. He'd turned toward Daphne and buried his face in the folds of her dress. His strong body sobbed violently. I wanted to go to him and hold him, but Daphne seemed able to handle it all just fine without me.

Branco said to his assistants, "I'll finish with him later. Let's call it quits for today."

"Can I take him away now?" said Daphne.

"Sure," replied Branco.

While his assistants put their papers in order, Branco came over to me. I stood up.

"Lieutenant, I really did sleep alone last night."

"It's all right, Stan," he said. "You're a big boy."

"But I'm not like that."

"Like what?" said the cop.

"When I'm involved with someone, I'm monogamous."

Unless they hide out in my bedroom and jump my bones in the dark.

"It takes all kinds," he said dismissively.

His remark confused me. Then again, if Branco had really employed prostitutes, and had beat them no less, he certainly didn't have much argument against anyone else's sexual mores.

Branco said, "I'd like that security report back now."

"Sure," I said as I handed him the report.

"Find anything interesting?"

"I'm not sure," I said. But in truth I'd found a tasty tidbit that I planned to follow up on the next morning.

Branco said, "Just remember, while you're working for me, I'm the first one you tell whenever you find something. Is that clear?"

"Oh yeah," I replied.

"Good," said Branco, and he returned to his assistants.

There was no need to tell him that I'd withheld the story of Daphne's wayward brooch, and how its subsequent discovery had caused friction between Daphne and Marcella Ostinata. I'd learned all that before I was officially Branco's deputy, so as far as I was concerned, it didn't officially come under category of "Tell me first."

By the time the three cops had packed up and were leaving the house, Daphne met them in the foyer. She discreetly detained Branco after the two assistants were out the door.

"Would you like to stay for dinner, Lieutenant?"

Branco wavered. "I wouldn't think you'd want to see much more of me around here, not after that last session."

"Lieutenant, I realize you were just doing your job."

"That's right, ma'am. There's nothing personal intended." Branco looked around the vast foyer and said, "But I think dinner in a place like this might be a little too formal for me."

"Don't worry about that," said Daphne. "We don't usually dress for dinner here."

That sounded provocative, especially with Branco at the table.

Then Daphne added, "Though I'll bet you're smashing in a dinner jacket."

Branco nodded pleasantly. "Right now, Ms. Davenport, I think socializing in your house could be construed as a conflict of interest."

"Goodness," said Daphne. "That bad?"

Branco said, "The fact is, someone killed that woman, and the person may be under this roof right now."

"Then I should think you'd want to stay for dinner as part of your investigation," replied Daphne.

Branco smiled. "I'll take a rain check."

"And I'll hold you to it, Lieutenant. You saved my life today."

"I saved you from falling, ma'am. That's all."

"I might have broken my neck."

"Glad to have spared you that."

"I should say so!" said Daphne with a chortle.

As Branco was halfway out the door, he turned back and asked Daphne if he could see Bruce David.

"But he's under sedation," said Daphne. "I thought I told you."

"You did," said Branco. "I just want to see him."

"Are you checking up on me, Lieutenant?"

"Like you said, ma'am, I'm just doing my job."

So Daphne took Branco upstairs. I watched them ascend the staircase together, and I recalled Alfred Hitchcock's *Notorious*. Sometimes I think I have an Ingrid Bergman complex.

Minutes later Branco was cantering down the stairs alone. At the front door he stopped and spoke to me, a murmur for my ears alone.

"Ms. Davenport is staying with Bruce David now. I saw him, and he does appear to be semiconscious. Still, I'd like you to keep an eye on him for me. Try to get some more facts on his condition. I want to be sure that woman isn't protecting him."

"I feel like a spy, Lieutenant."

"You're a natural," said Branco.

I didn't know whether to be flattered or insulted.

But then he was gone.

21

After Lieutenant Branco left I went upstairs. I wanted to see Bruce David myself, and since Daphne was still up there with him, I'd have a chance to talk to her as well. I stopped outside what I thought was Bruce's room, and knocked on the door. From within I heard a male voice call out, *"Avanti!"*

I opened the door and immediately realized that I'd mistakenly stopped at Maestro Toscanelli's room instead. The maestro was sitting near an open window. In the distance outside the window was the Atlantic Ocean, often dark and moody, but at that moment rolling lazily under the early evening sky. In one hand the maestro held a lit cigarette and in the other a small tumbler half full of whiskey. He turned his head to me and said, *"Ciao, ragazzo."* He gestured with his hand. "Come. Sit. Look at the water, how beautiful it is here in your country."

I entered and took the armchair opposite him. He offered me a cigarette, and I was about to refuse, but then figured, Why not? It might even be perceived as goodwill to smoke with the old man. I took a cigarette from the package he held out to me. I prepared to light it myself, but seemingly out of nowhere the maestro produced and struck a match for me. Again I wondered what had happened to the solid gold lighter he'd had the other day. He smiled as he held the match in front of my cigarette.

"Finalmente I light it for you," he said with a chuckle.

I drew cautiously on the shaft to keep from inhaling the smoke and coughing—not exactly a show of manliness.

"Where is your lighter?" I asked.

"Eh?" he replied.

"La fiamma d'oro," I fumbled in Italian.

He chuckled and corrected me. *"L'accendino d'oro."* Then he flushed with sudden embarrassment and muttered, "Er . . . *è perduto."* Then he smiled and said quickly, "Whiskey?"

I agreed, and he poured me some from the nearby liquor cart. The social niceties completed, it was time to improvise some commerce.

"Maestro," I said. "When you spoke with the police just now, you said that this opera festival would probably be the last time you would ever conduct an opera again. Why is that?"

The old man nodded. "For me soon it will be *finito."*

"But you still have so much energy."

"No, no." He waved his hand in front of himself. "I am tired now. When I was a young man, I had much fire in my blood. But now, it is only smoke." He looked at his cigarette and chuckled, as though he had made a joke.

"Why did you decide to make your last appearance with Madama Ostinata?"

He made a slight shrug. "I know Marcella for many, many years. I know there will be trouble—Marcella always makes trouble—but there will be no surprise."

Except for a couple of bodies, I thought.

I said, "So it was for old times' sake."

"Eh?"

"I mean, you chose Marcella because you were old friends."

The maestro made a vague *hmph,* but said nothing.

"But why would you conduct your final production in America instead of Italy?"

"I did not want," said the old man. "It is my last opera, but it is the first time I have the chance to come to America. Finally they will know who is Toscanelli. And this lovely woman, Miss Davenport, she pays for everything and makes our travel *molto lussuoso*—very much luxury. So how can I refuse?"

"Have you been to the states before?"

"Never," he said sharply.

"That's surprising, especially for someone of your stature." At least, I assumed the maestro had stature. I wasn't much of an opera buff, so I didn't really know. "It's too bad your first trip here turned out like this."

"Eh?" he said again.

"I mean, with Madama Ostinata's death."

"Ah, yes." Then the maestro shook his head despondently. "I cannot understand who can do such a thing. Marcella was a difficult woman, but she was an artist. In Europe it can never happen like that, that a great artist is killed like a dog."

We sat quietly as the smoke curled gracefully upwards from our two cigarettes. Outside the window the night sky was fast consuming the last reflected rays of sunset, making the ocean barely visible. I confessed to the maestro that I wasn't an aficionada of opera, but that since I'd met him in person, I looked forward to collecting his recordings.

He said, *"Non è possibile."*

"I know," I said. "They're very difficult to find in this country. But I'm going to Europe soon, and I'll find them there."

"No," he said, shaking his head emphatically. "There is no recording. I never make one."

"No?"

"Never."

"But why not?"

"Who knows?" he said. Then he made a cynical little shrug. "Perhaps before I die some big American company will ask me to make a contract. And then at last I will record every opera of the great Verdi." He punctuated his fantasy with a fey wink.

I countered, "But aren't most of the big recording companies based in Europe? Especially for opera."

"Yes," he whispered with a defeated nod. "That is true."

And I realized that despite the maestro's so-called stature, perhaps he had never been invited to make a recording.

There was a knock on the door.

"Avanti!" said the maestro, his voice once again full of energy and life.

Daphne entered, saw me sitting with the old man, and then exclaimed to me, "You smoke?"

"Sometimes," I said, cowering a bit.

"I wonder what other secrets you harbor."

"None, really," I said, but I sounded defensive—not the best attribute for a double secret agent. I extinguished the cigarette and recalled a similar guilt-ridden moment in my distant childhood, when I'd stayed overnight at my aunt Letta's house, and the cool starched cotton sheets on the guest bed had caused a throbbing erection, and there was no way to conceal my pronged state when she came in to say good night to me.

Daphne said, "I was checking on Bruce next door, and I heard voices coming from the maestro's room. And here I find you both, chewing the fat and having a relaxed smoke before dinner, just like two confirmed bachelors."

I was about to protest that I *was* married in a sense, although lately I hadn't been thinking much of my lover.

Daphne continued, "It's been a nightmare for me today, and I could use some pleasant company myself. Do you think we might move this little party downstairs to the library? Parker can serve cocktails, and perhaps we can chase away some of that horrid police energy from the room."

I said, "I thought you liked the lieutenant."

"Oh, I do, my dear. I like him very much. And it appears there's quite a bit of him to like too. But he certainly does bring a host of shadows with him."

"I never thought of it quite that way," I said.

The maestro spoke up. *"Il tenente?"*

"Yes," replied Daphne.

"Ah, sì," said the maestro. *"Un cavaliere scuro."*

"A dark knight, certainly," said Daphne. "It seems we're all smitten with him." And then she released a cascade of laughter like a flirtatious diva trilling about the joys of love.

"I'd better go wash for dinner," I said flatly.

"You can use the washroom at the end of the hall, dear."

I left Daphne and the maestro to compare notes on the Dark Knight. As Branco's deputy, I'd already learned that indulging the frivolous emotions would only impair my duties to him. And who would I have to answer to but the Dark Knight himself?

Next door to the maestro's quarters was Bruce David's suite. I opened his door quietly, just to peek in on him. I called his name but got no answer, so I entered the bedroom and tiptoed to his bedside. Bruce was sound asleep, breathing deeply and regularly. The sedative Daphne had given him was doing its job well. Bruce looked almost cherubic lying there under the covers. As I left the room I reminded myself to ask Daphne what she'd used on him. You never know when you might want to turn someone into a cherub.

On the way to the washroom I also passed the top landing of the staircase and the late Marcella Ostinata's chambers. Those rooms were still sealed off by the police. But coming from behind the next door along the hall, a door that was partially ajar, I overheard a female voice humming an operatic aria. The music was unfamiliar, but the voice was agile and resonant. I stopped outside the door to listen. It was a soprano, and she seemed to be moving around the room as fluidly as her voice did around the notes she was singing. Was there another singer staying at Daphne's house whom I hadn't met yet? My question was answered when the voice approached close to the door, and then suddenly the door flew open away from my face.

"*Aiy!*" squealed Mathilde, and she dropped the stack of folded garments she'd been holding. I guess finding me outside the door had shocked her, and she was speechless for a moment.

I said, "You have a lovely voice."

"Oh," she said, as she tried to collect herself. "I did not know you were there. I would not, er . . ."

"I didn't know you could sing."

Mathilde smiled awkwardly, then stooped down to pick up the clothing she had dropped. "I do not sing for others," she said.

"With a voice like that, why not?"

"Oh, no, no," she said. "Never."

"That's too bad," I said, and I thought how strange it was that the servant of a great diva should have a more pleasing voice, at least for the pedestrian world, than the larger-than-life woman who'd had the great career.

I knelt down to help Mathilde pick up the things on the floor. I noticed among the clothes a pair of men's pants made of tropical-weight worsted wool. I reached for them, but Mathilde quickly grabbed them up before I could get them.

"No help!" she said. "Please!" She pushed the pants under the clothes already in her arms and concealed them. Then she said, "Some things are very personal here."

I apologized to her, then said, "Did you ever sing onstage?"

Her tired but wary eyes glanced nervously at me. "Why do you ask me this?" she said. "What does it matter how I sing, or where I sing, or if I ever sing again? Who is asking this?"

"I was just curious," I said. "Your voice surprised me, that's all."

Mathilde and I stood up together, and I handed her the few items she'd allowed me to refold myself.

"Thank you," she said. "You pretend very well to be kind. Most people do not understand sometimes that is important."

"Apparently I've really offended you. I'm sorry."

"No," said Mathilde. "I am not offended. No one can offend me. My soul has been covered with so many scars, now they are all joined together like leather. Even a knife cannot penetrate my soul. Perhaps some person did cut Madama's neck and kill her, but nothing can hurt me. No one can hurt me now."

"Did Madama Ostinata know that you could sing?"

Mathilde's eyes flashed full of hatred.

"Of course she knew! That is what attracted her to me at the beginning. I was a poor girl, a servant in a villa. Marcella was a guest there, and she heard me singing as I did my work. That is when she decided to save me. But in her heart, Marcella wanted only to silence me, to kill my voice. If I had the chance, *I* would be the prima donna *assoluta.*"

Did I dare tell Mathilde that her life was a cliché?

She went on. "How many years I took care of her! All that traveling, the cities, the hotels, the theaters. Countless admirers, countless liaisons, always a scandal. Then the critics, the impresarios, the other singers. The ailments, the complaints. *Akh!* Thank God it is finished. Perhaps now I will have some small life of my own."

"And what will you do?" I said.

A wan little smile appeared on her face. "I know she will leave me nothing. She thought only of herself. So I will write a book and tell the world the truth about Marcella Ostinata. I will become rich, finally, from her disgusting life."

I couldn't ask what I was thinking: Will anyone care?

Instead I said, "What will you do then?"

"Then," said Mathilde. "Then I will . . . I will . . ."

Apparently she hadn't quite planned what she was going to do with the avalanche of money from her torrid bestseller.

"Maybe you can sing," I offered. After all, many careers in the arts were subsidized to the point of critical acclaim when talent alone proved insufficient.

"Perhaps," she said faintly.

"There's still time," I said. "But you have to write it first."

"Yes," she said. "I must write it all someday."

"Don't wait too long."

"No," said Mathilde. "I will do it soon. It will be like a confession, and I will be free when every black deed of the great Marcella Ostinata has been told."

With that she closed the door.

I continued to the washroom, washed my hands and face, and then went downstairs for cocktails before dinner. Daphne greeted me in the library.

"Before the maestro joins us," she said, "I want to thank you for saving my skin this afternoon."

"You're welcome," I said. "But what did I do?"

"It's what you didn't do, my dear, or more precisely what you didn't say. You very generously neglected to tell the lieutenant about the little disagreement I'd had with Madama Ostinata regarding my brooch, the one that showed up on her dress a few days ago."

"Well," I said. "There really wasn't any choice. I'm not a snitch, not when friends are involved. But you should know that Mathilde did mention the brooch to the cops."

"Implicating me?"

"Not exactly. She just announced in a general accusatory way that the brooch was missing from Marcella's jewelry box."

Daphne said, "That's too bad. I can't very well claim it as my own now, can I?"

"I was wondering if you already had."

"You mean with the police?"

"I mean with your hands."

Daphne chortled. "My dear, what do you take me for?"

"I only meant—" Why was my face suddenly burning? "I only meant that the brooch was rightfully yours to take back, if you had wanted to."

"Of course it was!" Daphne said with another loud laugh. "Those are my sentiments exactly. My dear, I think you may be playing your role of deputy far too seriously."

That's when the maestro entered. And for the rest of the evening, throughout cocktails and dinner, just for a change of pace, we avoided all talk of murder and the police, and spoke only of pleasant things, like music, and the glorious old days of opera, and the maestro's favorite from another era, Celestina Boninsegna. Polite conversation was always a heady challenge for me, but that evening I faced the task squarely.

After dinner I once again considered calling Rafik in Paris. But what would I have to tell him about, except for another dead body and the return of Lieutenant Branco into the sphere of my life? And the fact that I loved him and, given half a moment's peace, that I even missed him. Well, I did finally surrender to my destiny and called Paris that night. But as my destiny would decree, there was no answer at the number Rafik had given to me. So then I wondered, Where in hell is he?

22

The next morning was damp and chilly, even though it was the first Friday in June. As I walked to the big house for breakfast, I saw two Boston police cruisers parked in the wide circular driveway. Branco's Alfa was not there with them. With the New England weather playing its usual tricks, I wasn't surprised that Daphne was taking breakfast in the garden room rather than outside in the gazebo. She however, unlike the weather, was in her usual chipper mood.

After we greeted each other, she said, "The police are here cleaning up the last bits in Marcella's room. Perhaps the house will return to normal soon." Then she shuddered slightly. "Although I don't know if I'll ever forget the image of the dead woman on that bed."

I offered one solution: Paint the walls and rearrange the furniture to help the dreadful image fade more easily.

"That may work," said Daphne. "Or perhaps I should remodel the room completely, turn it into a solarium or a library or anything besides a bedroom."

"Or," I said, "you could seal the room up, leave everything exactly as it is, blood and all, and create a shrine to gothic horror."

Daphne looked askance at me. "Have some coffee," she said as she filled my cup. "From that last remark, I think you might still be asleep and dreaming. Shrine to gothic horror indeed!"

I took a warm blueberry muffin, split it, and spread butter on both halves. As I bit into one piece, my teeth punctured an extra-plump berry and sent an arc of purplish-red juice into the air. Fortunately the long spurt landed on the white plate in front of me, and spared the linen tablecloth. The juice was the color of veinous blood.

"Sorry," I said. "Close call."

"It could happen to a bishop," said Daphne.

"How is Bruce David?" I said.

"Not so good. It's likely I'll be admitting him today."

"What exactly is the problem?"

"Anxiety, my dear. He believes that what happened to Marcella is going to happen to him. He can't separate himself from what's happened to someone else."

"Maybe he did it," I said without thinking.

Daphne gave me a worried look. "Maybe he did."

"I guess he won't be singing then."

"If ever again. It looks as though we'll have two understudies singing opening night." Daphne shrugged helplessly. "There's nothing else to do. I just hope this is the end of it. I'm getting a bit old for this kind of excitement and challenge."

"I assume the maestro is all right today."

"Yes," said Daphne. "Though he'll never admit it, he's strong as a horse. He's taking breakfast in his room as usual. I've observed that he's extremely private in the morning. It's no wonder he never married. Never mind the pillows or the bathroom, he can't even face another person over coffee."

Was that all it was? A need for privacy?

"By the way," Daphne continued, "I'll be driving you and the maestro to the opera house from now on. Since there's only the two of you going there now, there's no need for Maurizio to take you in the jitney. He has plenty to do around here."

"Daphne, with all that's happened now, have you considered halting the production?"

"Oh, my dear. That would be admitting defeat."

"But murder . . ."

Daphne silenced me with a raised finger.

"Yesterday, while you were at the opera house, I called an emergency meeting for our board of directors. Many of those people are also our investors, and to a person they unanimously agreed to continue with the production. In fact, they believe the notoriety of Marcella's death would only help ticket sales."

"Morbid economics."

"The sad thing is," Daphne said, "they were right. You'd think by now I'd understand human nature, but I'll never fathom why grisly events attract people so much. Last night after dinner, the woman who is managing tickets called to tell me that every performance of *Ballo* is now sold out, and there are waiting lists. I don't know what those people expect to see when they come for the opera. There will simply be a new Amelia. Marcella Ostinata certainly won't be making a return engagement."

I nodded agreeably, but I still found Daphne's objective stance about the festival a bit disturbing in the face of murder.

Later, when Daphne drove the maestro and me to the performance center, I sat in back while they conversed together in Italian up front. It may have been a mistake, since the maestro was as oblivious to the rules of good driving as Daphne was. But they did both share the knack of keeping their conversation lively and in forward motion. So what if the Bentley meandered a bit? There was hardly a quiet moment during that drive, but neither was it filled with idle chatter. What occurred was two intelligent people expressing ideas to each other, and using pleasant sounds to do it.

I was eager for my first gumshoe task that morning. It had come to me the day before, when I was studying the security report during Branco's interrogations in Daphne's library. Within the huge matrix of numbers and codes in that report, I'd uncovered a few interesting comings and goings, or lack thereof. First among them was that during the entire twenty-four hour period before the discovery of Marcella Ostinata's body, and the four hours following it, neither April Kilkus nor Hwang Young Cho had used an electronic key to enter or leave the performance center residences. Obviously they had both stayed somewhere else, and I wanted to know where and why.

Both April and Hwang were scheduled for rehearsal that morning, but neither one was in the opera house auditorium or the backstage area. I went downstairs into the subterranean world of the warm-up rooms. I wandered through the maze of corridors and listened outside the doors for the distinct sounds of a baritone and a soprano singing together. Even with the other singers vocalizing, it was easy to identify April and Hwang by the timbre of their voices and the unity of their phrasing. They sang as though they were joined at the hip. I waited until they stopped singing to discuss a point of interpretation. That's when I knocked and entered the small chamber. It was very warm in there. The faces of both singers were moist and flushed from heavy exertion, though neither was out of breath. I suppose that was one advantage of the athletic rigors of operatic singing—you never gasped for air, at least not visibly to your audience.

I apologized for interrupting them and told them quickly that I was now working as an official deputy to the Boston police. Then I told them what I'd discovered on the security report.

Hwang said angrily, "I don't care what you found. And if the police want to question us, let them come in person. I'm not wasting time with some self-appointed lackey."

"I am not self-appointed," I protested.

"Then where's your identification?" demanded Hwang.

"It's on its way. I only started working yesterday."

As if to ease the situation, April interceded and spoke calmly to me. "The explanation is very simple. We needed some privacy."

Hwang said to me, "You're not staying here at the center, so you wouldn't know. But the place is more like a dormitory than a hotel. You can't do anything without some damn computer and video camera recording it."

I stared at Hwang Yung Cho like a shocked schoolmarm. "Are you saying you spent the night with this woman? I thought your culture deplored extramarital sex."

Hwang said, "It's the nineties, man. Get with the program."

How strange to hear American pop-talk spoken with perfect elocution by a trained operatic voice.

April added, "Besides, interracial couples are sanctioned now."

Nice word, I thought. Sanctioned. Implied all kinds of approval by government, community, even church. Maybe someday we'd be able to say it about same-sex couples too. Sanctioned.

April went on, "And Hwang and I wanted to celebrate my recording contract."

"Tell him the truth," spat Hwang. "We got married."

"What recording contract?" I said. First things first.

April explained, "Deutsche Phonogram International had planned to record this production of *Ballo*, and now that I'm to be singing Amelia at the festival, they've asked me to do the recording as well."

Hwang said, "I'll be singing Renato, and the maestro will be conducting. It's his first recording too."

"It's a first for all of us," said April. "A real historic event."

"I see," I replied.

"The maestro's name will help sales tremendously," said April.

Hwang took up the reins and impelled their enthusiasm to a full gallop. "And now that April is singing Amelia, there will be someone young and beautiful in the role, as there should be. So, Deutsche Phonogram has promised a videotape too. They're even talking about a live satellite broadcast for one of the performances. Imagine that? Television, around the world!"

April was soaring too. "This is going to put us high on the list of world-class desirables."

I said, "And how convenient that Madama Ostinata is out of the picture. You'll excuse the pun."

Suddenly two large operatic jaws were gaping loosely at me.

I said, "When did all this happen?"

April said, "I got my contract yesterday afternoon. But as far as I know, Deutsche Phonogram has been negotiating with the festival for weeks."

"The maestro too?" I said.

Hwang replied, "We only know what we heard yesterday."

"Did Marcella know about it?"

"Probably," said April somewhat cautiously.

"Who else?" I said.

Both singers shrugged. April said, "I imagine everyone knows by now. We haven't been exactly quiet about it." She laughed nervously.

"Funny," I said. "I haven't heard a thing."

They both sniggered.

Hwang said, "Well, you're not exactly in our crowd."

"You realize I'll have to tell all this to the police."

April said, "You can do whatever you want. But now just leave us alone. We want to try this scene one more time before rehearsal."

I left them and headed upstairs to the backstage area. Rick Jansen was at the stage manager's booth, clipboard in hand, talking with Ronda Lucca. He was trying to convince her about something. For her part Ronda nonchalantly rearranged the cue sheets on her desk. As I passed by them I overheard Rick saying, "Of course we know what the original specs were, but Sir Jonathan wants a minor change to the set, now that there's going to be a new Amelia. He wants to show her off more. She's going to be dancing. He's going to change some of the lighting too."

"We'll see about that," said Ronda.

"You'll do it," said Rick. "You know the stage director has the final word in everything."

"He's not God," said Ronda.

"He is as far as you're concerned." When Rick saw me passing by, he said to Ronda, "I'll finish with you later." Then he left her and caught up to me.

"I owe you an apology for what happened yesterday," he said. "I don't know what came over me."

I said, "Let's just stay clear of each other."

"I have nothing against you, and I didn't mean to hit you."

"Fortunately you missed."

"I have this problem."

"Obviously," I said. "There are people who can help you."

"I just need to talk about it, and I was hoping you'd—"

"Hey, pal," I interrupted. "I barely know you, and after our encounter yesterday, I certainly don't trust you."

"Maybe that can change."

"Not for me."

"You see," he said with a desperate look in his charming eyes. "Jon wants to get rid of me. He says I'm a fake."

"Didn't he know your credentials when he hired you?"

"I mean he's throwing me out of his bed," said Rick emphatically. "But I'm not a fake. I like men, and I'm not ashamed of it. I just don't like all that girly stuff, the kissing and the lovey-dovey talk. And that's really what Jon wants me to be—his girl."

"Leave him then," I said curtly.

"I can't. He's done a lot for me, gave me this job, got me on my feet."

"You mean on your back."

"I told you, I'm not the woman!"

"It's not being a woman. It's being a receptive man. Some people find a lot of strength in the receptive role."

Rick considered the idea a moment. Then he made a loathsome frown and said emphatically, "No! That kind of thing is for femmes, not for me."

I refrained from telling him about the burly trucker I once dated whose bootprints were always marring the ceiling of his sleeper cab.

"Hey, it's cool," I said in my clinical voice, the one that was comfortable telling lies. "Anal sex isn't for everyone."

"How about you?" asked Rick.

"That's hardly your business."

"So you think it's disgusting too."

"I don't share your opinion," I said, as though I led the most balanced, integrated sex life on earth.

"Then maybe you can help me."

"Yesterday you wanted to pulverize me. Today you want sex therapy." I suppose for some there was little difference.

Rick said, "The truth is, I think I like you."

"What!"

"I just don't know how to show it."

"Then I'd suggest you let it go," I said, hoping he'd relate to a cliché of psychobabble.

"Let what go?" he said.

"It," I replied. "Whatever it is you think you like about me, just let it go." I wanted to quell Ricky's dubious new ardor fast, and I wanted to get away from him before he started swinging again. With violent people, you never know what's going to set them off. "Besides, I already have a partner," I said, then added with finality, "And I don't play around."

"It can't hurt if we talk," he said. "We might have something in common."

"Like what?" I said.

"Well, I have a great body and a really thick—"

"*Why!*" I suddenly heard myself screaming. "Why are we talking about this?"

Ronda called out from her desk, "Quiet please over there!"

Rick leaned toward me and whispered like a secret lover. "You're very passionate. I like that. And I think maybe you really want me too."

I pressed my face toward his, as if to surrender to my hidden desire. I whispered, "I'll tell you what I want, okay?"

"Oh yeah. Tell me."

"What I really want from you . . ."

"Yeah . . . ?"

"What I really hope you're going to do for me . . ."

"Oh, baby, will I ever!"

"Is tell me where you were when that soprano was murdered."

Rick said, "I'll tell you anything you want, baby. Just let me be hard inside you."

"Alas, doll, those stakes are too high."

He pulled away suddenly and looked at me with disgust.

"You know," he said, "you flirt like a coy little bitch, but you're really hung up about sex. You're probably no damn good anyway. I'll bet you lose out on a lot of good dick."

"I don't keep count."

"Someone like you doesn't have to."

Well, despite his bad manners, Ricky-thing *had* identified a singular void in my life, at least from the traditional gay perspective: My celebration of sex in terms of sheer body count was relatively low. Fortunately our debate on the inherent virtues of promiscuity was curtailed by a loud argument coming from the auditorium, loud enough to snake its way backstage. I peered out from the wings to see what was going on, and I saw the two most improbable opponents—Jonathan Byers and Maestro Toscanelli—going at each other.

"The music!" said the maestro with a strangulated voice. He was standing beside the rehearsal piano, gripping its edge for support. "Always in the music is the answer. Here is Amelia in danger for her life. So what do you do? She must be afraid, not make a dance. You cannot make her dance around the stage. You will make her be a fool."

But Jonathan Byers was adamant. "Look, old man. I never considered putting it in before because I didn't have the raw material for it. But now I've got an Amelia who can sing and act *and* dance. I want to show that even in the face of death, it's her lust for the younger man that's driving her. She'll be singing regrets to her husband, but her body will be telling the truth. Just look at her yourself, for Christ's sake!"

Jonathan Byers pointed to April Kilkus, who had taken her position onstage with Hwang Yung Cho.

"She's a real woman," said Byers. "Not a brisket of beef like that other one was. So how can you sit there and fuss about the bleeding notes?"

The maestro persisted. "Verdi knows what he wants."

"Verdi would have done the same thing in my shoes."

"You are breaking sacred laws of opera."

"Balls!" said Sir Jonathan. "Let's ask her, eh? What do you say, April? Do you want to stand there like a statue while you're singing? Or do you want to put some blood between your legs?"

April responded like a penitent who was entrusting her fate to the archbishop. "You can do whatever you want with me, Sir Jonathan. Anything. Just don't let me sound like Callas at the end."

At the end of what? The opera? Or Callas's career?

"Don't worry about that, love," replied Byers. "They'll compare you to Callas, and then forget who she ever was."

Meanwhile the maestro was shaking his head in anguish. "How can you do this to Verdi?"

April turned toward the maestro with remorse in her eyes. She seemed genuinely distressed to be going against his wishes, or else she was rehearsing and perfecting her new role as a prima donna. She tried to placate him with her silken voice. "Maestro, please under-

172

stand. It will only be for the stage production. When we make the recording, you will have the final word. I promise."

The maestro said, "Who are you to promise me something? You are a *singer!*" His voice cracked at the word. "Do you think I care about a recording? I care only what the audience will see when the curtain goes up. *That* is opera. Not on a recording."

Jonathan Byers said, "Maestro, please, I'm sure we can reach some agreement between us later on, eh? But for now, just indulge me, and let's get on with the rehearsal, shall we?"

"I will do better," said the maestro. "I will ignore you."

He turned from his place near the piano and walked offstage, but just as he entered the wings, he turned back and made his final pronouncement to the assembled cast and crew.

"I am no longer needed here."

There should have been a final chord and an ominous rumble from the timpani as the maestro exited backstage.

"Oh, cock and balls," spluttered Jonathan Byers. Then he called for his assistant director to oversee things for a few minutes, while he went out and tried to appease the maestro. As Byers left the auditorium I heard him mutter angrily, "One prima donna after another."

When Marcella Ostinata had been alive, her petulance had provoked everyone else to distraction. But now those same people were vexing each other with a new peevishness, and I wondered what psychic vise had been released by the first diva's death.

I went downstairs to do time in the wig room. I wanted to question Daniel Carafolio anyway, on his whereabouts the night of the murder. That security report had shown me that Daniel had left the performance center around midnight, and didn't return until after seven o'clock the following morning, about an hour before Mathilde had discovered Marcella Ostinata's body.

But when I got to the wig room, Daniel wasn't there and the door was still locked. I guess he intended to mourn the diva's death a full forty days. Well, with him out of the picture maybe I'd do some real work, the work I was originally hired for and paid to do, if I could just get inside. So back upstairs I went to find someone to open the locked door. The best bet would be Ronda Lucca with her big ring of keys.

I asked her to open the wig room, and she said, "No Daniel today?"

"Missing in action I guess."

"Gimme a minute," she said.

While I waited for her, I noticed Maurizio hanging around the lock rail backstage. He seemed to show up everywhere, like a stage sprite. He looked toward Ronda's booth where I was standing. I waved to him. But when he recognized me, he turned and bolted to the side wall, then leaped up onto one of the steel ladders. The nimble young man climbed up, up, up toward the catwalks high overhead.

"Don't worry about him," said Ronda when she saw what I was looking at. "He's always hanging around back here, and he's always up there too. I think he likes the thrill of looking down on everything."

"Isn't it dangerous?"

"For some people."

"What's up there?"

"You wanna see? We can go for a little climb later."

"No, no," I said quickly. "Just curious."

Ronda spoke like a shop foreman. "Up there is every line and pulley that's connected to anything and everything that flies from this stage. Lights, scrims, scenery, curtains." She was clearly proud of her domain backstage. "The grid is like the spinal cord of the stage."

"Do you ever go up there?"

"Of course. I want to know about every corner and cable on my stage."

"It doesn't bother you, the heights?"

"Me?" she said, and then brayed a loud *hah!* "I go rock-climbing just to relax."

"To relax! The only rock-climber I ever knew did it for the life-and-death thrill of it, man against nature and all that."

"Not me," said Ronda. "After running a show like this one, climbing a sheer slab of rock will be downright relaxing."

I watched Maurizio vanish into the overhead world of steel mesh and girders. "He moves like a monkey," I said. "I thought you had to be in the union to do that work."

174

Ronda said, "He's a paid-up member of the rigger's and floorman's local."

"He is?"

Ronda looked around to see who was listening, then said surreptitiously, "Compliments of the same woman who's footing the bill for the rest of the festival."

"How did she get Maurizio into the union?"

"How else?" said Ronda, rubbing her thumb and first two fingers together. "Besides, when we had the riggers here working on the grid, that kid climbed right up there after them. I guess they took a shine to him. A lot of people lose their cool when they get up there, but he was right at home—jumping around the beams, hanging onto cables. He's not afraid of anything."

"Then why does he keep running away from me?"

Ronda grinned. "Are you kidding? Anyone can see he's soft on you."

"Hardly soft," I said. "But I'm already spoken for."

"You sound like a goddamn maiden." Then she cackled and said, "That's not going to stop how he feels. Don't you know anything?"

"What am I supposed to do?"

Ronda snorted. "What, you need lessons?"

Eventually I got her to unlock the wig room, and I did some high-productivity fussing around in there for a few hours. Then I got restless, which usually happens when I'm working alone too long. So I figured I'd go and find Daniel Carafolio. He was probably shut away in his room at the performance center, wearing his widow's weeds and weeping in the darkness. I found him there all right. And his condition wasn't far from what I'd imagined.

23

I rang Daniel's room and announced myself to him over the intercom.

"No visitors today," he said. "I'm not well."

"I'll only stay a few minutes," I said. "It's very important."

"What's it about?"

"The wigs," I replied, and he buzzed me in.

Even though I knew the room number, it was easy to find his place along the hallway. I was directed by the unmistakable voice of Maria Callas penetrating through the door.

As soon as I saw him I knew he'd been crying. His eyes were swollen and red. He was dressed completely in black. He'd even dyed his hair black for the occasion of Marcella Ostinata's death. The curtains over the windows were drawn to keep the room dark and still—still except for Maria Callas's recorded attempt to sustain a high B-flat against a full orchestra.

He stood in the half-open door and asked, "What happened?"

"I'd like to talk to you."

"You said the wig room . . ."

"I lied. I had to see you."

He raised his eyebrows slightly. "So impetuous," he said with a wan smile. "It's been years since anyone *had* to see me."

I said, "Can I come in?"

"It's about Marcella, isn't it?"

"Yes. I'm assisting the police to find her killer."

"So," he said with an arched brow. "Does that mean you get to work with that hot cop?"

"I'm helping the Boston police," I said flatly.

Daniel sneered. "Then by all means, come in and ask your questions."

I went in, but there was nowhere to sit. The bed and the two chairs were strewn with clothes. Even the floor was covered with piles of them. The stuff was all first-rate too, designer labels and current fashion. For the extent of his pricey wardrobe, Daniel Carafolio dressed pretty crummy.

"The only question I have," I said, "is kind of personal. But it has a direct bearing on the case."

"I know what you're going to ask. Where was I when Marcella was murdered? Isn't that it? That's exactly what the police wanted to know."

"Not quite. I want to know whom you were with."

"What?"

"The security report shows that you left the performance center at midnight the night before last and didn't return until seven o'clock the following morning."

Daniel said, "So? Is this a boarding school? Do I need a permission slip to roam off campus?"

"If Madama Ostinata hadn't been killed, nobody would care what you did."

"But you do?"

"I'm doing this for the police, not myself."

"Well I'll tell you exactly what I told the police, then," said Daniel. "I had a trick that night."

"A trick?"

"Yes. Remember those? Or do you find tricks too déclassé in your high-and-mighty married state?"

I was about to say, Not at all. But Daniel's question caused a tinge of regret. See, in my so-called monogamous partnership I had been the one to break the pledge, not my lover. Based on the flimsiest evidence, I had assumed that he'd fallen first. That done, I saw no reason for me to hold to the original agreement. The irony was, seeing us as a couple—with him so sexy and me so ordinary—no one would guess that I was the libertine.

I said to Daniel, "What was his name?"

"I never kiss and tell."

"Your alibi will have to be corroborated."

"Such *big* words you use, now that you're working for that—" Daniel sucked air in through his clenched teeth. "That *big* Italian stud. Is he big? Do you get to see him in the locker room? Yes? No? Ohhhh, I can tell by the look on your face you don't. Too bad. I bet it's a juicy one."

"Daniel, you might as well tell me the guy's name. You're going to have to tell the police anyway."

"Then I'll wait for the beefcake to ask me."

"Suit yourself. He'll have a good time at your expense."

Daniel frowned and considered what I'd said. "I think I know the type. Huge closet door. Right? Solid bronze, with barricades and trenches and lots of ammunition aimed directly at us. Are you consorting with the enemy?"

Was I? Branco had used that word too—ammunition. Perhaps the ammunition he was keeping from his fellow officers was being turned against every other gay man. But that wasn't true either. Branco was beginning to show signs of tolerance for us—acceptance even, for me at least. One at a time was better than none.

"By the way," said Daniel. "Just to save that redheaded little brow of yours some worry, the trick's name was Butch."

"Butch?"

"That's right. Butch. Do you have trouble with English?"

"Butch what?" I said.

"Just Butch."

"Might as well have been Dick."

"I had Dick the night before," said Daniel.

"I'll bet you did. What about Rick? Have you had him too?"

Daniel's beady eyes shot a nasty glance at me. "Rick Jansen? That tired thing?"

From my position, the pot was calling the kettle black.

I said, "You know Rick, then?"

"Been there, done that," he said affectedly.

"I take that to be a yes."

"Yes, yes, yes! Who are you, Dr. Ruth? You need footnotes? Yes, Rick Jansen gave me a long hard ride in Spoleto last summer. Yes, he's got a tight smooth body. And yes, among the family jewels lies an extra-wide choker."

"Then maybe you wanted a little reunion with him out here in Abigail, a stroll to the candy store for old times' sake."

"You don't know anything!" roared Daniel. Then he laughed derisively and said, "Rick Jansen is wearing blinders these days. He's in love, if that's what you can call it, with Jonathan Byers. *Sir* Jonathan Byers. It began last year in Spoleto, when Ricky started flirting with the recently dubbed Sir Jon. A year-long chase ensued, and Jon finally gave in. But the price for knight-fucking is damn high. Jon has made Rick swear off casual sex, which is certainly unfair given the Sir's own blatant lechery, that pig—and certainly tragic for the rest of us, given Rick's natural talents with his thing, the prince."

"I guess I didn't realize how lucky I was," I said. "I just turned down an offer to get acquainted with his princely thing."

Daniel spat the word, "When?"

"Backstage, maybe half an hour ago."

"You're lying."

"No. Rick told me exactly what he wanted to do to me."

"You're trying to provoke me, aren't you?" He was seething. "Who instigated it? You?"

"He did. I never make the first move."

Daniel eyed me slyly. "Did he pull it out and show you?"

Now maybe Daniel was just trying to verify my claim, and have me recite the specs of Ricky's thing. But I took his vulgar question as my cue to get back to work.

I said, "When was the last time you saw Madama Ostinata?"

It caught him off-guard, and he spun at me with an angry glare. "What kind of question is that?"

"A very simple one. It's not even incriminating, unless the last time you saw her was when you sliced her throat."

"I told you where I was that night."

"But when did you see her?"

"The last time I saw Marcella was in rehearsal." Then he added smugly, "I believe you were there too."

But Daniel Carafolio's alibi was nonexistent unless some guy named Butch stepped forward and confirmed that he had spent the night with him. And what self-respecting faggot would admit to such a thing except under grave duress?

"And now," said Daniel, heaving an exasperated sigh, "If you don't mind, I'm really tired of you."

I replied, "I could use some air myself."

I left him and headed back to the opera house. So much for my two hot leads from the security report. All I'd got from them was more tangles that led nowhere. I already knew why Rick Jansen and Sir Jonathan Byers weren't on the report. They were sharing digs at Abigail's oldest luxury hotel, the Abigail Arms. Then I wondered, since the hamlet of Abigail-by-the-Sea didn't offer any hopping nightspots for people with active sex lives, did Daniel Carafolio perhaps spend the night with one—or even both—of the other two men? He claimed to know Rick already. Perhaps he also knew Jonathan Byers. I'd heard Spoleto was a lively place. Perhaps the threesome had been frolicking in reunion the very night Marcella Ostinata's vocal cords were being severed. Anything was possible in the suburbs, even among people who didn't particularly care for one another.

Back at the opera house the musicians were still rehearsing. Apparently Jonathan Byers had placated the maestro into staying on with the production, because the old man was seated next to Carolyn Boetz at the piano, as though nothing had happened that morning. I sat in the back of the auditorium and watched awhile. With all the seats empty, the stage was like a huge shadow box, but with living creatures inside. There they were onstage—April Kilkus, Hwang Yung Cho, the nameless tenor, assorted other soloists, a rousing chorus, and the maestro and Carolyn Boetz at the piano—all in the work of making beautiful sounds about the horrors of betrayal and murder. Yet one of those very people had likely committed the dreadful deed in real life, perhaps more than once. Still, I found myself enjoying it all.

The rehearsal broke earlier than usual because the first lighting run-through was scheduled that evening. That first session is always done without singers to save wear and tear on the supposedly delicate creatures. Daphne was waiting outside the opera house to drive the maestro and me back to the mansion. During the drive the maestro excitedly told Daphne about the sacrilege that was being committed against Verdi in this production. At one point he raised his voice vehemently, just as he had done that morning.

"This Byers, he makes a sin against opera. He will burn in hell for what he does to Verdi."

Apparently the truce between the maestro and Jonathan Byers had been conditional. And it was quite a different stance from before, when the maestro had tried to quell Madama Ostinata's outrage over the preposterous interpretation of Verdi's work. Now the maestro was condemning Sir Jon to hell, just as Madama had done.

But Daphne answered him brightly, "Times are different, Maestro." She faced him as she continued talking. "Perhaps Verdi himself would have set things differently if he were alive now. There's nothing to do but bend with the wind. Otherwise grand opera will become as brittle as an old museum piece. And then it will shatter and vanish. You don't want that, do you?"

Shatter and vanish is what almost happened to us in the Bentley, since Daphne had let the car wander precariously close to the edge of the ocean road. From the back seat I made a strangled kind of croaking sound to alert her, but she smoothly maneuvered the car back on course. She glanced in the rearview mirror and said, "Thank you, dear. But I do know the road."

The maestro, absolutely unperturbed, smiled wanly.

"Verdi should live forever," he said. "But he must have respect. These musicians are like children. They want to play with him, but they do not know what they are doing."

Daphne said, "Be thankful that Verdi appeals to them at all. They're bright and they'll keep him alive and fresh."

I knew that her words reflected the hope that a progressive approach to opera might assure the festival's success this year and forever after. Somehow her words, or more likely the delivery of them, placated the old man, and he nodded and smiled.

Then Daphne said to me, "How are the wigs? I hope that things have settled down into a nice routine with your boss."

"Er, yes," I said tentatively. "Just fine."

"That's nice," said Daphne. "I'm afraid at home the developments have been a little less pleasant. I decided to admit Bruce David to McLean Hospital this afternoon. He'll receive the best care possible there."

The maestro brightened suddenly and said, "The second Riccardo is very good, very dramatic. He will sing well."

Daphne said, "Yes, but at what cost to dear young Bruce?"

I imagined that Bruce's cover, a serviceable if uninspiring tenor, would probably blossom under the maestro's renewed verve and attention to the music. It also helped that the tenor would have April Kilkus as his new and certain partner. It almost seemed too good to be true, or too good to be coincidental. But the nameless tenor was hardly a suspect in killing Madama Ostinata. He'd simply gained by her death, just the way April Kilkus had the good fortune to get that recording contract and the televised broadcast. It was a law of physics made into a law of survival, that every event, no matter how good or bad, had some opposite event connected to it, to balance its effect.

Guru-babble meant I was tired and hungry.

When we arrived at the house I was both elated and uneasy to see Lieutenant Branco's Alfa in the driveway.

Daphne exclaimed, "Oh dear. Now what?"

As it turned out, Mathilde had vanished from the premises. Parker explained to Daphne that he had called the Boston police to report the disappearance.

He said, "I wasn't sure what to do in your absence, Miss Davenport. It was hardly an emergency, but it did seem to call for action. I hope I did the correct thing."

"Well done, Parker," Daphne assured him. "Of course you had to call the police." Then she turned toward Branco and offered her hand.

"And now the lieutenant has returned here sooner than we might have expected."

Branco said, "I'd be talking with my deputy anyway." He nodded toward me, and my bosom swelled with pride, just like Della Street's after a crumb of attention from Perry Mason.

The maestro excused himself for a rest before dinner, and Parker escorted him up to his room. Daphne took Branco and me into the library, where she offered us drinks. Branco resisted, and Daphne insisted. Finally he yielded.

"Seltzer," he said. "I'm driving."

"Surely one little drop can't hurt," said Daphne.

"I don't let my crew drink on duty," said Branco. "The same goes for me. When this case is settled, then I'll celebrate."

What exactly did that mean for Branco? To celebrate?

He and I sat in the two wing-back armchairs facing the fireplace, while Daphne made our drinks at the liquor cart. Once she served us, I gave her my seat and sat on the arm of the chair. Then Branco asked Daphne if she'd known of Mathilde's plans to leave Abigail.

"Not at all," said Daphne. "It's so sudden. I hope she isn't in any danger."

"Not yet," said Branco. "She took her bags with her, so she clearly planned this escape."

"Escape?" blurted Daphne.

"That's how I see it," said Branco.

Daphne said, "Do you have any idea where she went?"

"I've got an APB out on her now." I knew that meant an all points bulletin, which was a search of near-global bounds. "We'll find her," said Branco. "She didn't get much of a start. I sure hope she has a good reason for this, because I'm just about ready to nail her."

I said, "For the murder?"

Branco nodded.

"On what evidence?"

"Basically on her statement. You may recall her admission that she had purposely oversedated the victim."

I nodded. "At Madama's request."

Branco went on. "I think she planned that story too. She sounded too glib about it. After administering that same potion countless times to the same high-strung woman, that maid should have known exactly what increased dosage was needed that particular night. But she acted as though it was the first time for both of them. After reconsidering her testimony, I think she was lying. Besides, she had a good motive."

At that moment I noticed that Parker had appeared in the library. "Is everyone served?" he asked.

Daphne said, "Yes, thank you, Parker."

He lingered at the liquor cart checking the ice and seltzer.

"What was Mathilde's motive?" I said to Branco.

He replied, "Marcella Ostinata was about to relieve her servant of her duties."

"After twenty-five years of faithful service?" I said.

"Yup," went the cop.

"To be replaced by . . . ?"

"Her personal accompanist, Rick Jansen."

Silence all around.

I said, "What did he have to say about that?"

"Jansen claims the singer hadn't told him anything about it. I talked with Byers right away too, before the two of them could collaborate on a story."

"Unless they already had," I said.

"No," said Branco. "I don't think Byers knew anything either. He got pretty agitated when I told him. I guess he expects Jansen to hang onto him forever."

That wasn't the story I'd heard from Rick earlier, when he claimed that Sir Jon was ready to throw him out of his bed.

"What about Mathilde?" I said. "Was Madama Ostinata going to provide for her in any way?"

"Not a cent," said Branco.

"After all those years," I said.

Discomforted glances passed between Daphne and Parker.

Parker said, "I'll see to dinner, Miss Davenport."

Daphne said, "Thank you," but she sounded unsettled.

When Parker had left us, Daphne asked the lieutenant, "How did you learn all that about Marcella releasing Mathilde from service?"

"I spoke to her attorneys in Milan," replied the cop. "I called them today about the woman's will. I thought there might be something useful there."

Branco sipped his seltzer.

I said, "Was there?"

"Was there what?" he said.

Cat and mouse.

"Was there anything incriminating in the will? I mean, did anyone here at the festival stand to gain or lose anything by Marcella's death?"

Branco smirked. "You'll have to hone your technique, Stan. That's two separate questions." Then he said, "I'll answer the second one first. Somebody obviously expected to gain something or else prevent its loss, which is why the woman was murdered."

"And the will?" I said.

"In terms of the will, nothing. No individual is named in her will."

"So where's all her money going?" I asked.

"That's the strange thing," said Branco. "She bequeathed her entire estate to two institutions. Half goes to an opera house in Bari, the one where Marcella Ostinata made her debut and had her first success."

"And the other half?" I said.

"To an orphanage in the same town," said Branco.

"Well," said Daphne. "At least no one can be accused of killing Marcella for her money."

Branco drained his glass and said, "I still haven't ruled it out completely."

Daphne asked him to stay for dinner with an apology. "I'm afraid it's going to be vegetarian," she said. "I don't think I can quite stomach the sight of meat yet."

But as I expected, Branco declined the invitation. Before he left, he wanted to talk to me privately. Daphne let us use the library, since she wanted to freshen up before dinner. Branco thanked her for the drink and said good night to her.

She said, "But it was only water."

"It's the thought," he replied.

Then I related my day's work to him: the argument at the opera house between Jonathan Byers and the maestro; the security report on April Kilkus, Hwang Yung Cho, and Daniel Carafolio; Maurizio's high-flying act on the backstage catwalks; and even Rick Jansen's crass offer of sex.

Branco laughed and said, "You get them coming and going."

"I don't want any of it, Lieutenant. I just want home and hearth."

He said, "Obviously you're not ready for that." But then he complimented me on my work, that I was on the right track chasing down people's whereabouts that night. "It's all a matter of timing," he said, and told me the results of the autopsy report, that Marcella Ostinata had died around four o'clock in the morning, based on the temperature of the body when the police got to her, and on the state of the stomach contents, and on the time she had supposedly last eaten.

"Unfortunately," said the cop, "That last bit comes from the maid's testimony, which as you know, I don't believe at all."

I told Branco what I'd learned from Mathilde the night before, how she'd always wanted to be a singer, and how Madama Ostinata had promised from the beginning to help nuture her talent, but over the years managed to thwart every possibility of Mathilde's ever singing.

Branco said, "Good work, Stan. Now we've got one more motivation for the maid. Revenge."

"What's my next assignment?" I said.

"Just keep nosing around. You're doing fine."

Branco departed, and minutes later Daphne and the maestro came into the library for a last cocktail before dinner. Parker took our drink orders, and I congratulated the maestro on the news of the big recording contract. He squinted one eye at me like a wary rodent.

Daphne exclaimed, "Isn't it wonderful? Finally the maestro will have a recording. The opera world has been waiting so long for this."

I kept my eye on the maestro and said, "I wonder why I was the last to know."

"But my dear," Daphne exclaimed. "Why would you? It has nothing to do with you."

"Daphne, I've spoken with everyone at the festival, both before and after Madama's death, and no one ever said a word about a recording contract. Now suddenly it's headline news."

"Oh, I think you're taking it too seriously. With all the horrid events of the last few days, it completely slipped my mind too."

Then the maestro turned himself toward me and addressed me with the candor of a Dutch uncle.

"Young man, it is better not to talk about such a thing until it is certain. But now," he said with a beneficent smile. "Now we have signed the papers and it is certain. So we can talk. Yes, I am happy." He smiled a wide, bright smile that showed off his excellent teeth. His eyes radiated the joy of attaining a long-sought success after a lifetime of struggle. Or was it a lifetime of deception?

Daphne quickly asked Parker to open some champagne to celebrate the signing of the contract. But the whole thing—the excuses, the pronouncements, the champagne—all seemed an afterthought. If I hadn't said anything to the maestro, would we be celebrating at all? Still, Parker popped the cork and we all enjoyed the vintage bubbly. And for a brief while no one thought about the late Marcella Ostinata.

I asked Daphne about Maurizio's membership in the stagehand's union, and she explained blithely, "He has an interest and a talent for that kind of work, so I helped the wheels turn a little faster and more smoothly in his favor. What else is money for but to help people?"

"Maybe your intervention spoiled a chance for him to prove that he can do things for himself."

"Bosh!" said Daphne. "Maurizio has enough challenge in his daily life without a catalog of union rules on top of it."

Matter closed.

After that the evening progressed pleasantly, a marked change from the perpetual conflicts of the earlier hours. The maestro even enjoyed the vegetarian dinner. But how could he not? Parker had filled our plates with steaming fresh produce—native grown, no less—in artistic arrangements that would have challenged the culinary deities of California.

However, matters changed when I headed back to the cottage that night. I felt uneasy the moment I left the big house, and the feeling worsened the further I got from it. It was that same inexplicable fear that had gripped me the first night I had been on the estate. I felt pursued. I told myself it was irrational, that I was completely safe, that no one had hurt me that time and no one would hurt me now. In fact, that first night I had been visited by the sexy Maurizio. Perhaps he was about to pay another call. Dynamic monogamy.

I had just turned down the last leg of the pathway to the cottage when I realized that one of the lamps on the path had gone out. It was extremely dark there, and I quickened my step. But I sensed it was in vain. I felt it coming just as it happened—a rustle from the dense prickly vegetation, and then an arm was wrapped around my neck, pulling me off balance. Before my eyes, in the moonlight, flashed the glint of steel, the blade of a big knife aimed at my throat.

"*Muori!*" said the voice in a hoarse whisper. He pulled the knife back, ready to strike. "*Muori!*"

My thoughts raced not to my mother, or to my lover, or my friends, or even my cat, but instead fled to Tosca and Scarpia in those final fatal seconds of their rendezvous. And then, at the exact moment when the blade should have begun its arced traversal of my throat, and the warm blood would flow freely and my life would ebb away, that's when I grabbed behind myself, for balance I guess—for something—a last hold on some earthly object before my pitiful farewell to the mortal coil. And what I felt in my grasp was as stark and as familiar as my own DNA, identifiable even in those last moments of cognizance. I heard my final breath come out as an ironic little laugh at the ultimate joke that life had played on me. For I had grabbed hold of my assailant's erect cock, which was sticking out the front of his trousers.

"Jesus," I muttered.

And then my savior did appear, though not garbed in flowing white robes. In fact, I saw nothing, save the knife from my attacker's hand fly upwards into the air, and then land safely away from us with a loud clank on the paved path. I swooned and fell to the ground. I sensed a brief tussle between savior and assailant, but I recognized neither one. The sole identifying clue came just before they both ran off— when my attacker grabbed his knife and my rescuer bolted after him.

It was the familiar nasal sound made by only one person among all the people I'd met in Abigail. I had been saved by Maurizio.

I lay on the path for a few minutes to catch my breath. Then I jumped up in a final surge of adrenaline and ran to the cottage. Once inside I closed and locked all the windows and doors, as though that would ensure my safety. I telephoned Daphne at the big house and told her what had happened. She said she would call the police, and I agreed, for whatever good it did. I'd expected Lieutenant Branco to show up and save the day, but instead the Abigail police came and took the report. They made a halfhearted search around the path where I'd been jumped, but of course they found no knife. My attacker had taken it. And since the path was paved, there was no evidence of a struggle either. I showed them the bruise on my forearm, where I'd fallen on it, but I knew they didn't believe me. Fine, I thought. When Maurizio turns up he'll explain everything. But he didn't turn up, not that night anyway.

Daphne insisted that I stay with her in the big house. I told her it hardly mattered to me, since it was no safer there than in the cottage, not after the recent crisis. Then I realized that she wanted me to be in the big house to comfort her, as much as for my own safety. So I packed my overnight kit and went to stay with her. The one small hitch was that the only guest quarters ready on such short notice were the ones Bruce David had just vacated. What an act to follow.

24

By the next morning Maurizio still hadn't shown up. And although he hadn't been absent long enough to be officially reported as a missing person, Daphne had convinced the local police to begin a search for him.

"He might be seriously hurt," she had argued to them. "Will you assume responsibility if he's lying injured somewhere?"

And just as she had done on those other occasions, Daphne somehow got the Abigail police to do her bidding.

She drove the maestro and me to the opera house, but when we arrived there, the maestro didn't get out of the car.

Daphne explained, "He's rehearsing his orchestra today." Then she added, "In the concert hall. The stage crew in the opera house has to prepare for the other productions too, you know."

I did know, and I also knew the wigs for those other productions were included with their costumes, and it would be someone else's job to style and dress them.

My first stop inside the opera house was the wig room, but the ridiculous black wreath was still hanging there, and the door was still locked. I knew there was plenty of work to be done inside, even if the wig master was too distraught in mourning. What kind of professional was Daniel Carafolio? I was only a hairdresser, and even I knew the show had to go on.

I went backstage to get Ronda Lucca to unlock the wig room, but she wasn't there. Her harried assistant told me I might find Ronda at the orchestra rehearsal in the concert hall on the far side of the performance center. Or she might be at the stage rehearsal in the building next door to the opera house. The assistant didn't try much to hide her annoyance that Ronda was elsewhere that morning, and not where she was sorely needed backstage. I asked the assistant if she could unlock the wig room for me, but she said there just wasn't time. So I set off to find Ronda Lucca. My first stop was the stage rehearsal in the studio building adjacent to the opera house. It was a short walk there, and once inside I found the large open studio easily. Rehearsal was already under way. The studio floor was set up to resemble the opera house stage, but with platforms and chairs and other makeshift objects, instead of the actual scenery. Jonathan Byers was in charge, and I was surprised to see at the piano not Carolyn Boetz, but Rick Jansen. It had been a while since I'd heard him abuse a keyboard. The rest of the singing cast was present, all assembled and seemingly eager to work. Perhaps the assurance of the new recording contract and the fast approach of opening night had begun to invigorate them with keen anticipation. The only potential worry was Jonathan Byers's detached, almost callous treatment of Rick, who floundered his way through the score note by perilous note.

But there was no Ronda there to unlock the wig room for me. So I continued to the concert hall, across the quadrangle of the performance center. Once inside that building, I got a sonic thrill I hadn't felt for years. Up to that point, all the supporting music I'd heard through all the rehearsals had been with a piano. But that morning the maestro was rehearsing the opera with a full orchestra. And in spite of the high-tech soundproofing of the concert hall, the old man had the musicians shaking the walls of the outer lobby with Verdi's music. I slipped into the hall to watch and listen.

The audience portion of the auditorium was dark, but the stage was brightly lit. The maestro stood on a podium before the orchestra. Gone was the old body that had day after day curled up in a chair next to the piano to conduct a single player. The maestro now stood erect and strong, an indisputable authority to all the musicians under his baton. Carolyn Boetz sat in a high stool next to the podium. Laid before her was a full orchestral score into which she made numerous notes in pencil, either in response to signs from the maestro—some subtle, some imperative—or from her own expert ear.

Once my eyes had adjusted to the darkness, I perceived Ronda Lucca sitting in one of the last rows of the house, also watching the rehearsal. I took the seat behind her, where I could whisper over her shoulder.

"I need the key to the wig room."

With nary a word or a jangle, Ronda unclipped the big ring of keys from her belt and handed it back to me. One key was singled out from the others.

"Thanks," I whispered. "When do you want them back?"

"Keep 'em," she said. "I'll be back there in half an hour."

I was about to leave when I realized there was no hurry for me to return to the opera house either. No one was around to scold me, so I could sit behind Ronda and listen to the music as long as I wanted to. And that's exactly what I did.

Watching the maestro was a thrill. I would never have guessed the old guy still had so much fire in him. He waved his arms energetically, and the orchestra responded with raw musical power. Then he would hush them suddenly while he mimicked the lyrics of Amelia in a high floating falsetto, followed by those of Renato in a faint hoarse grumble. Then he would fly into animation again, urging more thunder from the orchestra, all to support his whimpering, barking, keening imitations of the singers. It was almost a burlesque of real opera, but all in deadly seriousness. Verdi was well served.

And though I was sitting behind Ronda Lucca, I knew she was watching Carolyn Boetz. The intent stillness of her body gave it away. The music might be shaking the rafters, but Ronda was still and quiet. But then would come that moment, when far away onstage Carolyn Boetz would make a small gesture—a turn of the page, a tilt of the head—and Ronda would respond in some similar way, with her own head or body moving ever so slightly, only to settle down on a new vantage point on her beloved, until the next small motion that prompted an echo.

About half an hour later, halfway through the music of act one, Ronda checked her watch, then got up to leave. She showed only the slightest surprise that I was still sitting behind her.

"I'll walk you back," I said.

On our return to the opera house I said, "The orchestra sounds great, eh?"

"Yeah," said Ronda.

I pressed her with another question.

"Do you like her a lot?"

"Is the sky blue?" said Ronda with a sigh.

"Does she know?"

"It doesn't matter," she replied. "Whether or not Carolyn ever feels the same way I do, I'd still do anything in the world for her."

That was certainly one version of love.

I told Ronda that I'd just heard about the big recording contract for the production of *Ballo.*

"That's old news," she said. "Everybody knows by now."

"Not me."

"Maybe you don't travel in the right circles."

"That seems to be the general concensus among the singers."

"Well don't let *them* get to you," Ronda said with a laugh.

"You seem in a good mood."

"Yeah, well sure. Since Carolyn is the maestro's assistant, she's going to be involved with the recording as well. That's a big break for her."

"Sounds like the whole cast got hired for this recording."

"Yeah," said Ronda. "It turned out kind of lucky for everyone."

"Except the dead diva."

Ronda smiled tentatively. "Well, I guess someone's gotta take the bad luck."

"It wasn't luck that slashed her throat, Ronda. Someone wanted her out of the way."

"Maybe it was the record company," said Ronda. "They sure wouldn't want that cow in full digital sound."

"Was she supposed to sing on the recording?"

"Never," said Ronda assuredly. "Everyone knew Marcella Ostinata was a has-been. But she made her usual big noise about the recording. That's what held up the contract—the cow and her lawyers."

Once again I wondered, if Madama Ostinata had such a bad reputation, why had she been hired to sing in the first place? And how far would Ronda Lucca go in her unrequited love for Carolyn Boetz? With Marcella Ostinata out of the way, the record company had moved quickly to engage the whole cast along with Maestro Toscanelli. Ronda knew it was inevitable that he would take Carolyn along for that bonus as well. Had she hastened her paramour's success by killing the older singer?

I said, "Too bad for you the record company doesn't need a stage manager. You'd probably have a contract now too."

"Nah," said Ronda. "They use production assistants, and I've already done that. It's like boot camp."

Back in the wig room I settled down to get some real work done, and I became so engrossed with my projects that I forgot to have any lunch or my usual afternoon snack. Now that's dedication. At the rate I was going, even if Daniel never showed up again, the cast would be fabulously coiffed by soon to be slender and fabulous *moi*. I was just putting the finishing touches on a woman's wig for the last scene of the opera, which is the actual masked ball of the title. That was the one scene in the production where the costumes and wigs didn't have to be consistent with the rest of the eccentric setting—contemporary Manhattan. In fact, the sets for the first three acts were quite gray and dismal, but the costumes were vividly colored, supposedly to reflect the hidden passions among the players in a hostile, oppressive environment. In contrast, the finale was set in a bright and colorful ballroom, while all the costumes for the ball, however elegant, were strictly black and white, supposedly to reflect the stark hidden motives of the characters in a festive atmosphere. It was a hackneyed exercise in theatrical contrast. But if Jonathan Byers could blithely set Verdi's *Un ballo in maschera* in contemporary Manhattan, who was I to worry about anachronism? I intended to style the wigs to hold the audience rapt. In fact, the one in my hand was truly de trop, with ringlets and waves set off by an extravagant bouffant. It would have done Louis XVI proud, and I was pleased with my unexpected inspiration. That's exactly when an unexpected visitor arrived— Lieutenant Branco.

Branco hadn't shown up the previous night when Daphne had

called the police after my attack, and I was still a little miffed. I was his deputy, after all. Didn't that count for anything? Branco very rationally explained why he hadn't come himself to take the report: He'd been confirming the whereabouts of Bruce David, and then he had become entangled in a search for the maid, Mathilde. But the cop's words came out easily—without apology, almost flippant—as though he was talking shop with another cop. I suppose such apparent equality should have pleased me, but from where I stood, Lieutenant Branco had performed his professional duties to the ultimate degree of dedication for two complete strangers, albeit suspects. But when a more personal contingency had arisen, in the form of *me*—his deputy—being attacked, Branco had washed his hands of it and sent in the Abigail police.

"I read the report about that incident last night," he said. "Is everything okay now?"

"Sure," I said.

Branco gave me a skeptical look, then he said, "By the way, do you remember what you had to eat and drink?"

"I wasn't drunk," I protested. "It really happened."

"Sometimes an odd combination can make you hallucinate."

"Just like love."

"Maybe that's all you wanted from him."

"Who?"

"That little guy who shows up and disappears a lot."

"Lieutenant, Maurizio saved my life."

"Sure," he said. "I'm just glad you weren't hurt."

At a previous juncture of my life, a remark like that from Branco would have sent me running for my trousseau. But that afternoon the lieutenant's comment sounded like a polite brush-off to someone with unpredictable behavior.

"Lieutenant," I said, "I *was* attacked. The guy had a knife."

"I believe you," he said.

"No you don't. I can tell by your voice."

"Stan, we have to keep our trust here."

"I'd rather hear that you don't believe me if that's the truth, instead of a cautious lie that says we're supposed to trust each other."

I watched his strong jaw clench and release. I had created an instant showdown between us, small but serious. Branco wasn't used to this kind of thing—one man asking another for spikey honesty rather than bland trust—certainly not with the guys back at headquarters, who probably thrived on team spirit and manly bonding. But now Branco was dealing with me, Stan Kraychik—master hairdresser, poetic wigmaker, irksome homosexual.

Branco said, "Okay, Stan. I'll be completely honest with you, if that's what you want. I'm a little concerned about how you always seem to be in the wrong place at the wrong time. That's something you're going to have to recognize if you keep working for me. You could get yourself in a real dangerous position. And you're not armed."

"I was in danger last night, and where were you?"

"Sometimes I wonder if you put yourself in that kind of situation on purpose, just to see what might happen."

"What, you think I was out looking for sex in the bushes?"

"I don't know what I think, Stan."

"That's enough, Lieutenant. Thanks."

Branco frowned unhappily. "What did you want me to say?"

"I wanted the truth."

"That was the truth. What else do you want?"

"I want you to believe I was attacked last night, even if there wasn't supporting evidence in the report."

"That's asking me to lie, Stan."

"I'd do it for you."

"You'd lie to me?"

"If the situation called for it."

"Then that's where we're different," said the cop. "I wouldn't ever want you to lie to me."

"Not even to spare your feelings?"

"Not then, not ever!" he said fiercely. The air became still between us. When Branco spoke again, his eyes looked a little sad, a little disappointed. "You know," he said, "I actually let myself think I might become a better cop for having you work with me."

Heedless of my higher self, I retorted, "That sounds like one of

196

those movies where a man dresses up like a woman and has an epiphany."

The cop bristled.

I said quickly, "I'm sorry. That wasn't fair."

"You think you're the only one in the world with feelings."

"It's a survival tactic," I offered weakly.

"Look Stan," said my hero, "if we're going to work together, you have to accept things the way they are. I can't start saying things to you I don't mean. I thought you'd know that by now."

I blushed. He was right. I did know it.

My head lowered, I asked, "Should I hand in my badge?"

"Is that what you want?"

"No," I squeaked.

"Then just keep throwing me those good leads the way you have so far, and I'll listen. But that's the only guarantee I can make—that I'll listen. As far as what I say to you, well . . ." He trailed off without finishing.

"Lieutenant, you were right about one thing. I do get into jams sometimes. But I didn't imagine that attack last night. When we find Maurizio, he'll verify the whole thing."

"In the meantime," said Branco, "you'd better be extra careful."

Branco scanned the wig room with its stockpiles of hair and nets and lacquer and dummies, and the shelves full of finished wigs, and the tables full of works in progress. It would appear to be chaos to the unknowing eye.

He said, "So this is where you work."

I nodded.

He turned to leave the room and was almost out the door when he stopped and said, "I'll call you later."

"Thanks," I said.

I listened to his footsteps go down the hall and up the stairway to the stage door. Then I went back to work.

Before leaving the opera house that day, I explored some of the uncharted corridors on the upper floors and found a dance rehearsal in progress. Watching the dancers and the choreographer, I felt a sudden yearning for my lover. What was he doing in Paris at that moment? Why were we separated? What did the wigs matter? Or a diva's murder? The dancers in rehearsal seemed immune to mundane worries. Their only concern was movement and music. I stood outside the rehearsal studio and watched them sliding and turning along the floor, then becoming airborne and carefree. I should have been heartened by them and the lightness of their existence. Like some of the other artists in the opera house, their sights were still set on the work at hand and on opening night. It was a good life to be working in the arts. So why did I feel so bad? Hell, I was Branco's assistant in training. That should have been cause to rejoice and join in with the dancers. But instead I found myself watching them and almost sobbing. I fought hard to hold back the tears, and for an instant I felt that I understood a tiny bit why Lieutenant Branco always seemed so austere. Perhaps that cool façade wasn't his nature. Perhaps it was his work that required him to hold his emotions down, push them back, disregard them, just like a surgeon does. Sometimes there was no room for feelings. How else could one person slice open the body of another in the name of healing? Or pursue and convict and even kill someone else in the name of justice? The only way to prevail was with distance—a cold and calculated distance laid between you and the object of your attention. That's what I needed. Objectivity. Psychic distance. About a mile's worth.

But for all my faulty reasoning, I still wanted to cry when I left the opera house. Then I realized that I hadn't eaten all day. My emotional distress was simply low blood sugar.

25

Though I had spent the previous night with Daphne in the big house after the attack, all my clothes and other things were still in the cottage. I hadn't moved everything to the big house because I intended to return to the cottage once Daphne felt comfortable being alone again. Honestly, I enjoyed the independence the cottage offered me. And despite the illusion of "safety in numbers" at the big house, I didn't really like the energy that lingered in Bruce David's rooms after his uncertain residency there. So when Daphne and the maestro and I got back to the estate that evening, I went to the cottage to wash and change for dinner. But I wasn't prepared for what awaited me.

Maurizio was lying in my bed. I knew he was naked under the covers, yet there wasn't a single erg of sexual energy in the room. That was the first clue he was in trouble. I moved toward the bed and saw the sheets around his right shoulder stiff and maroon with dried blood. For an awful moment I imagined a reprise of Marcella Ostinata's death scene. But I was wrong. Maurizio was alive all right, but semiconscious and moaning quietly. He was in serious trouble, burning with fever. His eyes looked at me. They were glassy and unfocused. The knife wound on his shoulder gaped at me, a deep cut running from the middle of his collarbone diagonally through the pectoral muscle and across his upper arm. The gash was crusted and scabby, and it was oozing a bloody yellow slime. Portions of the sheets were still damp with the muck. Maurizio must have returned to the cottage after saving my life the previous night, and had been there since, suffering a knife wound and harboring an infection.

I telephoned the big house immediately and explained to Parker what had happened. I told him to call an ambulance and that I would wait in the cottage until it arrived. And for the next quarter hour or so until the medics arrived, I cradled Maurizio in my arms, using the blankets like swaddling clothes. That's when I also noticed something on my night stand that hadn't been there the last time I looked. A small folding silver frame displayed two photographs side by side—one a dark-haired, dark-eyed infant in a billowy white christening gown, and the other a curly-haired, impish boy of about two in a sailor's outfit. They were clearly the same person, and then I realized they were images, however distant, of the young man I held in my arms.

I was about to fold the frame and place it in the drawer of the night stand when Daphne arrived at the cottage. She saw me holding Maurizio, and marvelled for a moment at the queer picture we must have made. Then she noticed Maurizio's wound and quickly turned her head away.

She said, "Did you know he was here?"

"No. He must have come last night after chasing my attacker off. I guess they fought and he got hurt."

"It looks badly infected," Daphne said. "He'll need antibiotics."

Her gaze wandered to the silver-framed photos.

I said, "Those weren't here before." I sounded defensive. "Maurizio must have put them there last night."

Daphne said, "You don't have to explain, dear. We all have photographs of the people we love."

But her remark reminded me that I never carried a photo of my man Rafik with me. Worse, I'd always had one of Sugar Baby in my wallet instead, a tattered old snapshot taken when she was a five-week-old puff ball. Even then she had her magical powers.

The medics arrived and got Maurizio onto a gurney, then wheeled him back up the path to the waiting ambulance. Daphne and I followed close behind. I wondered about the two of us going to the hospital too, but Daphne said that extra bodies in the emergency room would only be in the way. I agreed, although I did worry that Maurizio might come out of his delirium with no familiar face nearby.

Daphne assured me that he'd be fine for the time being, and she'd drive us down to see him later, right after dinner. I still wanted to shower and change, but she insisted that we had little time to spare.

"Besides," she added, "You'll enjoy your shower more after we're back from the hospital. Did you bring the photos?"

"Which photos?"

"The ones of Maurizio that were on the bedstand."

"Why would I do that?"

"Oh, you must," said Daphne. "More than ever, now that he is ailing, you really must keep his image close to you. It will help him get well. Don't you see?" She smiled brightly. "Oh, to be young again! I'm afraid I'd be seen as a real quack the second time around, researching and proving the power of ESP to heal."

So much for Harvard Medical School.

Daphne sent me back to the cottage to get the photos while she continued on to the big house. When I got to the house, I found her in the library with the maestro—no cocktail in her hand that evening. She asked to see the photos immediately. As I handed her the silver frame, I asked why she was so interested in them.

She answered, "I can't say exactly, except that there's something compelling about that young face, something almost disturbingly familiar."

"It's not as if you don't know him," I offered.

"It's something else," said Daphne. "Something troubling."

The maestro asked to see the photos. He gazed on the pair of portraits for only a moment, then he blanched.

"It cannot be," he said, shaking his head dismally. "It is not possible."

Only an ominous timpani roll was lacking.

Che cosa? said Daphne, as if the maestro's native tongue would encourage him to speak.

He carefully folded the silver frame like a holy relic. Then he said, "I think this boy is the son of Marcella."

"So!" said Daphne.

"Huh?" said I.

The maestro nodded. "I am sure now. I have seen these photographs before, many years ago. Marcella did have a son. He was this boy. But she did not keep him."

"But how? When?" said Daphne. "Why?"

The maestro's remarks had unsettled her, as though they had agitated an old and dormant fear. He explained further.

"Marcella had this son, but she did not marry the father. It was accepted for her to do this because she was a great artist. But the infant was very sick, and after that he could not hear anything. He was *sordomuto*. Marcella cannot have a son who is like that, who does not hear her. It was a great shame for her. So she gives the baby to, er, *l'orfanotrofio*."

"Oh dear God," said Daphne. "That explains why she left half her estate to that orphanage in Bari."

"Yes," said the maestro. "I know about that, but Marcella made me promise I would never tell. Now what does it matter? She is dead, and the boy is here."

"But who is the father?" said Daphne.

"Ah," said the maestro. "The father was *americano*, a businessman, married already. He could not marry Marcella so instead he gave her much money."

"Oh dear, oh dear," said Daphne. "I don't like what I'm thinking."

The maestro said, "For many years I tried to find the boy, but he ran away and then no one could find him."

"Until he showed up here," said Daphne. "Two years ago, right after Sid's death." Then she added, as if in a trance, "He gave me a card on which he had written *Ho tornato a casa*. How could I turn him away when he said, 'I've come home'?"

For my part, a bit of mental arithmetic verified Lieutenant Branco's earlier report of Marcella Ostinata mysteriously leaving the opera stage for a single season about twenty-five years ago. My guess had been right. She had done so to have a baby.

I said, "Do you think Maurizio knew that Marcella was his mother?"

"How could he?" replied Daphne.

I shrugged. "I've heard there's an immutable bond between mother and child that nothing can erase. Kind of like ESP."

Daphne snapped at me. "Don't bandy my theories, young man."

"I didn't mean to. I just wonder if Maurizio had some instinctive sense about her. She did abandon him, after all. That may have left an imprint on his primal psyche."

"An imprint," said Daphne. "Like the Shroud of Turin."

"*Ah, sì,*" said the maestro.

"But I wonder," said Daphne. "I've known Maurizio for two years, and I never saw this frame or these photos."

"Maybe they were his special secret," I said.

"Imprint," she said and pondered a moment longer. "I wonder if this isn't the very thing that Marcella Ostinata had claimed was missing from her room that awful morning I found her wearing my brooch. If Maurizio had seen this frame in her room, he would certainly have recognized himself in the photos. We all retain that imprint. He might very possibly have taken it from Madama's room for himself."

"But when?" I said. "How?"

"Oh, he can climb anywhere," she said.

Then Daphne snatched the frame from the maestro's hands, flipped it open, and scrutinized the photos inside. After many silent seconds, she said, "I suppose I'm seeing exactly what I want to. I wish Maurizio was here right now, so that I could study his face directly. I must make sure."

"Of what?" I said.

Daphne lapsed into stream of consciousness about her second husband Sid, how he had traveled a lot during those early years, especially overseas, where his company had won many contracts to set up state-of-the-art processing and freezing plants.

"He went to Italy many times," she said.

Then her voice was almost suffocated when she recalled, "And then my brooch disappeared. And now, looking at these photographs of Maurizio, I'm certain. I'm certain that those young eyes belong to none other than Sidney Blaustein." She paused a moment, then muttered, "That snake!"

The maestro gasped. *"Gran Dio!"*

They say things come in threes. What would be discovered next? That Maurizio had recognized Marcella Ostinata as his own mother and then killed her to avenge the lifelong suffering that her cruel desertion had caused him? If the story of his birth was true, he was still half Italian, and such things happened all the time in opera. Maybe they happened in real families too.

"On the bright side," said Pollyanna Kraychik, "you and Maurizio have found each other and have become family."

Daphne scowled at me. "I love the boy dearly, but he is not my flesh and blood."

"Almost," I said unctuously.

"Almost not!" said Daphne.

After an extremely quick dinner, during which Daphne ate nearly nothing and was brusque to everyone, she called the hospital to check on Maurizio. The report came back that his wounds had been cleaned, stitched, and dressed; he was on an antibiotic drip, along with saline and glucose; and he was resting peacefully.

Daphne hung up and said to me, "Well, he may not be flesh and blood, but I'm going to see him. You're welcome to come along."

I accepted without hesitation, for I hoped during the ride to the hospital that I might ease the friction that had crept between us. The maestro declined to join us because the next day's rehearsal would be difficult. It was the *Sitzprobe,* when the singers and the orchestra would work their way through the complete score for the first time together.

In the hospital, Maurizio was sleeping quietly. His color had already returned a bit, and his long eyelashes drew me helplessly toward his face, as though I should kiss him. But I didn't. Instead I forced myself to gaze impassively and wonder if it was possible that such a beautifully formed young man could sever the neck of his estranged mother in a fit of pique. But no answer came.

On the ride home Daphne told me that starting the next morning a hired driver would be taking the maestro and me to the performance center.

"I'm afraid I've been overextending myself," she said. "And with opening night only a week off, I expect all kinds of last-minute contingencies, and I've got to be sharp. You understand, don't you, dear?"

"Of course," I said.

In fact, I'd never quite understood why Daphne had insisted on driving us around in the first place. Whether out of hospitality or responsibility, her chauffering the maestro and me had seemed incongruous to her rank as benefactress of the opera festival. And given Daphne's driving, it would be a relief to have a nice, taciturn, professional driver at the wheel.

"If you'd like," she said, "I can rent a car for you, so you can drive yourself."

"No," I said tentatively. "I'll ride with the maestro."

But then it occurred to me that a rented car would provide independence that no chauffeur-driven vehicle could. Besides, as Lieutenant Branco's deputy, I could use a set of wheels until I got my own cruiser.

"On second thought," I said, "a rental car for the next week or so might be a good idea."

In the amber glow of the Bentley's dashboard lights I saw Daphne smile. "I thought so too," she said. "Tell me what you'd like, and I'll have it brought round tomorrow morning."

My reply came out so fast it sounded as though I'd been waiting for that moment all along. Perhaps I had been, unconsciously.

"An Alfa," I said.

"A red convertible?" said Daphne. "Like my Bentley?"

"Black," I said. "Black goes better with my hair."

"Black it shall be then," said Daphne with a soothing cluck, like a mother hen who had found her long-lost chick. Correction. Her second long-lost chick.

She made all the arrangements as soon as we got back to the estate. And at her insistence I stayed again in the big house that night. I preferred the cottage to Bruce David's rooms, but I could hardly refuse Daphne's request after her easy generosity about the rental car.

26

The next day was Sunday, and I realized I'd been in Abigail exactly one week. Only a week, and look what had transpired. Whatever could be said about my life, it certainly wasn't dull. Then I realized that the illusion of a dull life had been my excuse for postponing my letter to Rafik in Paris. But in truth, I had no excuse. It was high time to send that aerogram, for what if Rafik wrote first? Or worse, what if he telephoned me? How would I explain the absence of any communication? By trying to avoid saying things like murder, Maurizio, and Branco? It would be easier to finish the letter, no matter how stilted, and mail it on the way to the opera house.

Though it was Sunday, a rehearsal was scheduled. Even the "day of rest" could not stay the progress of an opera production. And the union crew would see an exorbitant bonus too.

After breakfast a hired car and driver arrived to take the maestro to the opera house. I, however, got to drive myself in a roguish Italian roadster. It had been delivered during breakfast, and Daphne urged me outside to see it. The top had been lowered as if to entice me inside right away. I did hop in, and the tan leather seat embraced my back and fanny and thighs with a comforting, almost sexual familiarity. The exterior's glossy black paint mirrored the clear blue morning sky. That day was off to a good start. The only odd thing I noticed was the Alfa's odometer, which read fifty-three miles. Daphne had managed to rent a brand-new car for me.

Driving to the performance center gave me a feeling of optimism, and I knew the Alfa was certainly part of it. The car responded like a pliant and eager partner. Driving it was more than a pleasure. It was invigorating, almost arousing. No wonder Lieutenant Branco had never traded his vintage Alfa. They'd passed too many years and cruised too many miles together.

But beyond the car itself, it felt good to be on my own. Since arriving at the festival, I had always been in the company of others, which is usually fine for us ultrasocial Geminis. But sometimes we like to get away from people too, almost to the point of an absolute retreat from society. And what better way to do that, to feel at one with nature, than by zipping along a high serpentine coast road in a sporty little capsule of a car? Top down, of course.

Thank you, Daphne.

At the opera house I went downstairs to the wig room, where I found the black wreath still hung on the door. But the door was open. Apparently Daniel Carafolio was back in residence. He didn't hear me come in, but I sure heard him behind the high metal shelves, grunting and huffing and swearing. I peeked around one of the tall units to see him fiendishly undoing some of the fine work I had completed in his absence. He was unfurling and even slashing off some of the long hanks of hair that I had so lovingly teased and beehived. But instead of using shears the way they were designed, Daniel held one of the blades open like a carving knife and hacked away at the wigs with it. He was so preoccupied in his destructive frenzy that he didn't even notice me.

"How dare he!" he muttered. "No, no, no!" he raged as he tore into another of my masterpieces of excess. "All wrong!"

Such were the consequences of not following the costume designer's instructions to the letter. I had tried to be creative, and look what happened. I certainly wasn't about to confront Daniel at that moment, not with that open blade in his hand, and not after the good day's start I'd had driving the Alfa. So I sneaked out and went up to the backstage area.

Ronda Lucca wasn't there yet, and with the cat away, the mice did play. That morning the mice—members of the stage crew—were playing poker, even at that early hour. Because of the *Sitzprobe* the crew would have a fairly easy work day, but thanks to the wonder of unions, they'd still receive a Sunday bonus, which they seemed to be wasting no time in gambling away. I overheard them talking amongst themselves.

"Too bad Lucca's not in this game. She always bids high."

"Yeah, but if she was back here now, we wouldn't be playing, would we?"

"I guess not."

"What the hell's she doing out there anyway?"

"Whaddya think? She's watching that other broad."

"Can't hardly believe she's like that. Lucca's a good-looking girl. You ever see her up there on the ladders?"

"Yeah, so?"

"I'd sure like to slap that fat little butt of hers."

That was my cue to leave.

Out in the auditorium the *Sitzprobe* was getting under way. Energy was high, since this was the first time that voices and orchestra would make music together. All the principal singers and the *comprimarios*— the secondary soloists—were seated in chairs arranged under the proscenium. Behind them was the chorus, also seated. The maestro was in the orchestra pit with his players. Directly to his side sat Carolyn Boetz with a full orchestral score. There would be no stage action whatever that morning, for the *Sitzprobe* was a practical, almost intellectual exploration of the opera score with all musical forces at hand. Still, for me that German term conjured a much different image: a highly animated session of seated coupling with lots of bouncing around in the lap and raucous operatic screaming.

The maestro tapped the music rack with his baton to get everyone's attention.

"Numero quattro," he announced, indicating that the orchestra would play the last few bars of the *preludio* leading into the first scene of act one. Then he lifted his arms, and with a tranquil yet deliberate downbeat, he commenced to weave the magic spell that Verdi had initiated with his pen over a hundred years ago. The strings made a quiet declaration of the love theme, a last sigh that marked the imminent close to the *preludio.* The phrase was answered by the flute and oboe, then extended and repeated twice by both strings and winds. As the strings began their graceful arpeggiated ascent to the

final cadence, the maestro said, *"Sipario,"* which was a cue to the chorus that the curtain would rise at that moment, and they should be ready to sing. A tingle ran across my shoulders as I realized I was witnessing the birth of a live staged opera.

The scene itself opened with a placid men's chorale, as if to indicate that all was well in the city of New York. But any opera-going veteran knows that peace onstage usually portends serious trouble elsewhere. And with *Un ballo in maschera,* despite the well-wishing opening lyrics of Riccardo's entourage, murderous plots were already afoot. And despite the absence of staging for this rehearsal, the sound of voices combined with the orchestra synthesized a drama that almost belied the need for physical action.

Listening to the music that morning I realized that each succeeding step of the rehearsal period had added another dimension to the opera. Each day provided another new and unexpected sensation, just like a good lover who can keep you slightly off-balance with yet another surprise, and then make you hungry for more. Maybe that's what kept all these people at it, despite the daunting odds of success in the world of opera. There was always the anticipation of the unexpected thrill, when a moment of performance traveled to a place or came from a place that no one had even imagined yet. Maybe that's what they called inspiration. I know, because it happened at the styling chair too.

I scanned the seats in the darkened auditorium and spotted Ronda Lucca about midway up in an aisle seat. I tiptoed my way around the side aisle, then scooted across an empty row to get a seat next to her.

I whispered, "I've never been to one of these before. It's almost like a concert performance."

"But even better," said Ronda, "because you know it's on the way to being staged."

I nodded agreeably, as if I knew all about such things.

Ronda said, "This is usually the rehearsal when some tenor marches to the edge of the apron and sings his aria full out." She chuckled quietly. "Some singers just don't get it."

"Don't get what?"

"This rehearsal is for the conductor and the orchestra and the singers to perform *together* for the first time. It's a group effort. It's not a private concert for some button-dick tenor who can only sing his big solo when the house is empty."

I assumed she was referring to the new Riccardo, who was about to sing his first aria of the opera.

I said, "You think that guy has a button dick?"

"No," said Ronda. "Not him. The other one—David what's-his-name."

I corrected her. "You mean Bruce David."

"David, Bruce, what does it matter when someone has two first names? But *this* guy is going to be good. He's just about ready to sing from his balls, and when that happens, he's going to be great. And that'll make April look even better."

"April?" I said. "I thought you liked Carolyn."

"Oh, yeah," said Ronda. "Carolyn's my girl. At least I hope so, someday. But April and Carolyn are a team. They're planning a concert tour together, after the recording sessions are over."

"I heard about that."

"Yeah, well whatever is good for April is good for Carolyn. And that's good for me." Ronda punctuated her words with a wink.

I watched Carolyn Boetz sitting dutifully near the maestro in the pit, just as she had during the orchestra rehearsal the other day. And just as the maestro had done during that rehearsal, he leaned toward Carolyn at various odd moments with a word or a gesture, which she duly transcribed into the score for later reference.

Meanwhile the new tenor was in excellent form, as though the orchestra was nourishing him with royal jelly. Ronda had been right. He was about ready to emerge from his cocoon as an understudy to become a *primo tenore*. After the first ovation from a live audience, he would soar to Olympus.

I told Ronda about the guys backstage missing her in their card game, then repeated the comment one of them had made about her climbing up the ladders to the catwalks.

"I guess I'd better watch my bum," she said. "Some of those guys have no manners. They'll just grab a handful of whatever they want."

"So you do go up on the catwalks sometimes?"

"Yeah," she said. "I told you before, I been up there."

"What about around the time of Adam Pierce's accident? Did you go up then?"

"Hey," said Ronda. "You still think I had something to do with that?"

I said, "I never got to see the police reports, so I don't know what really happened, and I'm still trying to find out."

"Yeah, well," she said. "Just for your information I did go up on the grid myself, after the police finished their reports. I wanted to see what went wrong with my own eyes. I'm kind of like you that way. Seeing is believing."

"And?" I said.

Ronda grinned and her teeth shone in the darkness of the auditorium. "Everything was just fine up there."

I think as far as she was concerned, the matter was settled. The pulleys and the cables and the computer circuits were A-OK. So what more could I want? But Ronda's glibness about the technicalities of her stage sounded less like actual knowledge and more like the bluster of false confidence. It all convinced me that she might be concealing some embarrassing or even incriminating truths.

"And now," she said, "if my crew is playing cards I'd better get back there and crack the whip."

"Don't tell them I told you."

"What, are you afraid of them guys? You gotta toughen up."

Ronda stood up, and as she squeezed past me I noticed her suede gloves hanging from her belt.

I asked her, "You use those gloves for climbing the ladders?"

She turned back to me with a scowl. "I use them for everything," she said. "I might come off as butch, but I still like soft feminine hands."

She swaggered down the center aisle to go backstage and bully her crew, or else kick their butts and take their money. Maybe if I acted more like Ronda Lucca, Lieutenant Branco would respect me more.

I went back downstairs to the wig room. Daniel Carafolio was still in there. Apparently he'd finished pillaging the work I'd produced in his absence. He was seated at his workbench, demure as you please, serenely reweaving strands of hair into a net base. He looked up at me as I entered the room.

"You're not allowed in here," he said. "Get out."

So much for the gentle maiden.

"What have I done now?" I said.

"You were born. That was the first big mistake."

"I did some damn good work while you were gone."

He said, "I agree. Your work is the work of the damned, and I've had to destroy it all. Now, are you going to leave? Or am I going to have to call the head of costume?"

Was that supposed to be a threat? The Head of Costume?

I said, "I'll leave. But I've got to tell you, Daniel, you really should lock yourself away in some SoHo loft with your Maria Callas recordings."

"Spare me your judgments."

"It's a fact, Daniel, not a judgment. Some of us enjoy our work. We don't all use art as an outlet for our neuroses."

"That's fine coming from you," he spluttered. "You're the laziest, most untalented, undependable, untrustworthy, and *neurotic* person I have ever met."

"You ought to check the mirror sometime—if you can find one that won't crack in your face."

"Get out!" he screeched. "Get out before you get what you deserve."

He picked up a heavy hairbrush from his workbench and flung it at me. I ducked. The brush whizzed by overhead and struck a mirror behind me. The glass shattered and fell to the floor. It was all predictable, like a scene from a cheap television serial.

I clucked my tongue. "Seven more years of bad luck."

Daniel glowered from his bench. "I'll get you for this."

"You attempted the assault, pal, not me."

"I'll see you in court!" he shrieked. He grabbed the heavy shears from the bench and threw them wildly—so wildly that they spun far off their intended mark and flew out through the doorway and crashed loudly on the corridor floor. Seconds later two faces peered around the jamb of the open door, one a man's, one a woman's. The female head spoke first.

"We heard some noise from down in the costume room. Do you guys need help?"

Daniel exclaimed, "He tried to kill me!"

The male head said, "I'd better go get the security guard," and he left quickly.

I called after him, "He's lying. He threw those shears at *me.*" But the man didn't come back. I debated whether I should leave the scene myself, in my own best interest. It's hard to convince anyone that you're innocent when you're being falsely accused, especially by a raging queen. You always come out sounding defensive, as though you're scrambling to cover up your heinous deeds, the ones you never committed.

The security guard, a bulky female bodybuilder, came down and took a long and convoluted report. She was the nadir of an unrealized cop, completely enchanted with petty power and bureaucracy, a pretender wearing the mask of the law rather than earning a legitimate appointment, like me. In fact, she was everything I didn't like in a man.

Fortunately, the two people from the costume room had overheard most of the heated exchange between Daniel and me, and they reported the facts as they had happened, without embellishment. I reminded the guard that those flying shears could have injured anyone passing by the door. So although I didn't come out smelling like roses—there was no denying that I'd provoked Daniel—neither did I look or sound like a first-degree murderer. Small blessing.

I went back upstairs to the auditorium, where the first act was just coming to a close. During the following break, I found Carolyn Boetz and congratulated her on her appointment as the maestro's assistant and on the recording contract as well. She blushed when she told me how fortunate she felt, and it was almost convincing.

Then I said, "It's too bad a diva had to die for any of it to happen."

Carolyn retorted, "That had nothing to do with my getting the appointment."

"Maybe not directly. But if Marcella Ostinata was still around, that recording contract might not have happened so easily."

"That's not true," insisted Carolyn. "Deutsche Phonogram was planning to engage April Kilkus from the beginning."

"But Madama Ostinata was interfering with that. And then her death conveniently eliminated any problem."

Carolyn replied, "If you're implying that I killed that woman, you are a fool. Her death meant nothing to me, either personally or professionally. And furthermore, if you don't stop this harassment, I'll get a restraining order on you."

"That's not going to be easy since I'm working for the police."

"Oh!" she cried in exasperation. "I hate people like you."

"Look, Carolyn," I said. "Someone here killed Marcella Ostinata. The same person might have killed Adam Pierce too. If my questions offend you, I apologize. But there's a killer loose. Doesn't that bother you at all?"

"Let the police handle it," she said, as blasé as Marie Antoinette with a cake plate.

"The police includes me."

"Then I'd suggest," she snarled, "if you like playing cops and robbers so much, that you go and become a security guard, and leave the rest of us alone. Some people make better use of their time."

Suddenly Ronda Lucca appeared between us. She might as well have been wearing a neon sign that read: TO THE RESCUE.

"Is there a problem here?" she said.

Carolyn replied, "He's tormenting me."

Her neon sign read: SAVE ME!

Ronda said to me, "Aren't you needed downstairs?"

I considered regaling her with my recent escapades in the wig room, but instead asked her, "Have you seen Jonathan Byers or Rick Jansen today?"

"They took the day off," said Ronda. "Maybe you should do the same. You're beginning to act like the gestapo."

"Took the day off where?" I said.

"I don't keep track of other people's lives," said Ronda. "You oughta try it sometime."

214

"Not my nature," I said with a shrug. Then I spied April Kilkus and Hwang Yung Cho on the other side of the stage. "Bye-bye for now," I said, and set off to stalk the new quarry that had just emerged. But the two singers had already seen me coming toward them, and they bolted from the backstage area. I ran after them, but was foiled by the sudden descent of a gigantic Styrofoam mountain across my path—a deus ex machina, literally, for April and Hwang. From behind me I heard Ronda Lucca yell to one of the crew members.

"That's it, Vinny! Leave it right there for now."

I turned around to see her standing alongside Carolyn Boetz and smiling broadly.

Their tandem sign read: SMALL COP FALL DOWN GO BOOM.

Thanks, Ronda, for your many small kindnesses.

I decided to go outside for some fresh air. In fact, with my recently acquired wheels, I could do some off-campus sleuthing, maybe even find Johnny Byers and his boy-thing in their swank motor hotel, exercising and exorcising their psychosexual selves. With that appalling vision in mind I departed through the stage door, only to find an extraordinary and complementary vision awaiting me outside: Lieutenant Branco was rapt with the shiny new Alfa roadster that Daphne had rented for me. I could almost perceive his younger self face to face with the car of his dreams.

"You like it?" I said.

Branco replied, "Who wouldn't?"

"Some people prefer the Japanese equivalents."

"Too flimsy," said Branco.

A man after my own heart. Now if only I could acquire a lesbian swagger and keep the sports car, Branco and I might become buddies and share manly things like car talk.

Branco said, "There's still no sign of that maid. She sure found a good place to hide."

"You don't think she flew away?"

The cop shook his head. "There's no trace," he said. "Usually when people run, they leave a trail."

"Where do you think she might be?"

Branco nodded toward the performance center.

I said, "In there?"

"It's a big complex with lots of rooms that haven't been used yet. I've got a crew here now sweeping the place from the top floor down. If she's in there, we'll find her."

"At least we know Bruce David and Maurizio aren't in there."

"Funny you should mention those two," said Branco. "I did a follow-up on Bruce David at McLean Hospital. Now, I'm no expert on these matters—with that fancy degree of yours you'd probably know better than me—but I can't help thinking he's faking this breakdown of his. It's like he's acting out the whole thing."

I added, "And badly too."

Branco nodded with a smile, then said, "As soon as I get permission from his doctors, I'm going to grill him good."

"You think he might have killed the soprano?"

Branco said, "I have nothing to go on yet. It's just a feeling that he's hiding behind that mental breakdown."

Just a feeling? Branco had never acknowledged such a thing before.

"Talk about hiding something, Lieutenant." I told him about the photos of Maurizio as an infant and a toddler, and the startling revelations that had followed—that he was not only Marcella Ostinata's son out of wedlock, but that the father had been Daphne Davenport's second husband while they were married.

When I finished Branco made a quiet whistling sound.

Then he said, "You sure found out a lot more than I did. Even with a sign language interpreter all I got from the kid was that he had jumped whoever attacked you that night, and that's how he got hurt himself."

"Any idea who it was?"

"Nothing more from the kid," said Branco.

"Maybe it's your technique."

Grunt went the cop.

"But you do believe now that someone attacked me?" I said.

Branco skewed his mouth into a half smile, then after a vexing pause said, "I guess I do. But I wonder if all this business with photographs doesn't implicate the Davenport woman."

"Daphne?" I said. "It's not possible. What would be her motive?"

"It's obvious, isn't it?" said Branco. "Passion."

"Lieutenant, why would she kill the mother of the child? Wouldn't she have killed her husband?"

"Maybe she did," said Branco. "Do you know how her second husband died?"

"No."

"Well I do," he said. "I checked the records. Ms. Davenport and her second husband were dining alone at their Beacon Hill flat when it happened. Apparently the man choked on a chunk of frozen spinach that wasn't completely thawed."

"That's not funny, Lieutenant."

"I wouldn't make up something like that," he said. "You can read the files yourself."

He offered me a manila envelope, which I refused.

Branco said, "Maybe you don't approve of my theory, but from what you just told me about the husband and the singer and their boy, it's entirely possible that Ms. Davenport took justice into her own hands both times."

It couldn't be. Not Daphne. Surely Branco was toying with me. Perhaps he envied my easy friendship with her, and this was a way to derail me a bit.

Branco ruminated for a moment. "It could even have been the kid, for that matter."

"You think Maurizio killed his own mother?"

"After slicing his mother's throat, it would be relatively easy to cut his own shoulder and make up a story to go with it. I had a case once, open and shut. A fifty-five-year-old guy killed his eighty-six-year-old mother with an ice pick. Multiple wounds to the head. When we got to the scene, all he kept saying was, 'She got what she deserved.'"

"That was then, and this is now," I said. "Maurizio didn't kill Marcella Ostinata, and neither did Daphne. I've already been through all that myself. There's no evidence, both their motives stink, and neither one has the personality of a killer."

"And just what is that?" said Branco.

"They care too much."

"About what?"

"About anything," I said.

I pulled the keys to the Alfa from my pocket and unlocked the driver's door. Branco almost fainted.

"Is this yours?" he gasped.

"For the time being," I said nonchalantly.

"How'd you manage that?" he said.

"It was easy," I said with a shrug. "I needed a car. I visualized it. I affirmed it. I got it."

Branco struggled to make sense of my nonsense.

"Daphne rented it for me," I said. "That's what I meant about her personality. Would a killer do something like that?"

"Depends," said Branco, "on what was at stake."

"At least you're using your imagination, Lieutenant."

Branco grimaced. "You just keep up the good work and maybe I'll even learn to tolerate your insults."

"You want a ride?"

"No, thanks," he said. His voice was flat.

"You can drive," I offered coyly.

Branco wavered a moment. "Maybe another time."

Gotcha.

I hopped in, dropped the top, and zoomed off in my best impersonation of a college fraternity brat. In the rearview mirror I saw Branco shaking his head lamentably.

I decided to go for a drive up along the high coast road. The fresh air and the ocean would help me sort things out. I felt that I was getting nowhere in the quest for Marcella Ostinata's killer. Not that I had any personal interest in finding him or her. But as Branco's deputy, I did want my merit badge sewn on with gold thread. And the only way to get that would be to deliver the killer to Branco, in name if not in person.

Many people stood to benefit in some way from the death of Marcella Ostinata. What I hoped to uncover during my drive that afternoon was the link between her death and the apparently accidental death of Adam Pierce. But the only person who had gained from his death was Rick Jansen, and even that gain was questionable considering the tenuous, one-dimensional nature of his relationship with Jonathan Byers. What was to stop Jonathan Byers from dumping Ricky again and running off with the next tawny-skinned Apollo he met? Despite Rick Jansen's cultivated muscles, he would never be tan enough to satisfy Jon Byers's apparent fondness for dark-skinned men.

So, if only for simplicity, I had to assume that Adam Pierce's death had been accidental, just as the police had determined. But I still believed the accident had been with the victim, not with the event. The intended victim had been Marcella Ostinata, but a fluke had occurred and Adam Pierce was slain instead.

I was back to square one.

Who could have released that scrim to fall on Marcella at that moment? One name leaped out from all the others, and I felt kind of bad about it, because I was beginning to see Ronda Lucca as a possible new role model. How could I continue to do that if she turned out to be a murderer? (Sorry, Ronda. Murderess.) Well, I suppose even mentors have foibles. What I needed was objectivity. I would have to rely on cool reason, just like Branco, if I was to be a good deputy for him. And I knew that with her expert knowledge of stagecraft and her all-powerful computer, Ronda Lucca could easily have released that scrim. The only problem is that she had badly miscalculated its trajectory. So instead she found another opportunity, and that's where her rock-climbing came in. With those skills Ronda could easily have scaled the back wall of Daphne's house and got into Marcella Ostinata's bedroom.

The only real problem with Ronda Lucca as the killer is that her motive was null. It was all tangled up with the career of Carolyn Boetz. And to me unrequited love just wasn't a strong enough reason to kill a third person. Ronda was too entrenched in pragmatism for such sentimental mush. That's why I chose her as my role model—to learn how to become strong and manly. Then again, when cornered, she sure could be a passionate little beast.

While I was being coldhearted, I realized that Maurizio could have released that scrim too. According to Ronda he spent a lot of time backstage, which gave him ample opportunity. But then, Ronda may have been deflecting suspicion from herself. Even if Maurizio had released that scrim and missed his intended target, could he have later executed his mother with a knife? He seemed too much like a terrified wild animal to commit a violent act that required such fortitude and planning. Running away he was good at. A strategically devised beheading, not so. In fact, I wondered if he really knew Marcella Ostinata was his mother. It was only the maestro's words that said so.

Could *he* have killed Marcella? But why would he? Did she have some hold on him? His directorial powers did seem to revive after her death, as though he had been freed from great mental and emotional constraints. Was killing Marcella the maestro's final victory over her?

Jonathan Byers had been openly relieved by Marcella's death. She would have ruined his production, and with her out of the picture, his self-serving vision of Verdi's opera could be realized. But why not just break her contract? Pay her off and send her packing. In fact, why had she been engaged in the first place for a production that was so blatantly opposed to her temperament? There was murkiness to be cleared up there. Perhaps as a British knight Sir Jonathan had seen Marcella Ostinata as a dragon to be slain. His sense of duty had prevailed, and off came her head. But who was the metaphorical damsel in distress?

And what about Carolyn Boetz? April Kilkus? Hwang Yung Cho? Like Ronda Lucca, their motives were too weak. The only benefit of Marcella's death was to their careers, and none of the three seemed hell-bent enough on success to kill for it—not like Marcella herself. Then again, the two singers were excellent actors.

Then there was Daniel Carafolio. A small untamed voice inside me said, Too bad he didn't get it in the neck. Who would miss him anyway? All he did was rage like a mad queen. Just as Jonathan Byers had done for Marcella, I would probably express good riddance to a dead Daniel.

And finally I could make no sense of Daphne killing Marcella. For what? A stolen brooch? An infidelity committed over twenty-five years ago? Besides, Daphne was incapable of killing someone. She couldn't even look at blood, or so she claimed. Then again, she had got through medical school, which meant she would know how to kill effectively. And she was a psychiatrist too, among whom rank some of the world's most accomplished actors. So the whole story about fainting at the sight of blood could have been just that: a magnificent feint. And anyone can pretend to faint, especially into Lieutenant Branco's big strong arms. And I also wondered to what extent Daphne's maternal, womanly, jealous instincts had been awakened by the discovery of Maurizio's father being her late husband Sid. Had they kicked in to the point where she'd kill her rival?

Facts, theories, and hallucinations, and none of them pointed anywhere. I quickly became tired of trying to reason the matter out. It's a Gemini shortcoming anyway, the brief attention span with logic. And though I yearned to become tougher and more manly—macho mentor be damned—it was time to summon a forgotten ally: good old-fashioned feminine intuition. Intuition told me there was no sense going back to the opera house that afternoon. I'd been fired anyway, so I could devote myself full-time as Branco's deputy in the pursuit of truth, justice, and the American Way.

27

My first stop that afternoon was a visit to Maurizio in the local hospital. It seemed the least I could do, since the young man had been hurt while saving my life. Besides, as Lieutenant Branco had already observed, I had a certain affinity for puppylike young men from other countries, though my partner Rafik was more the lone panther type.

The small Abigail hospital was an exercise in upscale architecture. Perhaps medical science was evolving to the point where decorative veneer was challenging technology in terms of healing power. The lobby was a glass-walled atrium landscaped with grassy hillocks, ground shrubbery, and some deciduous trees, all to maintain a sense of season, I guess. I half expected to hear birds twittering among the overhead branches and to see small animals scampering along the Turkish carpets that graced the marble floors. Along the corridor to Maurizio's room I saw that no patient's room had more than two beds, and no room had more than one occupant. Abigail appeared to be a healthy town.

Maurizio was asleep when I entered his room, but as I approached his bed, his eyes snapped open. He gazed at me and made quiet mewling sounds. The arm of the injured shoulder had been immobilized with a rigid splint, and an IV rig was attached to it. But Maurizio's free hand wasted no time in finding one of my own and grabbing it and pressing it onto his crotch. I jerked back reflexively while a vision flashed through my mind of Carmen Miranda patriotically comforting all those lonely injured GIs. Maurizio gave me his sad-eyed look, and I knew what he wanted, but it just wasn't something I could do for him. I was there to visit, not to grope. My aunt Letta liked to tell the story of when her husband was sick for the last time, and whenever she'd go to see him he always tried to unbutton her blouse. But he was so weak that he fumbled, so she'd oblige him and haul out one of her substantial breasts for him to fondle. I suppose it was a way of passing the time or easing the pain or something like that. It sure as hell disavowed any notion that the body's power to heal was a mystical and sacred process, and that a hospital was like a church. Aunt Letta was never idealistic, especially in mundane matters like sex. Maybe that's why coming out of my distracted reverie I found my hand comfortably resettled in the hospitality suite of Maurizio's anatomy.

I stayed with him for a half hour, and nothing more happened, no dramatic splashing or anything like that. Just some warm, friendly strokes until he drifted off. Then I slipped my hand out from under the blanket—he stirred only slightly—and I left the room. At the nurse's station I learned that Maurizio would have to stay another day or so until the deep flesh wound was healing properly and his white blood count had fallen. At least I knew he was in good hands, so to speak.

I drove into downtown Abigail, where I hadn't been since my arrival at the train station eight days ago. I wanted to find a gift for Daphne, something that would help relieve the effects of the horrible events during the previous week. I found the perfect thing in a small weaver's shop nestled within an artisan's cooperative building. My find was a summer shawl of raw silk, woven with bold colorful rectangles of varying sizes along its six-foot length. I could easily see Daphne draping that length of silk—as inspired as a work of art—luxuriously about herself.

As the young woman who had created the piece wrapped it for me, she admitted modestly that she felt it was the best thing she had ever done. "And it was almost effortless," she added.

I told her I occasionally shared the same experience when a hairstyle worked itself out that way, as though some divine spirit guided my hands, and all I had to do was snip, snip, snip until the masterpiece was finished.

After shopping I felt the need for coffee, and I found a small café tucked in a faraway upstairs corner of the cooperative building. It was the perfect place for a discreet rendezvous. And as though my observation had the power of induction, I discovered two familiar faces in a cozy tête-à-tête at one of the small café tables—Jonathan Byers and Rick Jansen.

I said to Byers, "I missed you today at the opera house."

He replied acidly, "A man can take a day off."

"Especially with his boy," I added.

"No one's complaining about that," said Rick. He glanced at Sir Jon as if to seek confirmation. "Are they?" he said.

Byers remarked, "It's no one's bloody business!"

As I had guessed earlier, Jonathan Byers and Rick Jansen had spent the morning and afternoon together, probably in their hotel room, dancing the horizontal tango while the rest of the cast was rehearsing. It was not a pretty picture in my mind, the two of them coupling. But when is penetrative sex ever really pretty?

I said, "I was just visiting my friend at the hospital."

"Is that so?" said Byers, hardly interested. "Aren't you the good little Samaritan."

I said, "He got hurt trying to rescue me from an attacker the other night."

"How chivalrous!" said Sir Jonathan.

"Was he hurt bad?" asked Rick.

"Bad enough," I said. "The wound got infected."

Rick said, "I had a friend once, died from blood poisoning."

I said, "Well, my friend is recuperating."

"He's lucky," said Rick.

"What is this?" spat Sir Jon. "A screen test for Doctor Fucking Kildare?" He pushed his chair back so violently he almost upset the flimsy café table. "Let's get out of here," he said to Rick. "Now that our privacy has been violated."

I said, "You're not exactly an exemplar of etiquette."

"The difference is," said Byers, "I've earned the right to behave the way I do. I have genius. And what are you besides twaddle?"

"Come on," said Rick, coaxing the other man away from the table. "Don't make any more trouble."

Jonathan Byers brushed Rick's hand away sharply. Then he set off by himself from the café, and none too steadily.

Ricky spoke quietly to me. "Sorry about that. He's been drinking all night and all morning. This usually happens just before the first run-through."

"No problem," I said. But I was puzzled that the boy was suddenly apologizing for the daddy's behavior. They seemed to switch roles easily. "Will he be all right tomorrow?"

"Oh, sure," said Rick pleasantly. "I'll see to that. That's my real job anyway, taking care of Jon. The rest of it is just, er . . ."

"Recreation?" I offered.

Ricky cocked his head. "Yeah," he said. "I guess that's a good word for it. Recreation."

I added, "For pay."

"So what?" he snarled. "Everything has a price."

"Even devoted love."

"Yeah," he said, his hackles raised now. "Even that. You don't have to act so superior. It's just another job, except this one's a damn good gig."

I said, "Then you'd better watch out that someone doesn't snatch it from you."

"Go fuck yourself," he said. He tried to squint menacingly, but it didn't work. Poor Ricky still didn't realize that blonds cannot be menacing. Dyed blonds can. But natural blonds come off hopelessly silly when they try to look dangerous.

He tromped off after Jonathan Byers.

And I wondered just how far he'd go to remain daddy's boy.

When I arrived back at the estate that evening, I first ran down to the cottage to hide the shawl I'd bought for Daphne. If I gave it to her that same night, it might appear that I was just playing tit for tat: You rent me a sports car, I'll buy you a shawl. I figured I'd wait a few days, so she'd still have it in time for the opening night performance.

I just about got in the door to the big house when she met me in the foyer.

"I thought I heard the car," she said, "but I didn't see you. Is it running all right?"

"It's a dream come true," I said.

"Oh, good," she said. "The maestro is in the library, and we've already been celebrating the success of his rehearsal today." Then she leaned close and said, "But I wanted a moment with you alone."

She led me into the cloak room directly off the foyer and closed the door behind us. We sat on an upholstered bench, and Daphne told me what had happened that afternoon. Apparently she had received news of the altercation between Daniel Carafolio and myself in the wig room that morning, and also that I had been promptly dismissed from my duties as his assistant. I explained to her that after such a violent incident I had no intention of showing up to work for him anymore.

"Of course not," said Daphne. "Tomorrow morning I shall see about dismissing him instead."

"Don't," I said quickly. "They'll all scream nepotism."

"Let them," said Daphne. "I don't care."

"I don't mean to sound ungrateful, but the job just isn't that important to me."

"Well then," she said, "damn the wigs and let that horrid little man do them all by himself! But wouldn't you like to stay here with me until opening night and help the lieutenant with his case?"

Does a wild bear shit in the woods?

I'd get to drive the Alfa while I earned my deputy badge with Lieutenant Branco. And no more Daniel Carafolio!

Things were really looking up.

28

The next morning I headed to the opera house as usual, even though technically I was no longer employed by the opera festival. I was, however, still Branco's deputy.

The rehearsal schedule posted for that day read: PCA +, which meant piano, chorus, principal artists, and others. That rehearsal, sometimes called the "piano dress rehearsal," was a major milestone in the production schedule. It required the singers to prove their mettle under the added pressure of a run-through without a book or score at hand. Where the *Sitzprobe* of the previous day had been the maestro's first opportunity to bring all his musical forces together, the first staged run-through of the opera would be Jonathan Byers's moment of truth. For a final brief moment in the entire production, the music would be subordinate to the staged drama. There would be no orchestra that day, for it was too expensive to pay all the players for a trial run. Instead two pianos would be used in the pit, with Carolyn Boetz and Rick Jansen at the keyboards. The maestro would conduct from there.

I found a place to watch from backstage, on the far side of Ronda Lucca's booth. I'd be out of the way, and I'd have a relatively clear view of everything happening onstage, and even of the orchestra pit. I saw Rick Jansen trying to settle down at his piano in the pit. He seemed almost clumsy and uncoordinated, with none of the muscular astuteness or feisty volatility he'd displayed in our previous encounters. Perhaps the immense musical task he faced, coupled with his lack of skill to execute it, had forced him to dose up with tranquilizers—the American version of Dutch courage. Or perhaps he'd been lobotimized during a kinky session of limit-seeking with Sir Jonathan the night before. Whatever the reason for Rick's sluggishness, poor Carolyn Boetz would have to be doubly alert with him playing that morning.

Once rehearsal was under way, I made another discovery. Unlike the *Sitzprobe* of the previous day, when the music produced by the voices and the orchestra often rose divinely above the ordinary creatures who were making the sounds, the first staged run-through was utter chaos. Everything that could go wrong onstage did. Entrances and exits were fumbled, musical cues missed, whole segments of solos and ensembles omitted, and blocking was reinvented willy-nilly. In short, as an opera, the show had become a sudden mess.

For his part throughout the first act, Jonathan Byers sat in the auditorium and said nothing. Either he was seething inwardly from the apparent disorder onstage, or else he was coldly analyzing in molecular detail every aspect of his direction that would ultimately succeed and those that were doomed to fail. Whichever it was, Sir Jon made no critical comment whatsoever, save an occasional remark about a curtain cue, or a light cue, or a costume cue. But for the stage action itself, for his very own creation, Jonathan Byers that morning remained a cipher.

Not so some other folks, for that first run-through was also an opportunity to try out some costume mock-ups for the soloists, as well as the trickier wigs for the chorus members. However, without my expert assistance, Daniel Carafolio had been unable to fit all the wigs properly. As a result many of them had slipped around on the heads of the singers while they were singing onstage. Now, it's an involuntary reflex when you feel something on your head about to fall off, you put your hand up there to grab it and hold it. But with Miss Hissy Fit of the wig room, such a reflex had dire consequences. During the short break after act one, Daniel appeared onstage to address the chorus members. His first words came out as though he had just endured the biggest disappointment of his life, and he was fighting to hold back bitter tears.

"You people are just not cooperating." He sounded desolate. "How many times did I tell you this morning, you do *not* touch your wig."

One unsuspecting chorus member protested, "But they don't stay put. It's hard to sing with a big blob moving around on your head."

"My wigs do not move," Daniel said quickly. "Your scalp must have shriveled."

Another singer remarked, "We have a lot to do onstage, and the wigs are too loose."

"My wigs fit perfectly," contended Daniel. "If you knew how to move properly, you wouldn't have these problems."

"Why can't you just make the wigs tighter?" came another naive voice. "It's an easy enough job for someone who knows how."

"I am doing my job perfectly!" snapped Daniel. "If you insist on complaining and touching your wigs, one of us is going to have to leave." A hush descended among the culprits onstage. "The question is," continued Daniel, "is it going to be me or you? Because *I'll* leave, and gladly. I don't deserve this kind of treatment from anyone, least of all a bunch of *chorus* singers."

Dead silence throughout the house.

Daniel said, "Is that what you all want then? Shall I just go now?"

There were clear murmurings of "yes" and "amen" among the chorus members.

"Fine then!" said Daniel, and he stormed offstage.

As Daniel rushed past Ronda Lucca at her desk, she turned toward me and drew her finger across her throat. "I'll finish him off if you want," she said. "Then you can have the wig room all to yourself."

"No need," I said. "I've been fired."

"When?"

"Yesterday."

"Who?"

"Him."

"Then why are you hanging around here? You got the opera bug or something?"

"No," I said. "I have other work to do."

"For that cop," said Ronda.

I nodded.

"Yeah," she said. "It figures you'd like working for him."

"Not for," I protested mildly. "With."

"*Hah!*" went Ronda Lucca.

And just as she was about to announce a break for the cast and crew, a man appeared at her desk. He was from costumes, the same one who'd caught Daniel and me fighting the day before. He asked Ronda if he could make an announcement before the break.

"Sure," she said. "Ask and you shall receive."

Meanwhile the guy was looking sideways at me, as if to say, How dare you show your face in this theater again? Then he went onstage and announced that a pair of very expensive leather gauntlets was missing from the costume department, and if anyone knew their whereabouts, to please return them to him.

I said to Ronda, "I wonder if they're for the show, or from his private collection."

"Definitely not his," she said. "Unless they're elbow-length white lace."

When he walked back past the desk he thanked Ronda, then asked me if I'd seen the gauntlets.

I shrugged at his accusing tone and said, "You'd have to ask my husband. He's in charge of the family toys."

"Where is he?" said the man, unwittingly seizing the bait.

"In Paris," I said dryly.

He walked off in a huff.

I remarked to Ronda, "Was it something I said?"

"Babe," she answered, "I think it's something you are."

Then she announced over the public-address system that the cast and crew could take a twenty-minute break before running act two. As everyone dispersed for the break, I saw Hwang Yung Cho and

April Kilkus on the opposite side of the stage. They seemed to be inseparable, like an interracial version of the Bobbsey twins. Okay, they were supposedly married. But don't married couples ever walk and talk and wet separately? I headed across the stage toward them, but this time I was prepared for them to run away, so I readied myself to run too. What a surprise then, when only April vanished, and Hwang stayed and braced himself for a confrontation with me, the indelicate deputy.

"Do you have a minute?" I asked.

"When are you going to stop bothering us?" he said.

"When I find out who killed Marcella Ostinata."

"Then you can leave me alone," he said. "Because I assure you I'm not your man. I am an artist, a singer, and a refined human being. But I am not an executioner."

"Art isn't a protective shield, Hwang. Once upon a time I saw a movie. It was set in one of those agricultural outreaches in Central Asia, and the sheep herders used an unusual and extremely refined method of slaughtering their animals. First, they would play a game to catch the animal to be killed. I guess the period of playful romping was supposed to put the chosen animal at ease to face its destiny. And once they caught it, they'd hold it close to them, almost in a loving embrace, as a reward for being such a good sport. And then they'd take a very sharp knife—a stiletto really—and pierce the live animal's chest. But the blade was so sharp the animal didn't even feel it cut through the flesh. Then they'd reach inside the chest cavity and find the animal's beating heart. And then they'd strangle the living heart with their bare hand until the animal expired peaceably in their arms, within seconds."

Hwang said, "Why are you telling me this?"

"Because it proves how refined, even artistic some people can be about death."

"Are you saying I could do something like that because I'm Asian?"

"No," I replied. "But I do believe you could do it based on your claim, as you just now said, that you are an artist and you are so very refined."

Hwang said, "You don't have a shred of evidence against me. No one does. I've been completely cooperative with the police, and they believe me. Now if you don't cut this out and leave April and me alone, I'm going to report you to the police and get you thrown off the premises. You're becoming a menace."

"Hardly a menace," I said. "An annoyance, perhaps."

"I don't care what you call it. I just want you to stop."

I said, "You'd have to ask Lieutenant Branco to take me off the case. I work for him."

"I'll do that," said Hwang.

He turned and started walking away.

"By the way," I said. "You and April sounded great yesterday."

He turned back to face me. "What's that supposed to mean?"

"It means that as awful as I appear to be, I still enjoy hearing you and April sing."

"If you really like our singing," he said, "that's your one and only saving grace." And he walked away.

Then from out in the auditorium came the loud, accusing voice of Daniel Carafolio. And the rest of us couldn't help overhearing from the stage area. He was addressing Jonathan Byers. Rick Jansen was with them.

"Why don't you just return them?" Daniel said sharply.

"Return what?" said Byers.

"Don't they pay you enough to buy your own sex toys?"

Byers said, "What are you jabbering about?"

"I mean you pilfered those gauntlets from the costume department."

"That's outrageous!" said Byers.

"I agree," said Daniel. "It's as petty as taking paper clips from a law firm. But I saw you do it."

"You saw nothing," said Byers.

"You might as well keep them," said Daniel. "They're replaceable. And who would want them now with your sex juices all over them?"

"You watch your filthy mouth," said Rick.

But even Daniel seemed to recognize idle threats coming from a natural blond.

"Look, junior, I saw your old man coming out of the costume room last week, and he looked mighty suspicious."

Byers said, "You didn't see me take anything."

"But I saw you take something in Spoleto," said Daniel.

Rick said, "You'd better shut up now."

"Oooh," cooed Daniel. "Are you threatening me? Or are you demanding satisfaction? Is that it? Is there some code of honor at work here? When is the duel going to be? And will you wear your *gauntlets?*" Then he cackled and crowed loudly as he walked away from them. "Beware! Beware! Thieves among us!"

Rick made an aggressive move toward Daniel, but Jonathan Byers restrained him and quieted him down. I guess it was his turn to be the pacifist. If Sir Jonathan ever needed more theatrical grist for this production, he could certainly exploit the day-to-day occurrences offstage.

In the pit, hardly affected by the commotion over the gauntlets, the maestro and Carolyn Boetz returned to their quiet conference about the score.

Ronda announced ten minutes to the act two curtain.

And life in the theater went on.

I stayed through to the end of the rehearsal, out of respect for Verdi if no one else. It was the first staged run-through of his opera, after all. This show would never again be in such a raw, wounded state, and it needed all the psychic help it could get. At the end of the day, moments after the cue for the final curtain, Ronda Lucca made a closing announcement over the PA system.

"Thank you everyone," she said. "Congratulations on getting through a really difficult rehearsal. Thank you for your patience. And thank you all for your cooperation. This is going to be a great show. See you all tomorrow at ten."

I was bewildered. As the stage manager, Ronda was the last person I'd expect to show such pleasantness after a day like that one.

It was after four o'clock when I was heading out the stage door. Just inside that doorway is the glass-panelled booth where the security guard sits. I saw Lieutenant Branco in there going through the guard's reports, probably for the one describing my waltz around the wig room floor with Daniel Carafolio on the previous day. Branco looked up, saw me, and then motioned me inside.

"Have you eaten yet?" he said.

"No."

"Wanna grab a bite with me?"

Oh, would I.

"Let me call Daphne," I said.

"Why? You got a curfew or something?"

"I just want to tell her I won't be home for supper."

"She's not your mother," said Branco.

"Wouldn't you call your patrol mate?"

"I haven't had one for a long time," he said. Then he made a scornful little grunt, as if to imply that fellow cops were further up the evolutionary ladder than friends anyway.

Fifteen minutes later we were reading the menus in a cruelty-free charcuterie that had just opened in the performance center complex. As a promotional special they were offering two for one on everything, including all beverages. Still, with no animal tissue available for consumption, I was surprised that Branco had agreed on it. We ordered deluxe vegiburgers, which the menu guaranteed would "satisfy like the real thing." I wondered why anyone would want vegetables to satisfy like meat? It was like looking for secular Christmas cards to send to atheist friends.

We both ordered beers, which I assumed were also cruelty-free. Then while we waited for the food to arrive, Branco told me that his search for Mathilde within the performance center had proved fruitless. He asked me what had happened since we saw each other the previous afternoon. I started to tell him everything—the attempted assault by Daniel Carafolio, the defensive posturings of Jonathan Byers and Rick Jansen, the professionalism of Ronda Lucca, the serenity of the maestro—but he interrupted my litany.

"I'd like facts," he said brusquely. "Not interpretations."

"Okay," I said. "How about the fact that Daniel Carafolio claims he saw Jonathan Byers steal a pair of leather gauntlets from the costume room?"

Branco replied sharply, "That's hearsay." But when he saw how his bluntness had startled me, he added, "But it's intriguing hearsay. I'll talk to Carafolio about it." Then he thought a moment and said, "Leather gauntlets, eh? I wonder why Byers would want something like that."

"I'll find out," I said defiantly. "And it won't be hearsay this time. I'll get it straight from the horse's mouth."

"Don't get touchy, Stan. I know you're working hard on the case, but you've got a lot to learn."

"So how do I learn? Do I have to go to police school?"

Branco paused uncertainly before saying, "I'm not sure it would benefit someone like you."

"You think I can't cut it?"

The faux burgers arrived before he could answer. As we seasoned them and assembled them into sandwiches, our conversation took an abrupt turn.

Branco asked, "How's that car running?"

"If I had money to burn, I'd probably buy it."

He took a big bite from his burger, chewed a few moments, then swallowed with some effort.

"This tastes like it's good for you," he said. He opened the roll and sprinkled hot sauce liberally on the burger.

Then he reminded me to keep the Alfa's engine revved high.

"They're tough," he said. "You can really push them hard, but you've gotta do it with finesse. Do you know how to power-shift?"

"Nope."

"I'll show you how sometime. That'll give you a real charge."

Somehow I wasn't sure I'd ever be ready for a driving lesson with Mr. Vito Branco. Meanwhile he attacked his sandwich again and washed it down with some beer.

"Nothing a good dose of hot pepper can't fix," he said, then flashed his dazzling white teeth at me.

After that we talked about his house and his garden and my forthcoming vacation in Europe, and gradually I realized that I was actually being a pal with Branco, shooting the breeze of real life over burgers and beer. And then, inexplicably, a wave of nausea washed over me, and I broke out in a cold sweat. I tried a sip of ice water, but it didn't help. And I realized there was no way I would get another thing into my mouth and down my throat while I was at that table. In fact, I could hardly talk. Branco noticed and asked if I was all right, but all I could do was excuse myself and leave the restaurant pronto.

I drove back to the estate and went directly to the cottage. I couldn't even face Daphne in my strange condition. I drew a warm bath, dumped in a handful of mineral salts, then slid into the water. Within seconds I found myself weeping quietly.

Even then I didn't recognize what had happened to me.

29

Next morning I was having breakfast in the gazebo with Daphne. It seemed a long while since we had enjoyed the morning ocean together. Then I realized the last time had been the morning Marcella Ostinata's body had been discovered.

Daphne said, "I missed your 'good night' last night."

"I was in a state," I said apologetically.

"A state?"

"I think the Victorians called it hysteria."

"Yes," said Daphne. "Freud too. Quite sexist, you know."

"I know," I said. "But it's the only way to describe my behavior. There I was, calmly having a burger and a beer with Lieutenant Branco, friendly-like. And then without warning I had an uncontrollable urge to flee."

Daphne said, "I think the moderns call it a panic attack."

"But it was beyond anything mental and emotional," I said. "It was physical, and it was in my whole body."

"Adrenaline is strong stuff," said Daphne.

"But what caused it?"

"Ah," she said knowingly. "That's quite another matter."

At that moment Parker appeared at the gazebo with the portable telephone. "For Mr. Kraychik," he said.

It was Branco. He told me to report to the opera house immediately. He didn't even ask me how I was, which shouldn't have surprised me. Real men probably didn't do that either. I apologized to Daphne and left my breakfast unfinished.

"I understand dear," she said coolly. "Duty calls."

The front of the opera house was lined with police cruisers. When I pulled around to the back parking lot, near the stage door, I found the area cordoned off. An ambulance was parked and awaiting its tenant. I identified myself at the stage door and was admitted inside. I found Lieutenant Branco downstairs in the wig room. On the floor was the body of Daniel Carafolio. Sticking up out of his chest was the jewel-encrusted handle of a stiletto. The knife appeared to be larger than life, like a theatrical prop whose sinister aspect had to chill viewers far up in the second balcony. A pair of suede work gloves had been jammed into his mouth. They were disturbingly familiar.

Branco saw me standing in the doorway. He came over to me and said quietly, "How do you feel this morning?"

"It must have been that vegiburger."

"I thought it might be something else," he said with a peculiar warmth in his eyes. Then he was all business again.

"What about this?" he said, pointing to Daniel's body. "No love lost there either, right?"

That one word—*either*—gave me pause. Either Daniel or whom?

"I won't miss him," I said. "I suppose that's a sorry thing to say about any dead person."

Branco grunted. "Have you seen those gloves before?"

"I'm not sure," I lied.

"Well, I have," said the cop. "I'd like you to go and do a little excavating before I talk to her."

"You mean the stage manager?"

Branco nodded. "That's right. I knew you'd seen those gloves before."

"No, I just assumed—"

He interrupted me. "You've got your assignment. Now go do it." Branco returned to his manly duties. Just then one of his assistants called out, "Lieutenant!" and ran up to him. "You might want to see this." He held up a sealed plastic bag. As Branco took the bag I saw that it contained a pair of leather gauntlets. The assistant said, "We found them in the costume room."

Branco studied the contents for a moment. "Looks like blood," he said.

"That's what I thought," said the assistant eagerly.

"Get it to the lab," said Branco. "And remind them to look inside too."

The assistant said, "I'm sure they will, sir."

"Just remind them!" snapped Branco. He turned back into the wig room, leaving the poor rookie to wonder why his zeal hadn't been appreciated. I followed Branco into the wig room.

"There's something else you should know, Lieutenant."

"What's that?" said Branco, his patience clearly spent.

"Regarding those gauntlets, yesterday I overheard Daniel mention something to Jonathan Byers about Spoleto."

"The opera festival in Italy?"

"I guess so. He alluded that Byers had stolen something there as well."

"More hearsay," said Branco.

"But Daniel had also told me the other day that Spoleto is where Jonathan Byers and Rick Jansen first met each other."

Branco ruminated awhile on those tidbits, then said, "I'll put a data search on it." He scribbled a note in his little black book. Then he looked up at me. "Something else?" he said.

"No."

"Then get to work."

"Yes, boss," I said, feigning a salute.

Branco just turned away.

I trotted upstairs to the backstage area to dispatch my mission with Ronda Lucca. I acted surprised to see her there.

"You're here," I said.

"We've got a tech rehearsal in an hour. Where the hell is everybody?"

"Ronda, the cops are all over the place downstairs."

"I know. I called them." She shrugged. "Big deal. The wig man is dead. Is the world supposed to stop turning?"

"He was murdered."

"I'm not surprised," she said. "My big problem this morning—actually I got two big problems. One, where is everybody? And two, where are my work gloves?"

"The gray suede ones?" I said.

"Yeah," Ronda replied. "You seen 'em?"

"Don't look now, doll, but that body downstairs in the wig room . . . ?"

"Yeah?"

"I think your gloves are in his mouth."

"Jesus, Mary, and Joseph. Are you shittin' me?"

"No. They were sticking right out there, like a big old leather tongue."

"Cripes, I didn't even see them. All I seen was that knife stuck in his chest, and I ran like hell. It was like something on TV, y'know? All I could think was, Call the fucking cops."

"You did that right, at least."

"Yeah, well, now I need them damn gloves. I ought to just go and pull them out."

"Uh, Ronda, you might want to reconsider."

"What? You think just because some asshole takes my gloves and shoves them down some guy's throat the cops are gonna say I'm guilty? That's not procedure, pal. That's bad writing."

"I agree, Ronda. But like you said, this is like something on TV."

Heedless of my words, she headed toward the stairway, then suddenly stopped and turned around. She looked back at me with a resigned sort of half-grin.

"Y'know," she said. "Maybe I don't need them gloves so bad right now."

"Good thinking," I said and walked over to her. "But I wonder how they got in his mouth?"

Ronda said, "How do you think? Someone put them there."

I eyed her suspiciously. "Who might that be?"

She said, "If you're thinking what I think you're thinking, you're full of shit."

"Then why are your gloves in Daniel's mouth?"

Ronda said, "Obviously someone wants to frame me."

"Who?"

"How should I know?"

"Ronda, no one knows better than you who it might be."

"Hey, what is this? Twenty questions?"

"Branco wants to know."

"Then let *him* ask me."

I'd got her defenses up too high even for me to scale them. Maybe Branco was right. Maybe I didn't have what it took to be a good investigator. Fine, then. Let him do his own questioning.

There was still an hour until the ten o'clock rehearsal. Under the circumstances it should have been cancelled, but since Jonathan Byers had continued rehearsing the same day Marcella Ostinata's body had been found, it was unlikely that he'd halt the schedule just because the wig master had been exterminated. So I went back downstairs. I figured I could stand around the stage door and note everyone's reactions as they arrived at the opera house and found yet another corpse in their midst. But there was nothing much to discover. The whole lot of them—the maestro, Carolyn Boetz, April Kilkus, Hwang Yung Cho, Jonathan Byers, Rick Jansen, the new tenor—they were all unfazed by Daniel Carafolio's death. If anything, they were all annoyed by the inconvenience of identifying themselves to the police and then explaining why they were there. The most important aspect of their lives at the moment was the day's rehearsal, and beyond that, the swift approach of opening night, only three days away.

The run-through that day was the official technical rehearsal. It was the full opera, done all the way through, including lights, blocking, set changes, special effects, props, and some costume changes. But everything was performed cue-to-cue rather than note-by-note. So rather than have, say, April Kilkus come onstage and sing one of Amelia's arias, during tech April would get her cue to enter, then make the entrance and start the aria. But then the operatic clock would stop while all the hundreds of little operations of stagecraft that comprised that scene would be activated and run and rerun until every element was securely established. Lights and gels were adjusted, sight lines re-examined, props were placed and replaced, costume mock-ups applied, and then all was run again from the start of the cue. Then finally the operatic clock would start up again and race forward to the next cue, where the same thing would happen all over again. Tech rehearsal was like watching a film on a VCR by using the fast forward button to locate a scene, and then playing that scene in excruciating frame-by-frame slow motion to watch the molecular components of the movie, and then zoom-zooming on to the next scene. You'd almost think it would take less time, since very few notes were being sung. But tech always took longer than the full-length show because of the endless starting and stopping. Rafik once told me it's especially agonizing for the performers because it works against the natural momentum that comes from building a character onstage, in the continuum of moment-to-moment growth. In fact, it's very common after tech for performers to be suddenly insecure about their roles.

At one point the costume designer approached me in a desperate panic and offered to rehire me at Daniel's salary, if I would agree to make all the necessary adjustments to the wigs. Of course I accepted, but on two conditions. The first was that they hire someone else for the rest of the run, since I had plans to be in Europe with hubby. The designer agreed to that one easily. The second condition was that I have some creative freedom with the styling. As I expected he resisted on that point, then reconsidered his position, and then reluctantly agreed. And from that moment every wig behaved perfectly under my expert hand.

After rehearsal Branco met me outside the stage door.

"Is that offer of a drive still good?" he asked.

"Sure," I said. "You want to drive?"

"I'll ride this time."

I said, "I'm not exactly a hotshot driver."

"In time," said Branco.

We headed up along the ocean road, and Branco told me that the medical examiner had established Daniel Carafolio's time of death to be sometime between five and six o'clock the previous evening, right around the time when Branco and I were having vegiburgers.

I said, "At least I have a perfect alibi. I was dining with a cop."

"Except," said Branco, "you had that damn panic attack and ran out on me. I can't testify where you went after that."

"Testify? Are my whereabouts in question?"

"Probably not," said Branco. "What's more important right now are the lab reports."

More important than my alibi?

Branco continued, "The lab just called from Boston. As I'd suspected, the blood on those leather gauntlets is Marcella Ostinata's."

"So you're assuming the killer wore the gauntlets when he slashed Marcella's throat."

Branco corrected me. "He or she," he said. "But yes, that's the way I see it. The lab also examined the inside of the gauntlets, and they came up with a fragment of hair in one of the fingers. I'm betting it came off the knuckle of the killer."

"Or anyone else who had his—or her—hand in there at any time."

"That's true," said Branco with an ambiguous nod. "But all I care about is whether it came from someone on my list."

"Who's on that list?"

"You know the cast as well as I do."

He named the names I'd named before.

I downshifted into a tight turn. The road wasn't banked and I took it a bit too fast, causing the rubber to squeal.

"Tires need air," I said breezily, but when I looked at Branco his face was flat.

I said, "Is the hair fragment a man's or a woman's?"

"Hard to tell," said Branco. "It's just a small piece."

"But you're hoping it's the killer's," I said.

"If we get a match it would make things real easy," replied Branco. "I'm still waiting for a DNA analysis. Then I'll know whose it is, since the gauntlets had direct contact with the skin of the wearer."

"Just like underwear," I said.

Branco grunted.

We approached another turn, this one on an incline. I saw Branco brace his foot against the floorboard. But this time I revved the engine high enough for a smooth downshift and then maneuvered the corner as though the Alfa was on rails. Branco made a tiny nod, then gazed out over the water as we climbed higher.

I said, "What about the suede gloves? Was there anything in those?"

"Too soon," said Branco. "But I haven't eliminated the stage manager as a suspect. She's one tough little cookie, certainly strong and agile enough to jump a man like Carafolio from behind and stab him through the front of his chest."

"But what would be her motive?"

"I'll worry about that later," he said. "Right now, I just want some physical evidence to book someone."

"That sounds a little reckless."

Branco glared.

"Sorry," I said. "What are you going to do next?"

"What do you think? Get hair samples from everyone."

"Isn't that an invasion of privacy?"

"I've got search warrants."

"Already?"

"I have some clout," said the cop.

I half expected Branco to grab my hand and pluck one of the coppery hairs from a finger knuckle. But he didn't.

"What really concerns me," he said, "is that no one around that place has said 'too bad' about that guy, not even once. It was the same with the singer."

"That's not surprising, Lieutenant. None of the victims was exactly lovable."

"But I think it goes beyond that, Stan. I see a general attitude of relief around that place—relief instead of worry. And we're talking two separate instances of first-degree murder."

"Maybe three, if you count that set designer."

"That was an accident," said Branco.

"Maybe not."

We were on a straight and level stretch of road, so I opened up the engine and made it roar, just the way the cop might have done with his Alfa. I glanced his way. He looked content.

"What I'm saying," said the cop, "is that the blasé attitude these people have is going to make it a lot harder to crack this case, because no one really cares who killed any of the victims."

"Except maybe their insurance companies."

Branco looked me straight in the eyes.

"And me," he said.

I returned his look and said, "Then me too."

"Good," he said. "Now get your eyes back on the road."

Always the cop.

We headed back to the opera house, where I dropped Branco off. His parting words were, "You handle the car okay. Next time I'll show you that power shift technique."

"It's a date," I blurted.

Branco scowled and closed the door. I watched him walk away from the car, and I admired his long, deliberate stride, and the way he carried himself proudly. Then I drove back to Daphne's place.

30

D aphne greeted me in the foyer.
"How horrible!" she said. "The maestro has been telling me all about it. Another body! It's just not possible!"

I shrugged. "On the bright side, you didn't have to fire him and I got my job back."

Daphne scoffed, "Is that all you can think of? That's a very selfish attitude, young man. There's an entire opera festival at stake. Our opening season may flounder because of the murders being committed here."

"But none of it is any worse than what happens onstage with opera," I said. "The media scandal may even help the festival. You know how people are. Sex and violence sells."

Daphne grimaced. "It's a sad state of affairs to admit that you may be right about that."

"At least the investors will be happy," I said.

"But at what cost, my dear?"

She led me into the library, where the maestro was sitting by the fireplace. He was bristling with rage more incendiary than the flames from the hearth.

I said good evening.

He replied angrily, *"Il tenente è un fascista."*

Daphne explained that everyone at the opera house had to submit to a rather humiliating procedure with the police that afternoon, and the maestro found it unpardonable.

"I know," I said. "He's resorted to plucking hair now."

The maestro said, "How can he think I kill Marcella? I tell him, that girl is the dangerous one. She thinks she is a man."

"You mean Ronda, the stage manager?"

"*Sì,*" said the maestro. *"La Ronda.* Very dangerous. After the *Sitz-probe* I stay backstage for a little while. I am very tired, so I want to be quiet. And then I see her with a big knife in her hand. She is playing with it, like a toy."

"What did it look like?"

"It was the dagger which kills Riccardo."

"A prop," I said.

"Sì, a prop," said the maestro. "Not real."

"It was real enough to penetrate Daniel Carafolio's heart."

"Oh, dear," exclaimed Daphne. "He was murdered with one of the props?"

"It gets worse," I said. I told her about the bloody gauntlets that had vanished and then reappeared in the costume room, and why the lieutenant needed the hair samples. "To match the fragment he found in one of the gauntlets," I said.

"La Ronda is a dangerous woman," repeated the maestro. "When I see her with that dagger, I think of Marcella when she sings Lady Macbeth. Some people like very much sharp knives."

Daphne remarked, "And now someone is using props to kill people in the production. I hope we don't run out of people before opening night."

"Or props," I said.

"Touché," said Daphne. "Now I'm being selfish."

"At least the victims haven't been people who are crucial to the production, like Jonathan Byers, or the maestro here."

The maestro and Daphne exchanged dubious glances.

"Or me, for that matter," said Daphne. "Madam Moneybags."

"Or you," I allowed.

Parker entered the library and announced a telephone call.

"Lieutenant Branco calling for Mr. Kraychik."

Daphne's eyebrows rose accusingly. "Twice in one day," she said. "My, my, my."

I took the call in the library, in full view of Daphne and the maestro, just to prove I had nothing to hide from them. But then, why was I feeling defensive about it?

Branco had the DNA analysis from Boston. The hair fragment in the gauntlet matched the sample taken from Jonathan Byers's hand.

Branco said, "I'm about to confront him with the evidence. You want to come down here and see how it's done?"

"Uh, sure," I said. "Where should I meet you?"

"The Abigail Arms. I've got men posted all around the place, just in case Byers gets an itch to wander out before I get there. I'm heading over there now."

"Okay," I said uncertainly. "I'm on my way too."

But with his message successfully dispatched, Branco had already hung up, just the way Nicole often did.

I excused myself to Daphne with the explanation that Branco was about to confront Jonathan Byers with incriminating evidence, and he thought I might learn something by watching him.

She said, "It almost sounds as though he wants to perform for you."

I blushed. Her remark had struck home. It was hardly standard procedure for someone like me to be invited to an arrest. Perhaps Branco did want me to witness his version of theater: a matinee idol cop in the arena of police brutality.

It took me half an hour to find the Abigail Arms, and by then the cops had taken Jonathan Byers to the police station. When I got there Branco had already begun interrogating Byers. The two of them were in a soundproof room along with an assisting sergeant. I wasn't allowed in there, of course, but Branco had instructed the local police to let me observe the whole process through the one-way glass. It was like watching big-screen television in 3-D.

Branco said, "Why don't you just admit you stole the gauntlets." The tiredness in his voice implied it wasn't the first time he'd said it.

Byers replied, "I told you before, and I'll tell you again. I did not steal them. Where is my attorney?"

"He's on his way, but it doesn't matter. We have proof."

"I don't care what you have. I am not going to incriminate myself by saying the words *you* want me to say."

Branco paused as though he'd heard Byers's remark for the first time.

"All right," he said. "Then why don't you tell me what you did in your own words."

"Ah," said Byers. "That's better."

"Go on," said Branco.

"Well, if you must know . . ."

"Yes . . . ?"

"I *borrowed* the bloody things."

"All right."

"I intended to return them, but they were stolen from my hotel room."

"Go on," said Branco.

"That's it," said Byers.

"Nothing else?"

Byers was mute, but he gave the cop a puckish grin, as if to prompt him to ask the precise question to receive a desired response. Branco seemed to catch on to the game immediately.

"For what purpose did you borrow them?" he said.

"To wear them," replied Byers. "What else would I do with them?"

Branco said, "Where did you wear them?"

"Clever, clever," said Byers. "You learn fast. Have you ever acted, Lieutenant?"

"Where did you wear the gauntlets?" repeated Branco.

"You really want to know, don't you?"

"I do," said Branco.

"Then I'll tell you. And I'm telling you because it's a little quirk of mine, and I have a sense you might share an understanding about such things."

"Go on," Branco said coldly.

"Yes, well I did use them for sex." Byers then made a sinister theatrical laugh.

Branco just said flatly, "Please go on."

"I'd love to, Lieutenant. I'm beginning to think I really have your attention here. Or else you are a damn good actor. Are you sure you were never on the boards? Well it doesn't matter. I can't say I'm displeased. You are a handsome devil."

"I'm listening," said Branco.

"Yes, I suppose you are. Well, then," he said, and paused and took a big breath, as though preparing for a virtuoso display of oratory. "Let the big black box record the fact that Sir Jonathan Byers, Her Majesty's own knight-errant, likes to have sex with a prop, any prop, but preferably an important prop that's to be used onstage opening night!"

The last sounds of his stentorian voice echoed in the small chamber. He'd surely overloaded the tape recorder's circuits.

Branco said, "A prop? Or a person?"

"My dear Lieutenant, I thought the Puritans were extinct."

"I can see how someone like you might think that."

"Pity. We were getting on so well until you started being judgmental. Now I'm afraid you've spoiled it."

"I'm arresting you for the murder of Marcella Ostinata."

"On what grounds?" he said with a braying laugh.

"A fragment of your hair was found inside one of the gauntlets that was drenched with her blood."

"You fool!" said Byers. "Of course my hair was in that gauntlet! I just told you I wore them during sex."

Branco stood up and leaned toward Byers for his next question.

"What stage prop did you use during sex at Spoleto?"

Sir Jonathan shrank slightly in his chair. "Who told you about that?" he said. "That sniveling wig maker?"

"Which one?" said Branco, wounding me to the quick. Perhaps I whined, but I never sniveled.

Byers said, "There's only one bloody wig man, and he's dead."

"There's the redhead too," said Branco.

How strange to hear myself referred to in the third person.

"Ah, yes," said Byers. "Your little deputy."

Branco winced but pressed on. "Carafolio reported that you had some trouble in Spoleto. We followed up on it and found nothing."

A wave of relief washed over Byers's face. "I'm not surprised," he said.

"Nothing," said Branco. "Except that one of the stagehands at the opera house there died in a mysterious accident. Perhaps Carafolio knew some particulars about that accident."

Byers said, "If I'd known he was going to open his fat piggy mouth, I would have stuffed it myself, and not with any damn gloves, you can be sure."

Branco recited his next line flatly. "I have to advise you that anything you say may be used in evidence."

Byers replied, "Lieutenant, do you realize the potential consequences of this desperate little arabesque of yours?"

Branco remained stony.

Byers went on. "Then I hope you are prepared to face the most gargantuan lawsuit of your career."

Branco told the assisting sergeant to book him. Then he left the room. I intercepted him outside. Branco's eyes were like embers, and there was a moistness coming from his body, imbued with his familiar scent of balsam and clean cotton. I guess he got a physical rush whenever he arrested someone. Still, he looked plenty dissatisfied about something.

I said, "What's wrong?"

"Something is definitely not right," he said. "We've got two pairs of gloves, both pairs stolen and used in the killings of two different people that no one else gives a damn about. And I've just booked the director of the show for one of the murders on very flimsy evidence." He shook his head. "I know it's a mistake."

"Then why did you do it?"

"Because of that damn hair fragment! It was the only piece of evidence I had."

"Maybe you put too much store in physical stuff."

Branco gave me a withered look. He really looked tired.

"Wanna go for a beer?" he said.

"I haven't eaten yet," I said stupidly.

Then too quickly he replied, "Never mind. Another time."

As he walked away from me, I made a move to catch up with him. But then what was I going to say? Was it my place to comfort a cop because he was lonely for his mom and dad? I watched him go out the side door—the cop's door—of the Abigail police station. I left by the front door and took the Alfa for a short drive before returning to the estate. With the top down and the night air flying around me, at least my sensual self was getting some attention.

I stopped in at the hospital to see Maurizio, but they'd released him late that afternoon. Parker's daughter had picked him up and taken him back to her place to nurse him. I didn't know the way there, and I didn't feel like finding out, so I went home.

When I got back, I learned from Daphne that Jonathan Byers's attorney had already telephoned her and explained the seriousness of the situation. She immediately offered to pay bail for Byers's release, and the lawyer had already been by to pick up the check.

"He sure didn't waste any time," I said.

"Of course not," said Daphne. "I told you before, my whole festival is at stake. The bail was astronomical, but I am certain of Sir Jonathan's innocence. His only concern is the production, not an indictment or a trial. And as for you, my dear, I'd be very cautious."

"About what, Daphne?"

"About the lieutenant. Though he's probably quite unaware of it himself, I suspect that he is courting you."

"Daphne!" I said. "He's straight. I think he's just very lonely. He needs a friend, and he's really awkward about it."

"Weren't you lonely once?" she said.

"Yes, but my loneliness was different. I wanted a lover. Branco's loneliness is more familial. See, he lost both his parents only a few months ago."

"That's very tragic, my dear, and I'm sure it's affecting the man deeply. But losing one's parents is a natural course of events that one must face and adapt to. I think the death of his parents is irrelevant to the lieutenant's recent behavior toward you, except that perhaps now he feels more liberated about certain aspects of himself."

"Daphne, are you saying he likes me?"

"I think it's time you faced the facts, my dear. There's a deep conflict in that man—I'm sure it's plagued him for years—and now he's on the verge of confronting it again."

"But maybe losing his parents—"

"Please let me finish! Until the lieutenant can face those uncharted regions of his psyche and seek some resolution there—and I'm not suggesting he's going to find an easy answer one way or the other—if only it were so simple that all we had to do was make a choice. But until the lieutenant is willing at the very least to acknowledge what his recent behavior toward you indicates—and it's been blatant enough for an old coot like me to recognize what's going on—then you're going to continue walking this razor's edge between attraction and aversion to each other."

If this had been an opera, the score would have said *lunga pausa*.

"But what can I do, Daphne? I can't be Branco's therapist."

"My dear, it goes far beyond that."

"I can't face this now," I said. "I'm hungry and I'm tired."

"Very well. But the longer you wait, the longer everything will stay exactly as it is."

"That's fine with me," I said.

She shook her head with a look of grave disappointment.

"Where is your spunk?" she said.

I replied, "My spunk is in Paris convincing his parents that I'm worthy of him."

"Bah!" said Daphne. "Parents again! What do you care about his parents' approval? Why should he care? If you have a partner he should be here with you now, pursuing you, including you in his life, exactly the way the lieutenant is trying to do."

Gosh, I thought. Branco? I hadn't expected this little deviation on the storyboard of my life. In my long years of loneliness I had waited and yearned for a lover to appear, and somehow, wishing upon that star night after night, I finally saw my dream come true. As far as I was concerned, it was a fait accompli. I had a man I loved, and that was that. I certainly wasn't expecting to face the raging beast again, and most certainly not with Lieutenant Branco. No, Daphne was wrong. She had to be. In spite of her stellar credentials, when all was said and done, it was only her high-flown theory in contest with the physical evidence, or lack thereof, from Branco. I certainly didn't feel any physical attraction coming from him, at least nothing recognizable. In my eyes we were trying to build a comfortable working relationship, maybe even becoming friends, if such a thing was really possible between a cop and a hairdresser. But attraction to me? From him? Leading to what? Sex? Marriage? Daphne was projecting. No doubt about it. Even a world-class analyst was susceptible to psychofoibles.

So I resolved that there was nothing to do except to carry on as I was. I would maintain the status quo with the cop. For no matter what action I took based on Daphne's theory—either toward Branco or away from him—I felt I would be defending against a phantom.

31

My job in the wig room reinstated, the next morning I returned to the opera house for a full day's work. I also intended to continue my investigation as Branco's deputy because, like Daphne and even Branco himself, I suspected that Jonathan Byers had not killed Marcella Ostinata. How could he be a killer and remain so focused on an opera production? Besides, there was still no clue who had killed Daniel Carafolio. Certainly not Jon Byers. He had no motive, unless Daniel had known something that would prove Byers had killed Marcella. And there was still—at least from my perspective—the unresolved death of Adam Pierce. It was more likely that Jonathan Byers was unwittingly involved in someone else's morbid real-life opera, playing some unidentifiable role. But he was hardly the central character in that opera. The rash of killings was someone else's story, and somehow the libretto had gone awry. And by the fluke of a hair fragment left in a leather gauntlet, Jonathan Byers had been accused of killing Marcella Ostinata.

The rehearsal schedule posted inside the stage door that morning read: OCA +, which meant a staged run-through with orchestra, chorus, principal artists, and others, including scenery, props, but only some costumes, and none of the lighting.

I spent the first part of the morning in the wig room mounting and adjusting the wigs for all the chorus members. They were the only people I had to enwig that day, since the principal singers wouldn't have their wigs and final costumes onstage until the next night's rehearsal, the full orchestra dress. There'd even be an audience for that one, by invitation only. Even little old me had been allowed to invite two guests—Lieutenant Branco and my friend Nicole.

After I finished with the chorus, I made some last-minute adjustments to some of the more extravagant wigs for the final scene, the masked ball. Then I took a break and went upstairs. The rehearsal was well into act one when I entered the backstage area. I found the place riddled with video and audio monitors that relayed every sound and motion coming from the stage or the pit. Gone forever were the days when a cue was missed because of physical distance.

Ronda Lucca was at her desk, wearing her headset and briskly calling out the cues from her sheets to the crew members at their remote stations backstage and elsewhere in the theater. She looked like the editor of the city desk of an urban newspaper.

When there was a pause in her activity, I commented on her new gloves, adding, "Do the police know about the other ones?"

Ronda said, "What are you, crazy? You think I told some cop my gloves were shoved down a dead guy's throat? I sure hope you didn't say anything either."

I sensed a veiled threat in her voice.

"If you remember," I said, "I'm the one who warned you."

"I do," she said. "Now, you got something else to say, you should say it fast, I don't have time for guessing games today."

Ronda referred to her cue sheets, then spoke into her headset. "Preparation cue for scrim number seven. Prepare scrim seven." Then she turned to me and said, "Before you start laying into me today, let me tell you something. If I was gonna waste somebody, I wouldn't go shoving my work gloves down their throat. And if I did, I wouldn't leave them there. That would be pretty stupid, wouldn't it? So as far as I'm concerned, the cops found the guy who did it, and they arrested him. The case is closed."

Ronda spoke into the headset again. "Ready cue for scrim number seven. Ready scrim seven."

I said, "But Jon Byers is out on bail, Ronda. How do you feel about that?"

"Feel about it? What are you, some kind of shrink?"

"I almost was, once. But doesn't it bother you that a killer is back at work here in the opera house?"

"No. As a matter of fact, it doesn't."

"Is that because you know Jonathan Byers didn't kill anybody?"

"It's because I know I can take care of myself." Then she put her hand up to stop me from talking while she spoke into her headset. "Holding scrim seven," she said. Her hand still up to stop me, she listened intently to the orchestra and concentrated on the video monitor in front of her. "Holding . . ." she said again, waited another moment, then said sharply, "Go scrim seven!"

From the flies high above, a gauzy scrim the entire width of the massive stage plummeted to the floor without a sound. Its silent flight seemed almost magical, until I realized it was the very scrim that had killed Adam Pierce over a week ago.

"Perfect," Ronda said to herself.

"Not like the first time," I said, "when the pipe on that thing wiped out the set designer."

Ronda spun her face toward me and said, "You know, I got this bad feeling that you're trying to blame me for something. And frankly, I think you're jerking off. Now that's fine with me, because you seem to need to do that. But this is my stage. So if you want to mess up your pants, why don't you go downstairs and take care of it there, in your own room. Okay?"

But something about the previous few minutes was wrong. And then I realized what it was.

"Ronda, I'm wondering why you were just giving cues for that scrim when you told me before that everything on this stage was controlled by computer."

"Huh?" she said.

"You told me this stage was state-of-the-art, and all that business of manual timing was eliminated."

"It is. I'm just giving cues to my assistant. She has a remote terminal up in the control booth."

"Oh," I said. "That must explain it. I'll catch you later."

I had just turned to leave when she mumbled, "You'll catch me never."

But when I turned back to her, she was readying another cue.

I watched awhile from backstage, but that next scene was a dark one, and the scrim made it even more difficult to perceive any detail over the monitors. I knew it was the scene in the fortune-teller's cave, although in Jonathan Byers's version of the opera, Ulrica the witch had become a New Age psychic healer, and her cave had been transformed into an open workshop for interactive growth and grope. Poor Verdi.

I was about to wander out front to the auditorium when I saw Rick Jansen standing near one of the exits. His gaze was intent on one of the video monitors. I walked over to him.

"Your boyfriend had a bit of a jam with the cops."

Rick said, "He didn't do anything wrong."

"How are you so sure?"

"Because I know him. I know Jon the way no one else does."

I said, "I'm surprised you're not out front with him now."

"He doesn't want me near him."

"Why not?"

"The bastard thinks I testified against him at the police. He'll never know how much I've done for him—sacrificed for him! He doesn't appreciate me, never has."

"Maybe you should remind him how much you care."

Rick snorted and said, "It's obvious you don't know him at all." Then he gave me an uneasy look and said, "You've never done leather sex, have you?"

"Not at the Olympic level," I said.

"I didn't think so. It doesn't show in your eyes. You only play at it. You never did it for real. You never went to that place."

"What place?"

"That place where your mind and body connect during sex. And when you get there you find out what you're really made of. What you really want. Where your limits are. It's not the kind of sex typical people have, that vanilla stuff from the movies. Leather sex is what sex was meant to be, but very few people know how to handle it."

So much for genetically encoded drives and instincts.

I taunted him. "I never realized leather had so much power."

"One thing's for sure," he said. "You're not ready for it."

"Seems to me it's just one person giving orders and another one taking them, with lots of ritual attached."

"That just shows your ignorance," said Rick.

"I readily admit that," I said. "But maybe you can give me the inside scoop. See, I've always suspected that the boy—the bottom, the slave, whatever—is the one who's really calling the shots. Is that true?"

"It's too complex for someone like you."

"Tell me, Rick. Is it complex enough to kill another person? Which one of you gives the order to kill? Jonathan or you? And which one carries it out? Or are you both versatile and switch roles? That's always fun, even for us pedestrians."

Rick Jansen said bluntly, "Your sex life must be awful. Did you ever think of going into therapy?"

"What would you recommend? Primal harness?"

"For starters I recommend you drop dead," he said. Then he went out the exit.

Alone, I watched the monitor that showed the pit. The maestro was wielding his baton like a mace. Somehow the power behind Verdi's music permeated his aged body and conferred youthful vigor to it. For occasional moments, Maestro Toscanelli became the fiery youth who had made a sensational debut at La Scala almost fifty years ago.

The monitor also showed occasional glimpses of Carolyn Boetz, who was in the first row of orchestra seats directly behind the maestro. She was mesmerized by him, and she imitated his conducting gestures, as though preparing herself to take his place if the need should arise. In truth, Carolyn Boetz seemed to have little motive for killing any of the three people who had been murdered.

I realized I had to get back downstairs to unwig the chorus members when the first act was finished. Then I'd spend most of act two putting the wigs on the singers for act three, so my investigative time would be severely curtailed. It hardly mattered, since the two people I had wanted to approach—April Kilkus and Hwang Yung Cho—would be utterly unapproachable until after the rehearsal.

The masked ball finale of act three actually brought scattered applause from the crew backstage and elsewhere in the house. I felt proud because I knew the startling effect was partly due to my fantastic wigs. Of course, the music and the sets and the chorus members' costumes helped too. The only odd thing was the lack of a dagger for Renato to kill Riccardo with. There was no replacement yet for the prop that had been used to kill Daniel Carafolio in real life. And the new tenor was understandably skittish about rehearsing with any stage weapon whatsoever, especially considering the distinctive finale the previous "safe" prop had conferred upon our dear departed Daniel. The prop department was designing and building a completely different one with a foil blade that would crumple upon impact, and then release a large quantity of stage blood at the site of the fraudulent wound. No one would be killed, either accidentally or purposely, with that new dagger.

After rehearsal my first task was to de-wig the chorus and mount the masterpieces on dummies. By the time I was done, April and Hwang had fled from the opera house, as had all the other musicians. As there was no one else to confront that afternoon, I left too.

32

Before returning to the estate, I stopped by Lieutenant Branco's temporary office in the performance center residence building. The opera festival had set up a suite of rooms for him and his staff to conduct their investigation. The doorman of the building called Branco, who let me in right away. I expected the office to be abuzz with activity, but instead I found Branco packing up the place to return back to Boston.

"No reason to stick around now," he said. "I made my arrest and within an hour I was thwarted."

I knew he was referring to Daphne.

"She had to do it," I said. "The success of the festival depends on Jonathan Byers."

"One thing's for sure," he said. "That Davenport woman's money sure talks loud in this town."

"She's the local industry, Lieutenant."

"And *he* was my prime suspect."

"But didn't you say you weren't really convinced about him yourself?"

"That was a personal and confidential aside to you, Stan. It's definitely not my official stand. I don't go around trying to look like a fool."

"I know that," I said. "You acted on the evidence you had."

"There wasn't much else I could do."

"No," I said. "I guess there wasn't."

"Though maybe I did kind of jump the gun."

"Maybe."

"But I can't very well continue my investigation here if I've already booked a suspect."

"Why not? They do it on television all the time."

"This isn't television, Stan. It would look bad."

"Well . . . ," I said.

"What?"

"You could continue investigating unofficially."

Branco said, "I probably will."

"Have you considered using intuition to help your logic?"

Branco grunted. "I can't afford to waste time on that."

"But at this point you almost have no choice. Logic is what got you a prime suspect you don't wholeheartedly believe in. Maybe using another part of your mind would—"

"Cut it right now! Okay? That kind of yack is for amateurs. I'm a professional. I have years of training and experience. This is a job I do. A real job. Do you know what that is? I'm not about to start looking into crystal balls to find out who's been killing these people."

Branco was clearly upset about the turn of events. I couldn't blame him. Based on the evidence he had, he'd arrested his suspect. How was he to know that a wealthy dowager would bail the guy out within an hour? If he continued with his investigation now, officially at least, then he *would* look like a fool. I waited a few moments for the air to cool down, and during those moments I searched Branco's face for a sign that Daphne's hidden-love theory about him was true. But all I could perceive coming from the man was anger.

"Lieutenant, I'm not suggesting a crystal ball. I don't believe in that stuff either. But I do know from my limited experience that some-times we can't see the answer to a difficult problem because we keep looking at it from the same angle."

"I know that," he said irritably. "I use that technique, looking at a situation from the points of view of all the suspects, trying to see their motives."

"But that's still using logic. I'm talking about something else," I said. "I'm suggesting that you take all the facts you've gathered so far, and instead of organizing them into categories and lists—instead of trying to inflict a neat and tidy formula on what you have—I'm saying you might throw everything together, like in a big stock pot, and then turn up the heat to a rapid boil to see what happens."

"I'll tell you what'll happen," he said. "A mess will happen, that's what." He threw the last of the dossiers into a metal attaché case.

"Just try it, Lieutenant. You don't have to tell anybody about it. Do it like an experiment in the kitchen. Something might combine or congeal in a way you hadn't expected."

"You know what?" he said. "You're nuts."

He snapped the latches on the attaché case. Then he packed up the portable computer and printer that were on his desk. I thought I saw a tiny shudder when he disconnected a thin gray wire that had run from the computer to a phone jack in the wall. Apparently Branco had been online with Boston headquarters, and, for all I knew, the rest of the fact-laden, computerized world. Logic, logic everywhere. But without his electronic lifeline, Branco was just another flesh-and-blood man, typically refusing to recognize the potential power of intuition.

I said, "Does this mean the case is closed?"

Branco wavered before saying, "It's not closed until we get a conviction."

"What about my badge? If I didn't help you arrest Byers—"

"Don't worry," said Branco. "You did good work."

Then I reminded him that I'd left a complimentary ticket at the box office for the full dress rehearsal the following night.

"Nicole will be coming too," I said.

Branco smiled. "Is that so? I'll give her a call when I get back to town. Maybe we can ride out here together tomorrow."

"She'd like that."

Who wouldn't?

Branco headed toward the door, and I followed him out the building to his car. He got in his old Alfa and started it. The engine purred like a big tiger.

He spoke through the open window. "You're staying around, right?"

"I still have work to do. In spite of what you think, Lieutenant, creating beauty is a real job too. It's just different from yours. I make people beautiful, you put them in jail."

"Right," said Branco, with a grunt.

He revved the engine.

I said, "Maybe by the time you come back tomorrow you'll have had a revelation about the killer."

"Sure I will."

He put the car in reverse. As it rolled backwards away from me I said, "You never showed me how to power-shift."

"There's time," he replied.

Then he put the car in first gear and drove off.

At Daphne's house Parker greeted me at the door. For some odd reason he informed me that the maestro was tired and was taking a light supper in his room. It wasn't really my concern. I suppose the old man was exhausted by spending the day with—at least in his eyes—a convicted killer. Perhaps Maestro Toscanelli didn't under-stand the concept of "innocent until proven guilty." Then again, it was only a concept, hardly ever implemented in real life.

Parker continued, saying that Daphne was in the library, and if I wanted to join her, I was welcome. I said I would.

I went in and found her sitting in front of the fireplace. Daphne turned in her chair to greet me, but she didn't stand.

"Ah, you're back," she said with a chill that even the cheery fire couldn't dispel.

"Yes," I said.

Then she told me matter-of-factly that Maurizio had been released from the hospital and was staying with Parker's daughter. I told her I already knew that.

"When did you find out?" she said.

"Last night."

"Why didn't you tell me then?"

For an old girl, Daphne could sure make a room bristle with tension.

"I guess we got to talking about Branco, and I forgot."

Daphne grimaced. "Yes. That man. He almost destroyed my festival. I'm sorry to admit it, but I was mistaken about him. His presence is so powerful you forget yourself. But now I'm inclined to agree with the maestro's assessment. When faced with a stressful situation, the lieutenant becomes a brute. He needs absolute power and control."

"Daphne, I don't think Lieutenant Branco arrested Jonathan Byers just to ruin the festival."

Daphne said, "Are you defending his actions now?"

"I'm trying to be reasonable."

"Well, don't be. This is not a reasonable situation. Reason is what the lieutenant used to arrest Sir Jonathan."

I had to agree with her there. Branco's blunder was almost irresponsible, a desperate move to do something, anything to maintain his copness.

"Daphne, if it's any consolation, even Lieutenant Branco realizes that arresting Jonathan Byers may have been a mistake. But he was frustrated and had to do something. You can understand that at least."

"I expect an officer of the law to behave professionally, according to the law, not on some whimsical need to be right."

"But he was acting according to law," I said.

Yet Daphne was right too.

I said, "I'm sure everything will be fine. The run-through this afternoon was inspired. Even Sir Jonathan was pleased."

Daphne made a quiet little mewing sound that I hoped marked the end of our disagreement. But then said, "I'm afraid that bodes only trouble then. Surely you know the stage lore that says a good dress rehearsal augurs a bad opening night?"

"But today wasn't the dress rehearsal, Daphne. That's tomorrow night."

"Oh," she said. "Then I suppose there's still hope."

"Yes," I said agreeably, thinking how strange it was to be hoping for a bad rehearsal the following night. I hadn't realized that Daphne was superstitious.

"Would you like me to stay here, or in the cottage tonight?" I said.

"As you please, my dear."

Not the warmest welcome. I guess for consorting with Branco, I was now perceived as the enemy. I expected soon the maestro would be declaiming, *"Il pouffario è un fascista."* Although I suppose some hairstylists are like fascists in their quest for absolute control of a situation.

So what was left for me to do? Go to the cottage and sulk? Or continue with the case on my own? I had no vested interest in being right the way Branco did. I had no face to lose. So what if I came off the fool? Finding the killer was more important. And if I could do that, if I could get Branco back on track to the real culprit, then maybe I'd earn my merit badge after all.

I told Daphne that I wanted to go back to town and that I might be returning very late, so it was probably better if I stayed in the cottage that night.

"Are you sure that's wise?" she said.

"You mean about going out?"

"Yes."

"I'm not going prowling, or anything like that."

"I wasn't suggesting that, my dear." She softened finally, when it came to my safety. "But if you believe as I do—and the lieutenant too, apparently—that the real killer is still at large, then there's certainly reason for extreme caution."

"I'll be careful."

"I want you to do more," she said. "Wherever you decide to stay tonight—here, or the cottage, or elsewhere—I want you to call Parker and tell him."

"I'll be okay, Daphne."

"You must promise me, or I'll have the car keys back right now. I don't like ultimatums, my dear, but you leave me no choice."

No wonder Branco's need for power had provoked Daphne. It took one to know one.

"Yes, ma'am," I said. "I promise I'll either call Parker or else come to the front door myself."

"Good. Now you take care."

Before I set off for town, I returned to the cottage to call Nicole in Boston. I told her to expect a call from Lieutenant Branco, and that the chances were very likely that she'd be riding out with him to beautiful Abigail-by-the-Sea.

"I'd like to be riding something else," she said. "But it's not in the cards for the lieutenant and me."

I pretended to ignore her remark. I'd heard enough speculation about Branco's sexual vagaries from Daphne. And I prefered it to stay that way—vague.

"How's Sugar Baby?" I said.

"She sits at the window and gazes northward over the harbor, like a lonely whaler's wife."

"Poor thing," I said. "Incarcerated in a duplex penthouse at Harbor Towers. Not even a decent widow's walk."

"She'll survive," said Nicole.

"Is she eating okay?"

"Better than me," replied Nicole.

"It'll be good to see you tomorrow night, Nikki."

"I wonder how I should dress," she said. "Like a temptress? Or a lady of refinement?"

"It's the opera, doll. Anything goes."

We said good-bye. Or rather, I said good-bye and Nicole hung up as usual. Then I headed into town for my supper.

33

Daphne's recent shift in attitude toward me had been a painful surprise. I'd expected her to comprehend Lieutenant Branco's behavior better, since she herself had fallen under his spell when she first met him. How unfair of her first to submit the theory that Branco might be harboring latent desire for me, and then to reprimand me and warn me to keep away from him, just in case he was. Perhaps Daphne was a frustrated mother, and the opera festival hadn't provided quite enough challenge, quite the insurrection to traditional family values that a surrogate gay son did. So, like any concerned mother, she told me how she wanted me to behave, and I, like any spoiled young rebel with a car, took off.

I drove into town on the excuse to get something to eat, but I also wanted to be on my own, try to sort things out with the killings and maybe even the Vito Branco love boat. I found a small pizzeria near the train station. It was a crummy old place, with blinding fluorescent lights and red plastic-topped tables, and I wondered how it had escaped the steamroller of gentrification that had run through the once sleepy town of Abigail-by-the-Sea to make way for the performance center and the ensuing opera festival. There were no gourmet toppings to be had in that place—no smoked shredded chicken or wilted arugula in balsamic marinade. And no fancy cheeses either— no chevre, no jalapeño jack, no low-fat nothing. The only cheese option on the menu was called "extra."

So under the culinary circumstances I was surprised to find among the local clientele that evening two of the principal singers from the opera, April Kilkus and Hwang Yung Cho. They didn't notice me go into the place, and I watched them together for a while as they ate pizza and drank beer. There was a sense of private celebration between them, great elation, as though they had won a great victory, despite the heavy cost. Just like the Macbeths after the banquet.

I put in my order for a plain cheese pizza with extra sauce and a burnt crust. Then I took my first beer with me and stopped by the singers' table, which was on the way to the only vacant seat in the place, in a far corner near the bussing wagon.

"I didn't expect to see you folks in a place like this," I said. "Especially the night before the full dress rehearsal."

Hwang looked up from the table-sized pizza in front of them. "We weren't exactly looking forward to seeing you either," he said with a snarl. Maybe he was just polishing the fine points of his stage role as Renato.

I said, "I watched some of the rehearsal today. You were both captivating. I guess working under a murder suspect hasn't affected your performances."

Hwang spat his reply. "Jonathan Byers isn't guilty of anything."

"Except maybe bad manners," I said.

"And you know plenty about that," replied Hwang.

April interjected, "And as for our singing, it's just another benefit of good technique. It helps you sing under any circumstances, no matter how extreme."

Hwang picked up the big cutting knife that had come with their pizza. He gripped it tightly in his big fist. Since their pizza had been mostly cut, I assumed he meant to threaten me. But it was an idle threat, and I wasn't frightened. What was he going to do? Stab me in the pizzeria?

"I'm sure you'll both always sing well," I said. "Provided you get the opportunity. Even if you have to create it."

"Are you still on that kick?" said Hwang.

"You have to admit," I said. "If Marcella Ostinata was still alive, you two wouldn't exactly be partying for April's good luck."

"That's all it was," said Hwang, with his teeth clenched. "Just plain luck. We didn't kill anyone. We were just lucky."

"Who's we?" I said. "April's the one who got the prize, not you."

April said quickly, "You forget that we're married. And what is good for me is good for my husband."

"I hadn't forgot that at all," I said. "In fact, it seems to strengthen your motive."

"We haven't done anything wrong," said April. "Why can't you accept that?"

I said, "Aren't either of you even a tiny bit concerned that there's a killer loose among the cast and crew?"

Hwang said, "We can take care of ourselves. But if you're so worried about safety, maybe you should leave town yourself." Then he stabbed the pizza viciously with the point of the cutting knife. "Before something happens to you."

It was the kind of excessive gesture that might work onstage, in costume, under bright lights, at the end of a sustained climactic note, with cymbals crashing and trumpets blaring. But in real life, in a small-town pizzeria, Hwang's attack on the pizza with that big knife was a travesty of a dangerous man. If he wasn't careful, such operatic histrionics could become a habit, and his life would become a caricature.

I went to my table. But while I sat there waiting for my pizza and picking the label off my beer bottle, I got an idea. Why should I sit in that dreary dingy place and eat my pizza all alone near a cart full of dirty dishes? Why not get the pizza to go with another beer, then drive up to one of the ocean bluffs and eat it out there, under the open night sky?

Which is exactly what I did.

As I sat out on a rocky ledge, pizza slab in one hand, beer bottle in the other, I looked out over the ocean and wondered about my lover Rafik. Somewhere across the vast miles of water before me, in Paris at that very moment, he was probably sleeping. Was he dreaming of me? Was he even alone?

That was when I had the first troubling sense of the possibility, however remote, that I might never see him again. Absurd, I thought. I'd see him within a week. Such irrational fear was probably nothing more than what my cat Sugar Baby experienced when gazing out the window from Nicole's penthouse. Did Sugar Baby ever wonder if I'd return? Or did she perceive me merely as the red-haired can opener, the one that sometimes went away and then came back? Was I only something expedient, a piece of good luck, convenient but imminently replaceable? Then I wondered if that's how I perceived Rafik—as Mr. Expedient, who had filled the void of love in my life.

I left the last few slices of pizza out on the rocks for the sea gulls, and disposed of the remaining debris properly. I got back to the estate by eleven o'clock, and rang the doorbell to the big house to tell Parker that I was home safe and would be staying in the cottage that night. Then the fun began.

The maestro's head and hand emerged from the library door just off the foyer. He beckoned me inside. I asked Parker if it was all right to go in, and all he said was, "As you please, Mr. Kraychik." I guess he had gone stuffy on me too.

Inside the library the maestro was having a whiskey and a cigarette. I complimented him on the rehearsal that afternoon, and told him how much I had enjoyed it. He nodded modestly.

"It is *il signor Verdi* you should praise."

I asked him what he wanted to talk about.

"Ah," he said with a smile. "You are too serious, like *il tenente.*" The maestro sipped his whiskey then said, "I think this Jon Byers is a brilliant man, and he is also a foolish man. But he is not a killer."

"So you don't believe he killed Madama Ostinata."

"Jon Byers kills no one."

"Then who did?" I said.

"I think still it was the girl," said the maestro.

"The girl?"

"La Ronda. I see her always with Carolyn. She is in love with Carolyn. Do you know that? I think maybe *La Ronda* kills Marcella for Carolyn."

"Carolyn? How is that connected to Madama Ostinata?"

The maestro smiled broadly. "You do not see?"

"No," I said.

"Then I will explain. Carolyn wants a great success for April. If April has a big career, Carolyn will follow her. So *La Ronda* kills Marcella to make for April her big chance to sing."

I had already examined that theory myself and it sounded too far-fetched. I had even put the test to myself: Would I kill someone else to benefit Rafik? And the answer was a fast and definite no. I wasn't even sure I'd give up my own life. That's when I got down to the nitty-gritty and asked myself, Why should I? Why would Rafik's life be any more worthy than mine? Just because he was sexier? Did that make him more worthy to live?

Then I wondered, Could Ronda feel an even stronger love for Carolyn than I felt for Rafik? As far as I knew, Carolyn had not even yielded to Ronda's attentions yet. Perhaps women were genetically encoded to sacrifice their lives more readily. Maybe it was connected with the mother stuff. Ronda had appeared suspicious enough to me. Maybe the maestro had a point. Then I wondered why the maestro was telling me any of this. Was he trying to distract me from something I wasn't seeing yet? Could he have killed both Madama and Daniel? He did admit to staying late after the rehearsal, which is when he claims he saw Ronda playing with the dagger. Maybe *he* was playing with the dagger himself, preparing to use it on Daniel, and was waiting that afternoon for Ronda to leave the premises before committing the deed. Perhaps he had the same motive he was attributing to Ronda—to further April's career. And perhaps as an afterthought he had seen the connection between Ronda and Carolyn as a convenient way to deflect any suspicion of himself onto Ronda.

But the question remained: Why would he kill Daniel? Why did anyone kill Daniel? What did Daniel know? Somehow I felt that was the key to finding out who had killed Marcella.

"What did Daniel know?" I heard myself asking him.

"Eh?" said the maestro.

"Daniel—the wig man who was stabbed—what did he know?"

The maestro shuddered.

"You must find *La Ronda,*" he said. "She can tell you everything."

"Thanks for the tip," I said.

Thanks for nothing.

I bade the maestro good night and went back to the cottage, where I took a warm bath and went to bed, only to be attended by visions of people shrieking and wielding knives and slashing throats and stabbing pizzas.

34

The next morning I went to the big house to have breakfast with Daphne. She was all aflutter, probably because of the full dress rehearsal scheduled for that evening.

After a perfunctory greeting she said, "Parker told me you got in safely last night."

"Yes," I said. "Long before midnight too, so my magic coach remained a roadster."

"How is the car running?" she asked. "Any problems?"

"None at all. In fact, Daphne, I apologize for my recent behavior. Without your generosity and the car, I wouldn't have been able to run off the way I did. I feel like a brash adolescent."

Daphne laughed heartily, a positive sign that we might be back on friendly terms.

"It's no wonder you fled," she said. "I've been a meddlesome old hen. I hope you'll forgive an old woman's maternal weakness."

"On the contrary, I welcome it."

"Oh, good," she said. "Because I have some awful news, and I need a willing ear."

Then Daphne told me of a grave disappointment she'd suffered the day before, when she discovered that a particular silk shawl she had intended to buy as part of her opening night ensemble had been purchased by someone else.

"I always make the same mistake when I see something I like," she said. "I hesitate, and then when I go back, it's gone." Her eyes drooped sadly. "I'd already had the gown made too, a perfect complement for the shawl. And now the shawl is gone. I suppose it was silly of me to plan my outfit around an accessory that I hadn't bought yet."

"Not at all," I said. But I realized what had happened. I had bought the shawl that Daphne had wanted. Knowing that a happy ending would result when I gave it to her, I could offer her breezy advice. "I'm sure something just as nice will turn up."

"Oh, it's impossible. This one was a work of art, a one-of-a-kind thing. You've never seen anything like it."

Oh yes I had. And it was sitting in the cottage, beautifully wrapped and waiting for Daphne to receive it.

She asked about the day's schedule ahead of me. I told her I had the rest of the morning and the early afternoon free. I wanted to be at the opera house by three o'clock.

"So early for an eight o'clock curtain?" she said.

"I want to feel at home by the time the curtain goes up."

Daphne chortled. "But you're not even performing."

"I am in a way. My work will be onstage, even if I'm not. And the wigs still need more work before opening night."

"How would you like to visit Maurizio with me this morning?"

She suggested that I should drive us both there in the Alfa. Actually I think she wanted an excuse to ride in it, which was fine with me. After a few days of zooming around Abigail in that peppy roadster, I wasn't too eager to be a passenger again, crawling, meandering, drifting along in Daphne's Bentley. So the plan was, she would direct me to Parker's daughter's place, where Maurizio was staying, and I would drive us. But I soon found that Daphne's navigating skill was as faulty as her ability to direct a vehicle under her own command. Partly, she was fascinated with the Alfa's instrumentation, and partly she was enjoying the scenic ride too much. As a result, her directions usually began with, "Oh, dear. I think you were supposed to . . ." And then would follow whichever step of our route we had already missed.

But we did arrive finally at Parker's daughter's cottage, which was located on a neck of land that formed one side of a cove along Abigail's northern shore. Parker's daughter was in her kitchen preparing hundreds of hors d'oeuvres for a reception she was catering that night. Even her small enterprise was benefitting from the opportunities provided by the opera festival. She told us Maurizio was resting outside on the back porch. Daphne and I went out there and found him reclined on a chaise longue basking in the late morning sun. He was wearing light cotton clothing and a straw sun hat, so that only his hands were directly exposed to the sun. He sensed our presence immediately and sat up. It was good to see him bright-eyed and alert again.

Daphne greeted him in their private sign language, and I greeted him with a hearty two-fisted handshake. I had the urge to hug him too, but I could tell by the way he moved that his injuries still hurt him. The three of us sat there for a few minutes, smiling happily while Daphne and I made affectionate little get-well gestures to Maurizio. Then Daphne spoke slowly and clearly to him.

"The police arrested Jonathan Byers."

Maurizio nodded energetically. He explained something to Daphne, and she turned to me and translated.

"He says it was Jonathan Byers who attacked you and then hurt him that night outside the cottage."

I said, "How does he know?"

Maurizio's translated reply: He was wearing a leather jacket.

"That's not enough," I said to Daphne. "Did he see his face?" I turned directly to Maurizio and said it to him. "Did you see his face?"

He shook his head no.

I asked, "What about his hair?"

He signed something to Daphne, and she translated.

"Light-colored," she said.

"Orange?" I asked. "Or yellow?"

Maurizio didn't know, but he seemed afraid to disappoint me, so he explained to Daphne that it was dark when they were struggling, and he didn't get a good look at my attacker.

"That's all right," I said. "Neither did I."

Then Maurizio added that the attacker had worn gloves.

"Gloves?" I said. "Or gauntlets?"

Maurizio looked baffled.

I mimed the shape of gigantic gloves on my wrists, then clenched my fists and puffed up my chest like a he-man.

"Big gloves," I said. "Macho. Tough."

Maurizio nodded wildly and made a loud nasal grunt.

Apparently Jonathan Byers had worn the gauntlets when he attacked me.

"Oh, dear," said Daphne. "I was hoping for evidence to the contrary."

"Why would Sir Jonathan want to hurt me?" I said. "It doesn't make sense."

"No, it doesn't," said Daphne.

"Is that why you wanted to come here?" I said. "To find out for sure?"

"I confess," she said with a defeated nod. "That was my secondary, though no less important motive for visiting Maurizio this morning."

Maurizio looked alarmed, as though he had said something wrong.

"No, my dear," Daphne said soothingly. She put her hand on his forearm. "You have been very helpful. Now you get well. Do you understand?"

Maurizio nodded.

I nodded too, as if to fortify Daphne's order.

Then she and I got up to leave, but Maurizio pulled me close to him for a hug. I could smell the antiseptic dressing on his wounds. But I could also smell his body's sylvan warmth mingled with the brisk ocean air. It was similar to the complex scent I often noticed around Lieutenant Branco. I sensed a little commotion in my nether regions, and I pulled back from Maurizio's embrace. Then Daphne and I left him to recuperate some more in the warm sun.

I drove us back to the estate, where Parker had a message for me. Nicole would be arriving on the afternoon train, alone. I had hoped that she and Branco would have driven out to Abigail together, especially since I had new evidence against Jonathan Byers that I wanted to tell the cop. When I went to meet Nicole at the train station, I learned why she'd come alone.

35

H e's not even sure he can come tonight," said Nicole, as she
plunged her fork into one of the grilled tiger prawns that were
strewn over a mound of fettuccine Alfredo. "And I didn't want to miss
an opportunity to see you and the opera just because of an unreliable
man."

"That's a strong word, doll."

"And Vito is a strong man," said Nicole. "But he was so indecisive
when he called me that I simply decided to come here on my own.
Now I wish I hadn't been so abrupt with him. That train ride was
awful."

"It's a local commuter train, Nikki, not the French TGV."

"I know," she said with a slight shudder, as though riding in a
working-class stock car had tainted her sensibilities.

I reminded Nicole that Branco was probably still recovering from
the loss of his parents, and that might partly explain his uncertain
behavior.

"I understand that, Stanley. But it's not as though driving out here
with me was going to affect the rest of his life. I thought it would be
a nice opportunity to catch up. We haven't seen each other for
months."

"Nikki, Branco was really unsettled after he arrested Jon Byers.
Maybe he's finally realizing that logic and evidence by themselves
aren't enough to convict someone."

"First his parents, then his job. What other reason are you going to
find to explain why he couldn't drive out here with me?"

I wavered. "I guess you're right. He's waffling."

"And you're defending him," she said. "Which is quite a change for you." She took another bite of her lunch. "Stanley, these shrimp are divine. Are you sure that tiny salad is enough for you?"

"Yes, doll. I'm purposely eating light because I have a big night ahead of me. I don't want to spend all my energy digesting food. And by the way, those are tiger prawns."

"Well, whatever they are, they look like big shrimp."

"That's an oxymoron, doll."

"I don't care what you call them, Stanley. They're luscious. And that was a ridiculous reason you just gave for having no lunch. I hope you're not trying to lose weight again."

"No, Nikki. I've resigned both my soul and my body to their respective destinies. I am a dumpling. It's my new mantra. *I am a dumpling.* It's genetic, and there's no twelve-step program to fix it."

"Nonsense, Stanley. You are healthy, and it shows. That's nothing to be ashamed of."

"Yeah, well, look who's talking. When was the last time you squeezed into a size four?"

"The difference is, darling, I don't care."

"But gay men do. Look at the icons we're exposed to—those big, beefy, chisel-bodied boys."

"That's just advertising, Stanley. Those people aren't real. You've said so yourself."

"I was wrong, doll. They are real. And in my world, they are very god of very god. Plump is anathema."

"You're being silly again, darling. It's only a few pounds. It could be much worse, and you know it. You could be sick and have your body show that instead."

Nicole's sobering words stopped my mouth, at least for the moment. That's when Lieutenant Branco entered the café, scanned the place for us, then made his way to our table.

"Look who's here," I said to Nicole.

"I can see," she said.

Branco made no hello and no apology when he got to the table. Just more logic.

"I figured there were only a few places I might find you two," he said. "And I was lucky on the first try."

"It's nice to know my magnet still works," replied Nicole.

"Mind if I join you?" said the cop as he settled into an empty chair. "Sorry we couldn't ride out here together," he said to Nicole, finally acknowledging his defection. "As it turned out, that work took a lot less time than I expected, so I could have picked you up after all. I'd be glad to drive you back."

"Certainly," said Nicole. "All is forgiven."

That was fast. Nicole always made me squirm and beg to earn back her friendship whenever we had a disagreement. I guess her rules changed when it came to Lieutenant Branco. Then again, so did mine. So did everyone's, for that matter.

I asked Nicole's indulgence while I told Branco what Maurizio had related to me and Daphne that morning—that he had identified my attacker the other night to be Jonathan Byers.

"I thought it might help with your conviction," I said.

Branco nodded agreeably. "It's probably not going to be much use since it's technically unrelated to the death of that soprano."

"How can it be unrelated if Byers intended to kill me?" I said. "And with a knife?"

Branco said, "We don't know for sure it was Byers or what he really intended to do."

"But he did hurt Maurizio, and Maurizio said—"

"I know," said Branco. "You just told me. And I'll take it for what it's worth—another version of what happened that night. But I still don't believe it."

"What more do you need!" I said too loudly.

Nicole said, "I see you're both getting along as usual."

"Nothing has changed," I muttered.

"Nothing?" said Branco.

Nicole tapped the sleeve of a passing waiter and asked him for a very large glass of the café's best red wine. She looked at Branco and me and said, "Anything for the sparring warriors?"

Branco declined, and I made excuses about having to be alert at work.

"Fine," said Nicole. Then she turned to the waiter and said, "On second thought, make it a half-bottle." The waiter went off quickly and Nicole said, "There! Now I shall be able to finish my lunch while you two proceed with whatever it is you do together."

"What I'm going to do," I said, "is go to work now."

"So soon?" said Nicole. "Will I see you again tonight?"

"Probably."

Branco offered, "Why don't the three of us have dinner before the show?"

"I can't," I said. "I'll be working."

"Then how about cocktails beforehand?" he said.

Even Nicole stared at the cop in disbelief. It would have been more credible for Branco to invite us to a quilting bee than to have cocktails.

"I'll take a rain check," I said. "It's a work night, and I really have to be on my toes."

Branco gave me an approving look, as though declining a cocktail was a mark of strength.

"Well, I don't have to be alert," said Nicole, and she pushed her plate away from her. "In fact, I'll save my appetite for later too." But she did take one last morsel of tiger prawn.

I got up from the table to leave.

"I'll make sure your tickets are at the box office," I said. "They'll be under my name. Enjoy the show."

Nicole said, "I'm sure we will."

Branco said, "Thanks."

And I left the two of them to proceed with whatever it was *they* were to do together.

36

First thing I did at the opera house was go to the box office and confirm the tickets I'd reserved for Nicole and Branco. My karma was working well, as it usually did whenever I helped others. They were fabulous seats, twelfth-row orchestra on a center aisle. If they'd been for my own use, the seats would probably have been somewhere in the topmost balcony along a side wall with an obstructed view.

The posted schedule for that night read: OCA + DRESS REHEARSAL, which translated to the penultimate moment before opening night for everyone involved in the production—orchestra, chorus, principal artists, and other singers—all done up for a real show. And there would be a nearly full house too, comprising festival benefactors and friends of the cast, along with the hordes of critics and students. I knew Daphne would be sitting among the festival dignitaries.

Before settling down in the wig room for the long stint ahead of me, I wandered upstairs to the backstage area. Ronda Lucca was there. I guess by that point in the production schedule she pretty much lived, ate, and slept backstage.

"You're here early," she said. "I saw you in the café with that cop friend of yours. Too bad he has a girlfriend, huh?"

"The girlfriend is my boss," I said.

"Oh? So maybe there's still a chance for you two."

I shook my head no. "He's straight."

Ronda smirked and said, "You never know."

I said, "You got your props all in order? Knives sharp?"

"Hey, nip it! I told you before, I had nothing to do with any of that stuff."

"You must be happy that the moment you've been waiting for is just about here."

"What moment is that?"

"April Kilkus will have her big debut, and all your work will finally come to fruition."

Ronda looked sideways at me. "What are you talking about?"

"You can fess up," I said. "I know all about it. With April's success comes Carolyn's success. And with Carolyn's success comes your chance for love."

Ronda said, "I think you got me confused with you and the cop."

"Admit it, Ronda. You love her."

"Who?"

"Carolyn."

"I already told you I do. But she's straight, just like your cop. The best I can hope for is that she has a satisfying life."

"But like you said about my cop, Ronda, you never know."

"What is it with you? You think everybody in the world is gay like us?"

"Ten percent," I said.

"Well figure it out, then," she said. "Ten percent of everybody here—"

"It's higher in the theater."

"Look," said Ronda. "I told you before. I didn't kill anybody. Okay? You're obviously stuck on finding a killer to please the lieutenant. But I'm not taking a bum rap just so you look good to a cop. You'll have to go find some other sucker."

"I guess I will," I said. "But there's a killer loose, and I'm still not sure how far you'd go to please Carolyn."

"Maybe that's the kind of motive a gay man would have. But me, personally, I would never kill for love. It's too chancy. I might do it for something more tangible though, like money or property. But it would have to be worth millions. Then I'd go looking for love afterwards. You got to be practical about these things. Who kills just for love anymore?"

"Someone did," I said.

"You got it wrong," said Ronda.

"There's all kinds of love."

Ronda hesitated. "Y'know, maybe you got that right after all."

I went downstairs to ready myself and the wigs for the first group of singers for act one. My assistant was already there too, a former stylist for the Radio City Rockettes. She was setting up her station, and she radiated that perfect combination of friendliness and professionalism that was going to make working together an easy pleasure. I reminded her always to ask before using hairspray around the singers. Then I showed her how I had organized the wig room to match the order of the costuming schedule. It was as close to an assembly line as I could manage, so we'd lose very little time running around searching for wigs.

Gradually, as more and more singers arrived and curtain time approached, the wig room became as bustling and exciting a place as the noisy corridors that interconnected the warm-up rooms among all the singers. Although the principals had their own personal makeup artists to fit their wigs, my assistant and I had just as important a job affixing wigs properly to all the chorus members and the *comprimarios*. We had a lot more opportunity for fun as well. At one point I overheard one of the noisy male chorus singers telling another one that on his way into the opera house he had seen Bruce David, the original tenor who had been institutionalized after Marcella Ostinata's murder.

"And he's in a wheelchair!" squealed the singer. "Can you imagine? He's probably planning to make a big fuss during Riccardo's first aria, just like what Callas did to Tebaldi."

Our work proceeded easily until curtain time. After that we got to watch the stage action on the AV monitor in the wig room. Everything was progressing smoothly until the momentary pause before Riccardo's first aria. That's when some loony ran all the way from the back of the house down to the front row yelling, *"Viva Marcella!"*

Sure enough, it turned out to be Bruce David. Apparently the wheelchair was a prop to ensure he'd have a clear run down the center aisle. He was summarily dragged from the theater screaming Italian expletives. The tenor onstage tried to regain his composure as the orchestra repeated the introduction to his aria. He faltered slightly on his first few notes, but then he was back on solid ground.

My assistant and I watched a few more scenes on the monitor, but after that the wig room began to feel claustrophobic. There would be no rush of work for a while, so I told my assistant I was going upstairs to watch from backstage. I figured she should get the sense of being in charge down there, since that's exactly what she would be doing in a few days, when she would have her own assistant, and I would be jetting my way to Paris to be reunited with my spouse.

When I got backstage the chorus was well into their big number just prior to the scene in the fortune-teller's cave, I mean the New Age healing workshop. That scene would require a radical set change, so things were about to get kind of hectic back there. That's when I spied a most unlikely observer in a faraway corner of the backstage area—Mathilde Morçeau, former maid to the late Madama Ostinata. She was standing near a marked exit door that opened onto a rarely used stairwell. She seemed to be looking for someone amidst the bustling set crew. Then she waved to someone, and I looked to see who it was. It was Rick Jansen. They disappeared together quickly into the stairwell. So, there was a connection! Maybe even a conspiracy among Jon Byers and Rick and Mathilde. There was no time to figure out their motive. There was nothing to do but follow. And what a shock to find them on the next landing up the stairwell, both down on the floor, struggling against each other. Rick was trying to strangle the woman. I went to break them up, and he pushed me away.

"Get out of here!" he yelled. "Get out!"

But I persisted until he got up and ran down to the backstage area. I asked Mathilde what had happened.

"Nothing," she said quickly. "A mistake."

But I noticed her concealing something in a tightly clenched fist.

"What have you got there?" I said.

"Nothing."

"Come on, let me see."

"It is not your business," she said sharply.

"It is now," I said. And then, just like something brutish that Branco might do, I pried her small hand open. Lying on her palm was a solid gold cigarette lighter. I recognized it as the one the maestro had used for a short while.

"Where did you get this?"

Mathilde said, "I find it."

"Where?"

"Here, in the opera house."

"Why didn't you turn it in?"

She made a loud cackle. "Because I know the value of such things."

"Who are you blackmailing?"

Mathilde spat her reply. "You are very stupid."

I grabbed the lighter from her hand and ran from the stairwell to Ronda Lucca's desk backstage. Mathilde was right behind me.

I asked Ronda, "Can you get an usher to alert someone in a certain seat from back here?"

"Depends," said Ronda.

"It's Lieutenant Branco," I said.

Mathilde had arrived at Ronda's desk. "You have something that belongs to me," she said.

"Au contraire," I said. "Anyone *but* you."

"What's the message?" said Ronda.

"Tell Branco to come backstage immediately."

There must have been something incontestable about my manner, because Ronda cooperated without a beat's pause.

"Sure," she said. "Do you know his seat number?"

I told her and she put a call out to the box office to get an usher to find Branco in the house.

Mathilde said, "If you do not return that object, I will tell the police."

"Just wait a minute, honey," I said, "and you can tell them the whole story."

I pressed the lighter into Ronda's hand.

"For Branco," I said.

She glanced at it and replied, "When's the wedding?"

Meanwhile my brain was trying to figure out why Rick had been trying to kill Mathilde. Was he protecting Jon Byers? As far as I knew, at that moment Byers was sitting in the last row of the audience, taking notes on the performance in progress. Which one of them was behaving like a criminal? The one doing his job? Or the one running away? In that moment I made a decision.

I said to Ronda, "Which way did Rick go?"

She pointed toward the lock rail that secured all the cables running up to the flies.

"That's where I saw him last," she said. "Why?"

"I got a feeling he might be the man, not Byers."

Mathilde began to walk away.

I said to Ronda, "Can you keep an eye on her?"

"Trouble?"

"Major," I said.

Ronda yelled, "Hey, Vinny! Grab that woman, will ya?"

Mathilde resisted, but was no match for the massive musculature of Vinny the floor man.

I scanned the backstage area frantically. Rick was nowhere around the lock rail. For some reason, maybe because of all the cables running up to the heavens, I looked upward too. And damn, there he was, on his way up a ladder to the catwalks high above the stage. I headed toward the same ladder.

Just then Ronda's headset beeped. She listened a moment, then called out to me, "Hey, Tinkerbell! Your girl needs you down in the wig room."

"Tell her she's on her own now," I called back.

"Where do you think you're going?"

"I'm not sure, doll. But it looks like I'm taking the hell-bound express to get there."

"You can't go up there," she said. "You're not in the union."

"So file a grievance."

Ronda said, "I can't hold the curtain while you guys play hide-and-seek up there."

"Just tell Branco where I've gone."

And then began the long climb.

37

Some higher force must have driven me to climb that ladder after Rick Jansen, because I am severely acrophobic. But the moment of truth had come, and there was no choice. I just kept reminding myself not to look down or behind me into the vast void of space above the stage floor. Far above me I saw Rick, who had almost reached the upper tier of the catwalks, the grid itself, where all the pulleys for the flies were attached. The whole huge space was dark and eery, lit only by a dim glow of work lights.

An inner voice reminded me, *Don't look down.*

I saw Rick make the short leap necessary to get from the ladder onto the metal beams of the grid. He was extremely agile. The columns along the back of Daphne's house would have been no challenge to him. I pressed my good Slavic limbs to climb faster. As I approached the top of the ladder, Rick must have felt the vibrations because he looked down and saw me coming up. His body jolted in surprise. Apparently he hadn't expected anyone to notice or to follow him up there.

He scrambled across the grid toward a ladder on the other side of the stage. That one led up to a skylight that opened onto the roof of the opera house. I wasn't about to dance around with him under a summer moon, so I propelled myself from my ladder to the first catwalk and scrambled after him. I thanked my Czech ancestors for passing on the genes for strong legs and springy feet. Rick was already partway up the higher ladder when I got there. I clambered up fast and caught one of his ankles. He tried to shake me off, but I used a trick to hang onto him. Rather than try to limit his motion, I held fast with my hand, but let my arm and shoulder swing loosely. So no matter how hard or wildly he kicked, my arm just followed.

"Why were you trying to kill Mathilde?" I said.

"Let me go!"

"What did she do?"

"She was blackmailing Jon."

"For what?"

He kicked wildly, but then I grabbed his ankle with both my hands. I had to get him down off that ladder. With my full weight on his leg, he wasn't going any further. And if we fell—when we fell—it was only a few feet to the surface of the grid.

Don't look down.

Rick tried to shake me off his leg, but my weight was too much for him. Thank God for those fifteen extra pounds! Finally his grip gave out and we tumbled down onto the grid. I got myself on top of him and pressed him down with my weight.

"Who killed those people? You or Jon?"

"Fuck off," he said. "You don't know anything."

"Don't talk fresh, Rick."

His strong body writhed under my weight. I wasn't going to be able to hold him down indefinitely. Where the hell was Branco?

"Why did you do it?" I said.

"Fuck off!" he said again.

I slapped his face. "Save that talk for daddy Jon. Does he know what you did?"

"Not yet," said Rick.

"He may not approve."

"He'll love it," said Rick. "Jon loves anything sick."

Case in hand.

Rick relaxed his body underneath me.

"I'll tell Jon everything right after opening night," he said. "After all the applause and the elation, when I've got him bound and gagged in our hotel room, that's when he'll finally hear everything I've done for him. Then let's see if he can leave me for someone else, some bodybuilding set designer without balls."

"You're pretty buffed yourself," I said.

"But I've got the balls to do whatever has to be done."

I wished I could have said something tough like that, but instead my inner voice repeated the same old message.

Don't look down.

This time though, it came too late.

I found myself looking past Rick's face, through the metal I-beams behind his head, and down, down, down to the stage floor that was miles away below us. Tiny little creatures were busily moving tiny little things around the stage. My stomach went gurgly and my muscles turned to cotton. Rick must have felt my body go lax, because an instant later he'd flipped me over.

"And now," he said with a crazed grin, "prepare to die."

"Don't, Rick," I said. "They'll know it's you. They can see us from down there."

"But no one ever looks up here."

"They will now," I said. "Help!" I screamed. *"Hellllllp!"*

Rick slapped my face. "Shut up! I'm in charge now."

I was about to scream again, but he put his hand over my mouth.

"No one can hear you up here. It's all designed to be soundproof. All your screams are going up, not down. But that's where you'll be going soon. Down. So save your breath. You're going to need it for that last long scream."

He cackled with glee, and I realized that Rick was the one who really enjoyed the sicker pleasures like torture and murder.

I also realized that facing upwards had decreased my vertigo, and I could think somewhat clearly again. I used the same technique that had worked before when I was pinned under Rick. I relaxed my body. And for a microsecond, without that resistance from me, his own body's pressure caused him to fall toward me ever so slightly, but also slightly out of his control. I used his body's weight to roll us both over. But this time he got his bearings fast and rolled us again. That's when I felt my legs and part of my butt suddenly without any support, hanging out into nothing over the edge of the grid, into the wide margin of air where it didn't quite meet the stage house wall.

"How do you like that?" he said, putting his face close to mine. "I can smell the panic coming off your body."

"And I can smell the tartar on your teeth."

He pushed me further over the edge. My whole butt and both legs were dangling free, then my lower back. I realized it was Rick's own strength that was keeping me from sliding over the edge at that moment. He knew it too. From my perspective it wasn't a good place to be. I thrashed wildly for a hold on something, but all I got was air. One shoulder went over the edge. The other was slipping fast.

"Where's the safety screen?" said Rick. "Oh, that's right. Your friend Daphne paid off the building inspector to get the theater open on time without it. Too bad for you she was such a naughty old girl."

"Don't, Rick."

"Bye-bye, faggot."

And he let me go.

But my fall was as brief as the half-life of a plutonium atom. In my random flailing I'd somehow grabbed hold of the wide flange at the bottom of the I-beams of the grid. Rick stood up and saw what had happened.

"Shit!" he said. "You still here?"

He stuck one of his feet over the edge of the grid and tried to kick at my hands.

Not the hands, I thought.

I moved. He moved. We both moved again.

I called upon the spirit of Fay Wray to bless me with an ear-splitting scream. Then I let loose with it. Quiet seconds followed, and I almost thought I had woken from a bad dream.

Then I heard Rick say, "That was good. You really don't want to die."

He seemed to be stimulated by my adrenaline.

It was fight or flight, I told myself. And since there was no way to fight, I took the alternative. I saw a nearby cable and I made a wild grab for it. I caught it. At least my hands were safe for the moment. But my weight was causing the cable to swing and jounce wildly. I lowered myself carefully the ten or so feet to the batten pipe at the end of the cable. From there I looked across the broad expanse of the fly space, and saw that I had set into motion a huge flat of scenery as wide as the entire stage. A few other cables were connected to that same pipe across its length. It took only a moment for the flat to settle into a slow, pendulous swing, the kind of motion you'd expect on a veranda on a lazy summer's night in the deep South.

Then I found myself looking down. A hundred feet below I saw the scene change methodically continuing onstage. Rick had been right. For all the noise and drama up there on the grid, not one member of the stage crew had looked up. Then I found my hands gripping the cable in terror, for my fear of heights had been reawakened.

Meanwhile, Rick was watching me, trying to figure out the next best way to kill me. But he was going to have to catch me first. And I still had enough nerve and strength to increase the swing of the batten and the wall of scenery, and then to play at changing the direction of its swing—anything to make it more difficult for Rick to grab the cable. Leave it to me to try and save myself with a trick I learned on a playground swing. Rick reached out for the cable, but kept missing it.

"Come little fishy," he said. "Come to papa."

I guess he was appealing to my inner child. Good thing I'd aborted the little monster long ago.

"I'm not a fish," I muttered.

Rick kept trying to grab the cable I was on, stretching himself further and further out over the grid.

"I'll get you, you bastard."

Then I watched him confidently calculating the period of the swing of my cable, the way a cat watches a string and can predict its path. And I knew when the moment was right, he would reach out and make a risky lunge for it. And that's exactly when I jolted myself midswing to change the path of the cable's arc. Rick reached too far and missed my cable. He lost his balance, fluttered for a moment, and then reached out and grabbed desperately at another cable. He caught it, and he was saved.

We faced each other, me swinging like Little Sally Saucer, and him analyzing the situation like a wily predator.

That's when I noticed another big difference between us. Where my cable connected to a batten pipe and a big piece of scenery, Rick's cable connected to a batten from which hung a flimsy gauzy scrim.

Far below us, the work lights onstage suddenly went out. Then came the sounds of the orchestra playing the tremendous opening chords to the dark scene in the New Age workshop. Those sounds meant only one thing. I watched Rick's eyes bulge in terror as he felt the snap of the computer-controlled release latch travel through the cable he was holding. On the other end of that cable was a counterbalance, but it was negligible against Rick's body weight on the cable. He went down, down, down toward the stage along with the scrim. I heard the cables whirring through the pulleys above me, and I was helpless to stop them. Rick screamed a long, tortured wail all the way down.

And then a miracle happened.

The cables stopped.

My logical self quickly surmised what had happened. The bottom of the scrim had reached the stage floor, and at that moment the cables had locked again. I looked down and saw that the sudden stop had thrown Rick off the scrim, and he had fallen to the stage floor. The dramatic music continued. I heard the sound of electrical motors and saw a tremendous wall of fabric rise up before me, and I realized the main curtain had come up. Down below the stage lights had set the spiritual mood of Ulrica's New Age healing studio. And from my desperate perch on a cable high up in the flies I heard Rick screaming out at the audience.

"What are you all staring at? Assholes!"

He tried to get up and run, but couldn't. He'd hurt his leg badly when he fell off the scrim. In that moment Ronda Lucca had assessed the situation and given the order to bring down the main curtain. So once more I got to watch the giant mechanics at work up in stage heaven.

Work lights flashed brightly to life everywhere around me, and I saw many people running to center stage. Among them I tried to recognize Lieutenant Branco, whose broad shoulders and dark curly hair would make him easy to identify. I called out over and over again, but no one heard me. I guess the sound really did go up. It was only after they got Rick Jansen off the stage that some of the crew looked up into the flies and saw me hanging there. After that my rescue was easy. Ronda very cautiously lowered the piece of scenery I was connected to, which turned out to be the back wall of Mimi's finale for the festival's production of *La bohème*. Then the crew brought out a big ladder and got me down.

The scrim that Rick Jansen had fallen from was the same one that had killed Adam Pierce.

Both the maestro and Jon Byers insisted that the show continue, but the police forbade it. The dress rehearsal was cancelled, April Kilkus never sang a note that night, and I found Daphne in the patron's lounge in tears.

Some opera.

38

I drove Nicole back to Boston that night, where I stayed awhile and visited with Sugar Baby. Then I returned to Abigail. But by the time I got back to Daphne's place, she had already retired, which didn't surprise me, given the evening's events.

The next morning I was having breakfast with her in the garden room, trying to ease her grief over the previous night's fiasco with a gentle reminder that a bad dress rehearsal usually meant a good opening night. And with that dress rehearsal behind us, opening night would surely make operatic history.

Daphne said, "I hope you're right, my dear."

"Have I ever been wrong?"

"You most certainly have."

Parker then entered to announce that Lieutenant Branco had arrived. To my surprise Daphne invited him in, and then followed a lively session of Daphne and Branco apologizing for the mutual difficulties they'd caused each other.

Daphne would protest, "You were doing your job."

Branco would counter, "I was too impulsive."

It was like a mother-son quarrel that finally ended in a friendly impasse.

Once we'd all settled down with coffee, Branco told us that Rick Jansen had confessed to killing Adam Pierce and Marcella Ostinata for the love of Jonathan Byers.

"For love?" I said.

Branco nodded. "He even broke down when he confessed. I never saw a man cry like that."

Apparently Rick had really wanted to prove his love for Jon Byers, and since the only thing that mattered to Byers was opera, Rick had killed Marcella Ostinata to make sure the show was a success. That all made me wonder about my appallingly single-minded quest for a merit badge to prove my worthiness to Branco.

"But how did he get into her room?" said Daphne.

Branco replied, "He'd been flirting with Marcella all along. At some point she told him her balcony door was always unlocked. It was an open invitation."

"And Adam Pierce?" I said.

Branco went on. "Adam Pierce's death was truly an accident. Rick had intended to hit Marcella with that scrim."

"He did it?"

"Yup," said Branco.

"How?" I said. "Ronda Lucca claimed that everything mechanical onstage was controlled by her computer."

Branco said, "It was. And apparently Rick Jansen knows just enough about computers to be dangerous."

"Ah yes," said Daphne. "I recall Sir Jon introducing the young man as though he had rescued him from computer school."

"But how did Rick know Ronda's password?" I said.

"He didn't," said Branco. "One thing Ms. Lucca never admitted was that she had left the console unattended for a few moments."

"Why would she lie about that?"

Branco said, "Because she was so preoccupied with one of the musicians that she accidentally left the computer in a ready state. And as the almighty stage manager, Ms. Lucca wasn't too eager to admit the lapse of attention to her job that also gave our killer his unexpected opportunity to kill Marcella. The only trouble was, in his urgency to use that chance, Rick Jansen missed his intended mark."

"So all Ronda's stories about reloading the software . . . ?"

"Fiction," said Branco.

Accident or not Rick had still managed to rid himself of a rival. And as for my theory about natural blonds being incapable of dastardly deeds—okay, so I was wrong. Rick Jansen wasn't just another boy-toy exploiting his good looks and body. He was a serial killer.

Daphne said, "At least we know Rick didn't kill poor Sonia Hatfield. He hadn't even arrived here yet."

"I supposed that's some consolation," I said.

"What about the other one?" said Daphne. "That awful wig man."

"Daniel Carafolio," I said.

Branco said, "He knew that Jon Byers had taken the gauntlets from the costume room. Rick was afraid that we—that's you and me, Stan—would eventually link the gauntlets to him. That's why he came after you too, with that knife. You were nagging him so much."

Branco smiled as if to approve of my meddling nature.

"And Mathilde?" I said.

"Innocent," replied Branco.

I never thought he could say the word.

Daphne added, "Except for that double dose of sleeping potion."

Branco said, "That's what made her panic and run. But now we can assume she really was telling the truth and following her lady's orders."

I said, "I wonder if Madama Ostinata had a premonition that her final moment was approaching, and she wanted to make sure she wouldn't be awake for it."

"What a morbid thought!" said Daphne.

"We'll never know," said Branco.

"What about that cigarette lighter?" I said. "Was Mathilde blackmailing Jonathan Byers with it?"

"No," said Branco. "It turns out the maestro had borrowed the lighter from Byers and forgot to give it back. Then he accidentally lost it through a hole in his pants pocket."

"That explains why Mathilde had that pair of pants tucked in with the rest of the clothes the other night. They were the maestro's."

"Right," said Branco. "She had mended the pocket for him. But the maestro never told anyone about the missing lighter, not even Byers, because he was so embarrassed to lose it."

"Didn't Byers miss it?" I said. "It was solid gold."

Branco replied, "Rick gave it to him without thinking that Byers never smoked. So in spite of its intrinsic value, the lighter was useless to Byers."

"Not even for sentiment, I guess."

"Hardly that!" said Daphne.

"But then Mathilde found it," I said.

"Right," said Branco. "In the opera house."

"So why didn't she just return it to Byers?"

"She didn't know it was his, but she did know it was solid gold and extremely valuable." Then Branco smiled. "And it was inscribed: TO THE QUEEN OF THE KNIGHTS FROM HER LOYAL PAWN, R.J."

"Quite a line from a manly man," I said.

"And a bad joke at Mozart's expense," added Daphne.

Branco finished. "It took Mathilde a while to make the wrong connection to Rick as the owner."

"The flower beneath the foot," I said.

Branco grunted, then went on. "But when Mathilde showed Rick the lighter, he assumed that she assumed Byers had killed Marcella and had accidentally left the lighter behind, and now she was going to blackmail both of them."

"Too much logic," I said.

"Probably," said Branco. "At least Byers got his lighter back."

"For whatever it's worth to him now," I said. "But why was Mathilde always so scared and defensive if she was innocent?"

Daphne answered that simply. "It was her whole life."

"The reality she created for herself," I said.

"Oh dear," said Daphne. "I'd hoped you were beyond that kind of thinking. The woman did the best she could. We're all dealt different hands in the Big Game, young man, and some of them, no matter how much we may want to, just cannot be played with the panache of a boulevardier."

That kind of talk was Branco's cue to exit. "I'd better get back to Boston now," he said.

"Lieutenant," said Daphne. "I hope you'll come back tomorrow for the opening night gala. I've set aside a pair of house seats for you."

Branco accepted her offer graciously. Then he said good-bye and left. I excused myself to Daphne and went after him.

I found him outside looking at my rented Alfa.

"Nice car," he said.

I settled my butt on the fender of his Alfa and said, "Nice vintage."

He hesitated as if trying to snag some evasive words, then he managed to say, "Thanks for your help."

"My pleasure, Lieutenant. Too bad I didn't learn how to power-shift."

"There'll be another time."

"I hope so."

Then Branco got into his car and drove off.

After breakfast that morning I presented Daphne with the silk shawl I'd bought for her. She was so thrilled that she wrapped it about herself immediately, then swirled around the entrance foyer of the mansion like Loretta Young.

"And my dear," she said. "I have a surprise for you too."

She led me into the library, then scurried to her desk, fished out a large envelope, and handed me the title papers to the Alfa along with a five-year maintenance agreement.

"It's yours," she said. "All paid for."

When I could speak, all I could manage was, "It's too much."

"It's nothing," she said. "You've put a lot of energy back in my life. There's hardly a way to return a favor like that. I hope this little car will give you some fun."

"Thank you," I said.

"And I have a confession too," she said. "I was wrong to pay that building inspector to overlook the lack of a safety screen around the stagehouse grid. You could have been seriously hurt."

"But you didn't intend—"

"The road to hell, my dear. I was wrong. Your brush with death made me see that. And another thing I've decided—I am going to formally adopt Maurizio. That poor boy was heartlessly abandoned by both his mother and his father—my second husband, no less! Finally I realize that when he appeared on my doorstep, he had truly come home. So you see, my dear, the sports car is only a trinket. I owe you a lot more than that for refocusing my vision so clearly. If you ever do want to return to school, I intend to help you in every way possible."

"Thank you," I said again. I fought to hold back tears because I realized in a way that Daphne had just adopted me too.

I spent the rest of the morning doing mundane things like laundry and clearing my debris from the cottage. Balance, always balance. Later that day I went to see Maurizio and tried carefully to explain that I would soon be leaving for Europe to be with my lover. Any hope of an affair between us in Abigail was nil. I felt like a cad, but Maurizio seemed to understand and accept it all, which made me feel even worse.

There was no rehearsal scheduled that day. The principal singers were supposed to be recovering from the great energy they had expended in the full dress rehearsal. But since the dress rehearsal had foundered, there was little for the singers to recover from, except perhaps high anxiety. I spent that afternoon and most of the next day putting the finishing touches on the wigs. Like all great artists, I work best under pressure.

Then finally came the evening of the biggest event of the entire festival, the official opening night performance. As I had predicted, after the bad dress rehearsal, the opening night show started out as a grand success, what the French call *un succès fou*. Lieutenant Branco and Nicole were present again, and Daphne was radiant in the silken shawl. And Ronda Lucca forgave me all my trespasses. She even gave my butt a slap for good luck before the opening curtain.

But the tide turned abruptly during the intermission after act one. Parker arrived at the opera house bearing a telegram for me. It was from Rafik's parents, two words only, "Come quickly." I telephoned them immediately, but they weren't home. Only the household staff were there. And in the best French I could manage, I asked what had happened to Rafik. Their answer fell like a brick of cold lead.

"Il est très très mal."

And like Jane Truelove in *The Rake's Progress,* I could not think. I could not explain. I could only say, "I go to him."

Branco sacrificed seeing the rest of the opera and offered to drive me to Logan Airport to catch a direct flight to Europe that night. It was during the ride that he suggested I might consider pursuing criminal investigation as a new career, maybe even go to police school.

"I can help you," he said.

But I was too distressed and distracted by the news from Paris to talk about it then. I'd never even considered a career change until Branco had mentioned it.

And I never got to see the full opera in performance. But later that summer, after I had returned from Europe, I got to read all the reviews of the New England Summer Opera Festival's production of *Un ballo in maschera.* Jonathan Byers had outdone himself and had created a contemporary stage masterpiece from a hackneyed chestnut of the operatic repertoire. April Kilkus had been hailed as the next great Verdi soprano. *Brava, bravissima,* etc. Maestro Toscanelli was spoken of in terms that implied divine resurrection. The entire festival was praised as the year's most significant operatic event in America, if not the entire globe. And last but not least, my fantastic wigs for the final scene, the masked ball itself, were celebrated by every critic as perfect models of trenchant wit in the modern operatic theater. *Bravo, bravissimo,* etc.

But by that time my life had changed so drastically that the kudos hardly mattered.